O X 8/08

Anthology of Chinese Literature

The Red Cliff, II

"In the same year, on the fifteenth of the tenth month, I went on
foot from Snow Hall on my way back to Lin-kao, accompanied
by two guests. When we passed the slope of Huang-ni the frost
and dew had fallen already. The trees were stripped of leaves,
our shadows . . ."

This is the Chinese text of the opening phrases of Su Shih's
prose poem which appears in translation on page 383 of the anthology. It is reproduced from a copy made by an outstanding
calligrapher and painter of the Yüan dynasty, Chao Meng-fu (Chao
Tzu-ang, 1254-1322). Chao made an album of his calligraphic text,
painted a portrait of Su Shih on the first page and added the date,
which corresponds to February 17, 1301. At right, below the title,
two of the many collectors' seals are partly visible.

A scroll exists of the first prose poem in the equally celebrated
calligraphy of Su Shih himself, but the close-written style lends itself
less happily to reproduction here.

Other Works by Cyril Birch
Published by Grove Press

Anthology of Chinese Literature, Vol. 2:
From the Fourteenth Century to the Present

Stories from a Ming Collection (Cyril Birch, translator)

Anthology of

Chinese Literature

from early times
to the fourteenth century

compiled and edited by
CYRIL BIRCH

associate editor
Donald Keene

GROVE PRESS
NEW YORK

Grove Press
841 Broadway
New York, NY 10003

This work has been accepted in the Chinese Literature Translations Series of the United Nations Educational, Scientific and Cultural Organization (UNESCO).

UNESCO Collection of Representative Works
Chinese Series

Library of Congress Catalog Card Number: 65-14202
ISBN 0-8021-5038-1 (pbk.)

Manufactured in the United States of America

Acknowledgments

To Glen W. Baxter, Sam Houston Brock, James I. Crump, A. C. Graham, J. R. Hightower, K. Y. Hsü and Burton Watson the editors wish to express a debt of gratitude for valued contributions of unpublished translations, made in many cases expressly for the anthology.

Acknowledgments are also made to the following: to the Joint Administration of the National Palace and Central Museums, Taiwan, for permission to reproduce the calligraphy by Chao Meng-fu as frontispiece; to Arthur Waley, George Allen and Unwin, Ltd., and Macmillan Co. for material from *The Book of Songs, Three Ways of Thought in Ancient China, The Temple and Other Poems, Chinese Poems, More Translations from the Chinese, Poetry and Career of Li Po* and *Life and Times of Po Chü-i;* to Ezra Pound, Harvard University Press and Faber and Faber for material from *The Classical Anthology Defined by Confucius;* to Burton Watson and Columbia University Press for material from *Early Chinese Literature, Sources of Chinese Tradition, Ssu-ma Ch'ien: Grand Historian of China* and *Records of the Grand Historian of China;* to David Hawkes and Clarendon Press for material from *Ch'u Tz'u: Songs of the South;* to J. R. Hightower and the editors for translations published in *Asia Major* and *Studia Serica;* to C. J. Chen, Michael Bullock and Abelard-Schuman, Ltd., for material from *Poems of Solitude;* to William Acker, Thames and Hudson, Ltd., and the Vanguard Press for material from *T'ao the Hermit;* to Gary Snyder, who in turn acknowledges the assistance of S. H. Chen, and Grove Press for translations appearing in the *Evergreen Review;*

to S. H. Chen and the Anthoensen Press for material from *Lu Chi: Essay on Literature;* to C. H. Kwôck and Vincent McHugh and the Golden Mountain Press for material from *Why I Live on the Mountain* and *The Lady and the Hermit;* to Witter Bynner and Kiang Kang-hu and Alfred Knopf, Inc., for material from *The Jade Mountain;* to Mrs. John K. Rideout for permission to print translations made by her late husband; to Ch'u Ta-kao and Cambridge University Press for material from *Chinese Lyrics;* and to Mrs. Gerald Bullett for material from *The Golden Year of Fan Ch'eng-ta,* translations made by her late husband with the assistance of his friend the late Tsui Chi. J. I. Crump's translation "Li K'uei Carries Thorns" is included in University of Michigan, Center for Chinese Studies: *Occasional Papers,* No. 1.

Thanks are also due to the Asian Literature Program of the Asia Society for support given the publication of this book.

Translators

WILLIAM ACKER
GLEN W. BAXTER
CYRIL BIRCH
SAM HOUSTON BROCK
GERALD BULLETT
MICHAEL BULLOCK
WITTER BYNNER
C. J. CHEN
SHIH-HSIANG CHEN
CH'U TA-KAO
J. I. CRUMP

A. C. GRAHAM
DAVID HAWKES
J. R. HIGHTOWER
K. Y. HSÜ
DONALD KEENE
C. H. KWÔCK
VINCENT MCHUGH
EZRA POUND
J. K. RIDEOUT
GARY SNYDER
ARTHUR WALEY

BURTON WATSON

To Arthur Waley

Contents

SUNG DYNASTY (960-1279)

YÜAN DYNASTY (1280-1367)

Anthology of Chinese Literature

Introduction

The *Complete T'ang Poems,* in its 900 sections, comprises over 48,000 *shih* poems by some 2,200 authors. When such capacity is required by the written accomplishment in a single genre for a single dynastic period, it is hard to be unimpressed by the sheer mass of Chinese literature. It is a heritage awesome not only in mass and range and chronological sweep, but in the intense degree to which it has been studied by all who have received and furthered it. Originality in letters was prized in China as elsewhere, but it was a quality to be refined and made aware by rigorous training. The profundity of a writer's understanding of the tradition and the delicacy of his reference to it would inform his own advances, which without such guidance would be mere antlike scurryings.

The written character was a most powerful agent. A world in a syllable, it held over the centuries its own semantic history within its own form, aesthetically satisfying and endlessly durable in its independence of phonological change. An alphabetic script might speed the accomplishment of the child in school, but it could offer him no such induction into the thought and values of his civilization.

If we go back three and a half thousand years to the Shang dynasty we find only prototypes of the script form of later ages in the inscriptions on tortoise shells or the shoulder-blades of oxen. But since its standardization in the third century before Christ the character has undergone only minor modification. It began to be written on paper during the Han period, and to be printed by the use of wood blocks in the ninth century. From the Sung period there still survive some of the finest specimens of printed books ever made by man.

Bodied forth in this script is every conceivable form of literary composition, from the four-syllable epigram to the hundred-chapter novel and the hundred-volume history. In between lie folk ballads and metaphysical odes, epitaphs and commemorations of the siting of pavilions, love lyrics and shamanistic hymns, travel diaries and sermons, memorials to the emperor and letters to friends. Some of these genres, notably vernacular fiction and the "observation" (*pi-chi*), survive only in less developed form from the period covered by the present volume, but will be more conspicuous in the sequel.

Records give many indications of what must have been lost to fire and flood, strife and censorship. But countless generations of bibliophiles have collected, edited and transmitted the major corpus. Many works exist only in Chinese anthologies, from the *Book of Songs* through the *Wen hsüan* of the sixth century A.D. to the vast bibliographical undertakings of the eighteenth century, the mid-Ch'ing period.

Some earlier Western-language anthologies of Chinese literature are listed in our bibliography. None, obviously, can offer more than the sketchiest representation, and no doubt several could be compiled, each with as fair a coverage of three millennia, yet without the duplication of any particular item. This anthology, the most comprehensive in the English language, enjoys the additional advantage of being the work of a considerable variety of translators. But the degree of selectivity has had to be drastic, and some explanation should be made here of the principles on which we have worked.

Our definition of literature, first of all, has been modern Western rather than Chinese traditional, exclusive rather than comprehensive. Chinese bibliography recognized four major categories: *ching, shih, tzu, chi* or classics, historical writings, philosophical writings and "collections" (of the verse and prose of individuals). The last of these categories excludes fiction and drama (which were beneath the bibliographer's notice), but corresponds approximately to our concept of belles lettres; it is of course from this body of work that the bulk of our material, at least for this first volume, is drawn. Of the classics proper, the canonical corpus

of ancestral experience as Confucian scholars had shaped and de-
limited it by Han times, only the *Book of Songs* has engaged us.
There is an all-too-brief glance at the *Tso Commentary*, a canonical set of historical texts; but for the historians generally, we have
been content to rest with Ssu-ma Ch'ien. (In this at least we may
have the sanction of Chinese tradition, for the writing of history
as an art was felt hardly to have survived this gifted man.) The remaining class of philosophical writings we have almost entirely ignored. We would not wish to suggest any lack of literary merit in
Mencius or *Lieh Tzu* or even Chu Hsi, but we have preferred to exclude writings for whose appreciation the reader would first demand
an extensive interpretation of the ethical concepts and political
theory of the early Chinese world. In any case, it would be foolish
to imagine that one could blank out the philosophers, or the classics
either, merely by omitting them from the table of contents. Not one
of the authors represented in this volume received his formal education, his ethical training, or his literary style itself from anywhere
else. The thought of the classics and the philosophy of the immediately postclassical period nourish and suffuse the entire subsequent culture.

In our work of selection we have tried to avoid translations,
whether or not previously published, which are marred either by
lifeless English or by uninformed scholarship. We have regretfully
jettisoned fine translations of decades ago whose English style has
dated, and scholarly translations of pieces whose merits could be
glimpsed only through a thick fog of footnotes. Naturally we have
hoped to be reasonably representative, but not at the risk of presenting a writer of first rank in drab or ill-fitting garb. In particular,
we have tried to disperse the air of anonymity which the anthology
piece too often seems to exude. Each writer of worth, Chinese or
other, is an individual with an individual voice. For this reason we
have preferred to allow more space to each of a smaller total number of writers, even though as a result many names of high lustre
must drop out altogether. For this reason also the attempt has been
made where possible to link individual writer with individual translator, so that Watson speaks for Ssu-ma Ch'ien, Waley for Po Chü-yi,
Rideout for Han Yü, Bullett for Fan Ch'eng-ta.

The consequent variety of English styles, British or American,
measured or easy, muscular or fragile, will readily be apparent. What

may not present itself so easily to the reader's view is the considerable erudition and imaginative understanding which underpins many a brief set of simple lines. Chinese *is* a difficult language, Chinese literature *is* of great complexity. Partly to illustrate this and partly to explain the omission of many masterpieces—the truly "untranslateables"—we offer at this point a translation by A. C. Graham of a short lyric by the ninth-century poet Li Shang-yin. In the main body of the anthology Dr. Graham has a section of fourteen poems by this difficult writer. In the case of one poem there, "Peonies," he thoughtfully provides a prose paraphrase. In the present instance he prefaces his translation with an explanation of certain allusions, and appends a commentary in which verse and allusion are synthesized. The reader may regret that he is not offered more of texture so rich; he is invited to return to the following exercise whenever he feels himself disarmed by the smiling simplicity of our anthology pieces:

Li Shang-yin: THE PATTERNED LUTE

Background allusions:

The lute invented by Fu-hsi had fifty strings. When the Yellow Emperor commanded the White Lady to play the lute, he found it unbearably sad, so broke half the strings and left twenty-five.

Chuang Tzu once dreamed that he was a butterfly. Now he does not know whether is is Chuang Tzu who dreamed that he was a butterfly, or a butterfly dreaming that he is Chuang Tzu.

Wang-ti, King of Shu, committed adultery with the wife of a minister. In his shame he fled into exile and became the cuckoo. That is why, when the people of Shu hear a cuckoo call, they all rise to their feet saying: "That is Wang-ti."

When the moon waxes the oyster is full, when the moon wanes the oyster is empty.

Beyond the South Sea there are mermaids who live in the water like fish, but spin and weave like the women on land; their weeping eyes can exude pearls.

Her father the king was angry and would not let her marry, and Purple Jade died of grief. One day, when the king was dressing and combing his hair, suddenly he saw Purple Jade. "Can you be alive?" he asked in amazement, sad and happy at once. Her mother heard them and came out to embrace her, but Purple Jade dissolved like smoke.

Tai Hsü-lun (723-789) said that the scene presented by a poet is like the smoke which issues from fine jade when the sun is warm on Mount Lan-t'ien (Indigo Field); it can be seen from a distance but not from close to.

The Poem

Mere chance that the patterned lute has fifty strings.
One by one string and fret recall the blossoming years.
Chuang Tzu dreamed at sunrise that a butterfly lost its way;
Wang-ti's spring passion cries in the cuckoo's song.
When the moon is full on the vast sea a pearl sheds tears;
When the sun is warm on Indigo Field a smoke issues from jade.
Did it wait, this mood, to mature with hindsight?
Illusion was the whole of it, then as now.

Commentary

Lines 1, 2. The lute evokes a memory of the poet's youth. The fifty strings imply that the memory is painful, and hint at a private chronological reference which has defeated the commentators.

Lines 3, 4. The memory is of a love like Wang-ti's: like Chuang Tzu's dream, it sometimes seems unreal, sometimes more real than the rest of the poet's life; like the cuckoo which was once Wang-ti, the poet, changed by time, remembers it as though it happened to a different person.

"Chuang Tzu dreamed *at sunrise*" leaves open the question whether it was by night or by day that he dreamed.

Lines 5, 6. These lines combine two sets of implications:

(a) "A pearl sheds tears" paired with "A smoke issues from jade" suggests a woman who weeps and who dissolves like Purple Jade when the poet tries to fix her in memory.

(b) With time (full moon, midday sun) painful experience matures into poetry, which crystallises out of grief like the pearl from a tear, and depends for its beauty on distance, like the mountain mist.

In line 5, the assumption that pearls form as the moon waxes serves to fuse the images of pearl and mermaid in "A pearl sheds tears" suggesting that the mermaid is more precious than the gems which she exudes. The same piece of folklore is implicit in a line of "Written on a Monastery Wall," "The oyster before its womb fills thinks of the new cassia," where it helps to fuse the images of pearl and full moon. (The cassia tree, our "man-in-the-moon," becomes visible as the moon waxes.)

Lines 7, 8. Is this the mood of the experience itself, or did it begin with hindsight? Even at the time, this love was imagination without the hope of fulfillment.

This poem by Li Shang-yin is in the *lü-shih* or "regulated verse" pattern. No verse form ever achieved more intricate organization of language, and it is this structuring that makes possible the elaborate interplay of the poet's allusions, as witness the second set of parallels (lines 5-6): moon full || sun warm; vast sea || Indigo Field (mountain); pearl tears || jade smoke. We must remember also that the gifted poet danced freely in fetters which no translation, unfortunately, can do more than hint at: the rigid requirements of permissible rhyme and of the strictest patterning of tone for each successive syllable.

Not surprisingly, translators have shown a preference for the simpler poem which still in its very economy of means achieves tremendous power of suggestion. Yüan Chen sets a four-line "stop-short" poem in the ruins of an ancient "travel-palace."[1] This was a structure built especially for the visit of an emperor making a provincial tour. After his departure it could be used by no lesser mortal; and when the throne was occupied by a man who enjoyed his tours, the country must have been fairly dotted with decaying monuments to his brief sojournings. What interests Yüan Chen, though, is the human dimension, the pathetic figure of the palace woman, recruited locally for the service of the ruler, then left behind to moulder in company with the deserted terraces and pavilions. Flowers bloom red, but her hair is white. Her life is given over to boasting of the fleeting days of glory when she knew the emperor, Hsüan-tsung or Ming-huang, the *roi soleil* at whose court Tu Fu served. The whole inhuman waste is evoked by the poet in twenty

---

1. See p. 279 below.

syllables, words whose simplicity may yet be deceptive. For they unite both visual and aural dimensions with their semantic force. Seven of the twenty characters have the "roof" constituent, so that the calligraphy itself of the original brings the physical architecture of the palace before the eye; and the heavy sonorous rhyme is reminiscent of the bell or the gong of the night watches.

Chinese prose has its own kind of conciseness. The popular short anecdote, cut to the bone but of telling wit, is not much in evidence in the present volume, its place being rather in the bedside book[2] than in the general anthology. We pass rather quickly from the laconic prose of the early historical writings to the more discursive style of Ssu-ma Ch'ien. But the love of the concrete, and the power of the anecdote are still apparent in the structure of his biographies, as when incident by incident he builds up his portrait of General Li Kuang. Han Yü is the master of the spare, chiselled phrase, of taut logic; with the appearance of the fully-fledged *romancier,* represented here by a single incident from *The Men of the Marshes,*[3] we reach the opposite extreme of leisurely fluidity, of the unwearying exploration of every last ramification of plot, every last atmospheric nuance of dialogue.

The themes beloved of Chinese writers will of course present themselves in what follows. Here we need only underline certain recurring concerns. Love between man and woman runs the gamut from the pristine freshness of courtship in the *Book of Songs* to the laments for love unrequited or betrayed in the *tz'u* poets ("Poems in Irregular Metre") or the play *Autumn in the Palace of Han.* Given the social demands of marriage among the educated class, one would not expect to find much celebration of conjugal love, though Yüan Chen's moving memorial to his wife ("The Pitcher"[4]) is a notable exception to this observation. Even the courtesan could hardly provide that companionship which a man found with friends of his own sex; and for at least the middle part of our time-scale sexual love is seen to occupy the poet's brush far less than the concerns of friendship, the gatherings over wine, the partings and

---

2. E. D. Edwards' *Dragon Book* or Lin Yutang's *Importance of Understanding.*
3. *Shui-hu chuan,* translated by Pearl S. Buck as *All Men Are Brothers.*
4. See pp. 279-80 below.

reunions, the anticipation of pleasurable pursuits together (see Wang Wei's "Letter to P'ei Ti"[5]).

War, like the poor, is always with us, but the revulsion of Tu Fu is more characteristic, and a hundred times more moving, than any kind of martial ardour. We shall find little celebration of deeds of derring-do, at least after Ssu-ma Ch'ien, until we reach the storyteller of *The Men of the Marshes,* who recounts legendary feats for his comfortable street-corner audience when the perils are long past.

That harmony between man and nature which worldly concerns may disrupt but never destroy has informed much of the finest writing of the entire Chinese tradition. The teachings of Taoism made it possible for a man of understanding to accomplish an identification with the world of hills and streams which is almost inconceivable to the ego-ridden Westerner. Wordsworth's Lucy had to die to be

> Rolled round in earth's diurnal course
> With rocks, and stones, and trees

—but the living Wang Wei achieved so to say the obliteration of his own self in the landscapes he articulated. It comes as no surprise to learn that Wang Wei's painting won renown to rival his poems. Our frontispiece stresses the close link between literary composition and the art of calligraphy; landscape painting was merely an extension of the brush's function.

Ideally, the reader for whom our anthology will provide a first prolonged encounter with Chinese civilization would have at his elbow his general cultural and social history, his Grousset, Goodrich or Eberhard.[6] The spirit of the age is often very strong in the works that follow, and space remains only for us to make a few general comments and comparisons.

There is a golden glow of dawn over the *Songs* of our first section. Many of these pieces are the folk songs, spontaneous and direct, of an age on which later men looked back with a kind of awed nostalgia. There were giants in those days too, the great mythical or legendary heroes of the race who live on both in the

---

5. See p. 219 below.
6. René Grousset, *Rise and Splendour of the Chinese Empire;* L. C. Goodrich, *Short History of the Chinese People;* Wolfram Eberhard, *History of China.*

Book of Songs and in the *Songs of Ch'u.* These last, so different in prosody and in imagery, differ also in the intrusion, to mingle with the incantations of a magic-filled religion, of a new, sophisticated self-awareness. The meaning of life is questioned, as is the duty of an honest man in the world of political turmoil and naked greed in the power struggle which preceded the unification of China late in the third century B.C. Chia Yi's great *fu* "The Owl," whose form is a development from the modes of the earlier Ch'u poets, suggests that the *Chuang Tzu* and other works of the thinkers have brought the possibility of answers to some of the questions. Ssu-ma Hsiang-ju takes forward the genre of the rhyme-prose and extends the buoyancy of the mood: indeed, there is abundance of confidence about the Han, the vigour of the young nation, heir to the culture of the ancients. Ssu-ma Ch'ien, for all the tragedy of his personal life, writes with a fully realized philosophy of history and surveys the centuries of unrest from the vantage point of a settled and stable empire.

A development of prime importance for the subsequent grandeur of Chinese poetry was well under way when the Han came to its end. This was the evolution, out of the common four syllables of the folk-song metre, of the regular five-syllable line. Han songs and ballads (*yüeh-fu,* from the title of the imperial music bureau which supervised their collection) used the line, and by the hands of the poets of the post-Han era it was worked to that strength and flexibility which made it and kept it a staple metre as far as recent times.

We have stressed the theme of seclusion through the period of division which separates Han from Sui and T'ang. Through all these centuries parts of the north changed hands between one invader and another; in the south, native dynasties succeeded at longer or shorter intervals. From the north especially, Buddhism flooded in to extend the metaphysical and imaginative range of Chinese art and literature, whilst the courts of some southern emperors were made brilliant by poets and wits, by men like Lu Chi, fully—and fatally—committed to the political life of his day, yet able to crystallize his most subtle understanding of the creative process in his celebrated *Essay on Literature.* Yet the darkness persisted, and through it grew always stronger the yearning for the establishment of order and of strong imperial rule, for the restoration of the glories of Han. We can hardly speak of a decadence of four hundred years' duration. But such an impression would only be strengthened by examination of the prose of the period, over-elaborate, artificial, at its worst unbearably windy and trivial.

The accession of the T'ang broke the spell: the one great merit of the "curly-bearded hero" in that wistful late-T'ang story whose title he provides is his recognition of the heavenly ordination of the dynasty. A renaissance was ushered in whose equation with the Italian would not be too misleading. Even the old vices of artificiality were turned to good account in the supreme artistry now sought and attained by the poets. Tu Fu, the acknowledged master, created a large opus of astonishing strength of feeling, control of expression and nobility of thought. The graceful hyperbole with which he complimented a fellow-poet well characterizes his own verse:

> Your poem completed, each brush-stroke offers
> The sheen of a new pearl,
> The fresh polish of jade

—every detail at once a natural and true discovery and a proof of the painstaking refinement of art.

The age of Tu Fu and Li Po saw a brilliant reign plunged into disaster by the rebel armies of the frontier-general An Lu-shan. By the end of the eighth century the great catastrophe was only a memory to the generation of Han Yü, Po Chü-yi and Yüan Chen. It was a memory, though, which gave strong stimulus to their work of reconstruction. The educated elite they represented, created and authorized by the severe literary training of the system of bureaucratic examinations, held in its keeping the culture of the race—or, in their eyes, of the civilized world. Neither Han Yü, nor Su Shih (Su Tung-p'o) of the great Sung dynasty which eventually succeeded, could have conceived of writing as other than a means of service. The "classical style (*ku-wen*) movement," of which Han Yü was a leader, worked for the tempering of a precise and expressive prose through the observance of revered models from early times. But it was a movement with ethical, political, even religious ramifications. The instrument it developed, the prose style which the Sung brought to true perfection, was the means for definitive

statements of man's place in nature and of his duties to his fellows
and to the emperor at the centre of the cosmos.

Already by T'ang times, more markedly by Sung, the strictly
formalized grammar and vocabulary of the classical written style
had become divorced from the everyday language of the mass of
the people. We have only fragmentary relics of what must have
been a vast subculture. Of the great myths of antiquity only tan-
talizing traces remain scattered through the classics, the *Songs of
Ch'u* and Han geographies. There are *yüeh-fu* songs, referred to
above; ballads; and Buddhist and secular tales, more or less crude
and incomplete. Then, during the late T'ang and through the Five
Dynasties interregnum into the Sung, a new and vital verse-form
makes its appearance. The *tz'u* poem is marked by irregular length
of line, a wide variety of prosodic patterns and a hospitality to
elements from the contemporary spoken language. It originates
with the singing girls of the brothels and teahouses who fit the
words of their celebrations and (more often) laments to new tunes
coming in from beyond the frontiers. Taken up by enthusiasts, the
tz'u entered elite society "in a period of spiritual ruin, when faint-
hearted kings and officials, particularly in the south, drugged themselves with exquisitely voluptuous poetry and dolorous music."[7]

The elastic metrical potentialities of the *tz'u* are further ex-
ploited in the *ch'ü*, and the latter, taking often the form of dramatic
monologue, comes to constitute a prime element in the extraordinary amalgam of the drama. Orchestral music, acrobatics and
mime, gorgeous costume and elaborate make-up (in the absence
of stage sets) no doubt contributed greatly to the drama of Sung
times as they do to the modern schools today. The texts of the Sung
period have vanished, but from Yüan we have fully-fledged masterpieces in the *tsa-chü* genre of theatre.

When in 1127 the reigning Sung emperor made the fateful
"crossing to the south" of the Yangtze River, his act was no more
than an acknowledgment of the irresistible pressure of the "northern barbarians" whose successors were to engulf all China in the
next century. The hardships of the common people multiplied under
military service, the exactions of rapacious officials and armed in-

7. S. H. Chen, "China: Literature" in *Encyclopaedia Americana*.

vasion itself. Their plight is reflected in the experience of the three Juan brothers, the fishermen in our extract from *The Men of the Marshes.* Our modern editions of this great story-cycle date back no further than the sixteenth century; but the adventures of its bandit-heroes furnished material for storytellers and playwrights before the Yüan dynasty was established. The work of these men seized the imagination of more conventional—and more highly trained—men of letters, and popular fiction began to make its own contribution to the Chinese literary culture. Less elegant but more vital than the highly worked classical-style stories of T'ang and Sung, this fiction in the vernacular was to play, with its sister art of the drama, an ever more pervasive role in the ages to follow.

Chou Dynasty

1122-221 B.C.

Book of Songs

As Japanese literature begins with the Man'yōshū, so does Chinese literature, a millennium earlier, begin with a great collection of songs, hymns and ballads: the Book of Songs (Shih ching) was compiled at some time after 600 B.C., traditionally by Confucius himself. The oldest parts of the corpus from which it drew may go back some four centuries further, to the beginning of the Chou dynasty.

The first two poems in the present selection suggest the range of the three hundred and five songs, all the way from solemn dynastic hymn to unabashed love lyric. In between come songs of the hunt (number 27 below), of feasting (12), of grief (24), of folk wisdom (11, 25), of seignorial homage (14) or ancestral praise (31); a rural calendar (28), an epithalamium (22) and many songs of courtship. And such a song as the tenth of our sequence clearly recalls the tradition according to which officers of state toured the countryside to bring back such ballads as would inform the ruler of the mood of his people.

Numerous examples below reveal the most common form of Shih ching ballad: three stanzas, with near or complete repetition of certain lines particularly in the first two stanzas. The commonest length of line was four syllables, and rhyme was indispensable. We have no knowledge of the tunes of the songs.

English poetry has been created from the classic by two men, one of whom is better known as a translator, the other as an original poet. Each with his individual voice expresses the authentic beauty

3

of the songs. Arthur Waley translated Nos. 1-3, 6-8, 15, 18-20, 24, 28, 31 *and* 33; *and Ezra Pound Nos.* 4-5, 9-14, 16-17, 21-23, 25-27, 29-30 *and* 32.

●

1

She who in the beginning gave birth to the people,
This was Chiang Yüan.
How did she give birth to the people?
Well she sacrificed and prayed
That she might no longer be childless.
She trod on the big toe of God's footprint,
Was accepted and got what she desired.
Then in reverence, then in awe
She gave birth, she nurtured;
And this was Hou Chi.

Indeed, she had fulfilled her months,
And her first-born came like a lamb
With no bursting or rending,
With no hurt or harm.
To make manifest His magic power
God on high gave her ease.
So blessed were her sacrifice and prayer
That easily she bore her child.

Indeed, they put it in a narrow lane;
But oxen and sheep tenderly cherished it.
Indeed, they put it in a far-off wood;
But it chanced that woodcutters came to this wood.
Indeed, they put it on the cold ice;
But the birds covered it with their wings.
The birds at last went away,
And Hou Chi began to wail.

Truly far and wide
His voice was very loud.
Then sure enough he began to crawl;

Well he straddled, well he reared,
To reach food for his mouth.
He planted large beans;
His beans grew fat and tall.
His paddy-lines were close set,
His hemp and wheat grew thick,
His young gourds teemed.

Truly Hou Chi's husbandry
Followed the way that had been shown.
He cleared away the thick grass,
He planted the yellow crop.
It failed nowhere, it grew thick,
It was heavy, it was tall,
It sprouted, it eared,
It was firm and good,
It nodded, it hung—
He made house and home in T'ai.

Indeed, the lucky grains were sent down to us,
The black millet, the double-kernelled,
Millet pink-sprouted and white.
Far and wide the black and the double-kernelled
He reaped and acred;
Far and wide the millet pink and white
He carried in his arms, he bore on his back,
Brought them home, and created the sacrifice.

Indeed, what are they, our sacrifices?
We pound the grain, we bale it out,
We sift, we tread,
We wash it—soak, soak;
We boil it all steamy.
Then with due care, due thought
We gather southernwood, make offering of fat,
Take lambs for the rite of expiation,
We roast, we broil,
To give a start to the coming year.

High we load the stands,
The stands of wood and of earthenware.
As soon as the smell rises
God on high is very pleased:
'What smell is this, so strong and good?'
Hou Chi founded the sacrifices,
And without blemish or flaw
They have gone on till now.

2

Plop fall the plums; but there are still seven.
Let those gentlemen that would court me
Come while it is lucky!

Plop fall the plums; there are still three.
Let any gentleman that would court me
Come before it is too late!

Plop fall the plums; in shallow baskets we lay them.
Any gentleman who would court me
Had better speak while there is time.

3

That the mere glimpse of a plain cap
Could harry me with such longing,
Cause pain so dire!

That the mere glimpse of a plain coat
Could stab my heart with grief!
Enough! Take me with you to your home.

That a mere glimpse of plain leggings
Could tie my heart in tangles!
Enough! Let us two be one.

4

Mid the bind-grass on the plain
that the dew makes wet as rain
I met by chance my clear-eyed man,
                    then my
                    joy began.

Mid the wild grass dank with dew
lay we the full night thru,
                    that clear-eyed man and I
                    in mutual felicity.

5

Lies a dead deer on yonder plain
whom white grass covers,
A melancholy maid in spring
                    is luck
                    for
                    lovers.

Where the scrub elm skirts the wood,
be it not in white mat bound,
as a jewel flawless found,
                    dead as doe is maidenhood.

Hark!
Unhand my girdle-knot,
                    stay, stay, stay
                    or the dog
                    may
                    bark.

6

How you make free,
There on top of the hollow mound!
Truly, a man of feeling,
But very careless of repute.

Bang, he beats his drum
Under the hollow mound.
Be it winter, be it summer,
Always with the egret feathers in his hand.

Bang, he beats his earthen gong
Along the path to the hollow mound.
Be it winter, be it summer,
Always with the egret plumes in his hand.

7

Of fair girls the loveliest
Was to meet me at the corner of the Wall.
But she hides and will not show herself;
I scratch my head, pace up and down.

Of fair girls the prettiest
Gave me a red flute.
The flush of that red flute
Is pleasure at the girl's beauty.

She has been in the pastures and brought for me rush-wool,
Very beautiful and rare.
It is not you that are beautiful;
But you were given by a lovely girl.

8

I beg of you, Chung Tzu,
Do not climb into our homestead,
Do not break the willows we have planted.
Not that I mind about the willows,
But I am afraid of my father and mother.
Chung Tzu I dearly love;
But of what my father and mother say
Indeed I am afraid.

I beg of you, Chung Tzu,
Do not climb over our wall,
Do not break the mulberry-trees we have planted.
Not that I mind about the mulberry-trees,
But I am afraid of my brothers.
Chung Tzu I dearly love;
But of what my brothers say
Indeed I am afraid.

I beg of you, Chung Tzu,
Do not climb into our garden,
Do not break the hard-wood we have planted.
Not that I mind about the hard-wood,
But I am afraid of what people will say.
Chung Tzu I dearly love;
But of all that people will say
Indeed I am afraid.

9

He's to the war
for the duration;
Hens to wall-hole,
beasts to stall,
shall I not remember
him at night-fall?

He's to the war
for the duration,
fowl to their perches,
cattle to byre;
is there food enough
drink enough
by their camp fire?

10

Yellow, withered all flowers, no day without its march,
who is not alerted?
Web of agenda over the whole four coigns.

Black dead the flowers,
no man unpitiable.
Woe to the levies,
are we not human?

Rhinos and tigers might do it, drag it out
over these desolate fields, over the sun-baked waste.
Woe to the levies,
morning and evening no rest.

Fox hath his fur, he hath shelter in valley grass,
Going the Chou Road, our wagons our hearses, we pass.

11

Thorn-elm on mountain, white elm on slope,
the clothes you never wear,
carriages idle there
be another's fact or hope
        when you are dead, who now but mope.

Kao tree on crest, shrub in low-land,
dust in your courtly dancing place,

bells on rack and drums unlaced
shall be others' jollity
        when you've proved your mortality.

Terebinth stands high on the crest, chestnut in vale,
wine thou hast and lutes in array,
undrunk, unstruck today.
Who makest not carouse:
        another shall have thy house.

            12

"Salt
lick!" deer on waste sing:
grass for the tasting, guests to feasting;
strike lute and blow
pipes to show how
feasts were in Chou,
            drum up that basket-lid now.

"Salt
lick!" deer on waste sing:
sharp grass for tasting, guests to feasting.
In clear sincerity,
here is no snobbery.
This to show how
good wine should flow
            in banquet mid true
            gentlemen.

"Salt
lick!" deer on waste sing,
k'in plants for tasting, guests to feasting;
beat drum and strum
lute and guitar,
lute and guitar to get
deep joy where wine is set
mid merry din
let the guest in, in, in, let the guest in.

13

Thick, all in mass
bring drums, bring drums
bring leather drums and play
to T'ang, to T'ang
source of us all, in fane
again, again, pray, pray:
Tang's heir, a prayer
that puts a point to thought.

With thud of the deep drum,
flutes clear, doubling over all,
concord evens it all, built on
the stone's tone under it all.
T'ang's might is terrible
with a sound as clear and sane
as wind over grain.

Steady drum going on,
great dance elaborate,
here be guests of state
to us all one delight.

From of old is this rite
former time's initiate,
calm the flow
early and late
from sun and moon concentrate
in the heart of every man
since this rite began.

Attend, attend, bale-fire and harvest home,
T'ang's heir at the turn of the moon.

14

By curvèd bank
in South Mount's innerest wood
clamped as the bamboo root, rugged as pine,
let no plots undermine
this brotherhood.

Heir'd to maintain the lines
carnal and uterine;
doors west and south,
reared up the mile-long house
wherein at rest to dwell,
converse and jest.

Tight bound the moulds wherein to ram down clay,
beaten the earth and lime gainst rain and rat,
no wind shall pierce to cold the Marquis' state
nor bird nest out of place,
here is he eaved,
who moves as on winged feet,
sleeves neat
as a pheasant's wing,
prompt as the arrow's point
to the bull's-eye.
And here the audience hall,

Rich court in peristyle
with columns high
their capitals contrived right cunningly;
cheery the main parts,
ample the recess
where he may have repose in quietness.

Mat over mat, bamboo on rush
so it be soft, to sleep, to wake in hush,

from dreams of bears and snakes?
　　　　Saith the diviner:

Which mean
Bears be for boys; snakes, girls.
Boys shall have beds, hold sceptres for their toys,
creep on red leather,
bellow when they would cry
in embroidered coats
ere come to Empery.

Small girls shall sleep on floor and play with tiles,
wear simple clothes and do no act amiss,
cook, brew and seemly speak,
conducing so the family's quietness.

15

A moon rising white
Is the beauty of my lovely one.　　─
Ah, the tenderness, the grace!
Heart's pain consumes me.

A moon rising bright
Is the fairness of my lovely one.
Ah, the gentle softness!
Heart's pain wounds me.

A moon rising in splendour
Is the beauty of my lovely one.
Ah, the delicate yielding!
Heart's pain torments me.

16

At the great gate to the East
Mid crowds

be girls like clouds
who cloud not my thought in the least.

> Gray scarf and a plain silk gown
> I take delight in one alone.

Under the towers toward the East
be fair girls like flowers to test,

> Red bonnet and plain silk gown
> I take delight with one alone.

17

She:

> Curl-grass, curl-grass,
> to pick it, to pluck it
> to put in a bucket
> never a basket load

Here cn Chou road, but a man in my mind!
> Put it down here by the road.

He:

> Pass, pass
> up over the pass,

a horse on a mountain road!
A winded horse on a high road,
give me a drink to lighten the load.
As the cup is gilt, love is spilt.
> Pain lasteth long.

Black horses, yellow with sweat,
are not come to the ridge-top yet.
> Drink deep of the rhino horn
But leave not love too long forlorn.

Tho' driver stumble and horses drop,
we come not yet to the stony top.

Let the foundered team keep on,
How should I leave my love alone!

18

How it tapered, the bamboo rod
With which you fished in the Ch'i!
It is not that I do not love you,
But it is so far that I cannot come.

The Well Spring is on the left;
The Ch'i River on the right.
When a girl is married
She is far from brothers, from father and mother.

The Ch'i River is on the right,
The Well Spring is on the left;
But, oh, the grace of his loving smile!
Oh, the quiver of his girdle stones!

The Ch'i spreads its waves;
Oars of juniper, boat of pine-wood.
Come, yoke the horses, let us drive away,
That I may be rid at last of my pain.

19

If along the highroad
I caught hold of your sleeve,
Do not hate me;
Old ways take time to overcome.

If along the highroad
I caught hold of your hand,
Do not be angry with me;
Friendship takes time to overcome.

20

Tall stands that pear-tree;
Its leaves are fresh and fair.
But alone I walk, in utter solitude.
True indeed, there are other men;
But they are not like children of one's own father.
Heigh, you that walk upon the road,
Why do you not join me?
A man that has no brothers,
Why do you not help him?

Tall stands that pear-tree;
Its leaves grow very thick.
Alone I walk and unbefriended.
True indeed, there are other men;
But they are not like people of one's own clan.
Heigh, you that walk upon the road,
Why do you not join me?
A man that has no brothers,
Why do you not help him?

21

Some reeds be found by river's brink
and some by catchit pool
that she doth pull and pluck
to bring by basket-full;

Be her baskets round or square
she doth then all this catch prepare
in pots and pans of earthen-ware;

Then neath the light-hole of the shrine
she sets the lot in neat array

that all the family manes come
bless proper bride in ordered home.

22

Tall girl with a profile,
broidery neath a simple dress,
brought from Ts'i her loveliness
to Wei's marquisat.

Younger sister of Tung-Kung
("Palace of the East," crown-prince)
One sister of hers is the darling
of the great lord of Hing,
the other's man, T'an's viscount is.

Hand soft as a blade of grass,
a skin like cream, neck like the glow-worm's light,
her teeth as melon seeds,
a forehead neat as is a katydid's,
her brows and lids, as when you see her smile
or her eyes turn, she dimpling the while,
clear white, gainst black iris.

Tall she came thru the till'd fields to the town,
her quadriga orderly
that four high stallions drew
with scarlet-tasselled bits, and pheasant tails
in woven paravant.
Thus to the court, great officers, retire,
and let our noble Lord assuage his fire.

Ho tumbles north, tumultuous, animate,
forking the hills;
sturgeon and gamey trout
swim and leap out
to spat of nets and flap of flat fish-tails,

with Kiang dames' high hair-dos flashing bright
above the cortège's armèd might.

23

White the marsh flower that white grass bindeth,
my love's afar,
    I am alone.

White cloud and white dew shun,
amid all flowers, none.
Steep are the steps of heaven
    to him unknown.

The overflow seeps north from the pool,
rice hath its good therefrom;
singing I sigh
for a tall man far from home.

Are mulberries hacked to firewood for the stove?
A tall man, hard of head, wrecks my love.

Drums, gongs in the palace court
are heard by passers by,
yet if you think at all
of my pain, you think but scornfully.

Tall maribou stand at the dam,
cranes cry over dry forest
that a tall man teareth
the heart in my breast.

Drake at the weir spread a wing to the left in amity,
in man's unkindness his mind
is scattered as two against three.

These flat thin stones will not raise
me high enough to see
him who embitters my days.

24

Tossed is that cypress boat,
Wave-tossed it floats.
My heart is in turmoil, I cannot sleep.
But secret is my grief.
Wine I have, all things needful
For play, for sport.

My heart is not a mirror,
To reflect what others will.
Brothers too I have;
I cannot be snatched away.
But lo, when I told them of my plight
I found that they were angry with me.

My heart is not a stone;
It cannot be rolled.
My heart is not a mat;
It cannot be folded away.
I have borne myself correctly
In rites more than can be numbered.

My sad heart is consumed, I am harassed
By a host of small men.
I have borne vexations very many,
Received insults not few.
In the still of night I brood upon it;
In the waking hours I rend my breast.

O sun, ah, moon,
Why are you changed and dim?
Sorrow clings to me
Like an unwashed dress.
In the still of night I brood upon it,
Long to take wing and fly away.

25

Rabbit goes soft-foot, pheasant's caught,
I began life with too much élan,
Troubles come to a bustling man.
   "Down Oh, and give me a bed!"

Rabbit soft-foot, pheasant's in trap,
I began life with a flip and flap,
Then a thousand troubles fell on my head,
   "If I could only sleep like the dead!"

Rabbit goes soft-foot, pheasant gets caught.
A youngster was always rushin' round,
Troubles crush me to the ground.
   I wish I could sleep and not hear a sound.

26

So have I seen him in his service car
who now in war afar,
five bands on the curving pole, side shields and silver'd trace,
bright mats and bulging hub;
dapple and white-foot pace
into my thought. I see him neat as jade
in service shack, and in my thought confused.

Great dapples held, and by six reins restrained,
black-maned,
the darker pair outside,
locked dragon shield and silver-ringèd rein
before my thought again
who now by border wall
moves suave as once in hall.

Team in an even block, gilt trident-haft
with silver-basèd butt, and emboss'd shields,
bow-case of tiger's fell, graved lorica;
the bows are bound to laths inside their case;
Shall he not fill my thought,
                by day, by night,
whose mind and act are right,
whose fame, delight?

27

Shu's to the field, the reins of his double team
seem silken strands;
His outer stallions move
as in a pantomime. Thru thicket and marsh
flare beaters' fires.
Stript to the waist he holds a tiger down
for the Duke's smile and frown:
                "This once, but not again.
                I need such men."

Shu's to the hunt,
his wheel-bays pull strong.
The other pair are as twin geese a-wing.
He comes to marsh, the beaters' fires flash out.
Good archer and good driver to control,
The envy of all, be it to drive or shoot.

Again to hunting, now with the grays,
Pole pair show even head,
Outer pair like a hand outspread.
Shu to the break,
thru thicket swamp flare the fires.
Then driving slow,
Quiver set down, shoot comes to end.
Envy of all, he cases his bow.

28

In the seventh month the Fire ebbs;
In the ninth month I hand out the coats.
In the days of the First, sharp frosts;
In the days of the Second, keen winds.
Without coats, without serge,
How should they finish the year?
In the days of the Third they plough;
In the days of the Fourth out I step
With my wife and children,
Bringing hampers to the southern acre
Where the field-hands come to take good cheer.

In the seventh month the Fire ebbs;
In the ninth month I hand out the coats.
But when the spring days grow warm
And the oriole sings
The girls take their deep baskets
And follow the path under the wall
To gather the soft mulberry-leaves:
'The spring days are drawing out;
They gather the white aster in crowds.
A girl's heart is sick and sad
Till with her lord she can go home.'

In the seventh month the Fire ebbs;
In the eighth month they pluck the rushes,
In the silk-worm month they gather the mulberry-leaves,
Take that chopper and bill
To lop the far boughs and high,
Pull towards them the tender leaves.
In the seventh month the shrike cries;
In the eighth month they twist thread,
The black thread and the yellow:
'With my red dye so bright
I make a robe for my lord.'

In the fourth month the milkwort is in spike,
In the fifth month the cicada cries.
In the eighth month the harvest is gathered,
In the tenth month the boughs fall.
In the days of the First we hunt the racoon,
And take those foxes and wild-cats
To make furs for our Lord.
In the days of the Second is the great Meet;
Practice for deeds of war.
The one-year-old boar we keep;
The three-year-old we offer to our Lord.

In the fifth month the locust moves its leg,
In the sixth month the grasshopper shakes its wing,
In the seventh month, out in the wilds;
In the eighth month, in the farm,
In the ninth month, at the door.
In the tenth month the cricket goes under my bed.
I stop up every hole to smoke out the rats,
Plugging the windows, burying the doors:
'Come, wife and children,
The change of the year is at hand.
Come and live in this house.'

In the sixth month we eat wild plums and cherries,
In the seventh month we boil mallows and beans.
In the eighth month we dry the dates,
In the tenth month we take the rice
To make with it the spring wine,
So that we may be granted long life.
In the seventh month we eat melons,
In the eighth month we cut the gourds,
In the ninth month we take the seeding hemp,
We gather bitter herbs, we cut the ailanto for firewood,
That our husbandmen may eat.

In the ninth month we make ready the stack-yards,
In the tenth month we bring in the harvest,
Millet for wine, millet for cooking, the early and the late,

Paddy and hemp, beans and wheat.
Come, my husbandmen,
My harvesting is over,
Go up and begin your work in the house,
In the morning gather thatch-reeds,
In the evening twist rope;
Go quickly on to the roofs.
Soon you will be beginning to sow your many grains.

In the days of the Second they cut the ice with tingling blows;
In the days of the Third they bring it into the cold shed.
In the days of the Fourth very early
They offer lambs and garlic.
In the ninth month are shrewd frosts;
In the tenth month they clear the stack-grounds.
With twin pitchers they hold the village feast,
Killing for it a young lamb.
Up they go into their lord's hall,
Raise the drinking-cup of buffalo-horn:
'Hurray for our lord; may he live for ever and ever!'

29

Speed, speed the plow
on south slopes now
grain is to sow
            lively within.

Here come your kin,
baskets round
baskets square,
millet's there.

With a crowd of rain-hats
and clicking hoes
out goes the weed
to mulch and rot
on dry and wet,
crop will be thicker on that spot.

Harvest high,
reapers come by
so they mow
to heap it like a wall
comb-tooth'd and tall

an hundred barns to fill
till wives and childer fear no ill.

At harvest home kill a yellow bull,
by his curved horn is luck in full
(be he black-nosed seven foot high,
so tall's felicity).

Thus did
men of old
who left us this land
to have and to hold.

30

Heaven conserve thy course in quietness,
Solid thy unity, thy weal endless
that all the crops increase and nothing lack
in any common house.

Heaven susteyne thy course in quietness
that thou be just in all, and reap
so, as it were at ease, that every day
seem festival.

Heaven susteyne thy course in quietness
To abound and rise as mountain hill and range
constant as rivers flow that all augment
steady th'increase in ever cyclic change.

Pure be the victuals of thy sacrifice
throughout the year as autumns move to springs,

above the fane to hear "ten thousand years"
spoke by the manes of foregone dukes and kings.

Spirits of air assign felicity:
thy folk be honest, in food and drink delight;
dark-haired the hundred tribes concord
in act born of thy true insight.

As moon constant in phase; as sun to rise;
as the south-hills nor crumble nor decline;
as pine and cypress evergreen the year
be thy continuing line.

31

So they appeared before their lord the king
To get from him their emblems,
Dragon-banners blazing bright,
Tuneful bells tinkling,
Bronze-knobbed reins jangling—
The gifts shone with glorious light.
Then they showed them to their shining ancestors
Piously, making offering,
That they might be vouchsafed long life,
Everlastingly be guarded.
Oh, a mighty store of blessings!
Glorious and mighty, those former princes and lords
Who secure us with many blessings,
Through whose bright splendours
We greatly prosper.

32

When he planned to begin a spirit tower
folk rushed to the work-camp and overran
all the leisure of King Wen's plan;

old and young with never a call
had it up in no time at all.

The king stood in his "Park Divine,"
deer and doe lay there so fine,
so fine so sleek; birds of the air
flashed a white wing while fishes splashed
on wing-like fin in the haunted pool.

Great drums and gongs
hung on spiked frames
sounding to perfect rule and rote
about the king's calm crescent moat,

Tone unto tone, of drum and gong.

About the king's calm crescent moat
the blind musicians beat lizard skin
as the tune weaves out and in.

33

Don't escort the big chariot;
You will only make yourself dusty.
Don't think about the sorrows of the world;
You will only make yourself wretched.

Don't escort the big chariot;
You won't be able to see for dust.
Don't think about the sorrows of the world;
Or you will never escape from your despair.

Don't escort the big chariot;
You'll be stifled with dust.
Don't think about the sorrows of the world;
You will only load yourself with care.

Early Historical Writings

Of the excerpts in this section, the first is from the Tso Commentary (Tso chuan), *the second from the* Conversations from the States (Kuo yü) *and the "Three Persuasions" is from the* Intrigues of the Warring States (Chan kuo ts'e). *Each of these works is venerated in the corpus of early Chinese historical writings. Only the first, however, was actually collected into the classical canon, its contents having been arranged to form a "commentary" to the* Spring and Autumn Annals (Ch'un ch'iu) *which old traditions credited to the authorship of Confucius. This* Commentary *by Tso Ch'iu-ming is believed to have been compiled in the third century* B.C., *shortly before the close of the Chou dynasty whose earlier history it narrates.*

The Conversations *"cover roughly the same period as the* Tso chuan, *deal with many of the same persons and events, and even contain passages that are almost identical with the* Tso *narrative," according to our translator.*

"Warring States" is the name given to the fourth and third centuries B.C., *the late years of the Chou brought to an end by the unification of China by the First Emperor (of Ch'in) in 221* B.C. *The* Intrigues *draw historical persons and events from this period, but are concerned less with the narration of history than with supplying instances of rhetoric and guile in the service of statecraft. The "Persuasions," then, are highly characteristic of the work as a whole, and show a more sophisticated level of literary inventiveness than earlier prose can offer: Fan Sui (Ying-hou) in the first*

extract from the Intrigues, *like Sable P'o in the second, is believed by the translator to be a fictitious character.*

The Faults of Ch'in *is taken from a celebrated essay by the poet and statesman Chia Yi (201-169* B.C.). *Since the inexorable rise of Ch'in to its brief tenure of imperial power was the central reality of the entire late Chou period, it is fitting that this historical section should close with a moral homily on the downfall of the Ch'in dynasty.*

●

The Tso Commentary

The Death of Duke Ching of Chin

Duke Ching dreamt that he saw a huge ogre with disheveled hair hanging to the ground, who beat his chest and leapt about, screaming, "You killed my grandsons—you will suffer for your evil deed! Heaven has promised me revenge!" The ogre broke down the main gate of the palace, then the door of the inner apartments. The duke fled in terror to his chamber, but the ogre broke down the chamber door as well. At this moment the duke awoke. He at once sent for the sorcerer of Mulberry Field. The sorcerer, without asking what had happened, described the duke's dream exactly as it had occurred.

"What will become of me?" asked the duke.

"You will not live to eat the new grain!" replied the sorcerer.

Soon afterwards the duke fell gravely ill. He sent for a doctor to the state of Ch'in, whose ruler dispatched a physician named Huan to treat him. Before the physician arrived, the duke had a dream in which his illness appeared to him in the guise of two little boys. One boy said, "Huan is a skilled physician. I am afraid he will harm us. How can we escape?" The other boy replied, "If we go to the region above the diaphragm and below the heart, what can he do to us?"

As soon as the physician arrived he told the duke, "I can do nothing for your illness. It is located above the diaphragm and below the heart. No treatment can affect it there: acupuncture will not penetrate, and internal medicine is useless. There is nothing I can do."

"You are a good doctor," said the duke and, after entertaining him with all courtesy, he sent him back to Ch'in.

On the day *ping-wu* of the sixth month, the duke decided he would like to taste the new grain and ordered the steward of his

32

private domain to present some. When his manservant had prepared the grain the duke summoned the sorcerer of Mulberry Field, pointed out the error of his prophecy and had him executed. Then the duke started to eat the grain, but his stomach swelled up and, hurrying to the privy, he fell down the hole and died.

One of the duke's servants had dreamt in the early morning hours that he was carrying the duke on his back up to Heaven. He was consequently delegated to bear the duke's body on his back out of the privy, after which he was executed so that his spirit might accompany the duke in death.

TRANSLATED BY BURTON WATSON

Conversations from the States

The Downfall of Prince Shen-sheng

[*Prince Shen-sheng—d.* 655 B.C.—*was the eldest son of Duke Hsien of Chin and had accordingly been designated crown prince to succeed his father. His mother, a noblewoman of Ch'i, had died some years before the narrative begins.*]

Duke Hsien divined to see whether or not he should attack the Jung barbarians of Mount Li. The historian Su, who conducted the divination, announced, "The attack will be victorious but unlucky."

Ignoring this prediction, the duke proceeded to attack and defeat the Jung barbarians. He brought back as a captive Lady Li, the daughter of the barbarian chief, and treated her with great favor, eventually making her his new consort.

One day the duke, dispensing wine to his ministers, ordered the master of ceremonies to fill a goblet and offer it to the historian Su. "I give you wine, but no meat to go with it," he said. "When I was planning my campaign against the Jung barbarians of Li you predicted that the attack would be victorious but unlucky. Therefore I reward you with this goblet of wine for your prediction of victory, but punish your false prediction of ill luck by withholding the meat. What could be more fortunate than to conquer a state and win myself a consort?"

The historian Su drained the cup, bowed his head twice and replied, "That was the oracle. I dared not hide it. I should be guilty of a double fault if by concealing the meaning of a prognostication I failed to carry out the duties of my office. How then could I serve my lord? I should call down upon myself a punishment far worse than being deprived of meat with my wine!

"Yet, my lord, even while you delight in this good luck I would have you also prepare for misfortune. If the misfortune never oc-

34

curs, what harm will there have been in the preparations? And if it should occur, the preparations will mitigate it. If my prediction proves to have been wrong, it will be a blessing to the state. How could I object to punishment for such a happy error?"

He drank the wine and departed.

[*The duke, having fallen under the spell of Lady Li, who has borne him a son named Hsi-ch'i, is persuaded to consider removing Shensheng from his position of heir and designating Lady Li's son in his place. In the following highly stylized scene, three ministers of Chin appear, as though upon a stage, and state their respective opinions on the proposed step.*]

Lady Li gave birth to Hsi-ch'i and her younger sister gave birth to Cho-tzu. The duke wished to remove his son Shen-sheng from the position of crown prince and establish Hsi-ch'i in his place. Li K'o, P'i Cheng and Hsün Hsi met one day. "The misfortune which the historian Su predicted would befall the state is about to strike us," said Li K'o. "What shall we do?"

"I have heard that he who serves his lord performs his duties to the best of his ability," said Hsün Hsi. "I have never heard that he goes about disobeying orders. Whomsoever the ruler establishes as his successor we should follow. What right have we to question this change?"

"I have heard," said P'i Cheng, "that he who serves his ruler follows what is right but does not flatter the ruler's delusions. If the ruler is deluded the people will be misled, and if the people are misled they will abandon virtue. This is nothing less than to cast the people aside. The reason the people have a ruler is that he may guide them in doing right. Right brings profit, and profit enriches the people. How can a ruler live with his people and still cast them aside? Shen-sheng must be retained as crown prince!"

Li K'o said, "I am no good at making speeches, but though I may not know what is right, neither will I flatter delusion. I had best remain silent."

With this the three ministers parted.

[*Lady Li, conspiring with one of the duke's palace actors named Shih, with whom she is carrying on a clandestine affair, plots the downfall of her son's rival. By means of deceit and hypocritical tears she succeeds in arousing the duke's suspicions against the crown prince Shen-sheng, and by various pretexts she manages to have him sent on several expeditions of conquest. From each of these he returns victorious. His success, however, only makes the duke contemplate the more anxiously his son's increasing fame and favor with the people. Finally Lady Li begins to slander Shen-sheng openly, playing upon the duke's fear that the prince may be plotting a revolt. In the following scene, as her scheme nears consummation, Lady Li attempts to discover which side the minister Li K'o will support in the event of an open break.*]

Lady Li said to the actor Shih, "The duke has already promised me that he will kill the crown prince and establish my son Hsi-ch'i as heir. But I am worried about what Li K'o will do."

"It will take me but one day to win Li K'o to our side!" said the actor. "Prepare a feast of the meat of a ram for me, and I will take wine and go wait upon him. I am an actor. I know how to avoid saying anything indiscreet."

Lady Li agreed to do as he suggested. When everything was prepared, she sent him to drink with Li K'o, and when the drinking had reached its height, the actor Shih rose from his place and prepared to dance. "Lady Meng," he said to Li K'o's wife, "if you will give me a bite to eat, I will teach this contented gentleman how to serve his lord." Then he began to sing:

> "Contented gentleman, aloof and solitary,
> No match for the flocks of birds:
> While others gather in the flourishing grove,
> You perch alone on a withered branch."

Li K'o laughed and said, "What grove do you mean? And what is the withered branch?"

"The mother a royal consort, the son a lord—is that not a flourishing grove? The mother long since dead, the son ill spoken of—is this not a withered branch? What is withered will be cut off!"

With this the actor took his departure.

Li K'o ordered the gifts of food taken away and, without eating any supper, retired to bed. In the middle of the night he sent for the actor Shih and said, "Were you only joking earlier? Or have you really heard something?"

"I have," replied Shih. "Our lord has already promised Lady Li that he will kill the crown prince and set up her son Hsi-ch'i as his heir. The plans are all settled."

"I could not bear to assist my lord in killing the crown prince," said Li K'o. "And yet, now that I know of the plot, I would not dare to associate with the crown prince as I have in the past. If I were to remain neutral, do you think I could escape harm?"

"You will escape," said Shih.

[*Lady Li is now ready to deliver the final blow. Shen-sheng, though fully aware of her machinations and the way she has managed to delude his father, remains throughout apprehensive but unwilling or unable to take any steps to combat the forces opposing him. He is the model of passive suffering, a figure tragically paralyzed by the ideal of filial piety.*]

Lady Li came to Shen-sheng with an order from the duke, saying, "Last night our lord dreamt of your mother, the princess of Ch'i. You must sacrifice to her spirit at once and bring him a portion of the sacrifice!"

Shen-sheng consented and, having performed the sacrifice at his fief in Ch'ü-wo, returned to the capital with the sacrificial meat and wine. The duke was out hunting and Lady Li received the offerings. Then she mixed poison with the sacrificial wine and soaked the meat in deadly aconite.

When the duke returned, he summoned Shen-sheng to present his offerings. The duke poured a libation of the wine on the ground, but the ground boiled up. Shen-sheng was frightened and left the palace. Lady Li threw some of the meat to one of the dogs and the dog died. She gave the wine to a servant to drink and the servant died too. The duke ordered the execution of Shen-sheng's tutor Tu Yüan-k'uan. Shen-sheng fled to the New City, his fief in Ch'ü-wo. . . .

Someone said to Shen-sheng, "You have committed no fault. Why do you not leave the realm?"

"I cannot," he replied. "If I were to evade the blame by departing, then it would fall upon my lord. This would be to defame my lord. If I were to expose my father's faults and make him a laughingstock among the other lords, what land could I look to for refuge? . . . I shall bow down and wait my lord's command."

Lady Li appeared before Shen-sheng and wept. "If you could bear to do this to your own father, what would you not do to your countrymen? You would sacrifice your father in order to curry favor with others, but who would favor such as *you*? You would kill your father in order to seek gain from others, but who would grant *you* gain? Deeds such as these all men despise. It will be a hard thing for you to live for long!"

After Lady Li had left, Shen-sheng hanged himself in the ancestral temple of the New City.

TRANSLATED BY BURTON WATSON

Intrigues of the Warring States

Three Persuasions

I

"Your majesty has doubtless heard about the Spirit of the Grove in the country of Hanker?" Ying-hou asked King Chao of Ch'in. "There lived in Hanker an extremely rash youth who got the Sacred Grove to gamble with him. 'If I beat you,' said the boy, 'you must lend me your genie for three days. If I lose to you, you may do as you please with me.' So saying, he cast the dice for the Grove with his left hand and for himself with his right. The Grove lost and lent the boy his genie for three days. But when the Grove went back to get his Spirit, he was turned away. Five days later the Grove began to rot and in seven it had died.

"The country of Ch'in is your majesty's Grove and power is its genie: is it not a course fraught with danger to lend it to others? Now I have never heard of a finger being greater than an arm nor of an arm being greater than a leg, but if such should exist it could only indicate a serious disease!

"A hundred men scrambling to fetch a gourd by cart will accomplish less than one man holding it in his hand and walking purposefully. For if the hundred actually managed to get it aboard their wagon you may be quite sure that the gourd would be split asunder when it arrived. Today the country of Ch'in is used by Lord Hua-yang, by Jang-hou, by the Queen Mother and by your majesty. If it is not to become a gourd with which any may dip his water this should stop. For you may be quite sure that when a country does become a gourd for all to dip with, it too will be split asunder.

"I have heard it said, 'when the fruit is heavy the bough is strained, when the bough is strained the trunk is harmed; when a capital is great it endangers the state, when a minister is strong

39

he menaces his king.' Yet in your city today every man worth more than a peck of grain is the minister's man—this includes your majesty's lieutenants, chancellors, and even personal attendants. Even in times of peace this should not happen, but should there ever be trouble, then I would certainly witness a king standing all alone in his own court.

"I have the temerity to feel fear for your majesty. And what I fear is that in the country of Ch'in, many generations hence, the rulers will no longer be descendants of yours.

"Your servant has heard that the awesome presence of great rulers in the past held their ministers in check at home and spread their control abroad over the land. Their government was neither troubled nor seditious and their deputies trod a straight path, fearing to do otherwise. But today the deputies of Jang-hou split the lords among themselves, and tallies given by his hand are recognized all over the land. He arrogates the power of a great state to muster troops and attack the lords, but the profits from his victories and gains all return to his own fief of T'ao, the spoils enter the treasuries of the Queen Mother and revenues from within your borders find their way to Lord Hua-yang. Surely what used to be called 'the road to danger and destruction for state and ruler' begins here.

"If three honored persons can drain the state to secure themselves, can the king's power be absolute? Will all commands originate with him? In truth, your majesty, only one in every three actually does."

II

A certain Sable P'o several times slandered T'ien Tan at court saying he was a small man without principles. When T'ien Tan heard of this he set out wine and summoned Sable P'o.

"What have I done to offend you, sir, that you should vilify me before my king?"

"When robber Chih's dog barked at Yao," replied the Sable, "it did not favor footpads like Chih and hold sages such as Yao worthless. A dog merely barks at those who are not its master.

"Suppose nowadays," he continued, "there were a Duke Noble who was worthy and a Mr. Tardy who was not. The two of them fight; Mr. Tardy's dog springs at Duke Noble and nips his heels, of course. But, further suppose the dog finally to leave the unworthy and serve the worthy master—perhaps then that dog would do more than just nip the heels of the unworthy!"

"I hear and respect your commands," replied T'ien Tan and the following day he commended Sable P'o to the king.

At the time the king had nine ministers he favored and it was they who wished harm to T'ien Tan. And so they said to the king:

"While Yen attacked Ch'i, the king of Ch'u sent to us his general and ten thousand troops to aid our country. Now the state is restored and its altars safe. Should we not send an emissary to the king of Ch'u to thank him?"

"Who among my attendants would be fit for this?" asked the king. And the nine men replied as one:

"Sable P'o is fit."

Sable P'o went to Ch'u and there the king honored and feasted him. And for many days he did not return.

The nine ministers all said to the king:

"Here is a common man who has impressed the king of a mighty country. Why should he not manage our state's affairs? For indeed, T'ien Tan's attitude toward your majesty has lacked the ceremony proper between sovereign and minister; the lower has not been distinct from the higher. In truth his ambition is to do 'that which is improper.'[1] Within the country he has received commoners and complied with their desires: he has prospered the poor, supplied the destitute, and spread a name for virtue among the citizens. Abroad he has won over the barbarians, and at home the worthies of the empire. Secretly he has allied himself with the mightiest and bravest among the feudal lords. He means to do mischief and we wish your majesty to examine him."

"Summon Tan the minister," cried the king when another day had gone by. T'ien Tan entered without cap or sandals and approached the king with his back bared for punishment. He withdrew and requested the death penalty.

On the fifth day thereafter the king announced: "Sir, you have not offended me to that extent, but you shall continue to observe only

---

1. A euphemism for seizing the throne.

that conduct which befits a king's minister and I only that conduct befitting a minister's king!"

Sable P'o returned from Ch'u and the king offered him wine with his own hand. And when they had both felt the pleasure of drink the king cried:

"Summon Tan the minister!"

Sable P'o left his mat and bowed down. "Your majesty, whence comes this style of speech proper to a doomed kingdom? Among kings, is your majesty the equal of Chou's King Wen?"

"I am not."

"That is so, your minister knows you are not. Among lesser rulers, is your majesty the equal of Ch'i's Duke Huan?"

"I am not."

"That is so, your minister knows you are not.

"However," continued Sable P'o, "King Wen had by him Lü Wang, whom he addressed as 'Grand Duke,' while Duke Huan had by him Kuan Yi-wu, whom he called 'Second Father.' Your majesty has by him the lord of An-p'ing, T'ien Tan, whom he insults, addressing him by his given name! Surely there has never been—since the creation of heaven and earth, since the beginnings of mankind—a minister more faithful than T'ien Tan, lord of An-p'ing. And yet your majesty cries 'Tan, Tan': whence comes this form of speech proper only to a state which is damned?

"When your majesty could not guard the altars of his ancestors, when the Yen armies rose and assaulted the bastions of Ch'i, your majesty fled to Chü in the mountains of Ch'eng-yang while the lord of An-p'ing held tiny Chi-mo—which trembled in fear—with seven thousand wearied soldiers. But from those three li of city wall and those five li of suburb he captured the Yen commander and recovered a thousand li of our country—such was the merit of Lord An-p'ing. At that time he could have sealed off your majesty in Ch'eng-yang and himself ruled—there would have been no one in the world to stop him. But his plans were conceived in virtue and tested against righteousness so he knew it could not be done. Therefore he made his way over the steeps and passes to welcome your majesty and his queen among the mountains of Ch'eng-yang. Thus your majesty was enabled to return and rule over his people. And so it is that today your country is ordered and your people at

peace! Your majesty now summons this man by calling 'Tan,' as
though he were an infant; but they were not plans of a child which
made all these things possible. If your majesty does not now execute those nine scheming men to vindicate the lord of An-p'ing, then
this state will truly be in peril!"

The king had the nine executed and drove their families from
the state. He added ten thousand families of Yeh-yi to the fief of
Lord An-p'ing.

III

The queen of Chao had just assumed authority when Ch'in
suddenly attacked. Chao sought succor of Ch'i, which country sent
word that the queen's son, Prince Ch'ang-an, must be sent as hostage[2] before the soldiers of Ch'i would come forth. The queen was
unwilling, but her ministers so strongly importuned that she cried
out to the courtiers: "Whosoever again urges that Prince Ch'ang-an
be a hostage, I will spit in his face!"

The elderly commander, Ch'u Che, asked audience of the
queen. She contained her anger enough to greet him. When he
entered he walked very slowly and having reached her he apologized for himself.

"It is because your minister's feet pain him that he cannot walk
quickly," he said, "and because of this it has been long since I have
had audience with your majesty. But while I was excusing my absence for this reason it occurred to me that perhaps your majesty's
own comfort might be similarly impaired, which is why I requested
an audience."

"I go about only in the palanquin," she replied.

"The quality of your majesty's meals has not diminished?"

"I eat only to live."

"Your minister lately had a similar disinclination for food, so
he forced himself to walk a short distance each day. This slightly
increased the appetite, and—it is good for one's health."

"I am not able to do it," said the queen whose color had somewhat subsided.

---

2. It was the custom at this time for sons of the royal family of one state
to reside as "pledges" or "hostages" at the courts of other states in order to
insure the continuance of friendly relations between the states.

"Your majesty," said the commander after a moment, "I grow old and though my son Shu-ch'i is worthless and quite young, I love him greatly and beseech your majesty to grant him the black uniform of the palace guards that he may win fame by risking his life for you."

"It is granted, of course," replied the queen. "How old is the boy?"

"Fifteen. But young as he is I want to put him in your majesty's care before I fill my shallow grave."

"Does a brave man love and cherish a young son then?" asked the queen.

"More than a woman!"

The queen laughed. "Ah, a woman is a different thing entirely!"

"Your majesty," said the commander, "in my ignorance I assumed you favored your daughter, the Queen of Yen, over Prince Ch'ang-an."

"My minister is completely mistaken! Prince Ch'ang-an is dearer to me."

"But when a parent loves his offspring he is ever mindful of planning far in advance for the child," replied the commander. "When your majesty parted from your daughter you clasped her feet and wept—wept for the distance that would separate you, and it saddened us. Nor did your majesty forget her when she had left, you thought of her at the time of sacrifice and prayed for her. Yet, this prayer was always, 'let her not return'! Was this not because your majesty was thinking far in the future for her child? . . . praying that her sons and grandsons would succeed each other as kings?"

"It was."

"But your majesty," continued the commander, "before the present three generations, and back as far as the beginnings of the kingdom of Chao have there been many sons and grandsons succeeding a king to his throne?"

"No, there have not," replied the queen.

"Has it been only Chao? Have any of the other lords been succeeded by their sons and grandsons?"

"I have not heard so."

"This is why it is said, 'an error of the present strikes the living, an error for the future strikes sons and grandsons,' " said the commander. "Certainly it is not that among rulers of men sons and grandsons *must* be bad! Is it not rather that high position is given where no merit exists; that favored treatment is won with no effort, and much wealth has come too easily to hand?

"Your majesty has raised Prince Ch'ang-an to high position, favored him with the richest lands and given him much wealth, but you do not order him in this present instance to show mettle for his country. When a new royal tomb is raised, what reasons will Prince Ch'ang-an have had to devote himself to Chao? This, your majesty, is why your minister assumed that you favored your daughter, the Queen of Yen, since your hopes for her were of longer range."

"Let it be done as my minister wishes," said the queen.

Prince Ch'ang-an was given a retinue of one hundred carts and went into Ch'i as hostage; whereupon the troops of Ch'i were sent forth.

TRANSLATED BY J. I. CRUMP

Chia Yi
[*Kuo Ch'in lun*]

The Faults of Ch'in

Duke Hsiao of Ch'in, relying upon the strength of the Han-ku Pass and basing himself in the area of Yung-chou, with his ministers held fast to his land and eyed the house of Chou, for he cherished a desire to roll up the empire like a mat, to bind into one the whole world, to bag all the land within the four seas; he had it in his heart to swallow up everything in the eight directions. At this time he was aided by Lord Shang who set up laws for him, encouraged agriculture and weaving, built up the instruments of war, contracted military alliances and attacked the other feudal lords. Thus the men of Ch'in were able with ease to acquire territory east of the upper reaches of the Yellow River.

After the death of Duke Hsiao, kings Hui-wen, Wu, and Chao-hsiang carried on the undertaking and, following the plans he had laid, seized Han-chung in the south and Pa and Shu in the west, acquired rich land in the east and strategic areas in the north. The other feudal lords in alarm came together in council to devise some plan to weaken Ch'in, sparing nothing in gifts of precious objects and rich lands to induce men from all over the empire to come and join with them in the Vertical Alliance . . . which united all the peoples of the states of Han, Wei, Yen, Ch'u, Ch'i, Chao, Sung, Wei and Chung-shan. . . . With ten times the area of Ch'in and a force of a million soldiers they beat upon the pass and pressed forward to Ch'in. But the men of Ch'in opened the pass and went out to meet the enemy, and the armies of the nine states were blocked and did not dare to advance. Ch'in, without wasting a single arrow or losing a single arrowhead, at one stroke made trouble for the whole empire.

With this the Vertical Alliance collapsed, its treaties came to naught and the various states hastened to present Ch'in with parts of their territories as bribes for peace. With its superior strength Ch'in pressed the crumbling forces of its rivals, pursued those who had fled in defeat, and overwhelmed the army of a million until their shields floated upon a river of blood. Following up the advantages of its victory, Ch'in gained mastery over the empire and divided up the land as it saw fit. The powerful states begged to submit to its sovereignty and the weak ones paid homage at its court.

Then followed kings Hsiao-wen and Chuang-hsiang whose reigns were short and uneventful. After this the First Emperor arose to carry on the glorious achievements of six generations. Cracking his long whip, he drove the universe before him, swallowing up the eastern and western Chou and overthrowing the feudal lords. He ascended to the highest position and ruled the six directions, scourging the world with his rod, and his might shook the four seas. In the south he seized the land of Yüeh and made of it the Cassia Forest and Elephant commanderies, and the hundred lords of Yüeh bowed their heads, hung halters from their necks, and pleaded for their lives with the lowest officials of Ch'in. Then he caused Meng T'ien to build the Great Wall and defend the borders, driving back the Hsiung-nu over seven hundred li so that the barbarians no longer dared to come south to pasture their horses and their men dared not take up their bows to avenge their hatred.

Thereupon he discarded the ways of the former kings and burned the writings of the hundred schools in order to make the people ignorant. He destroyed the major fortifications of the states, assassinated their powerful leaders, collected all the arms of the empire, and had them brought to his capital at Hsien-yang where the spears and arrowheads were melted down to make twelve human statues, all in order to weaken the people of the empire. After this he ascended and fortified Mount Hua and set up fords along the Yellow River, strengthening the heights and precipices overlooking the deep valleys. He garrisoned the strategic points with skilled generals and expert bowmen and stationed trusted ministers and well-trained soldiers to guard the land with arms and question all who passed back and forth. When he had thus pacified the empire, the First Emperor believed in his heart that with the strength of his capital within the Pass and his walls of metal extending a thousand miles, he had established a rule that would be enjoyed by his descendants for ten thousand generations.

For a while after the death of the First Emperor the memory of his might continued to awe the common people. Yet Ch'en She, born in a humble hut with tiny windows and wattle door, a day laborer in the fields and a garrison conscript, whose abilities could not match even the average, who had neither the worth of Confucius and Mo Tzu nor the wealth of T'ao Chu or Yi Tun, stepped from the ranks of the common soldiers, rose up from the paths of the fields and led a band of some hundred poor, weary troops in revolt against the Ch'in. They cut down trees to make their weapons, raised their flags on garden poles, and the whole world in answer gathered about them like a great cloud, brought them provisions and followed after them as shadows follow a form. In the end the leaders of the entire east rose up together and destroyed the house of Ch'in.

Now the empire of Ch'in at this time was by no means small or feeble. Its base in Yung-chou, its stronghold within the pass, was the same as before. The position of Ch'en She could not compare in dignity with the lords of Ch'i, Yen, Chao, Han, Wei, Sung, and Chung-shan. The weapons which he improvised of hoes and tree branches could not match the sharpness of spears and battle pikes; his little band of garrison conscripts was nothing beside the armies of the nine states; his plots and stratagems, his methods of warfare were far inferior to those of the men of earlier times. And yet Ch'en She succeeded in his undertaking where they had failed. Why was this, when in ability, size, power and strength his forces came nowhere near those of the states of the east that had formerly opposed Ch'in? Ch'in, beginning with an insignificant amount of territory, reached the power of a great state and for a hundred years made all the other great lords pay homage to it. Yet after it had become master of the whole empire and established itself within the fastness of the pass, a single commoner opposed it and its ancestral temples toppled, its ruler died by the hands of men, and it became the laughingstock of the world. Why? Because it failed to rule with humanity and righteousness and to realize that the power to attack and the power to retain what one has thereby won are not the same.

TRANSLATED BY BURTON WATSON

The Songs of Ch'u

Between the latest poems of the Book of Songs and the principal Songs of Ch'u (Ch'u tz'u) there is not only a time difference of some three to four centuries. We are faced also with a culture of considerable geographic divergence: the culture of the kingdom of Ch'u, which in the fourth and third centuries B.C. centered on the Yangtze valley and spread to the southern limits of the Chinese world at that time. Immediately different are the plants and flowers, rich in symbolic force in the use of the poets of Ch'u. The splendours of the Ch'u court, the joys of the good life of the age are described in rare detail in "The Summons of the Soul," uttered by a shaman for the benefit (the recall to life) of a dying king. The common Chinese spiritual heritage is enriched by local cults: the goddess of the Hsiang, major river of Ch'u and tributary of the Yangtze, is invoked in two songs of which, though one merely plays variations on the other, each has its own ground beat of religious yearning.

The tone of "The Lament for Ying" (Ying was the royal capital) and of the passage from "The Nine Arguments" is characteristic of the later parts of the corpus in its assertion of the purity, the incorruptibility of the poet, despite his rejection by his prince in a "mad and fearful age." The note is already sounded in the "Encountering Sorrow," the rare first specimen from early China of the long narrative poem. David Hawkes, whose translation is here reprinted, is inclined to accept the traditional attribution of this poem to Ch'ü Yüan, a minister whose loyalty to the king of Ch'u remained steadfast through slander, rejection and banishment. Ssu-ma Ch'ien records his suicide, in protest and despair, by drowning *in the river Mi-lo: it is this event which is commemorated in later centuries (and into modern times) in the annual Dragon-boat Festival. The last line of the poem has been taken as the poet's statement of his intention to drown himself—in the manner ascribed by tradition to the early shaman P'eng Hsien. Professor Hawkes however believes that to "join P'eng Hsien" for Ch'ü Yüan meant rather to devote himself to occult training. And certainly, from the astrology of the first stanza through to the advice of the god Wu Hsien, the spirit-journeys and the wooing of Fu-fei, goddess of the river Lo, there is magic enough in Ch'ü Yüan's poem to warrant such an interpretation.*

●

Encountering Sorrow

[*Li Sao*]

Scion of the High Lord Kao Yang,
Po Yung was my father's name.
When She T'i pointed to the first month of the year,
On the day *keng yin,* I passed from the womb.
My father, seeing the aspect of my nativity,
Took omens to give me an auspicious name.
The name he gave me was True Exemplar;
The title he gave me was Divine Balance.

Having from birth this inward beauty,
I added to it fair outward adornment:
I dressed in selinea and shady angelica,
And twined autumn orchids to make a garland.
Swiftly I sped, as in fearful pursuit,
Afraid Time would race on and leave me behind.
In the morning I gathered the angelica on the mountains;
In the evening I plucked the sedges of the islets.

The days and months hurried on, never delaying;
Springs and autumns sped by in endless alternation:
And I thought how the trees and flowers were fading and falling,
And feared that my Fairest's beauty would fade too.
'Gather the flower of youth and cast out the impure!
Why will you not change the error of your ways?
I have harnessed brave coursers for you to gallop forth with:
Come, let me go before and show you the way!

'The three kings of old were most pure and perfect:
Then indeed fragrant flowers had their proper place.

They brought together pepper and cinnamon;
All the most prized blossoms were woven in their garlands.
Glorious and great were those two, Yao and Shun,
Because they had kept their feet on the right path.
And how great was the folly of Chieh and Chou,
Who hastened by crooked paths, and so came to grief.

'The fools enjoy their careless pleasure,
But their way is dark and leads to danger.
I have no fear for the peril of my own person,
But only lest the chariot of my lord should be dashed.
I hurried about your chariot in attendance,
Leading you in the tracks of the kings of old.'
But the Fragrant One refused to examine my true feelings:
He lent ear, instead, to slander, and raged against me.

How well I know that loyalty brings disaster;
Yet I will endure: I cannot give it up.
I called on the ninefold heaven to be my witness,
And all for the sake of the Fair One, and no other.
There once was a time when he spoke with me in frankness;
But then he repented and was of another mind.
I do not care, on my own count, about this divorcement,
But it grieves me to find the Fair One so inconstant.

I had tended many an acre of orchids,
And planted a hundred rods of melilotus;
I had raised sweet lichens and the cart-halting flower,
And asarums mingled with fragrant angelica,
And hoped that when leaf and stem were in fullest bloom,
When the time had come, I could reap a fine harvest.
Though famine should pinch me, it is small matter:
But I grieve that all my blossoms should waste in rank weeds.

All others press forward in greed and gluttony,
No surfeit satiating their demands:
Forgiving themselves, but harshly judging others;
Each fretting his heart away in envy and malice.
Madly they rush in the covetous chase,

But not after that which my heart sets store by.
For old age comes creeping and soon will be upon me,
And I fear I shall not leave behind an enduring name.

In the mornings I drank the dew that fell from the magnolia:
At evening ate the petals that dropped from chrysanthemums.
If only my mind can be truly beautiful,
It matters nothing that I often faint for famine.
I pulled up roots to bind the valerian
And thread the fallen clusters of the castor plant;
I trimmed sprays of cassia for plaiting melilotus,
And knotted the lithe, light trails of ivy.

I take my fashion from the good men of old:
A garb unlike that which the rude world cares for:
Though it may not accord with present-day manners,
I will follow the pattern that P'eng Hsien has left.
Heaving a long sigh, I brush away my tears,
Grieving for man's life, so beset with hardships.
I have always loved pretty things to bind myself about with,
And so mornings I plaited and evenings I twined.

When I had finished twining my girdle of orchids,
I plucked some angelica to add to its beauty.
It is this that my heart takes most delight in,
And though I died nine times, I should not regret it.
What I do resent is the Fair One's waywardness:
Because he will never look to see what is in men's hearts.
All your ladies were jealous of my delicate beauty;
They chattered spitefully, saying I loved wantonness.

Truly, this generation are cunning artificers!
From square and compass they turn their eyes and change the
      true measurement,
They disregard the ruled line to follow their crooked fancies:
To emulate in flattery is their only rule.
But I am sick and sad at heart and stand irresolute:
I alone am at a loss in this generation.

But I would rather quickly die and meet dissolution
Before I ever would consent to ape their behaviour.

Eagles do not flock like birds of lesser species:
So it has ever been since the olden time.
How can the round and square ever fit together?
How can different ways of life ever be reconciled?
Yet humbling one's spirit and curbing one's pride,
Bearing blame humbly and enduring insults,
But keeping pure and spotless and dying in righteousness:
Such conduct was greatly prized by the wise men of old.

Repenting, therefore, that I had not conned the way more closely,
I halted, intended to turn back again—
To turn about my chariot and retrace my road
Before I had advanced too far along the path of folly.
I walked my horses through the marsh's orchid-covered margin;
I galloped to the hill of pepper-trees and rested there.
I could not go in to him for fear of meeting trouble,
And so, retired, I would once more fashion my former raiment.

I made a coat of lotus and water-chestnut leaves,
And gathered lotus petals to make myself a skirt.
I will no longer care that no one understands me,
As long as I can keep the sweet fragrance of my mind.
High towered the lofty hat on my head;
The longest of girdles dangled from my waist.
Fragrance and richness mingled in sweet confusion.
The brightness of their lustre has remained undimmed.

Suddenly I turned back and let my eyes wander.
I resolved to go and visit all the world's quarters.
My garland's crowded blossoms, mixed in fair confusion,
Wafted the sweetness of their fragrance far and wide.
All men have something in their lives which gives them pleasure:
With me the love of beauty is my constant joy.
I could not change this, even if my body were dismembered;
For how could dismemberment ever hurt my mind?

Then came my maidens with sobbing and sighing,
And over and over expostulated with me:
'Kun in his stubbornness took no thought for his life,
And perished, as result, upon the moor of Yü.
Why be so lofty, with your passion for purity?
Why must you alone have such delicate adornment?
Thorns, king-grass, curly-ear hold the place of power:
But you must needs stand apart and not speak them fair.

'You cannot go from door to door convincing everybody;
No one can say, "See, look into my mind!"
Others band together and like to have companions:
Why should you be so aloof and not take our advice?'
I look to the sages of old for inward guidance:
So, sighing with a bursting heart, I endure these trials.
I crossed the Yüan and Hsiang and journeyed southward
Till I came to where Ch'ung Hua was and made my plaint to him.

'In the Nine Variations and Nine Songs of Ch'i
The house of Hsia made revelry and knew no restraint,
Taking no thought for the troubles of the morrow:
And so it was that Wu Kuan made rebellion in his house.
Yi loved idle roaming and hunting to distraction,
And took delight in shooting at the mighty foxes.
But foolish dissipation has seldom a good end:
And Han Cho covetously took his master's wife.

'Cho's son, Chiao, put on his strong armour
And wreaked his wild will without any restraint.
The days passed in pleasure; far he forgot himself,
Till his head came tumbling down from his shoulders.
Chieh of Hsia all his days was a king most unnatural,
And so he came finally to meet with calamity.
Chou cut up and salted the body of his minister;
And so the days were numbered of the house of Yin.

'T'ang of Shang and Yü of Hsia were reverent and respectful;
The house of Chou chose the true way without error,

Raising up the virtuous and able men to government,
Following the straight line without fear or favour.
High God in Heaven knows no partiality;
He looks for the virtuous and makes them his ministers.
For only the wise and good can ever flourish
If it is given them to possess the earth.

'I have looked back into the past and forward to later ages,
Examining the outcome of men's different designs.
Where is the unrighteous man who could be trusted?
Where is the wicked man whose service could be used?
Though I stand at the pit's mouth and death yawns before me,
I still feel no regret at the course I have chosen.
Straightening the handle, regardless of the socket's shape:
For that crime the good men of old were hacked in pieces.'

Many a heavy sigh I heaved in my despair,
Grieving that I was born in such an unlucky time.
I plucked soft lotus petals to wipe my welling tears
That fell down in rivers and wet my coat front.
I knelt on my outspread skirts and poured my plaint out,
And the righteousness within me was clearly manifest.
I yoked a team of jade dragons to a phoenix-figured car
And waited for the wind to come, to soar up on my journey.

In the morning I started on my way from Ts'ang-wu;
In the evening I came to the Garden of Paradise.
I wanted to stay a while in those fairy precincts,
But the swift-moving sun was dipping to the west.
I ordered Hsi-ho to stay the sun-steeds' gallop,
To stand over Yen-tzu mountain and not go in.
Long, long had been my road and far, far was the journey:
I would go up and down to seek my heart's desire.

I watered my dragon steeds at the Pool of Heaven,
And tied the reins up to the Fu-sang tree.
I broke a sprig of the Jo-tree to strike the sun with:
I wanted to roam a little for enjoyment.

I sent Wang Shu ahead to ride before me;
The Wind God went behind as my outrider;
The Bird of Heaven gave notice of my comings;
And the Thunder God told me when all was not ready.

I caused my phoenixes to mount on their pinions
And fly ever onward by night and by day.
The whirlwinds gathered and came out to meet me,
Leading clouds and rainbows, to give me welcome.
In wild confusion, now joined and now parted,
Upwards and downwards rushed the glittering train.
I asked Heaven's porter to open up for me;
But he leant across Heaven's gate and eyed me churlishly.

The day was getting dark and drawing to its close.
Knotting orchids, I waited in indecision.
The muddy, impure world, so undiscriminating,
Seeks always to hide beauty, out of jealousy.
I decided when morning came to cross the White Water,
And climbed the peak of Lang Feng, and there tied up my steeds.
Then I looked about me and suddenly burst out weeping,
Because on that high hill there was no fair lady.

I thought to amuse myself here, in the House of Spring,
And broke off a jasper branch to add to my girdle.
Before the jasper flowers had shed their bright petals
I would look for a maiden below to give it to.
And so I made Feng Lung ride off on a cloud
To seek out the dwelling-place of the lady Fu-fei.
I took off my belt as a pledge of my suit to her,
And ordered Chien Hsiu to be the go-between.

Many were the hurried meetings and partings with her:
All wills and caprices, she was hard to woo.
In the evenings she went to lodge at the Ch'iung-shih Mountain;
In the mornings she washed her hair in the Wei-p'an stream.
With proud disdain she guarded her beauty,
Passing each day in idle, wanton pleasures.

Though fair she may be, she lacks all seemliness:
Come! I'll have none of her; let us search elsewhere!

I looked all around over the earth's four quarters,
Circling the heavens till at last I alighted.
I gazed on a jade tower's glittering splendour
And spied the lovely daughter of the Lord of Sung.
I sent off the magpie to pay my court to her,
But the magpie told me that my suit had gone amiss.
The magpie flew off with noisy chatterings:
I hate him for an idle, knavish fellow.

My mind was irresolute and wavering;
I wanted to go, and yet I could not.
Already the phoenix had taken his present,
And I feared that Kao Hsin would get there before me.
I wanted to go far away, but had nowhere to go to;
I longed for a little sport and amusement:
And I thought that before they were wedded to Shao K'ang,
I would stay with the Lord of Yü's two princesses.

But my pleader was weak and my matchmaker stupid,
And I feared that this suit, too, would not be successful:
For the world is impure and envious of the able,
And eager to hide men's good and make much of their ill.
Deep in the palace, unapproachable,
The wise king slumbers and will not be awakened;
And the thoughts in my breast must all go unuttered.
How can I bear to endure this for ever?

I searched for the holy plant and twigs of bamboo,
And ordered Ling Fen to make divination for me.
He said, 'Beauty is always bound to find its mate.
Who that was truly fair was ever without lovers?
Think of the vastness of the wide world:
Here is not the only place where you can find your lady.
Go farther afield,' he said, 'and do not be faint-hearted.
What woman seeking handsome mate could ever refuse you?

'What place on earth does not boast some fragrant flower?
Why should you always cleave to your old home?'
The world is blinded with its own folly:
How can you show men the virtue inside you?
Most people's likings and loathings are quite separate:
Only *these* men differ in this respect.
For they wear mugwort and cram their waistbands with it;
While the lovely valley orchids they say are not fit to wear.

Since beauty of flower and of shrub escapes them,
What chance has a rarest jewel of gaining recognition?
They gather up muck to stuff their perfume-bags with;
But the pepper-shrub they say has got no fragrance.
I wanted to follow Ling Fen's auspicious oracle,
But I faltered and could not make my mind up.
I heard that Wu Hsien was descending in the evening,
So I lay in wait with offerings of peppered rice-balls.

The spirits came like a dense cloud descending,
And the host of Chiu Yi Mountain came crowding to meet him.
His godhead was manifested by a blaze of radiance,
And he addressed me in these auspicious words:
'To and fro on the earth you must everywhere wander,
Seeking for one whose thoughts are of your own measure.
T'ang and Yü sought sincerely for the right helpers;
So Yi Yin and Kao Yao worked well with their princes.

'As long as your soul within is beautiful,
What need have you of a matchmaker?
Yüeh laboured as a builder, pounding earth at Fu Yen,
Yet Wu Ting employed him without a second thought.
Lü Wang wielded the butcher's knife at Chao Ko,
But King Wen met him and raised him up on high.
Ning Ch'i sang as he fed his ox at evening;
Duke Huan of Ch'i heard him and took him as his minister.

'Gather the flower of youth before it is too late,
While the fair season is still not yet over.

Beware lest the shrike sound his note before the equinox,
Causing all the flowers to lose their fine fragrance.'
How splendid the glitter of my jasper girdle!
But the crowd make a dark screen, masking its beauty.
And I fear that my enemies, who never can be trusted,
Will break it out of spiteful jealousy.

The age is disordered in a tumult of changing:
How can I tarry much longer among them?
Orchids and iris have lost all their fragrance;
Flag and melilotus have changed into straw.
Why have the fragrant flowers of days gone by
Now all transformed themselves into worthless mugwort?
What other reason can there be for this
But that they have no more care for beauty?

I thought that Orchid was one to be trusted,
But he proved a sham bent only on pleasing his masters.
He overcame his goodness and conformed to evil counsels:
He no more deserves to rank with fragrant flowers.
Pepper is all wagging tongue and lives only for slander;
And even stinking Dogwood seeks to fill a perfume bag.
Since they only seek advancement and labour for position,
What fragrance have they deserving our respect?

Since, then, the world's way is to drift the way the tide runs,
Who can stay the same and not change with all the rest?
Seeing the behaviour of Orchid and Pepper flower,
What can be expected from cart-halt and selinea?
They have cast off their beauty and come to this:
Only my garland is left to treasure.
Its penetrating perfume does not easily desert it,
And even to this day its fragrance has not faded.

I will follow my natural bent and please myself;
I will go off wandering to look for a lady.
While my adornment is in its pristine beauty
I will travel all around looking both high and low.
Since Ling Fen had given me a favourable oracle,

I reckoned a lucky day to start my journey on.
I broke a branch of jasper to take for my meat,
And ground fine jasper meal for my journey's provisions.

'Harness winged dragons to be my coursers;
Let my chariot be of fine work of jade and ivory!
How can I live with men whose hearts are strangers to me?
I am going a far journey to be away from them.'
I took the way that led towards the K'un-lun mountain:
A long, long road with many a turning in it.
The cloud-embroidered banner flapped its great shade above us;
And the jingling jade yoke-bells tinkled merrily.

I set off at morning from the Ford of Heaven;
At evening I came to the world's western end.
Phoenixes followed me, bearing up my pennants,
Soaring high aloft with majestic wing-beats.
'See, I have come to the desert of Moving Sands!'
Warily I drove along the banks of the Red Water;
Then, beckoning the water-dragons to make a bridge for me,
I summoned the God of the West to take me over.

Long was the road that lay ahead and full of difficulties;
I sent word to my other chariots to take a short route and wait.
The road wound leftwards round the Pu Chou Mountain:
I marked out the Western Sea as our meeting-place.
There I marshalled my thousand chariots,
And jade hub to jade hub we galloped on abreast.
My eight dragon-steeds flew on with writhing undulations;
My cloud-embroidered banners flapped on the wind.

I tried to curb my mounting will and slacken the swift pace;
But the spirits soared high up, far into the distance.
We played the Nine Songs and danced the Nine Shao dances:
I wanted to snatch some time for pleasure and amusement.
But when I had ascended the splendour of the heavens,
I suddenly caught a glimpse below of my old home.
The groom's heart was heavy and the horses for longing
Arched their heads back and refused to go on.

Envoi:

Enough! There are no true men in the state: no one to understand me.
Why should I cleave to the city of my birth?
Since none is worthy to work with in making good government,
I will go and join P'eng Hsien in the place where he abides.

From "The Nine Songs"

1. The Princess of the Hsiang

[*Chiu ko: Hsiang chün*]

My lady comes not but shyly waits:
Who is it tarries within the islet,
So wondrous beautiful and fair?
Skimming the waters in boat of cassia,
I bid the Yüan and Hsiang still their waves,
And the stream of the River softly flow.
I look for my queen, but she comes not yet:
Of whom do I think as I play my reed-pipes?
North I go, drawn by flying dragons,
Bending my course to the Tung-t'ing lake.
My sail is of fig-leaves, melilotus the rigging,
With iris for yard and a banner of orchids.
Far out I gaze to the mooring at Ts'en-yang,
And over the great River waft my spirit:
Waft, but my spirit does not reach her;
And the maiden many a sigh heaves for me:
While down my cheeks the teardrops in streams are falling,
As with grieving heart I yearn for my lady.
The cassia oars, the sweep of orchid
Churn the waters to foaming snow.
Would you gather the wild-fig in the water?
Or pluck the lotus-flower in the tree-tops?
Unless two hearts are both as one heart,
The matchmaker only wastes her labours;
And love not deep is too quickly broken.
Swift flows the stream through the stony shallows;
Fast beat the wings of the flying dragons.
When friendship is faithless, hate lasts the longer:

You break your tryst and you tell me you've not time.
In the morning I gallop beside the river,
And stop at dusk in the northern island.
The birds are roosting upon the rooftop,
And the water laps round about the hall.
I'll throw my thumb-ring into the river,
Leave my girdle-gem in the bay of the Li.
.Sweet pollia I've plucked in the flowering islet
To give to the maiden there below.
For time once gone cannot be recovered,
And I wish we could sport but a little longer.

2. The Lady of the Hsiang

[*Hsiang fu jen*]

The Child of God, descending the northern bank,
Turns on me her eyes that are dark with longing.
Gently the wind of autumn whispers;
On the waves of the Tung-t'ing lake the leaves are falling.
Over the white sedge I gaze out wildly;
For a tryst is made to meet my love this evening.
But why should the birds gather in the duckweed?
And what are the nets doing in the tree-tops?
The Yüan has its angelicas, the Li has its orchids:
And I think of my lady, but dare not tell it,
As with trembling heart I gaze on the distance
Over the swiftly moving waters.
What are the deer doing in the courtyard?
Or the water-dragons outside the waters?
In the morning I drive my steeds by the river;
In the evening I cross to the western shore.
I can hear my beloved calling to me:
I will ride aloft and race beside her.
I will build her a house within the water
Roofed all over with lotus leaves;
With walls of iris, of purple shells the chamber;
Perfumed pepper shall make the hall.
With beams of cassia, orchid rafters,

Lily tree lintel, a bower of peonies,
With woven fig-leaves for the hangings
And melilotus to make a screen.
Weights of white jade to hold the mats with,
Stone-orchids strewn to make the floor sweet:
A room of lotus thatched with the white flag
Shall all be bound up with stalks of asarum.
A thousand sweet flowers shall fill the courtyard,
And rarest perfumes shall fill the gates.
The hosts of the Chiu Yi come to meet her:
Like clouds in number the spirits come thronging.
I'll throw my thumb-ring into the river,
Leave my thimble in the bay of the Li.
Sweet pollia I've plucked in the little islet
To send to my far-away Beloved.
Oh, rarely, rarely the time is given,
And I wish we could sport but a little longer.

3. The Lord of the East

[*Tung chün*]

With a faint flush I start to come out of the east,
Shining down on my threshold, Fu-sang.
As I urge my horses slowly forward,
The night sky brightens, and day has come.
I ride a dragon car and chariot on the thunder,
With cloud-banners fluttering upon the wind.
I heave a long sigh as I start the ascent,
Reluctant to leave, and looking back longingly;
For the beauty and the music are so enchanting
The beholder, delighted, forgets that he must go.
Tighten the zither's strings and smite them in unison!
Strike the bells until the bell-stand rocks!
Let the flutes sound! Blow the pan-pipes!
See, the priestesses, how skilled and lovely!
Whirling and dipping like birds in flight!
Unfolding the words in time to the dancing,
Pitch and beat all in perfect accord!

The spirits, descending, darken the sun.
In my cloud-coat and my skirt of the rainbow,
Grasping my bow I soar high up in the sky;
I aim my long arrow and shoot the Wolf of Heaven;
I seize the Dipper to ladle cinnamon wine.
Then holding my reins I plunge down to my setting,
On my gloomy night journey back to the east.

4. The Spirits of the Fallen

[*Kuo shang*]

Grasping our great shields and wearing our hide armour,
Wheel-hub to wheel-hub locked, we battle hand to hand.
Our banners darken the sky; the enemy teem like clouds:
Through the hail of arrows the warriors press forward.
They dash on our lines; they trample our ranks down.
The left horse has fallen, the right one is wounded.
Bury the wheels in; tie up the horses!
Seize the jade drumstick and beat the sounding drum!
The time is against us: the gods are angry.
Now all lie dead, left on the field of battle.
They went out never more to return:
Far, far away they lie, on the level plain,
Their long swords at their belts, clasping their elmwood bows.
Head from body sundered: but their hearts could not be vanquished.
Both truly brave, and also truly noble;
Strong to the last, they could not be dishonoured.
Their bodies may have died, but their souls are living:
Heroes among the shades their valiant souls will be.

5. The Ritual Cycle

The rites are accomplished to the beating of the drums;
The flower-wand is passed on to succeeding dancers.
Lovely maidens sing their song, slow and solemnly.
Orchids in spring and chrysanthemums in autumn:
So it shall go on until the end of time.

From "The Nine Declarations"

1. A Lament for Ying

[*Chiu chang: Ai Ying*]

High Heaven is not constant in its dispensations:
See how the country is moved to unrest and error!
The people are scattered, and men cut off from their fellows.
In the middle of spring the move to the east began.
I left my old home and set off for distant places,
And following the waters of the Chiang and Hsia, I travelled into
    exile.
I passed through the city gate with a heavy heart:
On the day *chia,* in the morning, my journey began.
As I set out from the city and left the gate of my village,
An endless turmoil started in my mind.
And as the oars slowly swept in time,
I grieved that I should never look on my prince again.
I gazed on the high catalpa trees and heaved a heavy sigh,
And the tears in torrents, like winter's sleet, came down.
We passed the head of the Hsia; and once, as we drifted westwards,
I looked back for the Dragon Gate, but I could not see it.
My mind was drawn with yearning and my heart was grieved.
So far! I knew not whither my way was leading.
But I followed the wind and waves, drifting on aimlessly,—
A traveller on an endless journey, with no hope of return.
As we rode on the Wave God's surging swell,
Oh, when, I thought, will this aimless wandering cease?
My heart was caught in a mesh that I could not disentangle;
My thoughts were lost in a maze there was no way out of.
I let my boat float on, following the current downstream,
South up to the Tung-t'ing lake, and then north again to the River.

67

I had left behind the home where of old I dwelt,
And now, at random drifting, I travelled towards the east.
But my soul within me longed to be returning:
Ah! when for one moment of the day have I not longed to go back?
I turned my back on Hsia P'u, and my thoughts went speeding
    westwards,
And I grieved that the great City grew daily more far away.
I climbed a steep islet's height and looked into the distance,
Thinking to ease the sorrow in my heart.
I was sad to see the island's soil so fertile,
Remembering the old ways of the land of the Great River.
Where shall I get to in my watery wanderings?
How cross to the south over this great waste of water?
In my exile I did not know that the palace was now a mound;
And who would have thought that East Gate would become a
    wilderness?
It is now a long time since my heart has known happiness;
Grief comes following sorrow and sorrow following grief.
I think how long and hard is the road to the Great City,
And the River and the Hsia how hard for me to cross.
Sometimes I no more believe that I have left it;
Yet now I have been here nine years without returning.
I am overcast with a sadness which cannot find expression;
I am tied to one spot and my mouth is full of gall.
When your favour was courted with outward show of charm,
You were too weak; you had no will of your own.
But when with deep loyalty I tried to go in before you,
Jealousy cut me off and blocked my way to you.
Though Yao and Shun excelled in noble actions,
So that their glory reaches to the skies,
The crowd of backbiters were envious of their fame,
And gave them a false name, saying they were not kind.
You hate the deep and studious search for beauty,
But love a base knave's braggart blusterings;
And so the crowd press forward and each day advance in your
    favours,
And true beauty is forced far off, and retires to distant places.

Envoi:

Long my eyes rove, upon the distance gazing.
I long but once to return; but when will that time be?
The birds fly home to their old haunts where they came from;
And the fox when he dies turns his head towards his earth.
That I was cast off and banished was truly for no crime.
By day and night I never can forget.

2. In Praise of the Orange Tree

[*Chü sung*]

Fairest of all God's trees, the orange came and settled here,
Commanded by Him not to move, but grow only in the south
 country.
Deep-rooted, firm and hard to shift: showing in this his singleness
 of purpose;
His leaves of green and pure white blossoms delight the eye of the
 beholder,
And the thick branches and spines so sharp, and the fine round
 fruits,
Green ones with yellow ones intermingled to make a pattern of
 gleaming brightness.
Orange on the outside, but pure white within, the fruits yield a
 parable for human conduct!
Rich and beautiful, his loveliness is not impaired by any blemish.
Oh, your young resolution has something different from the rest.
Alone and unmoving you stand. How can one not admire you!
Deep-rooted, hard to shift: truly you have no peer!
Awake to this world's ways, alone you stand, unyielding against the
 vulgar tide.
You have sealed your heart; you guard yourself with care; have
 never fallen into error.
Holding a nature free from selfishness, you are the peer of heaven
 and earth.
I would fade as you fade with the passing years, and ever be your
 friend.

Pure and apart and free from sin, and strong in the order of your
    ways:
Though young in years, fit to be a teacher of men;
In your acts like Po Yi: I set you up as my model.

From "The Nine Arguments"

[*Chiu pien*]

High Heaven divides the four seasons equally:
But I grieve only at the chill autumn.
The white dew has fallen on the flowers of the field,
And these *t'ung* and catalpa trees will soon grow thin and bare.
Gone is the radiance of the bright sun,
And come the dreary watches of long nights.
I have left behind my blossom-burgeoning prime:
Sere and withered, I am full of melancholy.
First autumn heralds with warning of white dew;
Then winter redoubles rigour with bitter frost.
High summer's fecund forces are gathered up,
Then trapped and buried away in winter's prison.
The leaves are sickly and without colour;
The branches are all confused and crossed;
Things creep in hue towards their coming end;
The boughs are thin and withered-looking;
The tapering twigs are sad to see;
The whole appearance wasted away and sick.
I think of the rich profusion soon to fall,
And grieve that I missed the time when I might have met my master.
I seize my horses' reins and check their pace,
Thinking to take some pleasure in idle wandering;
But the years move quickly on and will soon be ended,
And I fear that a good old age will not be for me.
I mourn that I was not born in a better time,
And have fallen upon this mad and fearful age.
Silent and slow I pace on my own
As the cricket chirps here in the west hall.
But my heart is afraid and sorely shaken:
I have so many sources of sorrow.

I look up to the bright moon and sigh,
And walk beneath the stars until daylight comes . . .

I grieve for the orchid blossoms thickly spreading
That grow so gaily in the great courtyard.
Alas that these flowers should be without any fruits,
And fluttering, bow to every wind and shower!
I had thought that my lord would only wear these orchids;
But he treated them no differently from any other flower.
I was sad that my matchless thoughts could find no way to him,
And resolved to leave my lord and fly off high.
My heart was grieved and sorely pained within me;
I longed but once to see him, so that all might be made clear.
It grieved me to be estranged for no offence of mine;
And my breast was tormented with bitter pain.
How could I not be downcast and long for my lord?
But ninefold are the gates of my lord,
And fierce, snarling dogs run out from them and bark,
And the gate-beam is bolted, and none can go through.
High Heaven overflows, and the autumn rains are here,
And it seems that Earth will never be dry again.
I alone am kept thus barren of nurturing moisture,
And look up at the floating clouds with a heavy sigh.

The Summons of the Soul

[*Chao hun*]

> The Lord God said to Wu Yang:
> 'There is a man on earth below whom I would help:
> His soul has left him. Make divination for him.'
> Wu Yang replied:
> 'The Master of Dreams. . . .
> The Lord God's bidding is hard to follow.'
> The Lord God said:
> 'You must divine for him. I fear that if you any longer decline,
>   it will be too late.'
> Wu Yang therefore went down and summoned the soul, saying:

O soul, come back! Why have you left your old abode and sped
    to the earth's far corners,

Deserting the place of your delight to meet all those things of evil
    omen?

O soul, come back! In the east you cannot abide.

There are giants there a thousand fathoms tall, who seek only for
    souls to catch,

And ten suns that come out together, melting metal, dissolving stone.

The folk that live there can bear it; but you, soul, would be
    consumed.

O soul, come back! In the east you cannot abide.

O soul, come back! In the south you cannot stay.

There the people have tattooed faces and blackened teeth;

They sacrifice flesh of men, and pound their bones to paste.

There are coiling snakes there, and the great fox that can run a
    hundred leagues,

And the great Nine-headed Serpent who darts swiftly this way and
    that,

And swallows men as a sweet relish.

O soul, come back! In the south you may not linger.

O soul, come back! For the west holds many perils:

The Moving Sands stretch on for a hundred leagues.

You will be swept into the Thunder's Chasm, and dashed in pieces,
    unable to help yourself;
And even should you chance to escape from that, beyond is the
    empty desert,
And red ants as huge as elephants, and wasps as big as gourds.
The five grains do not grow there; dry stalks are the only food;
And the earth there scorches men up; there is nowhere to look for
    water.
And you will drift there for ever, with nowhere to go in that vastness.
O soul, come back! lest you bring on yourself perdition.
O soul, come back! In the north you may not stay.
There the layered ice rises high, and the snowflakes fly for a hundred
    leagues and more.
O soul, come back! You cannot long stay there.
O soul, come back! Climb not to the heaven above.
For tigers and leopards guard the gates, with jaws ever ready to
    rend up mortal men,
And one man with nine heads, that can pull up nine thousand trees,
And the slant-eyed jackal-wolves pad to and fro;
They hang out men for sport and drop them in the abyss,
And only at God's command may they ever rest or sleep.
O soul, come back! lest you fall into this danger.
O soul, come back! Go not down to the Land of Darkness,
Where the Earth God lies, nine-coiled, with dreadful horns on his
    forehead,
And a great humped back and bloody thumbs, pursuing men,
    swift-footed:
Three eyes he has in his tiger's head, and his body is like a bull's.
O soul, come back! lest you bring on yourself disaster.
O soul, come back! and enter the gate of the city.
The priests are there who call you, walking backwards to lead you in.
Ch'in basket-work, silk cords of Ch'i, and silken banners of Cheng:
All things are there proper for your recall; and with long-drawn,
    piercing cries they summon the wandering soul.
O soul, come back! Return to your old abode.
All the quarters of the world are full of harm and evil.
Hear while I describe for you your quiet and reposeful home.
High walls and deep chambers, with railings and tiered balconies;

Stepped terraces, storied pavilions, whose tops look on the high
    mountains;
Lattice doors with scarlet interstices, and carving on the square
    lintels;
Draughtless rooms for winter; galleries cool in summer;
Streams and gullies wind in and out, purling prettily;
A warm breeze bends the melilotus and sets the tall orchids swaying.
Crossing the hall into the apartments, the ceilings and floors are
    vermilion,
The chambers of polished stone, with kingfisher hangings on jasper
    hooks;
Bedspreads of kingfisher seeded with pearls, all dazzling in
    brightness;
Arras of fine silk covers the walls; damask canopies stretch
    overhead,
Braids and ribbons, brocades and satins, fastened with rings of
    precious stone.
Many a rare and precious thing is to be seen in the furnishings of
    the chamber.
Bright candles of orchid-perfume fat light up flower-like faces that
    await you;
Twice eight handmaids to serve your bed, each night alternating
    in duty,
The lovely daughters of noble families, far excelling common
    maidens.
Women with hair dressed finely in many fashions fill your
    apartments,
In looks and bearing sweetly compliant, of gentleness beyond com-
    pare,
With melting looks but virtuous natures and truly noble minds.
Dainty features, elegant bearing grace all the marriage chamber:
Mothlike eyebrows and lustrous eyes that dart out gleams of
    brightness,
Delicate colouring, soft round flesh, flashing seductive glances.
In your garden pavilion, by the long bed-curtains, they wait your
    royal pleasure:
Of kingfisher feathers, the purple curtains and blue hangings that
    furnish its high hall;

The walls, red; vermilion the woodwork; jet inlay on the
 roofbeams;

Overhead you behold the carved rafters, painted with dragons and
 serpents;

Seated in the hall, leaning on its balustrade, you look down on a
 winding pool.

Its lotuses have just opened; among them grow water-chestnuts,

And purple-stemmed water-mallows enamel the green wave's surface.

Attendants quaintly costumed in spotted leopard skins wait on
 the sloping bank;

A light coach is tilted for you to ascend; footmen and riders wait
 in position.

An orchid carpet covers the ground; the hedge is of flowering
 hibiscus.

O soul, come back! Why should you go far away?

All your household have come to do you honour; all kinds of good
 foods are ready:

Rice, broom-corn, early wheat, mixed all with yellow millet;

Bitter, salt, sour, hot and sweet: there are dishes of all flavours.

Ribs of the fatted ox cooked tender and succulent;

Sour and bitter blended in the soup of Wu;

Stewed turtle and roast kid, served up with yam sauce;

Geese cooked in sour sauce, casseroled duck, fried flesh of the great
 crane;

Braised chicken, seethed tortoise, high-seasoned, but not to spoil
 the taste;

Fried honey-cakes of rice flour and malt-sugar sweetmeats;

Jadelike wine, honey-flavoured, fills the winged cups;

Ice-cooled liquor, strained of impurities, clear wine, cool and re-
 freshing;

Here are laid out the patterned ladles, and here is sparkling wine.

O soul, come back! Here you shall have respect and nothing to
 harm you.

Before the dainties have left the tables, girl musicians take up their
 places.

They set up the bells and fasten the drums and sing the latest songs:

'Crossing the River,' 'Gathering Caltrops,' and 'The Sunny Bank.'

The lovely girls are drunk with wine, their faces flushed and red.
With amorous glances and flirting looks, their eyes like wavelets
    sparkle;
Dressed in embroideries, clad in finest silks, splendid but not showy;
Their long hair, falling from high chignons, hangs low in lovely
    tresses.
Two rows of eight, in perfect time, perform a dance of Cheng;
Their *hsi-pi* buckles of Chin workmanship glitter like bright suns.
Bells clash in their swaying frames; the catalpa zither's strings are
    swept.
Their sleeves rise like crossed bamboo stems, then they bring them
    shimmering downwards.
Pipes and zither rise in wild harmonies, the sounding drums thun-
    derously roll;
And the courts of the palace quake and tremble as they throw them-
    selves into the Whirling Ch'u.
Then they sing songs of Wu and ballads of Ts'ai and play the Ta
    Lü music.
Men and women now sit together, mingling freely without distinc-
    tion;
Hatstrings and fastenings come untied: the revel turns to wild dis-
    order.
The singing-girls of Cheng and Wei come to take their places
    among the guests;
But the dancers of the Whirling Ch'u find favour over all the others.
Then with bamboo dice and ivory pieces, the game of Liu Po is
    begun;
Sides are taken; they advance together; keenly they threaten each
    other.
Pieces are kinged and the scoring doubled. Shouts of 'Five White!'
    arise.
Day and night are swallowed up in continuous merriment of wine.
Bright candles of orchid-perfumed fat burn in stands of delicate
    tracery.
The guests compose snatches to express their thoughts as the
    orchid fragrance steals over them.
And those with some object of their affections lovingly tell their
    verses to each other.

In wine they attain the heights of pleasure, and give delight to the
  dear departed.
O soul, come back! Return to your old abode.

  Envoi:

In the new year, as spring began, I set off for the south.
The green duckweed lay on the water, and the white flag flowered.
My road passed through Luchiang and to the right of Ch'ang-po.
I stood on the marsh's margin and looked far out on the distance.
My team was of four jet horses; we set out together a thousand
  chariots strong.
The beaters' fires flickered skyward, and the smoke rose like a pall.
I trotted to where the throng was, and galloped ahead to draw them;
Then reined as we sighted our quarry, and wheeled around to the
  right hand.
I raced with the King in the marshland to see which would go the
  faster.
The King himself shot the arrow, and the black ox dropped down
  dead.
'The darkness yields to daylight; we cannot stay much longer.
The marsh orchids cover the path here: this way must be too marshy.'
On, on the river's waters roll; above them grow woods of maple.
The eye travels on a thousand li, and the heart breaks for sorrow.
O soul, come back! Alas for the Southern Land!

Summons for a Gentleman
Who Became a Recluse

[*Chao yin shih*]

The cassia trees grow thick
In the mountain's recesses,
Twisting and snaking,
Their branches interlacing.
The mountain mists are high,
The rocks are steep.
In the sheer ravines
The waters' waves run deep.
Monkeys in chorus cry;
Tigers and leopards roar.
One has climbed up by the cassia boughs
Who wishes to tarry there.
A prince went wandering
And did not return.
In spring the grass grows
Lush and green.
At the year's evening,
Comfortless,
The cicada sings with
A mournful chirp.
Wildly uneven,
The bends of the mountain:
The heart stands still
With awe aghast.
Broken and wild,
Chilling the heart.
In the deep wood's tangle
Tigers and leopards spring.

79

Towering and rugged,
The craggy rocks, frowning.
Crooked and interlocked
The woods' gnarled trees.
Green cyprus grass grows in between,
And the rush grass rustles and sways.
White deer, roebuck and horned deer
Now leap and now stand poised.
Sheer and steep,
Chill and damp:
Baboons and monkeys
And the bears
Seek for their kind
With mournful cries.
Tigers and leopards fight,
And the bears growl.
Birds and beasts, startled,
Lose the flock.
O prince, return!
In the mountains you cannot stay long.

TRANSLATED BY DAVID HAWKES

Chuang Tzu and Others on Death

In general the philosophers, with their ethical prescriptions, their recipes for good government and their parodies of each other's logic, must be omitted from the present anthology. The loss is great, not only of noble precept, intricate argument and picturesque anecdote, but of so many clues to the underlying concerns of later poetry and writing in all genres. But an adequate representation of the "hundred schools" of pre-Han thought alone would require too much space and too full an explanation of the historical background to be practicable.

The Chuang Tzu, however, as Arthur Waley says, "can be understood by anyone who knows how to read poetry." The book is attributed to the philosopher Chuang Chou, who lived in the late fourth and early third centuries B.C., and parts may well be from his own hand. It contains some of the most beautiful passages in all of Chinese literature. From the present selections, all of which concern death, we learn something of that Taoist interpretation of life which informs much of the finest poetry of every subsequent age. We learn too what poor Yorick's skull might have said had it not been too "chop-fall'n" to speak. And it may be of interest to compare the Chuang Tzu passages with the Taoist-inspired reflections of the Han Emperor Wen (d. 157 B.C.) and with those of the Confucianist Wang Ch'ung (A.D. 27-c.100).

●

Chuang Tzu

Three Dialogues

1

When Chuang Tzu's wife died, Hui Tzu came to the house to join in the rites of mourning. To his surprise he found Chuang Tzu sitting with an inverted bowl on his knees, drumming upon it and singing a song.

"After all," said Hui Tzu, "she lived with you, brought up your children, grew old along with you. That you should not mourn for her is bad enough; but to let your friends find you drumming and singing—that is going too far!"

"You misjudge me," said Chuang Tzu. "When she died, I was in despair, as any man well might be. But soon, pondering on what had happened, I told myself that in death no strange new fate befalls us. In the beginning we lack not life only, but form. Not form only, but spirit. We are blended in the one great featureless indistinguishable mass. Then a time came when the mass evolved spirit, spirit evolved form, form evolved life. And now life in its turn has evolved death. For not nature only but man's being has its seasons, its sequence of spring and autumn, summer and winter. If some one is tired and has gone to lie down, we do not pursue him with shouting and bawling. She whom I have lost has lain down to sleep for a while in the Great Inner Room. To break in upon her rest with the noise of lamentation would but show that I knew nothing of nature's Sovereign Law. That is why I ceased to mourn."

2

When Chuang Tzu was going to Ch'u he saw by the roadside a skull, clean and bare, but with every bone in its place. Touching it gently with his chariot-whip he bent over it and asked, "Sir, was it some insatiable ambition that drove you to transgress the law and brought you to this? Was it the fall of a kingdom, the blow of the executioner's axe that brought you to this? Or had you done some shameful deed and could not face the reproaches of father and mother, of wife and child, and so were brought to this? Was it hunger and cold that brought you to this, or was it that the springs and autumns of your span had in their due course carried you to this?"

Having thus addressed the skull, he put it under his head as a pillow and went to sleep. At midnight the skull appeared to him in a dream and said to him, "All that you said to me—your glib, commonplace chatter—is just what I should expect from a live man, showing as it does in every phase a mind hampered by trammels from which we dead are entirely free. Would you like to hear a word or two about the dead?"

"I certainly should," said Chuang Tzu.

"Among the dead," said the skull, "none is king, none is subject. There is no division of the seasons: for us the whole world is spring, the whole world is autumn. No monarch on his throne has joy greater than ours."

Chuang Tzu did not believe this. "Suppose," he said, "I could get the Clerk of Destinies to make your frame anew, to clothe your bones once more with flesh and skin, send you back to father and mother, wife and child, friends and home, I do not think you would refuse."

A deep frown furrowed the skeleton's brow. "How can you imagine," it asked, "that I would cast away joy greater than that of a king upon his throne, only to go back to the toils of the living world?"

TRANSLATED BY ARTHUR WALEY

3

Master Ssu, Master Yü, Master Li and Master Lai were all four talking together. "Who can look upon inaction as his head, upon life as his back, upon death as his rump?" they asked. "Who knows that life and death, existence and annihilation, are all parts of a single body? I will be his friend!"

The four men looked at each other and smiled. There was no

disagreement in their hearts and so the four of them became friends.

All at once Master Yü fell ill, and Master Ssu went to ask how he was. "Amazing!" exclaimed Master Yü. "Look, the Creator is making me all crookedy! My back sticks up like a hunchback's so that my vital organs are on top of me. My chin is hidden down around my navel, my shoulders are up above my head, and my pigtail points at the sky. It must be due to some dislocation of the forces of the yin and the yang."

Yet he seemed quite calm at heart and unconcerned. Dragging himself haltingly to the edge of a well, he looked at his reflection and cried, "My, my! Look, the Creator is making me all crookedy!"

"Do you resent it?" asked Master Ssu.

"Why no," replied Master Yü. "What is there to resent? If the process continues, perhaps in time he'll transform my left arm into a rooster: in that case I'll herald the dawn with my crowing. Or in time he may transform my right arm into a crossbow pellet and I'll shoot down an owl for roasting. Or perhaps he will even turn my buttocks into cartwheels: then with my spirit for a horse, I'll climb up and go for a ride, and never again have need for a carriage.

"I received life because the time had come; I will lose it because the order of things passes on. If only a man will be content with this time and dwell in this order neither sorrow nor joy can touch him. In ancient times this was called 'the freeing of the bound.' Yet there are those who cannot free themselves, because they are bound by mere things. Creatures such as I can never win against Heaven. That is the way it has always been: what is there to resent?"

Then suddenly Master Lai also fell ill. Gasping for breath he lay at the point of death. His wife and children gathered round in a circle and wept. Master Li, who had come to find out how he was, said to them, "Shoo! Get back! Don't disturb the process of change!"

And he leaned against the doorway and chatted with Master Lai. "How marvelous the Creator is!" he exclaimed. "What is he going to make out of you next? Where is he going to send you? Will he make you into a rat's liver? Will he make you into a bug's arm?"

"A child obeys his father and mother and goes wherever he is told, east or west, south or north," said Master Lai. "And the yin and the yang—how much more are they to a man than father or mother! Now that they have brought me to the verge of death, how perverse it would be of me to refuse to obey them. What fault is it of theirs? The Great Clod burdens me with form, labors me with life, eases me in old age and rests me in death. So if I think well of my life, by the same token I must think well of my death. When a skilled smith is casting metal, if the metal should leap up and cry, 'I insist upon being made into a famous sword like the sword Mu-yeh of old!'—he would surely regard it as very inauspicious metal indeed. In the same way, if I who have once had the audacity to take on human form should now cry, 'I don't want to be anything but a man! Nothing but a man!'—the Creator would surely consider me a most inauspicious sort of person. So now I think of heaven and earth as a great furnace and the Creator as a skilled smith. What place could he send me that would not be all right? I will go off peacefully to sleep, and then with a start I will wake up."

TRANSLATED BY BURTON WATSON

The Testamentary Edict of Emperor Wen

[*Shih chi* X: *Wen-ti yi chao*]

I have heard that of the countless beings beneath heaven which sprout or are brought to life, there is none which does not have its time of death, for death is a part of the abiding order of heaven and earth and the natural end of all creatures. How then can it be such a sorrowful thing? Yet in the world today, because all men rejoice in life and hate death, they exhaust their wealth in providing lavish burials for the departed, and endanger their health by prolonged mourning. I can in no way approve of such practices.

I, who am without virtue, have had no means to bring succor to the people. If, having passed away, I were to inflict upon them deep mourning and prolonged lamentation, exposing them to the cold and heat of successive seasons, grieving the fathers and sons of the people and blighting the desires of old and young, causing them to diminish their food and drink and to interrupt the sacrifices to the ancestors and spirits, I would only deepen my lack of virtue. What then could I say to the world?

For over twenty years now I have been allowed to guard the ancestral temples of the dynasty, and with my poor person have been entrusted with a position above the lords and kings of the empire. With the aid of the spirits of heaven and earth and the blessings of our sacred altars, peace has been brought to the region within the seas, and the empire is without armed strife. I, who am without wisdom, have been in constant fear that I might commit some fault to bring dishonor upon the virtue handed down to me by those rulers who went before me. As my years of rule grew longer, I trembled lest they should not reach a just conclusion. Yet now I have been permitted to live out the years which heaven granted to me, and graciously allowed to serve the ancestral temple of Emperor Kao-tsu. For one so unenlightened as I, is this not a cause for rejoicing? Why should there be any sadness or sorrow?

Let the officials and people of the empire be instructed that, whenever this order shall reach them, they shall take part in lamentations for three days, after which all shall remove their mourning garments. There shall be no prohibitions against taking a wife or giving a daughter in marriage, or against performing sacrifices or partaking of wine and meat.

As for those who shall take part in the actual funeral proceedings and lamentations, they need not wear the customary unhemmed robes, and their headbands and sashes should not exceed three inches in width. There shall be no display of chariots or weapons, nor shall men and women be summoned from among the people to wail and lament in the palace. Those whose duty it is to lament in the palace shall do so only in the morning and evening, raising their voices fifteen times on each occasion, and, when the funeral rites have come to an end, this practice shall cease. There shall be no indiscriminate wailing other than at these prescribed times. After the coffin has been lowered into the grave, deep mourning shall be worn for fifteen days, then all mourning clothes shall be removed. Matters which are not specifically covered herein shall be disposed of in accordance with the spirit of this order. All of this shall be announced to the people of the empire so that they may understand my will. The hills and rivers around my tomb at Pa-ling may be left in their natural state and need not be altered in any way. The ladies of the palace, from those of the highest rank down to the junior maids, shall be sent back to their homes.

TRANSLATED BY BURTON WATSON

Wang Ch'ung

A Discussion of Death

[*Lun heng, XX*]

People say that when men die they become ghosts with consciousness and the power to harm others. If we try to test this theory by comparing men with other creatures, however, we find that men do not become ghosts, nor do they have consciousness or power to harm. . . . Man lives because of his vital force (*ch'i*) and when he dies this vital force is extinguished. The vital force is able to function because of the blood system, but when a man dies the blood system ceases to operate. With this the vital force is extinguished and the body decays and turns to clay. What is there to become a ghost then? If a man is without ears or eyes he lacks faculties of consciousness. Hence men who are dumb and blind are like grass or trees. But when the vital force has left a man it is a far more serious matter than simply being without ears or eyes. . . . The vital force produces man just as water becomes ice. As water freezes into ice, so the vital force coagulates to form man. When ice melts it becomes water and when a man dies he becomes spirit again. He is called spirit just as ice which has melted changes its name to water. People see that the name has changed, yet they then assert that spirit has consciousness and can assume a form and harm others, although there is no basis for this assertion.

People see ghosts which in form appear like living men. Precisely because they appear in this form, we know that they cannot be the spirits of the dead. How can we prove this? Take a sack and fill it with millet or rice. When the millet or rice has been put into it, the sack will be full and sturdy and will stand up in clear view so that people looking at it from a distance can tell that it is a sack of millet or rice. Why? Because the shape of the sack bespeaks the contents. But if the sack has a hole in it and all the millet or rice runs out, then the sack collapses in a heap and people looking from a distance can no longer see it. The spirit of man is stored up in his bodily form like the millet or rice in the sack. When he dies and his body decays, his vital force disperses like the grain running out of the sack. When the grain has run out, the sack no longer retains its shape. Then when the spirit of man has dispersed and disappeared, how could there still be a body to be seen by others? . . .

From the beginning of heaven and earth and the age of the sage rulers until now millions of people have died of old age or have been cut off in their prime. The number of men living today is nowhere near that of the dead. If men become ghosts when they die, then when we go walking we ought to see a ghost at every step. If men see ghosts when they are about to die then they ought to see millions of them crowding the hall, filling the courtyards and jamming the streets, and not just one or two of them. . . . It is the nature of Heaven and earth that, though new fires can be kindled, one cannot rekindle a fire that has burned out, and though new human beings can be born, one cannot bring back the dead. . . . Now people say that ghosts are the spirits of the dead. If this were true, then when men see them they ought to appear completely naked and not clothed in robes and sashes. Why? Because clothes have no spirits. When a man dies they all rot away along with his bodily form, so how could he put them on again? . . .

If dead men cannot become ghosts, then they also cannot have consciousness. How do we prove this? By the fact that before a man is born he has no consciousness. Before a man is born he exists in the midst of primal force (*yüan-ch'i*), and after he dies he returns again to this primal force. The primal force is vast and indistinct and the human force exists within it. Before a man is born he has no consciousness, so when he dies and returns to this original unconscious state how could he still have consciousness? The reason a man is intelligent and understanding is that he possesses the forces of the five virtues [humanity, righteousness, decorum, wisdom, and faith]. The reason he possesses these is that he has within him the five organs [heart, liver, stomach, lungs, and kidneys]. If these five organs are unimpaired, a man has understanding, but if they are diseased, then he becomes vague and confused and behaves like a fool or an idiot. When a man dies, the five organs rot away and the five virtues no longer have any place to reside. Both the seat and the faculty of understanding are destroyed. The body must await the vital force before it is complete, and the vital force must await the body before it can have consciousness. Nowhere is there a fire that burns all by itself. How then could there be a spirit with consciousness existing without a body? . . .

Confucius buried his mother at Fang. Later there was a heavy rain and the grave mound collapsed. When Confucius heard of this he wept bitterly and said: "The ancients did not repair graves," and he never repaired it. If the dead had consciousness then they would surely be angry that people did not repair their graves, and Confucius, realizing this, would accordingly have repaired the grave in order to please his mother's spirit. But he did not repair it. With the enlightenment of a sage he understood that the dead have no consciousness.

TRANSLATED BY BURTON WATSON

Han Dynasty

206 B.C. — A.D. 219

Biographies by Ssu-ma Ch'ien

Ssu-ma Ch'ien, who lived from the year 145 to about 90 B.C., succeeded to his father's post of Grand Historian at the Han court. The Shih chi (Records of the Grand Historian) is his account of the history of China—that is, of civilization—from earliest antiquity down to his own day. Its one hundred and thirty chapters are organized into four major sections: annals of the ruling houses, chronological tables, treatises on individual topics such as music or rivers and canals, and biographies of eminent men. Our extracts are drawn from this last and longest section, for it is the dramatic power and didactic force of the biographies which, more than any other feature, have captured and moulded the minds of readers through twenty centuries.

Po Yi and Shu Ch'i are classic examples of men of honour forced by their high principles into retreat from the "muddy confusion" of the world. Brief though their joint biography may be, it prompts Ssu-ma Ch'ien to a pointed questioning.

Ching K'o figures among the "famous assassins" in Ssu-ma Ch'ien's grouping, despite the failure of his attempt on the life of the tyrant of Ch'in, later the First Emperor.

Hsiang Yü, who contended for the throne against the eventual founder of Ssu-ma Ch'ien's own dynasty, the Han, is given a noble though bloody death. His tragedy is still movingly celebrated on the stage today.

The last of these biographies concerns Li Kuang, a general of the generation preceding the author's own. From an age so close comes a figure to whom the biographer's art gives the warmth and breath of life.

The great calamity of Ssu-ma Ch'ien's own career is evoked not in his history itself but in a letter he wrote late in life to an old friend. This letter opens the selection from his writings.

•

Letter to Jen An (Shao-ch'ing)

[*Pao Jen Shao-ch'ing shu*]

The Grand Historian Ssu-ma Ch'ien, bowing repeatedly, addresses his worthy friend Shao-ch'ing:

Some time ago you deigned to send me a letter in which you advised me to be concerned for my social contacts and devote myself to the recommendation and advancement of qualified persons. You expressed yourself with considerable vigor, as though you expected I would not follow your advice but would be influenced by the words of the vulgar: I would hardly behave in such a way. I may be a broken hack, but I have still been exposed to the teachings handed down by my elders. However, I see myself as mutilated and disgraced: I am criticized if I act, and where I hope to be helpful I do harm instead. This causes me secret distress, but to whom can I unburden myself? As the proverb says, "For whom do you do it? Who are you going to get to listen to you?" Why was it that Po-ya never again played his lute after Chung Tzu-ch'i died? A gentleman acts on behalf of an understanding friend, as a woman makes herself beautiful for her lover. Someone like me whose virility is lacking could never be a hero, even if he had the endowments of the pearl of Sui and the jade of Pien-ho or conducted himself like Hsü Yu and Po Yi; he would only succeed in being laughed at and put to shame.

I should have answered your letter sooner, but when I got back from the East in the emperor's suite I was very busy. We were seldom together, and then I was so pressed that there was never a moment's time when I could speak my mind. Now you, Shao-ch'ing, are under an accusation whose outcome is uncertain. Weeks and months have passed until we have now reached the end of winter, and I am going to have to accompany the emperor to Yung. I am afraid that that may come to pass which cannot be avoided,

95

and as a result I will never have the chance to give expression to my grievance and explain myself to you. It would mean that the souls of the departed would carry a never-ending burden of secret resentment. Let me say what is on my mind; I hope you will not hold it against me that I have been negligent in leaving your letter so long unanswered.

I have been taught that self-cultivation is the mark of wisdom, that charity is the sign of humanity, that taking and giving is the measure of decency, that a sense of shame is the index of bravery, that making a name for oneself is the end of conduct. A gentleman who practices these five things can entrust his reputation to the world and win a place among outstanding men. On the other hand there is no misfortune so hurtful as cupidity, no grief so painful as disappointment, no conduct so despicable as disgracing one's forebears, no defilement so great as castration. One who has undergone that punishment nowhere counts as a man. This is not just a modern attitude; it has always been so. Formerly when Duke Ling of Wei rode in the same chariot with the eunuch Yung-ch'ü, Confucius left Wei to go to Ch'en; when T'ung-tzu shared the emperor's chariot, Yüan Ssu blushed. It has always been occasion for shame. Even an ordinary fellow never fails to be offended when he has business with a eunuch—how much the more a gentleman of spirit. Though the court today may want men, you surely do not expect one who has submitted to the knife to recommend the worthies of the empire for places?

It has been twenty years since I inherited my father's office and entered the service of the emperor. It occurs to me that during that time I have not been able to demonstrate my loyalty and sincerity or win praise for good advice and outstanding abilities in the service of a wise ruler; nor have I been able to make good defects and omissions, or advance the worthy and talented, or induce wise hermits to serve; nor have I been able to serve in the ranks of the army, attacking walled cities and fighting in the field to win merit by taking an enemy general's head or capturing his banners; nor have I been able to win merit through long and faithful service to rise to high office and handsome salary, to the glory of my family and the benefit of my friends. From my failure in all four of these endeavors it follows that I am prepared to compromise with the times and avoid giving offence, wholly ineffectual for good or ill.

Formerly as Great Officer of the third grade I once had the chance to participate in deliberations in a minor capacity. Since I then offered no great plans nor expressed myself freely, would it not be an insult to the court and an affront to my colleagues if now, mutilated, a menial who sweeps floors, a miserable wretch, I should raise my head and stretch my eyebrows to argue right and wrong? Alas, for one like me what is there left to say? What is there left to say?

It is not easy to explain just what happened. When I was young I had no outstanding abilities and I grew up unpraised by my fellow townsmen. Fortunately, however, thanks to my father's service, the emperor made it possible for me to put my inconsiderable abilities at his disposal, and I had access to the court. It seemed to me that one cannot get a good view of the sky carrying a platter on one's head, so I broke off relations with my friends and neglected my family affairs that I might day and night devote all my small abilities wholeheartedly to my official duties and so gain the liking and approval of the ruler. But then came the event when I made my big mistake and everything was changed.

Li Ling and I were both stationed in the palace, but we never had a chance to become friends. Our duties kept us apart; we never shared so much as a cup of wine, let alone enjoyed a closer friendship. But I observed that he conducted himself as no ordinary gentleman. He was filial toward his parents, honest with his colleagues, scrupulous about money, decent in his behavior, yielding in matters of precedence, respectful, moderate, and polite to others. Carried away by his enthusiasm he never thought of himself but was ever there where his country needed him: such was his constant concern. To me he seemed to have the bearing of a national hero. A subject who exposes himself to a thousand deaths without regard for his own single life, and rushes to the defence of his country—that is a great man. That men who had been solely concerned with keeping themselves and their wives and children safe and sound should go out of their way to stir up trouble for him when he had made a single mistake was something that really pained my inmost feelings.

Moreover Li Ling's troops numbered fewer than 5,000 when he led them deep into the territory of the nomads. They marched to the khan's court and dangled the bait in the tiger's mouth. They boldly challenged the fierce barbarians, in the face of an army of a million. For ten days running they fought the khan, killing more than their own number, so that the enemy were unable to retrieve their dead or rescue their wounded. The princes of felts and furs were all terror-stricken; they called on the neighboring lords to draft bowmen, and the whole nation joined to attack and surround Li Ling's troops. For a thousand miles they retreated, fighting as they went, until their arrows were exhausted and the road cut off. The relieving force had not arrived. Dead and wounded lay in heaps. But when Li Ling rallied his men with a cry, his soldiers rose to fight, with streaming tears and bloody faces. They swallowed their tears and brandishing their empty bows braved naked swords. Facing north they fought to the death with the enemy.

Before Li Ling had reached this extremity a messenger brought news to the court and all the lords and princes raised their cups to drink to his success. Some days later the message arrived announcing that he had been defeated. The news so affected the emperor that he found his food tasteless and took no pleasure in holding court. The great ministers were depressed and fearful, not knowing what course to take. When I saw the emperor in great distress of mind, I took no count of my own humble position, but wished to express my honest opinion: that Li Ling had always shared with his men, renouncing the sweet and dividing his short rations, so that he was able to get them to die for him—no famous general of antiquity surpassed him in this. And though he was now involved in defeat, it could be assumed that he intended to do what was right and make good his obligation to China. The situation was past remedying, but the losses he had already inflicted on the Hsiung-nu were such that his renown filled the empire.

· I wished to express these ideas but had no way to do so until by chance I was ordered to give an opinion. In these terms I extolled Li Ling's merits, hoping to get the emperor to take a wider view of things and at the same time to undo the charges of his enemies. I did not succeed in making myself clear, and the emperor, in his wisdom, did not understand, suspecting that I was criticizing the Second General Li Kuang-li, who headed the relief column, and that I was indulging in special pleading in behalf of Li Ling. As a result I was turned over to the judges, and despite all my heartfelt sincerity I was unable to justify myself. In the end it was decided that I was guilty of attempting to mislead the emperor.

Being poor, I had insufficient funds to pay a fine in lieu of punishment. None of my friends came to my aid. My colleagues and associates spoke not a word on my behalf. My body is not of wood or stone: and I was alone with my jailors. When one is shut up in the depths of prison is there anyone he can appeal to? You have experienced this yourself, do you think it was otherwise with me?

In giving himself up alive to the Hsiung-nu, Li Ling disgraced his family; in going to the silkworm chamber after his act I became doubly the laughingstock of the empire. Alas, alas! This is not a thing one can easily talk about to the vulgar. My father never earned tally and patent of nobility; as annalist and astrologer I was not far removed from the diviners and invokers, truly the plaything of the emperor, kept like any singing girl or jester, and despised by the world. Had I chosen to submit to the law and let myself be put to death, it would have been no more important than the loss of a single hair from nine oxen, no different from the crushing of an ant. No one would have credited me with dying for a principle; rather they would have thought that I had simply died because I was at my wit's end and my offence allowed no other way out. And why? They would think so because of the occupation in which I established myself.

A man can die only once, and whether death to him is as weighty as Mount T'ai or as light as a feather depends on the reason for which he dies. The most important thing is not to disgrace one's ancestors, the next is not to disgrace one's self, the next not to disgrace one's principles, the next not to disgrace one's manners. Next worse is the disgrace of being put in fetters, the next is to wear a prisoner's garb, the next is to be beaten in the stocks, the next is to have the head shaved and a metal chain fastened around the neck, the next is mutilation, and the very worst disgrace of all is castration. It is said that corporal punishments are not applied to the great officers, implying that an officer cannot but be careful of his integrity. When the fierce tiger is in the depths of the mountain, all animals hold him in fear, but when he falls into a trap he waves his tail and begs for food: this is the end result of curtailing his dignity. Hence if you draw the plan of a jail on the ground, a gentleman will not step inside the figure, nor will he address even the wooden image of a jailor. In this way he shows his determination never to find himself in such a position. But let him cross his hands and feet to receive the bonds, expose his back to receive the whip, and be incarcerated in the barred cell—by then when he sees the jailor he bows his head to the ground and at the sight of his underlings he pants in terror. And why? It is the result of the gradual curtailment of his dignity. If now he claims there has been no disgrace, he is devoid of a sense of shame and wholly unworthy of respect.

Wen Wang was an earl, and yet he was held prisoner in Yu-li; Li Ssu was prime minister and yet was visited with all five punishments; Han Hsin was a prince and yet he was put in the stocks in Ch'en; P'eng Yüeh and Chang Ao each sat on a throne and called himself king, and yet the one was fettered in prison, the other put to death. These were all men of high rank and office and widespread reputation, but when they got into trouble with the law they were unable resolutely to put an end to themselves. It has always been the same: when one lies in the dirt there is no question of his not being disgraced. In the light of these examples, bravery and cowardice are a matter of circumstance, strength and weakness depend on conditions. Once this is understood, there is nothing to be surprised at in their behavior. If by failing to do away with himself before he is in the clutches of the law a man is degraded to the point of being flogged and then wishes to rescue his honor, has he not missed his chance? This is no doubt why the ancients were chary of applying corporal punishment to a great officer.

Now there is no man who does not naturally cling to life and avoid death, love his parents and cherish his wife and children. But the man who is devoted to the right sometimes has no choice but to behave otherwise. I early had the misfortune to lose my father and mother; I had no brothers and was quite alone. You have seen how little my affection for my wife and children deterred me from speaking out. But a brave man will not always die for his honor, and what efforts will not even a coward make in a cause to which he is devoted? I may be a coward and wish to live at the expense of my honor, but I surely know how to act appropriately. Would I have abandoned myself to the ignominy of being tied and bound? Even a miserable slave-girl is capable of putting an end to herself; could you expect less of me, when I had so little choice? If I concealed my feelings and clung to life, burying myself in filth without protest, it was because I could not bear to leave unfinished my deeply cherished project, because I rejected the idea of dying without leaving to posterity my literary work.

In the past there have been innumerable men of wealth and rank whose names died with them; only the outstanding and unusual are known today. It was when King Wen was in prison that he expanded the *Chou yi;* when Confucius was in straits he wrote the *Spring and Autumn Annals;* when Ch'ü Yüan was banished he composed the "Encountering Sorrow"; Tso Ch'iu lost his sight and so we have the *Conversations from the States;* Sun Tzu had his feet chopped off, and *The Art of War* was put together. The general purport of the 300 poems of the *Book of Songs* is the indignation expressed by the sages. All of these men were oppressed in their minds, and, unable to put into action their principles, wrote of the past with their eyes on the future. For example, Tso Ch'iu without sight and Sun Tzu with amputated feet were permanently disabled. They retired to write books in which they expressed their pent-up feelings, hoping to realize themselves in literature, since action was denied them.

I have ventured not to look for more recent models, but with what little literary ability I possess I have brought together the scattered fragments of ancient lore. I studied the events of history and set them down in significant order; I have written 130 chapters in which appears the record of the past—its periods of greatness and decline, of achievement and failure. Further it was my hope, by a thorough comprehension of the workings of affairs divine and human, and a knowledge of the historical process, to create a philosophy of my own. Before my draft was complete this disaster overtook me. It was my concern over my unfinished work that made me submit to the worst of all punishments without showing the rage I felt. When at last I shall have finished my book, I shall store it away in the archives to await the man who will understand it. When it finally becomes known in the world, I shall have paid the debt of my shame; nor will I regret a thousand deaths.

However, this is something I can confide only to a person of intelligence; it would not do to speak of it to the vulgar crowd. When one is in a compromising situation, it is not easy to justify oneself; the world is always ready to misrepresent one's motives. It was in consequence of my speaking out that I met disaster in the first place; were I to make myself doubly a laughingstock in my native place, to the disgrace of my forebears, how could I ever have the face again to visit the grave of my father and my mother? Even after a hundred generations my shame will but be the more. This is what makes my bowels burn within me nine times a day, so that at home I sit in a daze and lost, abroad I know not where I am going. Whenever I think of this shame the sweat drenches the clothes on my back. I am fit only to be a slave guarding the women's apartments: better that I should hide away in the farthest depths of the mountains. Instead I go on as best I can, putting up with whatever treatment is meted out to me, and so complete my degradation.

And now you want me to recommend worthy men for advancement! Is this not rather the last thing in the world I would want to do? Even if I should want to deck myself out with fine words and elegant phrases, it would not help me any against the world's incredulity; it would only bring more shame on me. In short, I can hope for justification only after my death.

In a letter I cannot say everything. What I have written is a crude and general statement of my feelings. Respectfully I bow to you.

TRANSLATED BY J. R. HIGHTOWER

The Biography of Po Yi and Shu Ch'i

Confucius said, "Po Yi and Shu Ch'i never bore old ills in mind and had not the faintest feelings of rancor." "They sought to act virtuously and they did so: what was there for them to repine about?"

I am greatly moved by the determination of Po Yi. But when I examine the song that has been attributed to him, I find it very strange.

The tales of these men state that Po Yi and Shu Ch'i were two sons of the ruler of Ku-chu. Their father wished to set up Shu Ch'i as his heir, but when he died, Shu Ch'i yielded in favour of Po Yi. Po Yi replied that it had been their father's wish that Shu Ch'i should inherit the throne and so he departed from the kingdom. Shu Ch'i likewise, being unwilling to accept the rule, went away and the people of the kingdom set up a younger son as ruler. At this time Po Yi and Shu Ch'i heard that Ch'ang, the Chief of the West, knew well how to look after the old, and they said, "Why should we not go and follow him?" But when they came there they found that the Chief of the West was dead and his son, King Wu, had taken up the ancestral tablet of his father, whom he honored with the title of King Wen, and was marching east to attack Emperor Chou of the Yin. Po Yi and Shu Ch'i clutched the reins of King Wu's horse and reprimanded him, saying, "The mourning for your father is not yet completed and yet you take up shield and spear. Can this conduct be called filial? As a subject you seek to assassinate your lord. Is this what is called righteousness?" The king's attendants wished to strike them down, but the king's counselor, T'ai-kung, interposed, saying, "These are just men," and he sent them away unharmed.

After this, King Wu conquered and pacified the people of the Yin and the world honored the house of Chou as its ruler. But Po Yi and Shu Ch'i were filled with shame and outrage and considered it unrighteous to eat the grain of Chou. They fled and hid on Shou-yang Mountain, where they tried to live by gathering ferns to eat. When they were on the point of starvation, they composed a song:

> We ascend this western hill
> And pluck its ferns.
> He replaces violence with violence,
> And sees not his own fault.
> Shen Nung, Yü and Hsia,
> How long ago these great men vanished!
> Whom now should we follow?
> Alas, let us depart,
> For our fate has run out!

They died of starvation on Shou-yang Mountain. When we examine this song, do we find any rancor or not?

Some people say: "It is Heaven's way, without distinction of persons, to keep the good perpetually supplied." Can we say then that Po Yi and Shu Ch'i were good men or not? They clung to righteousness and were pure in their deeds, as we have seen, and yet they starved to death.

Of his seventy disciples, Confucius singled out Yen Hui for praise because of his diligence in learning, yet Yen Hui was often in want, never getting his fill of even the poorest food, and in the end suffered an untimely death. Is this the way Heaven rewards the good man?

Robber Chih day after day killed innocent men, making mincemeat of their flesh. Cruel and wilful, he gathered a band of several thousand followers who went about terrorizing the world. But in the end he lived to a great old age. For what virtue did he deserve this?

The import of these examples is perfectly apparent. Even in more recent times we see that men whose deeds are immoral and who constantly violate the laws and prohibitions end their lives in luxury and wealth and their blessings pass down to their heirs without end. And there are others who carefully choose the spot where they shall place each footstep, who "speak out only when it is time to speak," who "walk on no bypaths and expend no anger on what is not a matter of uprightness and justice," and yet, in numbers too great to be reckoned, they meet with misfortune and disaster. I find myself in much perplexity. Is this so-called "Way of Heaven" right or wrong?

Confucius said, "Those whose ways are different cannot lay plans for one another." Each will follow his own will. Therefore he said, "If the search for riches and honor were sure to be successful, though I must become a groom with whip in hand to get them, I would do so. But as the search might not be successful, I will follow after that which I love." "When the year becomes cold, then we know how the pine and the cypress are the last to lose their leaves." When the whole world is in foul and muddy confusion, then is the man of true purity seen. Then must one judge what he will consider important and what unimportant.

"The superior man hates the thought of his name not being mentioned after his death." As Chia Yi has said:

> The covetous run after riches,
> The impassioned pursue a fair name.
> The proud die struggling for power
> And the people long only to live.

"Things of the same light illumine each other; things of the same class seek each other out. Clouds pursue the dragon; the wind follows the tiger. The sage arises and all creation becomes clear."

Po Yi and Shu Ch'i, although they were men of great virtue, became, through Confucius, even more illustrious in fame. Though Yen Hui was diligent in learning, like a fly riding on the tail of a swift horse, his attachment to Confucius made his deeds renowned. The hermit-scholars hiding away in their caves may be ever so correct in their givings and takings, and yet the names of them and their kind vanish like smoke without receiving a word of praise. Is this not pitiful? People of humble origins living in village lanes strive to make perfect their actions and establish a name for virtue, but if they do not somehow ally themselves with a man of worth and importance, how can they hope that their fame will be handed down to posterity?

TRANSLATED BY BURTON WATSON

The Biography of Ching K'o

Ching K'o was a native of Wei, though his family came originally from Ch'i. He loved to read books and practice swordsmanship. He expounded his ideas to Lord Yüan of Wei, but Lord Yüan failed to make use of him.

Ching K'o once visited Yü-tz'u, where he engaged Kai Nieh in a discussion on swordsmanship. In the course of their talk, Kai Nieh got angry and glared fiercely at Ching K'o, who immediately withdrew. Someone asked Kai Nieh if he did not intend to summon Ching K'o back again. "When I was discussing swordsmanship with him a little while ago," said Kai Nieh, "we had a difference of opinion and I glared at him. Go look for him if you like, but I'm quite certain he has gone. He wouldn't dare stay around!" Kai Nieh sent a messenger to the house where Ching K'o had been staying, but Ching K'o had already mounted his carriage and left Yü-tz'u. When the messenger returned with this report, Kai Nieh said, "I knew he would go. I glared at him and frightened him away."

Again, when Ching K'o was visiting the city of Han-tan, he and a man named Lu Kou-chien got into a quarrel over a chess game. Lu Kou-chien grew angry and began to shout, whereupon Ching K'o fled without a word and never came to see Lu Kou-chien again.

In the course of his travels, Ching K'o reached the state of Yen, where he became close friends with a dog butcher and a man named Kao Chien-li, who was good at playing the lute. Ching K'o was fond of wine, and every day he would join the dog butcher and Kao Chien-li to drink in the marketplace of the Yen capital. After the wine had begun to take effect, Kao Chien-li would strike up the lute and Ching K'o would join in with a song. In the middle of the crowded marketplace they would happily amuse themselves, or if their mood changed they would break into tears, exactly as though there were no one else about. But, although Ching K'o spent his time with drunkards, he was a man of depth and learning. Whatever feudal state he traveled to, he always became close friends with the most worthy and influential men. When he went to Yen, Master T'ien Kuang, a gentleman of Yen who was living in retirement, treated him very kindly, for he realized that he was no ordinary man.

After Ching K'o had been in Yen some time, Prince Tan, the heir apparent of Yen, who had been a hostage in Ch'in,[1] escaped and returned home. Prince Tan had previously been a hostage in the state of Chao. Cheng, the king of Ch'in, was born in Chao, and in his youth had been very friendly with Prince Tan; later, when Cheng became king, Prince Tan went as a hostage to the Ch'in court. But the king of Ch'in treated him very shabbily until, in anger, he escaped from the state and returned to Yen. After his return, he looked about for some way to get back at the king of Ch'in for the insults he had suffered; but because Yen was small and powerless, there was nothing he could do. Meanwhile, Ch'in day by day dispatched more troops east of the mountains, attacking Ch'i, Ch'u, Han, Wei and Chao and gradually eating away at the lands of the other feudal lords, until it became obvious that Yen's turn would be next. The ruler of Yen and his ministers all feared imminent disaster, and Prince Tan likewise, worried by the situation, asked his tutor Chü Wu what could be done.

Chü Wu replied, "Ch'in's lands fill the world and its might overawes the rulers of Han, Wei and Chao. To the north it holds the strongholds at Sweet Springs and Valley Mouth, and to the south the fertile fields of the Ching and Wei river valleys; it commands the riches of Pa and Han, the mountain ranges of Lung and Shu to the west, and the vital Han-ku and Yao passes to the east. Its people are numerous and its soldiers well trained, and it has more weapons and armor than it can use. If it should ever decide to march against us, we could find no safety south of the Great Wall or north of the Yi River.[2] Angry as you are at the insults you have suffered, how can you dream of baiting such a dragon?"

"Then what should I do?" said Prince Tan.

"Let me retire and think it over," replied Chü Wu.

---

1. See footnote 2 on p. 43 above.
2. The boundaries of the state of Yen.

Shortly after, the Ch'in general Fan Yü-ch'i, having offended the king of Ch'in, fled to Yen, where Prince Tan received him and assigned him quarters. Chü Wu admonished the prince, saying, "This will not do! Violent as the king of Ch'in is, and with the resentment he nurses against Yen because of your escape, it is already enough to make one's heart turn cold. And what will he be like when he hears where General Fan is staying? This is what men call throwing meat in the path of a starving tiger—there will be no help for the misfortune that follows! Even if you had ministers as wise as Kuan Chung and Yen Ying, they could think of no way to save you! I beg you to send General Fan at once to the territory of the Hsiung-nu barbarians to get him out of the way. Then, after you have negotiated with Han, Wei and Chao to the west, entered into alliance with Ch'i and Ch'u on the south, and established friendly relations with the leader of the Hsiung-nu to the north, we may be able to plan what move to make next."

"The scheme you propose will require a great deal of time," said Prince Tan. "As anxious as I feel at the moment, I am afraid I cannot wait that long! And that is not all. General Fan, having been hounded throughout the world, has come to entrust his fate to me. No matter how much I might be pressed by Ch'in and its power, I could never bear, when he is in such a pitiful plight, to betray his friendship and abandon him by sending him off to the Hsiung-nu! This is a matter of life and death to me. I beg you to consider the question once more."

Chü Wu said, "To pursue a dangerous course and hope for safety, to invite disaster while seeking good fortune; with too little planning and too much hatred to disregard a serious threat to the whole nation because of some lately incurred debt of friendship to one man—this is what is known as 'fanning resentment and abetting disaster'! Drop a swan's feather into a burning brazier and pff!—it is all over in an instant. And when Ch'in, like a ravening hawk, comes to vent its anger, will Yen be able to last any longer? However, there is a certain Master T'ien Kuang in Yen who is a man of deep wisdom and great daring. He would be a good person to consult."

"I would like you to introduce me to him," said Prince Tan. "Can you arrange it?"

"With pleasure," said Chü Wu, and went to see Master T'ien, informing him that the crown prince wished to consult him on mat-

ters of state. "I will be happy to comply," said Master T'ien. He
went to call on the prince, who came out to greet him, politely led
him inside, knelt, and dusted off a mat for him to sit on.

When T'ien Kuang was settled on his seat and those about
them had retired, the prince deferentially moved off his mat and
addressed his request to his visitor: "Yen and Ch'in cannot both
stand! I beg you to devote your mind to this problem."

"They say," replied T'ien Kuang, "that when a thoroughbred
horse is in its prime, it can gallop a thousand li in one day; but
when it is old and decrepit, the sorriest nag will outdistance it. It
appears that you have heard reports of how I was when I was in
my prime, but you do not realize that my strength is by now wasted
and gone. Nevertheless, though I myself would not venture to plan
for the safety of the state, I have a friend named Master Ching who
could be consulted."

"I would like you to introduce me to him," said Prince Tan.
"Is it possible?"

"With pleasure," said T'ien Kuang and, rising from his mat, he
hurried from the room. The prince escorted him as far as the gate
and there warned him, "What we have been discussing is a matter
of vital concern to the nation. Please do not let word of it leak out!"

T'ien Kuang lowered his gaze to the ground and replied with a
laugh, "I understand."

Then, stooped with age, he made his way to the house of
Master Ching. "Everyone in Yen knows that we are good friends,"
he said. "The crown prince, having heard reports of me when I was
in my prime and unaware that by now my powers have failed, has
told me that Yen and Ch'in cannot continue to exist side by side
and begged me to devote my mind to the problem. Rather than refuse his request, I took the liberty of mentioning your name. May
I ask you to go call on him at his palace?"

"I will be glad to comply," said Ching K'o.

"They say," T'ien Kuang continued, "that a worthy man does
not act in such a way as to arouse distrust in others. Now the prince
has warned me that the matter we discussed was of vital concern
to the nation and begged me not let word of it leak out. Obviously
he distrusts me, and if my actions have aroused his distrust, then
I am no gentleman of honor!" T'ien Kuang had decided to commit
suicide in order to spur Ching K'o to action, and he continued:

"I want you to go at once and visit the prince. Tell him I am already dead, so he will know that I have not betrayed the secret!" With this he cut his throat and died.

Ching K'o went to see the prince and informed him of T'ien Kuang's death and last words. The prince bowed twice and then, sinking to his knees, crawled forward, the tears starting from his eyes. After some time, he said, "I only cautioned Master T'ien not to speak so that we could be sure of bringing our plans to a successful conclusion. Now he has actually killed himself to show me that the secret will never be betrayed—as though I could have intended such a thing!"

After Ching K'o had settled himself, the prince moved deferentially off his mat, bowed his head, and said, "Master T'ien, unaware of how unworthy a person I am, has made it possible for me to speak my thoughts to you. It is clear from this that Heaven has taken pity upon Yen and has not abandoned me altogether.

"Ch'in has a heart that is greedy for gain, and its desires are insatiable. It will never be content until it has seized all the land in the world and forced every ruler within the four seas to acknowledge its sovereignty. Now, having already taken captive the king of Han and annexed all his lands, Ch'in has mobilized its troops to strike against Ch'u in the south, while in the north it stands poised for an attack on Chao. Wang Chien, leading several hundred thousand troops, is holding Chang and Yeh, while Li Hsin leads another force against T'ai-yüan and Yün-chung. Chao, unable to withstand the might of Ch'in, will undoubtedly submit and swear allegiance to it. And when Chao has gone under, Yen will stand next in line for disaster!

"Yen is small and weak, and has often fared badly in war. Even if we were to mobilize the entire nation, we obviously could not stand against Ch'in; and once the other feudal lords have bowed to its rule, none of them will dare to become our allies. Nevertheless, I have a scheme of my own which, foolish as it may be, I would like to suggest—that is, to find a really brave man who would be willing to go as our envoy to the court of Ch'in and tempt it with some offer of gain. The king of Ch'in is greedy, and under the circumstances would surely listen to our offer. If this man could then somehow threaten the king, as Ts'ao Mo threatened Duke Huan of Ch'i,[3] and force him to return to the feudal lords all the land he has seized, that would be the best we could ask for. And if that proved impossible, he might still be able to stab and kill the king. With the Ch'in generals free to do as they wished with the troops in the outlying areas, and the Ch'in court in a state of confusion, dissension would surely arise between ruler and subject. The feudal lords could then take advantage of the situation to band together once more, and in that case the defeat of Ch'in would be inevitable. This is what I would like to see more than anything else, but I do not know who could be entrusted with such a mission. I can only ask that you give it some thought!"

After some time, Ching K'o said, "This is a matter of grave importance to the state. I am a person of little worth and I fear I would be unfit for such a mission."

The prince moved forward and, bowing his head, begged and begged Ching K'o to accept the proposal and not to decline any longer, until at last Ching K'o gave his consent. The prince then honored him with the title of Highest Minister and assigned him the finest quarters in the capital. Every day the prince went to call at his mansion, presenting gifts of food, supplying him with all manner of luxuries, and from time to time pressing him to accept carriages, rider attendants and waiting women, indulging his every wish so as to insure his cooperation.

Time passed, but Ching K'o showed no inclination to set out on the mission. Meanwhile the Ch'in general Wang Chien defeated Chao, took prisoner its king, and annexed its entire territory. Then he advanced north, seizing control of the land as he went, until he reached the southern border of the state of Yen. Crown Prince Tan, filled with terror, begged Ching K'o to set off. "Any moment now the Ch'in forces may cross the Yi River, and if that happens, though I might wish to continue to wait upon you, how could I do so?"

"I intended to say something, whether you mentioned it or

---

3. At a meeting of the rulers of Ch'i and Lu in 681 B.C., Ts'ao Mo, a Lu general, suddenly leaped forward and threatened Duke Huan of Ch'i with a dagger until he promised to return the lands he had earlier seized from Lu. Prince Tan's hope was that a similar promise could be extorted from the king of Ch'in.

not," said Ching K'o. "The trouble is that, if I set off now without any means of gaining the confidence of the king of Ch'in, I will never be able to get close to him. The king of Ch'in has offered a thousand catties of gold and a city of ten thousand households in exchange for the life of his former general, Fan Yü-ch'i. If I could get the head of General Fan and a map of the Tu-k'ang region of Yen, and offer to present these to the king of Ch'in, he would certainly be delighted to receive me. Then I would have a chance to carry out our plan."

But the prince replied, "General Fan has come here in trouble and distress and entrusted himself to me. I could never bear to betray the trust of a worthy man for the sake of my own personal desires. I beg you to think of some other plan."

Ching K'o realized that the prince would never bring himself to carry out his suggestion, and so he went in private to see Fan Yü-ch'i. "Ch'in's treatment of you has been harsh indeed!" he said. "Your father, your mother, and all the members of your family have been done away with; and now I hear that Ch'in has offered a reward of a thousand catties of gold and a city of ten thousand households for your head! What do you intend to do?"

Fan Yü-ch'i looked up to heaven and gave a great sigh, tears streaming down his face. "I think of nothing else, until the ache of it is in my very bones! But I do not know what I can do!"

"Suppose I said that one word from you could dispel the troubles of the state of Yen and avenge the wrong you have suffered?"

Fan Yü-ch'i pressed forward. "What is it?" he asked.

"Give me your head, so that I can present it to the king of Ch'in! Then he will surely be delighted to receive me. With my left hand I will seize hold of his sleeve, with my right I'll stab him in the breast, and all your wrongs will be avenged and all the shameful insults which Yen has suffered will be wiped out! What do you say?"

Fan Yü-ch'i bared his shoulder and gripped his wrist in a gesture of determination. Moving forward, he said, "Day and night I gnash my teeth and eat out my heart trying to think of some plan. Now you have shown me the way!" Then he cut his throat.

When the crown prince heard what had happened, he rushed to the spot and, throwing himself upon the corpse, wept in deep sorrow. But, since there was nothing that could be done, he took Fan Yü-chi's head and sealed it in a box. Earlier, he had ordered a search for the sharpest dagger that could be found, and had purchased one from a man of Chao named Hsü Fu-jen for a hundred catties of gold. He ordered his artisans to coat the blade with poison and try it out on some men; though the thrust drew hardly enough blood to stain the robe of the victim, every one of the men dropped dead on the spot. The prince then began to make final preparations for sending Master Ching on his mission. There was a brave man of Yen named Ch'in Wu-yang who had murdered someone at the age of thirteen, and was so fierce that no one dared even to look at him crossly. This man the prince ordered to act as a second to Ching K'o.

There was another man whom Ching K'o wished to have along in his party, but he lived a long way off and had not yet arrived in Yen. Meanwhile, preparations for the journey were completed but, though time passed, Ching K'o still did not set off. The prince began to fret at the delay and to suspect that Ching K'o had changed his mind. He therefore went to Ching K'o and pressed his request. "The day for departure has already passed, and I am wondering what you intend to do. Perhaps I should send Ch'in Wu-yang on ahead . . ."

"What do you mean, send Ch'in Wu-yang on ahead?" roared Ching K'o angrily. "Send that little wretch alone and you may be sure he'll never return successful—setting off with a single dagger to face the immeasureable might of Ch'in! The reason I have delayed is that I was waiting for a friend I wanted to go with me. But if you feel it is growing too late, I beg to take my leave."

Then he set out. The crown prince and all their associates who knew what was happening put on white robes and caps of mourning to see the party off, accompanying them as far as the Yi River. After they had sacrificed to the god of the road and chosen their route, Kao Chien-li struck up his lute and Ching K'o joined in with a song in the mournful *pien-chih* mode. Tears streamed from the eyes of the company. Ching K'o came forward and sang this song:

> "Winds cry *hsiao-hsiao,*
> Yi waters are cold.

> Brave men, once gone,
> Never come back again."

Shifting to the *yü* mode with its martial air, Ching K'o sang once more; this time the eyes of the men flashed with anger and their hair bristled beneath their caps. Then he mounted his carriage and set off, never once looking back.

In time he arrived in Ch'in, where he presented gifts worth a thousand catties of gold to Meng Chia, one of the king's favorite ministers. Meng Chia in turn spoke on his behalf to the king of Ch'in. "The king of Yen, trembling with awe before your majesty's might, has not ventured to call out his troops to oppose our forces, but requests that he and all his people may become vassals of Ch'in, so that he may be ranked among the other feudal lords and present tribute and perform labor services in the manner of a province; in this way he hopes to be allowed to continue the sacrifices at the temple of his ancestors, the former kings of Yen. In his terror he has not dared to come and speak in person, but has respectfully sent the severed head of Fan Yü-ch'i sealed in a box, along with a map of the Tu-k'ang region in Yen, to be presented to you. Bowing respectfully in his courtyard, he has sent these gifts, dispatching his envoys to inquire your majesty's pleasure. He awaits your command."

When the king of Ch'in heard this, he was delighted and, donning his court robes and ordering a full dress reception, he received the envoys of Yen in the Hsien-yang Palace. Ching K'o bore the box with Fan Yü-ch'i's head, while Ch'in Wu-yang carried the map case; step by step they advanced through the throne room until they reached the steps of the throne, where Ch'in Wu-yang suddenly turned pale and began to quake with fear. The courtiers eyed him suspiciously. Ching K'o turned around, laughed at Ch'in Wu-yang, and then stepped forward to apologize. "This man is a simple rustic from the barbarous region of the northern border, and he has never seen the Son of Heaven. That is why he shakes with fright. I beg your majesty to pardon him for the moment and permit me to complete my mission here before you."

"Bring the map he is carrying!" said the king to Ching K'o, who took the map container from Ch'in Wu-yang and presented it to the king. The king opened the container, and when he had removed the map, the dagger appeared. At that moment Ching K'o seized the king's sleeve with his left hand, while with his right he snatched up the dagger and held it pointed at the king's breast, but he did not stab him. The king jerked back in alarm and leapt from his seat, tearing the sleeve off his robe. He tried to draw his sword, but it was long and clung to the scabbard, and since it hung vertically at his side, he could not, in his haste, manage to get it out.

Ching K'o ran after the king, who dashed around the pillar of the throne room. All the courtiers, utterly dumbfounded by so unexpected an occurrence, milled about in disorder.

According to Ch'in law, no courtier or attendant who waited upon the king in the upper throne rooms was permitted to carry a weapon of any kind. The palace attendants who bore arms were ranged in the lower hall, and without a command from the king they were forbidden to ascend to the throne room. In his panic the king had no chance to give the command for the soldiers to appear, and thus Ching K'o was able to pursue him. Having nothing with which to strike at Ching K'o, the king in panic-stricken confusion merely flailed at him with his hands. At the same time the physician Hsia Wu-chü, who was in attendance, battered Ching K'o with the medicine bag he was carrying.

The king continued to circle the pillar, unable in his confusion to think of anything else to do. "Push the scabbard around behind you!" shouted the king's attendants, and when he did this, he was at last able to draw his sword and strike at Ching K'o, slashing him across the left thigh. Ching K'o, staggering to the ground, raised the dagger and hurled it at the king, but it missed and struck the bronze pillar. The king attacked Ching K'o again.

Ching K'o, wounded now in eight places, realized that his attempt had failed. Leaning against the pillar, his legs sprawled before him, he began to laugh and curse the king. "I failed because I tried to threaten you alive and get a promise from you that I could take back to the crown prince!" As he spoke, the king's attendants rushed forward to finish him off.

It was a long time before the king regained his composure. When at last he came to himself, he discussed with his ministers who deserved a reward for his part in the incident, and who deserved punishment. To the physician Hsia Wu-chü he presented two hundred taels of gold, "because Hsia Wu-chü, out of love for me, hit Ching K'o with his medicine bag."

After this the king in a rage dispatched more troops to join his army in Chao and commanded Wang Chien to attack Yen. Ten months later, the Ch'in army captured the city of Chi. King Hsi of Yen, Prince Tan, and the others of the court, leading their best troops, fled east to Liao-tung for safety. The Ch'in general Li Hsin pursued and attacked them with ever increasing fury.

King Chia of Tai sent a letter to King Hsi of Yen which read: "It is all because of Prince Tan that Ch'in is harrassing you with such vehemence. If you would only do away with the prince and present his corpse to Ch'in, the king's anger would surely be appeased and he would leave you in peace to carry on the sacrifices to your altars of soil and grain."

Shortly after this, Li Hsin pursued Prince Tan as far as the Yen River, where the prince hid among the islands in the river. Meanwhile the king of Yen sent an envoy to cut off the prince's head, intending to present it to Ch'in, but Ch'in dispatched more troops and reopened its attack on Yen. Five years later, Ch'in finally destroyed the state of Yen and took its ruler, King Hsi, prisoner. The following year [221 B.C.], the king of Ch'in united all the world under his rule and assumed the title of Supreme Emperor.

The Ch'in ruler then began a campaign to ferret out the associates of Prince Tan and Ching K'o, and as a result they all went into hiding. Kao Chien-li, who was among the group, changed his name, hired himself out as an indentured workman, and went into hiding in a household in the city of Sung-tzu, enduring for a long time the hardships of a laborer's life. Whenever he heard some guest of the family playing the lute in the main hall of the house, he would linger outside, unable to tear himself away, and after each performance he would say, "That man plays well," or "That man is not very good." One of the servants reported this to the master of the house, saying, "That hired man must know something about music, since he ventures to pass judgment on everyone's playing."

The master of the house summoned Kao Chien-li to appear and play the lute before his guests, and when he did so, everyone in the company praised his playing and pressed wine on him. Kao Chien-li thought of the long time he had been in hiding, and of the seemingly endless years of hardship and want that lay ahead; finally he went back to his room, got his lute and good clothes out of the trunk where he had stored them and, changing his clothes, appeared once more in the hall. The guests were overcome with surprise and, bowing and making room for him as an equal, they led him to the seat of honor and requested him to play the lute and sing. When the performance was over, there was not a guest who left the house dry-eyed.

Kao Chien-li was entertained at one home after another in Sung-tzu, and in time his fame reached the ears of the Ch'in emperor. The emperor summoned him to an audience, but when he appeared someone who had known him in the past exclaimed, "This is Kao Chien-li!" The emperor, unable to bring himself to kill such a skilled musician, ordered his eyes put out and commanded him to play in his presence. The emperor never failed to praise his playing and gradually allowed him to come nearer and nearer. Kao Chien-li then got a heavy piece of lead and fastened it inside his lute, and the next time he was summoned to play at the emperor's side, he raised his lute and struck at the emperor. He missed and was summarily executed, and after that the emperor never again permitted any of the former followers of the feudal lords to approach his person.

When Lu Kou-chien heard of Ching K'o's attempt to assassinate the king of Ch'in, he sighed to himself and said, "What a pity that he never properly mastered the art of swordsmanship! And as for me—how blind I was to his real worth! That time when I shouted at him in anger, he must have thought I was hardly human!"

The Grand Historian remarks: When people these days tell the story of Ching K'o, they assert that at the command of Prince Tan the heavens rained grain and horses grew horns. This is of course a gross error. They likewise say that Ching K'o actually wounded the king of Ch'in, which is equally untrue. At one time Kung-sun Chi-kung and Master Tung were friends of the physician Hsia Wu-chü and they learned from him exactly what happened. I have therefore reported everything just as they told it to me. Of these five men [4] from Ts'ao Mo to Ching K'o, some succeeded in carrying out their duty and some did not. But it is perfectly clear that they had all determined upon the deed. They were not false to their intentions. Is it not right, then, that their names should be handed down to later ages?

TRANSLATED BY BURTON WATSON

---

4. The five men whose biographies make up Ssu-ma Ch'ien's chapter on assassin-retainers.

The Death of Hsiang Yü

Hsiang Yü's army had built a walled camp at Kai-hsia, but his soldiers were few and his supplies exhausted. The Han army, joined by the forces of the other leaders, surrounded them with several lines of troops. In the night Hsiang Yü heard the Han armies all about him singing the songs of Ch'u. "Has Han already conquered Ch'u?" he exclaimed in astonishment. "How many men of Ch'u they have with them!" Then he rose in the night and drank within the curtains of his tent. With him were the beautiful lady Yüh, who enjoyed his favor and followed wherever he went, and his famous steed Dapple, which he always rode. Hsiang Yü, filled with passionate sorrow, began to sing sadly, composing this song:

> My strength plucked up the hills,
> My might shadowed the world;
> But the times were against me,
> And Dapple runs no more,
> When Dapple runs no more,
> What then can I do?
> Ah, Yüh, my Yüh,
> What will your fate be?

He sang the song several times through, and Lady Yüh joined her voice with his. Tears streamed down his face, while all those about him wept and were unable to lift their eyes from the ground. Then he mounted his horse and, with some eight hundred brave horsemen under his banner, rode into the night, burst through the encirclement to the south, and galloped away.

Next morning, when the king of Han became aware of what had happened, he ordered his cavalry general Kuan Ying to lead a force of five thousand horsemen in pursuit. Hsiang Yü crossed the Huai River, though by now he had only a hundred or so horsemen still with him. Reaching Yin-ling, he lost his way, and stopped to ask an old farmer for directions. But the farmer deceived him, saying, "Go left!" and when he rode to the left he stumbled into a great swamp, so that the Han troops were able to pursue and overtake him.

Hsiang Yü once more led his men east until they reached Tung-ch'eng. By this time he had only twenty-eight horsemen, while the Han cavalry pursuing him numbered several thousand.

Hsiang Yü, realizing that he could not escape, turned to address his horsemen: "It has been eight years since I first led my army forth. In that time I have fought over seventy battles. Every enemy I faced was destroyed, every one I attacked submitted. Never once did I suffer defeat, until at last I became dictator of the world. But now suddenly I am driven to this desperate position! It is because Heaven would destroy me, not because I have committed any fault in battle. I have resolved to die today. But before I die, I beg to fight bravely and win for you three victories. For your sake I shall break through the enemy's encirclement, cut down their leaders, and sever their banners that you may know it is Heaven which has destroyed me and no fault of mine in arms!" Then he divided his horsemen into four bands and faced them in four directions.

When the Han army had surrounded them several layers deep, Hsiang Yü said to his horsemen, "I will get one of those generals for you!" He ordered his men to gallop in all four directions down the hill on which they were standing, with instructions to meet again on the east side of the hill and divide into three groups. He himself gave a great shout and galloped down the hill. The Han troops scattered before him and he succeeded in cutting down one of their generals. At this time Yang Hsi was leader of the cavalry pursuing Hsiang Yü, but Hsiang Yü roared and glared so fiercely at him that all his men and horses fled in terror some distance to the rear.

Hsiang Yü rejoined his men, who had formed into three groups. The Han army, uncertain which group Hsiang Yü was with, likewise divided into three groups and again surrounded them. Hsiang Yü once more galloped forth and cut down a Han colonel, killing some fifty to a hundred men. When he had gathered his horsemen together a second time, he found that he had lost only two of them.

"Did I tell you the truth?" he asked. His men all bowed and replied, "You have done all you said."

Hsiang Yü, who by this time had reached Wu-chiang, was considering whether to cross over to the east side of the Yangtze. The village head of Wu-chiang, who was waiting with a boat on the bank of the river, said to him, "Although the area east of the river is small, it is some thousand miles in breadth and has a population of thirty or forty thousand. It would still be worth ruling. I beg you to make haste and cross over. I am the only one who has a boat, so that when the Han army arrives they will have no way to get across!"

Hsiang Yü laughed and replied, "It is Heaven that is destroying me. What good would it do me to cross the river? Once, with eight thousand sons from the land east of the river, I crossed over and marched west, but today not a single man of them returns. Although their fathers and brothers east of the river should take pity on me and make me their king, how could I bear to face them again? Though they said nothing of it, could I help but feel shame in my heart?" Then he added, "I can see that you are a worthy man. For five years I have ridden this horse, and I have never seen his equal. Again and again he has borne me hundreds of miles in a single day. Since I cannot bear to kill him, I give him to you."

Hsiang Yü then ordered all his men to dismount and proceed on foot, and with their short swords to close in hand-to-hand combat with the enemy. Hsiang Yü alone killed several hundred of the Han men, until he had suffered a dozen wounds. Looking about him, he spied the Han cavalry marshal Lü Ma-t'ung. "We are old friends, are we not?" he asked. Lü Ma-t'ung eyed him carefully and then, pointing him out to Wang Yi, said, "This is Hsiang Yü!"

"I have heard that Han has offered a reward of a thousand catties of gold and a fief of ten thousand households for my head," said Hsiang Yü. "I will do you the favor!" And with this he cut his own throat and died.

Wang Yi seized his head, while the other horsemen trampled over each other in a struggle to get at Hsiang Yü's body, so that twenty or thirty of them were killed. In the end cavalry attendant Yang Hsi, cavalry marshal Lü Ma-t'ung, and attendants Lü Sheng and Yang Wu each succeeded in seizing a limb. When the five of them fitted together the limbs and head, it was found that they were indeed those of Hsiang Yü. Therefore the fief was divided five ways, Lü Ma-t'ung being enfeoffed as marquis of Chung-shui, Wang Yi as marquis of Tu-yen, Yang Hsi as marquis of Ch'ih-ch'üan, Yang Wu as marquis of Wu-fang, and Lü Sheng as marquis of Nieh-yang.

With the death of Hsiang Yü, the entire region of Ch'u surrendered to Han, only Lu refusing to submit. The king of Han set out with the troops of the empire and was about to massacre the inhabitants of Lu. But because Lu had so strictly obeyed the code of honor and had shown its willingness to fight to the death for its acknowledged sovereign, he bore with him the head of Hsiang Yü and, when he showed it to the men of Lu, they forthwith surrendered.

King Huai of Ch'u had first enfeoffed Hsiang Yü as duke of Lu, and Lu was the last place to surrender. Therefore, the king of Han buried Hsiang Yü at Ku-ch'eng with the ceremony appropriate to a duke of Lu. The king proclaimed a period of mourning for him, wept, and then departed. All the various branches of the Hsiang family he spared from execution, and he enfeoffed Hsiang Po as marquis of She-yang. The marquises of T'ao, P'ing-kao, and Hsüan-wu were all members of the Hsiang family who were granted the imperial surname Liu.

TRANSLATED BY BURTON WATSON

The Biography of General Li Kuang

General Li Kuang was a native of Ch'eng-chi in Lung-hsi Province. Among his ancestors was Li Hsin, a general of the state of Ch'in, who pursued and captured Tan, the crown prince of Yen. The family originally lived in Huai-li but later moved to Ch'eng-chi. The art of archery had been handed down in the family for generations.

In the fourteenth year of Emperor Wen's reign [166 B.C.] the Hsiung-nu entered the Hsiao Pass in great numbers. Li Kuang, as the son of a distinguished family, was allowed to join the army in the attack on the barbarians. He proved himself a skillful horseman and archer, killing and capturing a number of the enemy, and was rewarded with the position of palace attendant at the Han court. His cousin Li Ts'ai was also made a palace attendant. Both men served as mounted guards to the emperor and received a stipend of eight hundred piculs of grain. Li Kuang always accompanied Emperor Wen on his hunting expeditions. The emperor, observing how he charged up to the animal pits, broke through the palisades, and struck down the most ferocious beasts, remarked, "What a pity you were not born at a better time! Had you lived in the age of Emperor Kao-tsu, you would have had no trouble in winning a marquisate of at least ten thousand households!"

When Emperor Ching came to the throne, Li Kuang was made chief commandant of Lung-hsi; later he was transferred to the post of general of palace horsemen. At the time of the revolt of Wu and Ch'u, he served as a cavalry commander under the grand commandant Chou Ya-fu, joining in the attack on the armies of Wu and Ch'u, capturing the enemy pennants, and distinguishing himself at the battle of Ch'ang-yi. But because he had accepted the seals of a general from the king of Liang without authorization from the Han government, he was not rewarded for his achievements when he returned to the capital.

Following this he was transferred to the post of governor of

Shang-ku Province, where he engaged in almost daily skirmishes with the Hsiung-nu. The director of dependent states Kung-sun K'un-yeh went to the emperor and, with tears in his eyes, said, "There is no one in the empire to match Li Kuang for skill and spirit and yet, trusting to his own ability, he repeatedly engages the enemy in battle. I am afraid one day we will lose him!" The emperor therefore transferred him to the post of governor of Shang Province.

At this time the Hsiung-nu invaded Shang Province in great force. Emperor Ching sent one of his trusted eunuchs to join Li Kuang, ordering him to train the troops and lead them in an attack on the Hsiung-nu. The eunuch, leading a group of twenty or thirty horsemen, was casually riding about the countryside one day when he caught sight of three Hsiung-nu riders and engaged them in a fight. The three Hsiung-nu, however, began circling the party and shooting as they went until they had wounded the eunuch and were near to killing all of his horsemen. The eunuch barely managed to flee back to the place where Li Kuang was. "They must be out hunting eagles!" said Li Kuang, and galloped off with a hundred horsemen in pursuit of the three Hsiung-nu. The Hsiung-nu, having lost their horses, fled on foot. After they had journeyed twenty or thirty li, Li Kuang caught up with them and, ordering his horsemen to fan out to the left and right of them, began to shoot at them. He killed two with his arrows and took the third one alive. As he had guessed, they were eagle hunters.

Li Kuang had bound his prisoner and remounted his horse, when he spied several thousand Hsiung-nu horsemen in the distance. The Hsiung-nu, catching sight of Li Kuang and his men, supposed that they were a decoy sent out from the main body of the Han forces to lure them into combat. They made for a nearby hill in alarm and drew up their ranks on its crest.

Li Kuang's horsemen were thoroughly terrified and begged him to flee back to camp as quickly as possible, but he replied, "We are twenty or thirty li away from the main army. With only a hundred of us, if we were to try to make a dash for it, the Hsiung-nu would be after us in no time and would shoot down every one of us. But if we stay where we are, they are bound to think we are a decoy from the main army and will not dare to attack!"

Instead of retreating therefore, Li Kuang gave the order to his men to advance. When they had reached a point some two li from the Hsiung-nu ranks, he told his men, "Dismount and undo your saddles!"

"But there are too many of them and they are almost on top of us!" his men protested. "What will we do if they attack?"

"They expect us to run away," said Li Kuang. "But now if we all undo our saddles and show them we have no intention of fleeing, they will be more convinced than ever that there is something afoot."

The Hsiung-nu in fact did not venture to attack, but sent out one of their leaders on a white horse to reconnoiter. Li Kuang mounted again and, with ten or so of his horsemen, galloped after the barbarian leader and shot him down. Then he returned to his group and, undoing his saddle, ordered his men to turn loose their horses and lie down on the ground. By this time night was falling and the Hsiung-nu, thoroughly suspicious of what they had seen, still had not ventured to attack. They concluded that the Han leaders, having concealed soldiers in the area, must be planning to fall upon them in the dark, and so during the night the Hsiung-nu chiefs and their men all withdrew. When dawn came Li Kuang finally managed to return with his group to the main army, which, having no idea where he had gone, had been unable to follow him.

After this Li Kuang was assigned to the governorship of several other border provinces in succession, returning finally to Shang Province. In the course of these moves he served as governor of Lung-hsi, Pei-ti, Tai, and Yün-chung Provinces and in each won fame for his fighting.

After some time, Emperor Ching passed away and the present emperor came to the throne. The emperor's advisers informed him of Li Kuang's fame as a general, and he made Li Kuang the colonel of the guard of the Eternal Palace, while allowing him to retain the governorship of Shang Province.

At this time Ch'eng Pu-chih was colonel of the guard of the Palace of Lasting Joy. Ch'eng Pu-chih had been a governor in the border provinces and a garrison general at the same time as Li Kuang. When Li Kuang went out on expeditions to attack the Hsiung-nu, he never bothered to form his men into battalions and companies. He would make camp wherever he found water and grass, leaving his men to set up their quarters in any way they thought convenient. He never had sentries circling the camp at night and beating on cooking pots, as was the custom, and in his headquarters he kept records and other clerical work down to a minimum. He always sent out scouts some distance around the camp, however, and he had never met with any particular mishap.

Ch'eng Pu-chih, on the other hand, always kept his men in strict battalion and company formation. The sentries banged on the cooking pots, his officers worked over their records and reports until dawn, and no one in his army got any rest. He likewise had never had any mishaps. Ch'eng Pu-chih once expressed the opinion, "Although Li Kuang runs his army in a very simple fashion, if the enemy should ever swoop down on him suddenly he would have no way to hold them off. His men enjoy plenty of idleness and pleasure, and for that reason they are all eager to fight to the death for him. Life in my army may be a good deal more irksome, but at least I know that the enemy will never catch me napping!"

Li Kuang and Ch'eng Pu-chih were both famous generals at this time, but the Hsiung-nu were more afraid of Li Kuang's strategies, and the Han soldiers for the most part preferred to serve under him and disliked being under Ch'eng Pu-chih's command. Ch'eng Pu-chih advanced to the position of palace counselor under Emperor Ching because of the outspoken advice he gave the emperor on several occasions. He was a man of great integrity and very conscientious in matters of form and law.

Some time later, the Han leaders attempted to entice the Shan-yü [leader of the Hsiung-nu] into entering the city of Ma-yi, concealing a large force of men in the valley around the city to ambush the Hsiung-nu. At this time Li Kuang was appointed cavalry general under the command of Han An-kuo, leader of the supporting army. As it happened, however, the Shan-yü discovered the plot and escaped in time, so that neither Li Kuang nor any of the other generals connected with the plot achieved any merit.

Four years later [129 B.C.] Li Kuang, because of his services as colonel of the guard, was made a general and sent north from Yen-men to attack the Hsiung-nu. But the Hsiung-nu force he was pitted against turned out to be too numerous and succeeded in defeating Li Kuang's army and capturing him alive.

The Shan-yü had for a long time heard of Li Kuang's excellence as a fighter and had given orders, "If you get hold of Li Kuang, take him alive and bring him to me!" As it turned out, the barbarian horsemen did manage to capture Li Kuang and, since he was badly wounded, they strung a litter between two horses and, laying him on it, proceeded on their way about ten li. Li Kuang pretended to be dead but managed to peer around him and noticed that close by his side was a young Hsiung-nu boy mounted on a fine horse. Suddenly he leaped out of the litter and onto the boy's horse, seizing his bow and pushing him off. Then, whipping the horse to full gallop, he dashed off to the south. After traveling twenty or thirty li he succeeded in catching up with what was left of his army and led the men back across the border into Han territory. While he was making his escape, several hundred horsemen from the party that had captured him came in pursuit, but he turned and shot at them with the bow he had snatched from the boy, killing several of his pursuers, and was thus able to escape.

When he got back to the capital, he was turned over to the law officials, who recommended that he be executed for losing so many of his men and being captured alive. He was allowed to ransom his life and was reduced to the status of commoner.

Following this, Li Kuang lived in retirement for several years, spending his time hunting. His home was in Lan-t'ien, among the Southern Mountains, adjoining the estate of Kuan Ch'iang, the grandson of Kuan Ying, the former marquis of Ying-yin.

One evening Li Kuang, having spent the afternoon drinking with some people out in the fields, was on his way back home, accompanied by a rider attendant, when he passed the watch station at Pa-ling. The watchman, who was drunk at the time, yelled at Li Kuang to halt.

"This is the former General Li," said Li Kuang's man.

"Even present generals are not allowed to go wandering around at night, much less former ones!" the watchman retorted, and he made Li Kuang halt and spend the night in the watch station.

Shortly after this, the Hsiung-nu invaded Liao-hsi, murdered its governor, and defeated General Han An-kuo. Han An-kuo was transferred to Yu-pei-p'ing, where he died, and the emperor forthwith summoned Li Kuang to be the new governor of Yu-pei-p'ing. When he accepted the post, Li Kuang asked that the watchman of Pa-ling be ordered to accompany him, and as soon as the man reported for duty Li Kuang had him executed.

After Li Kuang took over in Yu-pei-p'ing, the Hsiung-nu, who were familiar with his reputation and called him_"The Flying General," stayed away from the region for several years and did not dare to invade Yu-pei-p'ing.

Li Kuang was out hunting one time when he spied a rock in the grass which he mistook for a tiger. He shot an arrow at the rock and hit it with such force that the tip of the arrow embedded itself in the rock. Later, when he discovered that it was a rock, he tried shooting at it again, but he was unable to pierce it a second time.

Whatever province Li Kuang had been in in the past, whenever he heard that there was a tiger in the vicinity he always went out to shoot it in person. When he got to Yu-pei-p'ing he likewise went out one time to hunt a tiger. The beast sprang at him and wounded him, but he finally managed to shoot it dead.

Li Kuang was completely free of avarice. Whenever he received a reward of some kind he at once divided it among those in his command, and he was content to eat and drink the same things as his men. For over forty years he received a salary of two thousand piculs of grain, but when he died he left no fortune behind. He never discussed matters of wealth. He was a tall man with long, ape-like arms. His skill at archery seems to have been an inborn talent, for none of his descendants or others who studied under him was ever able to equal his prowess. He was a very clumsy speaker and never had much to say. When he was with others he would draw diagrams on the ground to explain his military tactics or set up targets of various widths and shoot at them with his friends, the loser being forced to drink. In fact, archery remained to the end of his life his chief source of amusement.

When he was leading his troops through a barren region and they came to water, he would not go near it until all his men had finished drinking. Similarly he would not eat until every one of his men had been fed. He was very lenient with his men and did nothing to vex them, so that they all loved him and were happy to serve under him. Even when the enemy was attacking, it was his custom never to discharge his arrows unless his opponent was within twenty or thirty paces and he believed he could score a hit. When he did discharge an arrow, however, the bowstring had no sooner sounded than his victim would fall to the ground. Because of this peculiar habit he often found himself in considerable difficulty when he was leading his troops against an enemy, and this is also the reason, it is said, that he was occasionally wounded when he went out hunting wild beasts.

Sometime after Li Kuang was made governor of Yu-pei-p'ing, Shih Chien died, and Li Kuang was summoned to take his place as chief of palace attendants.

In the sixth year of *yüan-so* [123 B.C.] Li Kuang was again made a general and sent with the general in chief Wei Ch'ing to proceed north from Ting-hsiang and attack the Hsiung-nu. Most of the other generals who took part in the expedition killed or captured a sufficient number of the enemy to be rewarded for their achievements by being made marquises, but Li Kuang's army won no distinction.

Three years later Li Kuang, as chief of palace attendants, was sent to lead a force of four thousand cavalry north from Yu-pei-p'ing. Chang Ch'ien, marquis of Po-wang, leading ten thousand cavalry, rode out with Li Kuang but took a somewhat different route. When Li Kuang had advanced several hundred li into enemy territory, the Hsiung-nu leader known as the "Wise King of the Left," appeared with forty thousand cavalry and surrounded Li Kuang's army. His men were all terrified, but Li Kuang ordered his son Li Kan to gallop out to meet the enemy. Li Kan, accompanied by only twenty or thirty riders, dashed straight through the Hsiung-nu horsemen, scattering them left and right, and then returned to his father's side, saying, "These barbarians are easy enough to deal with!" After this Li Kuang's men were somewhat reassured.

Li Kuang ordered his men to draw up in a circle with their ranks facing outward. The enemy charged furiously down on them and the arrows fell like rain. Over half the Han soldiers were killed, and their arrows were almost gone. Li Kuang then ordered the men to load their bows and hold them in readiness, but not to discharge them, while he himself, with his huge yellow crossbow, shot at the subcommander of the enemy force and killed several of the barbarians. After this the enemy began to fall back a little.

By this time night had begun to fall. Every one of Li Kuang's officers and men had turned white with fear, but Li Kuang, as calm and confident as though nothing had happened, worked to get his ranks into better formation. After this the men knew that they could never match his bravery.

The following day Li Kuang once more fought off the enemy, and in the meantime Chang Ch'ien at last arrived with his army. The Hsiung-nu forces withdrew and the Han armies likewise retreated, being in no condition to pursue them. By this time Li Kuang's army had been practically wiped out. When the two leaders returned to the capital, they were called to account before the law. Chang Ch'ien was condemned to death for failing to keep his rendezvous with Li Kuang at the appointed time, but on payment of a fine he was allowed to become a commoner. In the case of Li Kuang it was decided that his achievements and his failures canceled each other out and he was given no reward.

Li Kuang's cousin Li Ts'ai had begun his career along with Li Kuang as an attendant at the court of Emperor Wen. During the reign of Emperor Ching, Li Ts'ai managed to accumulate sufficient merit to advance to the position of a two thousand picul official, and under the present emperor he became prime minister of Tai. In the fifth year of *yüan-so* [124 B.C.] he was appointed general of light carriage and accompanied the general in chief, Wei Ch'ing, in an attack on the Hsiung-nu "Wise King of the Right." His achievements in this campaign placed him in the middle group of those who were to receive rewards and he was accordingly enfeoffed as marquis of Lo-an. In the second year of *yüan-shou* [121 B.C.] he replaced Kung-sun Hung as chancellor of the central court. In ability one would be obliged to rank Li Ts'ai very close to the bottom, and his reputation came nowhere near to equaling that of Li Kuang. And yet, although Li Kuang never managed to obtain a fief and never rose higher than one of the nine lower offices of the government, that of colonel of the guard, his cousin Li Ts'ai was enfeoffed as a marquis and eventually reached the position of chancellor, one of the three highest posts. Even some of Li Kuang's own officers and men succeeded in becoming marquises.

Li Kuang was once chatting with Wang So, a diviner who used configurations of the sky to foretell the future, and remarked on this fact. "Ever since the Han started attacking the Hsiung-nu, I have never failed to be in the fight. I've had men in my command who were company commanders or even lower and who didn't even have average ability, and yet twenty or thirty of them have won marquisates on the strength of their achievements in attacking the barbarian armies. I have never been behind anyone else in doing my duty. Why is it I have never won an ounce of distinction so that I could be enfeoffed like the others? Is it that I just don't have the right kind of face for a marquis? Or is it all a matter of fate?"

"Think carefully, general," replied Wang So. "Isn't there something in the past that you regret having done?"

"Once, when I was governor of Lung-hsi, the Ch'iang tribes in the west started a revolt. I tried to talk them into surrendering and, in fact, persuaded over eight hundred of them to give themselves up. But then I went back on my word and killed all of them the very same day. I have never ceased to regret what I did. But that's the only thing I can think of."

"Nothing brings greater misfortune than killing those who have already surrendered to you," said Wang So. "This is the reason, general, that you have never gotten to be a marquis!"

Two years later general in chief Wei Ch'ing and general of swift cavalry Ho Ch'ü-ping set off with a large force to attack the Hsiung-nu. Li Kuang several times asked to be allowed to join them, but the emperor considered that he was too old and would not permit him to go. After some time, however, the emperor changed his mind and gave his consent, appointing him general of the vanguard. The time was the fourth year of *yüan-shou* [119 B.C.].

Li Kuang accordingly joined the general in chief, Wei Ch'ing, and set off to attack the Hsiung-nu. After the group had crossed the border, Wei Ch'ing captured one of the enemy and learned the whereabouts of the Shan-yü. He therefore decided to take his own best troops and make a dash for the spot, ordering Li Kuang to join forces with the general of the right, Chao Yi-chi, and ride around by the eastern road. The eastern road was rather long and roundabout and, since there was little water or grass in the region, it presented a difficult route for a large army to pass over. Li Kuang therefore asked Wei Ch'ing to change the order. "I have been appointed general of the vanguard," he said, "and yet now you have shifted my position and ordered me to go around by the east. I have been fighting the Hsiung-nu ever since I was old enough to wear my hair bound up, and now I would like to have just one chance to get at the Shan-yü. I beg you to let me stay in the vanguard and advance and fight to the death with him!"

Wei Ch'ing had been warned in private by the emperor that Li Kuang was an old man and had already had a lot of bad luck in the past. "Don't let him try to get at the Shan-yü, or he will probably make a mess of things!" the emperor had said. Also, at this time Kung-sun Ao, who had recently been deprived of his marquisate, was serving as a general under Wei Ch'ing, and Wei Ch'ing wanted to take him along with him in his attack on the Shan-yü so that Kung-sun Ao would have a chance to win some distinction. For these reasons he removed Li Kuang from his post of general of the vanguard.

Li Kuang was aware of all this and tried his best to get out of obeying the order, but Wei Ch'ing refused to listen to his arguments. Instead he sent one of his clerks to Li Kuang's tent with sealed orders to "proceed to your division at once in accordance with the instructions herein." Li Kuang did not even bother to take leave of Wei Ch'ing but got up and went straight to his division, burning with rage and indignation; then, leading his troops to join those of general of the right Chao Yi-chi, he set out by the eastern road. Lacking proper guides, however, they lost their way and failed to meet up with Wei Ch'ing at the appointed time. Wei Ch'ing in the meantime engaged the Shan-yü in battle, but the latter fled and Wei Ch'ing, unable to capture him, was forced to turn back south again. After crossing the desert, he joined up with the forces of Li Kuang and Chao Yi-chi.

When Li Kuang had finished making his report to Wei Ch'ing and returned to his own camp, Wei Ch'ing sent over his clerk with the customary gifts of dried rice and thick wine for Li Kuang. While the clerk was there, he began to inquire how it happened that Li Kuang and Chao Yi-chi had lost their way, since Wei Ch'ing had to make a detailed report to the emperor on what had happened to the armies. Li Kuang, however, refused to answer his questions.

Wei Ch'ing sent his clerk again to reprimand Li Kuang in the strongest terms and order him to report to general headquarters at once and answer a list of charges that had been drawn up against him. Li Kuang replied, "None of my commanders was at fault. I was the one who caused us to lose our way. I will send in a report myself."

Then he went in person to headquarters and, when he got there, said to his officers, "Since I was old enough to wear my hair bound up, I have fought over seventy engagements, large and small, with the Hsiung-nu. This time I was fortunate enough to join the general in chief in a campaign against the troops of the Shan-yü himself, but he shifted me to another division and sent me riding around by the long way. On top of that, I lost my way. Heaven must have planned this! Now I am over sixty—much too old to stand up to a bunch of petty clerks and their list of charges!" Then he drew his sword and cut his throat.

All the officers and men in his army wept at the news of his death, and when word reached the common people, those who had known him and those who had not, old men and young boys alike, were all moved to tears by his fate. Chao Yi-chi was handed over to the law officials and sentenced to death, but on payment of a fine he was allowed to become a commoner.

The Grand Historian remarks: One of the old books says, "If he is an upright person, he will act whether he is ordered to or not; if he is not upright, he will not obey even when ordered." It refers, no doubt, to men like General Li.

I myself have seen General Li—a man so plain and unassuming that you would have taken him for a peasant, and almost incapable of speaking a word. And yet the day he died all the people of the empire, whether they had known him or not, were moved to the profoundest grief, so deeply did men trust his sincerity of purpose. There is a proverb which says, "Though the peach tree does not speak, the world wears a path beneath it." It is a small saying, but one which is capable of conveying a great meaning.

TRANSLATED BY BURTON WATSON

Rhyme-Prose of the Han Dynasty

Even for early Chinese literature, where the resistance to docketing or classification is strong and general, the term fu *is elastic. Typically, the* fu *presents an essay in varied verse with prose introduction and interludes: "rhyme-prose" is a fair representation of the generic name. The staple verse line stems from the longer line used in the* Songs of Ch'u *rather than from the archaic brevity of the* Shih-ching. *Chia Yi's "Lament for Ch'ü Yüan" suggests the strong link between the Ch'u poets and the Han rhyme-prose authors.*

The first fu *below is attributed to Sung Yü, courtier of Ch'u and disciple of Ch'ü Yüan. It is characteristic of the genre in its leaning towards description. With Ssu-ma Hsiang-ju (179-117 B.C.), the reader will note, the genre reaches the brilliant height of its development: his heady concoctions served as models for many imitators in later centuries.*

"The Shang-lin Park" is an excerpt of about half of one fu *by Ssu-ma Hsiang-ju. In wildly extravagant terms two gentlemen, "Master No-such" and "Sir Fantasy," compare the royal hunts of Ch'i and Ch'u. "Lord Not-real" then proceeds to cap even these descriptions with the splendours of the imperial hunting-ground, the Shang-lin Park. The catalogue of its marvels threatens to exhaust the poet's lexicon; but even so, in deference to the didactic convention, he finds it possible to conclude with a call for the return to thrifty ways and simple virtues.*

Four centuries later, rhyme-prose furnished the vehicle for a work of penetrating literary criticism. To this work, Lu Chi's Essay on Literature, *a separate section is devoted.*

●

Sung Yü

The Wind

[*Feng fu*]

King Hsiang of Ch'u was taking his ease in the Palace of the Orchid Terrace, with his courtiers Sung Yü and Ching Ch'a attending him, when a sudden gust of wind came sweeping in. The king, opening wide the collar of his robe and facing into the wind, said, "What a delightful breeze! And I and the common people may share it together, may we not?"

But Sung Yü replied, "This wind is for your majesty alone. How could the common people have a share in it?"

"The wind," said the king, "is the breath of heaven and earth. Into every corner it unfolds and reaches; without choosing between high or low, exalted or humble, it touches everywhere. What do you mean when you say that this wind is for me alone?"

Sung Yü replied, "I have heard my teacher say that the twisted branches of the lemon tree invite the birds to nest, and hollows and cracks summon the wind. But the breath of the wind differs with the place which it seeks out."

"Tell me," said the king. "Where does the wind come from?"

Sung Yü answered:

"The wind is born from the land
And springs up in the tips of the green duckweed.
It insinuates itself into the valleys
And rages in the canyon mouth,
Skirts the corners of Mount T'ai
And dances beneath the pines and cedars.
Swiftly it flies, whistling and wailing;
Fiercely it splutters its anger.
It crashes with a voice like thunder,
Whirls and tumbles in confusion,

135

Shaking rocks, striking trees,
Blasting the tangled forest.
Then, when its force is almost spent,
It wavers and disperses,
Thrusting into crevices and rattling door latches.
Clean and clear,
It scatters and rolls away.
Thus it is that this cool, fresh hero wind,
Leaping and bounding up and down,
Climbs over the high wall
And enters deep into palace halls.
With a puff of breath it shakes the leaves and flowers,
Wanders among the cassia and pepper trees,
Or soars over the swift waters.
It buffets the mallow flower,
Sweeps the angelica, touches the spikenard,
Glides over the sweet lichens and lights on willow shoots,
Rambling over the hills
And their scattered host of fragrant flowers.
After this, it wanders into the courtyard,
Ascends the jade hall in the north,
Clambers over gauze curtains,
Passes through the inner apartments,
And so becomes your majesty's wind.
When this wind blows on a man,
At once he feels a chill run through him,
And he sighs at its cool freshness.
Clear and gentle,
It cures sickness, dispels drunkenness,
Sharpens the eyes and ears,
Relaxes the body and brings benefit to men.
This is what is called the hero wind of your majesty."
"How well you have described it!" exclaimed the king. "But
now may I hear about the wind of the common people?" And Sung
Yü replied:
The wind of the common people
Comes whirling from the lanes and alleys,
Poking in the rubbish, stirring up the dust,
Fretting and worrying its way along.

It creeps into holes and knocks on doors,
Scatters sand, blows ashes about,
Muddles in dirt and tosses up bits of filth.
It sidles through hovel windows
And slips into cottage rooms.
When this wind blows on a man,
At once he feels confused and downcast.
Pounded by heat, smothered in dampness,
His heart grows sick and heavy,
And he falls ill and breaks out in a fever.
Where it brushes his lips, sores appear;
It strikes his eyes with blindness.
He stammers and cries out,
Not knowing if he is dead or alive.
This is what is called the lowly wind of the
        common people."

TRANSLATED BY BURTON WATSON

Chia Yi

The Owl[1]

[*Fu niao fu*]

The year was *tan-wo*, it was the fourth month, summer's first,
The thirty-seventh day of the cycle, at sunset, when an owl flew
    into my house.
On the corner of my seat it perched, completely at ease.
I marveled at the reason for this uncanny visitation
And opened a book to discover the omen. The oracle yielded
    the maxim:
"When a wild bird enters a house, the master is about to leave."
I should have liked to ask the owl: Where am I to go?
If lucky, let me know; if bad, tell me the worst.
Be it swift or slow, tell me when it is to be.
The owl sighed; it raised its head and flapped its wings
But could not speak—Let me say what it might reply:
All things are a flux, with never any rest,
Whirling, rising, advancing, retreating;
Body and breath do a turn together—change form and slough off,
Infinitely subtle, beyond words to express.
From disaster fortune comes, in fortune lurks disaster,
Grief and joy gather at the same gate, good luck and bad share the
    same abode.
Though Wu was great and strong, Fu-ch'ai met with defeat;
Yüeh was driven to refuge on Kuai-chi, but Kou-chien became
    hegemon.

---

1. Chia Yi had been tutor to the prince of Ch'ang-sha for three years when
one day an owl flew into his house and perched in a corner of his room. (In
Ch'u the word for owl is *fu*; it is a bird of ill omen.) This was after he had been
banished to Ch'ang-sha, a low, damp place, and he was greatly depressed at
what he took to be a sign that he had not much longer to live. On this occasion
he wrote this *fu* to console himself.

Li Ssu emigrated to become minister, but in the end he suffered
the Five Punishments.
Fu Yüeh was once in bonds, before he was minister to Wu-ting.
So,
Disaster is to fortune as strands of a single rope.
Fate is past understanding—who comprehends its bounds?
Force water and it spurts, force an arrow and it goes far:
All things are propelled in circles, undulating and revolving—
Clouds rise and rain falls, tangled in contingent alternation.
On the Great Potter's wheel creatures are shaped in all their
infinite variety.
Heaven cannot be predicted, the Way cannot be foretold,
Late or early, it is predetermined; who knows when his time will be?
Consider then:
Heaven and Earth are a crucible, the Creator is the smith,
Yin and yang are the charcoal, living creatures are the bronze:
Combining, scattering, waning, waxing—where is any pattern?
A thousand changes, a myriad transformations with never any end.
If by chance one becomes a man, it is not a state to cling to;
If one be instead another creature, what cause is that for regret?
A merely clever man is partial to self, despising others, vaunting ego;
The man of understanding takes the larger view: nothing exists
to take exception to.
The miser will do anything for his hoard, the hero for his repute;
The vainglorious is ready to die for power, the common man clings
to life.
Driven by aversions and lured by desires men dash madly west or
east;
The Great Man is not biased, the million changes are all one to him.
The stupid man is bound by custom, confined as though in fetters;
The Perfect Man is above circumstance, Tao is his only friend.
The mass man vacillates, his mind replete with likes and dislikes;
The True Man is tranquil, he takes his stand with Tao.
Divest yourself of knowledge and ignore your body, until, trans-
ported, you lose self,
Be detached, remote, and soar with Tao.
Float with the flowing stream, or rest against the isle,
Surrender to the workings of fate, unconcerned for self,
Let your life be like a floating, your death like a rest.

Placid as the peaceful waters of a deep pool, buoyant as an unfastened boat
Find no cause for complacency in life, but cultivate emptiness
   and drift.
The Man of Virtue is unattached; recognizing fate, he does
   not worry.
Be not dismayed by petty pricks and checks!

TRANSLATED BY J. R. HIGHTOWER

Lament for Ch'ü Yüan

[*Tiao Ch'ü Yüan*]

With awe I receive the imperial blessing,
And await chastisement at Ch'ang-sha.
I have heard men tell of Ch'ü Yüan,
And how he drowned himself in the Mi-lo.
I have come, and to Hsiang's flowing waters
With reverence entrust this lament for the Master.
You met with the evil ones of the world
And they have destroyed this body.
Pitiful, alas,
That you should fall upon such days.
Hidden are the phoenixes from sight,
While kites and owls flap abroad.
Now the dullard gains favor and fame;
The slanderer and the toady have their way.
The wise and sage they turn aside;
The righteous they have toppled over.
Now the world calls Po-yi greedy
And speaks of the purity of Robber Chih;[1]
The blade Mu-yeh, they say, is dull,
And praise for keenness knives of lead.
(Alas, Master, I am dumb—
You, who were without fault!)
Cast aside are the cauldrons of Chou;
Pots of clay are what men hold precious now.
Wearied oxen draw the carriages;

---

1. Po-yi and Robber Chih: see above, pp. 103-104.

To the chariot the lame nag is harnessed,
While the fine-blooded stallion droops his ears
And plods before a wagon of salt.
The caps of state are trod underfoot—
Confusion cannot be far off!
Ah, bitter, my Master,
That you met with this sorrow!

    Reprise:

"It is over.
There is none in the kingdom who knows me!"[2]
Alone in my woe,
To whom shall I speak?
Lightly the phoenix soars aloft;
Far off he withdraws, he departs.
The holy dragons of the nine-fold depths
Conceal their rareness in fathomless tides,
Deep their iridescence hide
Where leech and mudworm cannot bore.
The shining virtue of the sage
Must shut itself far from the filth of the world.
If the unicorn be leashed,
How does he differ from dog or ram?
Hesitation brought you to this fate;
Was this not the sin of my lord?
Roaming the nine lands to save your prince,
Must you yet long for the capital?
To the rarest heights the phoenix soars,
Alights where the light of virtue shines;
Spying the snares of petty goodness,
He beats his wings and flies away.
How in this shallow, mud-clogged fen
Should swim the giants of the sea?
The whale, stranded on the river shoals,
Ants and crickets feed upon!

                TRANSLATED BY BURTON WATSON

---

2. Quotation from Ch'ü Yüan's poem, "Encountering Sorrow."

Ssu-ma Hsiang-ju

From "The Shang-lin Park"

[Shang lin fu]

Have you not heard of the Shang-lin Park of the Son of Heaven?
To the east of it lies Ts'ang-wu,
To the west the land of Hsi-chi;
On its south runs the Cinnabar River,
On its north, the Purple Deeps.
Within the park spring the Pa and Ch'an rivers,
And through it flow the Ching and Wei,
The Feng, the Hao, the Lao, and the Chüeh,
Twisting and turning their way
Through the reaches of the park;
Eight rivers, coursing onward,
Spreading in different directions, each with its own form.
North, south, east and west
They race and tumble,
Pouring through the chasms of Pepper Hill,
Skirting the banks of the river islets,
Winding through the cinnamon forests
And across the broad meadows.
In wild confusion they swirl
Along the bases of the tall hills
And through the mouths of the narrow gorges;
Dashed upon boulders, maddened by winding escarpments,
They writhe in anger,
Leaping and curling upward,
Jostling and eddying in great swells
That surge and batter against each other;
Darting and twisting,
Foaming and tossing

142

In a thundering chaos;
Arching into hills, billowing like clouds
They dash to left and right,
Plunging and breaking in waves
That chatter over the shallows;
Crashing against the cliffs, pounding the embankments
The waters pile up and reel back again,
Skipping across the rises, swooping into the hollows,
Rumbling and murmuring onward;
Deep and powerful,
Fierce and clamorous
They froth and churn
Like the boiling waters of a cauldron,
Casting spray from their crests, until,
After their wild race through the gorges,
Their distant journey from afar,
They subside into silence,
Rolling on in peace to their long destination,
Boundless and without end,
Gliding in soundless and solemn procession,
Shimmering and shining in the sun
To flow through giant lakes of the east
Or spill into the ponds along their banks.
Here horned dragons and red hornless dragons,
Sturgeon and salamanders,
Carp, bream, gudgeon, and dace,
Cowfish, flounder, and sheatfish
Arch their backs and twitch their tails,
Spread their scales and flap their fins,
Diving among the deep crevices;
The waters are loud with fish and turtles,
A multitude of living things.
Here moon-bright pearls
Gleam on the river slopes,
While quartz, chrysoberyl
And clear crystal in jumbled heaps
Glitter and sparkle,
Catching and throwing back a hundred colors
Where they lie tumbled on the river bottom.

Wild geese and swans, graylags, bustards,
Cranes and mallards,
Loons and spoonbills,
Teals and gadwalls,
Grebes, night herons, and cormorants
Flock and settle upon the waters,
Drifting lightly over the surface,
Buffeted by the wind,
Bobbing and dipping with the waves,
Sporting among the weedy banks,
Gobbling the reeds and duckweed,
Pecking at water chestnuts and lotuses.
Behind them rise the tall mountains,
Lofty crests lifted to the sky;
Clothed in dense forests of giant trees,
Jagged with peaks and crags;
The steep summits of the Nine Pikes,
The towering heights of the Southern Mountains
Soar dizzily like a stack of cooking pots,
Precipitous and sheer.
Their sides are furrowed with ravines and valleys,
Narrow-mouthed clefts and open glens,
Through which rivulets dart and wind.
About their base, hills and islands
Raise their tall heads;
Ragged knolls and hillocks
Rise and fall,
Twisting and twining,
Like the coiled bodies of reptiles;
While from their folds the mountain streams leap and tumble,
Spilling out upon the level plains.
There they flow a thousand miles along smooth beds,
Their banks lined with dikes
Blanketed with green orchids
And hidden beneath selinea,
Mingled with snakemouth
And magnolias;
Planted with yucca,
Sedge of purple dye,

Bittersweet, gentians, and orchis,
Blue flag and crow-fans,
Ginger and turmeric,
Monkshood, wolfsbane,
Nightshade, basil,
Mint, ramie, and blue artemisia,
Spreading across the wide swamps,
Rambling over the broad plains,
A vast and unbroken mass of flowers,
Nodding before the wind;
Breathing forth their fragrance,
Pungent and sweet,
A hundred perfumes
Wafted abroad
Upon the scented air.
Gazing about the expanse of the park
At the abundance and variety of its creatures,
One's eyes are dizzied and enraptured
By the boundless horizons,
The borderless vistas.
The sun rises from the eastern ponds
And sets among the slopes of the west;
In the southern part of the park,
Where grasses grow in the dead of winter,
And the waters leap, unbound by ice,
Live zebras, yaks, tapirs, and black oxen,
Water buffalo, elk, and antelope,
"Red-crowns" and "round-heads,"
Aurochs, elephants, and rhinoceros.
In the north, where in the midst of summer
The ground is cracked and blotched with ice
And one may walk the frozen streams or wade the rivulets,
Roam unicorns and boars,
Wild asses and camels,
Onagers and mares,
Swift stallions, donkeys, and mules.
Here the country palaces and imperial retreats
Cover the hills and span the valleys,
Verandahs surrounding their four sides;

With storied chambers and winding porticoes,
Painted rafters and jade-studded corbels,
Interlacing paths for the royal palanquin,
And arcaded walks stretching such distances
That their length cannot be traversed in a single day.
Here the peaks have been leveled for mountain halls,
Terraces raised, story upon story,
And chambers built in the deep grottoes.
Peering down into the caves, one cannot spy their end;
Gazing up at the rafters, one seems to see them brush the heavens;
So lofty are the palaces that comets stream through their portals
And rainbows twine about their balustrades.
Green dragons slither from the eastern pavilion;
Elephant-carved carriages prance from the pure hall of the west,
Bringing immortals to dine in the peaceful towers
And bands of fairies to sun themselves beneath the southern eaves.
Here sweet fountains bubble from clear chambers,
Racing in rivulets through the gardens,
Great stones lining their courses;
Plunging through caves and grottoes,
Past steep and ragged pinnacles,
Horned and pitted as though carved by hand,
Where garnets, green jade
And pearls abound;
Agate and marble,
Dappled and lined;
Rose quartz of variegated hue,
Spotted among the cliffs;
Rock crystal, opals
And finest jade.
Here grow citrons with their ripe fruit in summer,
Tangerines, bitter oranges and limes,
Loquats, persimmons,
Wild pears, tamarind,
Jujubes, arbutus,
Peaches and grapes,
Almonds, damsons,
Mountain plums and litchis,
Shading the quarters of the palace ladies,

Ranged in the northern gardens,
Stretching over the slopes and hillocks
And down into the flat plains;
Lifting leaves of kingfisher hue,
Their purple stems swaying;
Opening their crimson flowers,
Clusters of vermilion blossoms,
A wilderness of trembling flames
Lighting up the broad meadow.
Here crab apple, chestnut and willow,
Birch, maple, sycamore and boxwood,
Pomegranate, date palm,
Betel nut and palmetto,
Sandalwood, magnolia,
Cedar and cypress
Rise a thousand feet,
Their trunks several arm-lengths around,
Stretching forth flowers and branches,
Clustered in dense copses,
Their limbs entwined,
Their foliage a thick curtain
Over stiff and bending trunks,
Their branches sweeping to the ground
Amidst a shower of falling petals.
They tremble and sigh
As they sway with the wind,
Creaking and moaning in the breeze
Like the tinkle of chimes
Or the wail of flageolets.
High and low they grow,
Screening the quarters of the palace ladies;
A mass of sylvan darkness,
Blanketing the mountains and edging the valleys,
Ascending the slopes and dipping into the hollows,
Overspreading the horizon,
Outdistancing the eye.
Here black apes and white she-apes,
Drills, baboons, and flying squirrels,
Lemurs and langurs,

Macaques and gibbons
Dwell among the trees,
Uttering long wails and doleful cries
As they leap nimbly to and fro,
Sporting among the limbs
And clambering haughtily to the treetops.
Off they chase across bridgeless streams
And spring into the depths of a new grove,
Clutching the low-swinging branches,
Hurtling across the open spaces,
Racing and tumbling pell-mell,
Until they scatter from sight in the distance.
Such are the scenes of the imperial park,
A hundred, a thousand settings
To visit in the pursuit of pleasure;
Palaces, inns, villas, and lodges,
Each with its kitchens and pantries,
Its chambers of beautiful women
And staffs of officials.
Here, in late fall and early winter,
The Son of Heaven stakes his palisades and holds his hunts,
Mounted in a carriage of carved ivory
Drawn by six jade-spangled horses, sleek as dragons.
Rainbow pennants stream before him;
Cloud banners trail in the wind.
In the vanguard ride the hide-covered carriages;
Behind, the carriages of his attendants.
A coachman as clever as Sun Shu grasps the reins;
A driver as skillful as the Duke of Wei stands beside him.
His attendants fan out on all sides
As they move into the palisade.
They sound the somber drums
And send the hunters to their posts;
They corner the quarry among the rivers
And spy them from the high hills.
Then the carriages and horsemen thunder forth,
Startling the heavens, shaking the earth;
Vanguard and rear dash in different directions,
Scattering after the prey.

On they race in droves,
Rounding the hills, streaming across the lowlands,
Like enveloping clouds or drenching rain.
Leopards and panthers they take alive;
They strike down jackals and wolves.
With their hands they seize the black and tawny bears,
And with their feet they down the wild sheep.
Wearing pheasant-tailed caps
And breeches of white tiger skin
Under patterned tunics,
They sit astride their wild horses;
They clamber up the steep slopes of the Three Pikes
And descend again to the river shoals,
Galloping over the hillsides and the narrow passes,
Through the valleys and across the rivers.
They fell the "dragon sparrows"
And sport with the *chieh-ch'ih,*
Strike the *hsia-ko*
And with short spears stab the little bears,
Snare the fabulous *yao-niao* horses
And shoot down the great boars.
No arrow strikes the prey
Without piercing a neck or shattering a skull;
No bow is discharged in vain,
But to the sound of each twang some beast must fall.
Then the imperial carriage signals to slacken pace
While the emperor wheels this way and that,
Gazing afar at the progress of the hunting bands,
Noting the disposition of their leaders.
At a sign, the Son of Heaven and his men resume their pace,
Swooping off again across the distant plains.
They bear down upon the soaring birds;
Their carriage wheels crush the wily beasts.
Their axles strike the white deer;
Deftly they snatch the fleeting hares;
Swifter than a flash
Of scarlet lightning,
They pursue strange creatures
Beyond the borders of heaven.

To bows like the famous Fan-jo
They fit their white-feathered arrows,
To shoot the fleeing goblin-birds
And strike down the griffins.
For their mark they choose the fattest game
And name their prey before they shoot.
No sooner has an arrow left the string
Than the quarry topples to the ground.
Again the signal is raised and they soar aloft,
Sweeping upward upon the gale,
Rising with the whirlwind,
Borne upon the void,
The companions of gods,
To trample upon the black crane
And scatter the flocks of giant pheasants,
Swoop down upon the peacocks
And the golden roc,
Drive aside the five-colored *yi* bird
And down the phoenixes,
Snatch the storks of heaven
And the birds of darkness,
Until, exhausting the paths of the sky,
They wheel their carriages and return.
Roaming as the spirit moves them,
Descending to earth in a far corner of the north,
Swift and straight is their course,
As they hasten home again.
Then the emperor ascends the Stone Gate
And visits the Great Tower,
Stops at the Magpie Turret
And gazes afar from the Dew Cold Observatory,
Descends to the Wild Plum Palace
And takes his ease in the Palace of Righteous Spring;
To the west he hastens to the Hsüan-ch'ü Palace
And poles in a pelican boat over Ox Head Lake.
He climbs the Dragon Terrace
And rests in the Tower of the Lithe Willows,
Weighing the effort and skill of his attendants
And calculating the catch made by his huntsmen.

He examines the beasts struck down by the carriages,
Those trampled beneath the feet of the horsemen
And trod upon by the beaters;
Those which, from sheer exhaustion
Or the pangs of overwhelming terror,
Fell dead without a single wound,
Where they lie, heaped in confusion,
Tumbled in the .gullies and filling the hollows,
Covering the plains and strewn about the swamps.
Then, wearied of the chase,
He orders wine brought forth on the Terrace of Azure Heaven
And music for the still and spacious halls.
His courtiers, sounding the massive bells
That swing from the giant bell rack,
Raising the pennants of kingfisher feathers,
And setting up the drum of sacred lizard skin,
Present for his pleasure the dances of Yao
And the songs of the ancient Emperor Ko;
A thousand voices intone,
Ten thousand join in harmony
As the mountains and hills rock with echoes
And the valley waters quiver to the sound.
The dances of Pa-yü, of Sung and Ts'ai,
The Yü-che song of Huai-nan,
The airs of Tien and Wen-ch'eng,
One after another in groups they perform,
Sounding in succession the gongs and drums
Whose shrill clash and dull booming
Pierce the heart and startle the ear.
The tunes Ching, Wu, Cheng, and Wei,
The Shao, Huo, Wu, and Hsiang music,
And amorous and carefree ditties
Mingle with the songs of Yen and Ying,
"Onward Ch'u!" and "The Gripping Wind."
Then come actors, musicians and trained dwarfs,
And singing girls from the land of Ti-ti,
To delight the ear and eye
And bring mirth to the mind;
On all sides a torrent of gorgeous sounds,

A pageant of enchanting color.
Here are maidens to match
The goddess Blue Lute and Princess Fu:
Creatures of matchless beauty,
Seductive and fair,
With painted faces and carved hairpins,
Fragile and full of grace,
Lithe and supple,
Of delicate feature and form,
Trailing cloaks of sheerest silk
And long robes that seem as though carved and painted,
Swirling and fluttering about them
Like magic garments;
With them wafts a cloud of scent,
A delicious perfume;
White teeth sparkle
In engaging smiles,
Eyebrows arch delicately,
Eyes cast darting glances,
Until their beauty has seized the soul of the beholder
And his heart in joy hastens to their side.

But then, when the wine has flowed freely and the merriment is at its height, the Son of Heaven becomes lost in contemplation, like one whose spirit has wandered, and he cries, "Alas! What is this but a wasteful extravagance? Now that I have found a moment of leisure from the affairs of state, I thought it a shame to cast away the days in idleness and so, in this autumn season, when Heaven itself slays life, I have joined in its slaughter and come to this hunting park to take my ease. And yet I fear that those who follow me in ages to come may grow infatuated with these sports, until they lose themselves in the pursuit of pleasure and forget to return again to their duties. Surely this is no way for one who has inherited the throne to carry on the great task of his forebears and insure the rule of our imperial house!"

Then he dismisses the revelers, sends away the huntsmen, and instructs his ministers, saying, "If there are lands here in these suburbs that can be opened for cultivation, let them all be turned into farms in order that my people may receive aid and benefit thereby. Tear down the walls and fill up the moats that the common folk may come and profit from these hills and lowlands! Stock the lakes with fish and do not prohibit men from taking them! Empty the palaces and towers, and let them no longer be staffed! Open the storehouses and granaries to succor the poor and starving and help those who are in want; pity the widower and widow, protect the orphans and those without families! I would broadcast the name of virtue and lessen punishments and fines; alter the measurements and statutes, change the color of the vestments, reform the calendar and, with all men under heaven, make a new beginning!"

TRANSLATED BY BURTON WATSON

Period of Division

220 - 589

On Seclusion:
Two Letters, a Dream, and a Satire

This section is prefaced by a letter from a Han official who in some ways anticipates the mood of the period of division. Burton Watson writes: "Yang Yün was the son of a prominent statesman and grandson of Ssu-ma Ch'ien. He rose to a position of importance at the court of Emperor Hsüan (74-48 B.C.), and because of the part he played in exposing the plot of the Ho family to dethrone the emperor he was enfeoffed as a marquis. In time, however, he was accused by a rival at court of various treasonable acts and utterances. The emperor forbore to impose the death sentence but stripped Yang of his position and title. Yang retired to the country, where he devoted himself to farming and speculating in grain. Some time later he received a letter from a friend, Sun Hui-tsung, reprimanding him for his way of life. A gentleman in disgrace, Sun wrote, should live in humble and abject seclusion instead of entertaining friends and engaging in that most disgraceful of human activities, the pursuit of material gain. The letter is Yang's reply."

Where Yang Yün celebrates the joys of private life, the poet Hsi K'ang (223-262) in his letter to Shan T'ao indulges a Taoist sense of fun by listing the afflictions to be endured by those who aspire to polite society. Both men, however, bear unmistakable witness to the ideal of seclusion.

"Peach Blossom Spring" rapidly became the classic expression, constantly quoted in later writing, of the longing for an earthly

157

utopia. Some of T'ao Ch'ien's poems would suggest that he succeeded in finding his way there in spirit.

That seclusion served sometimes as a cloak for the poseur is evident from the satirical "Proclamation" by K'ung Chih-kuei (447-501). In this essay the devices of parallel prose are used to great effect to pillory the pretensions of a would-be recluse, Chou Yung (d. 485), dignified by the writer as Chou Tzu, "Master Chou." This man built a retreat he called Grass Hut on the Bell Mountain named in the opening sentence of Kung's essay. He suffers at the writer's hands by comparison with various genuine immortals and sages whose names dot the piece, e.g. Wu Kuang who threw himself into the river rather than accept the throne when it was offered to him. Other names mentioned, e.g. Chang Ch'ang, Chao Kuanghan and the rest, are those of model local officials.

In explanation of the allusion to Mo Ti and Yang Chu, early philosophers: "Yang Chu wept on seeing a crossroad, because one could turn north or south; Mo Ti cried on seeing them dye plain silk, because it could become yellow or black."

Cranes were used by Taoist adepts for steeds in their flights through the air.

•

Yang Yün

Letter to Sun Hui-tsung

[Pao Sun Hui-tsung shu]

I am a man of paltry talent and unworthy actions, possessing neither refinement nor native ability. Yet I was fortunate enough, because of my father's achievements, to win a post in the palace guard, and later, happening upon a time of plotted disaffection, I gained the title of marquis. But I deserved neither of these, and so in the end I met with misfortune. Moved to pity by my stupidity, you have been good enough to write me a letter teaching me my shortcomings and how to correct them. Your heartfelt concern is truly generous. I am disturbed that, because you perhaps have not examined deeply enough into the circumstances of my case, you may be misled by the judgments of the common run of people, though I realize that if I speak out my unworthy thoughts too frankly I may appear to be contradicting you and attempting to gloss over my own errors. Nevertheless, if I were to remain silent, I fear I would be ignoring Confucius' injunction to let "each man speak his mind." Therefore I have ventured briefly to set forth my ideas in the hope that you will give them your consideration.

When my family was at the height of its power, ten of us rode about in the vermilion-wheeled carriages of high officials. I held a place in the ranks of ministers and was enfeoffed as a marquis. I had charge of the officials who waited upon the emperor and I took part in the handling of affairs of state. And yet at that time I was unable to contribute anything to the advancement and glorification of imperial rule, nor did I succeed in joining my efforts with those of my fellow officials in repairing defects and oversights in the government. For a long time I was guilty of stealing a post I did not deserve and enjoying a salary I had not earned, coveting my stipend, greedy for power, and quite unable to check

159

myself. Then I met with a sudden change of fortune and found myself faced with unbridled accusations. I was confined to the North Tower of the palace and my wife and children were thrown into prison. At that time I concluded that even the death penalty would be insufficient to atone for my guilt. Surely I never thought that I could keep head and body together and serve once more the grave mound of my father. And yet the mercy of our sage ruler knows no bounds!

The superior man practices the Way and delights in forgetting his cares. The mean man seeks to prolong his life and loves to forget his faults. Considering that my errors had been great and my actions far from what they should have been, I decided that it was best for me to end my days as a farmer. So I took my wife and family to the country where, pooling our strength, we plow, tend the mulberries, water the garden, and so produce enough to pay our taxes to the state. It never occurred to me, however, that such activities might arouse your censure.

One cannot put a stop to human emotions: even sages do not try. Therefore, although rulers or fathers command the greatest honor and affection, when they die the period of mourning for them must eventually come to an end. And it has already been three years since I incurred disgrace.

My family and I work hard in our fields, and when the summer and winter holidays come, we boil a sheep, roast a young lamb, bring out a measure of wine and rest from our labors. My own family came originally from Ch'in and so I can make music in the Ch'in style, while my wife is from Chao and consequently plays the lute very well. In addition we have several maidservants who sing. After I have had something to drink and my ears are beginning to burn, I gaze up at the sky and, thumping on a crock to keep time, I give a great *ya-a!* and sing this song:

> I sowed the southern hill
> But I could not keep back the weeds.
> I planted an acre of beans
> But they fell off the vine, leaving bare stems.
> Man's life should be spent in joy;
> Why wait in vain for wealth and honor?

At such times I flap my robes in delight, wave my sleeves up and down, stamp my feet and dance about. Indeed it is a wild and unconventional way to behave, and yet I cannot say that I see anything wrong in it.

I was lucky enough to have a little of my stipend left over, and with the amount I bought up grain cheap and sold it dear, making a ten per cent profit. This is a vile and merchantly thing to do, a sordid undertaking, and for me to engage in it personally places me among the lowest ranks of society and makes me the butt of censure. Though the weather is not cold, I tremble to think of the disgrace. Even you, who know me so well, appear to have followed along with the rest in reprimanding me. Under such circumstances, what business would I have trying to win a fair reputation?

The philosopher Tung Chung-shu has said, has he not: "To strive with all one's might for benevolence and righteousness, fearful always lest one fail to educate the people—this is the ambition of a statesman. To strive with all one's might for goods and profit, fearful always of poverty and want—this is the business of ordinary people." So, as Confucius said, "those who do not follow the same road cannot lay plans for each other." Why, then, do you come with the ideals of the statesman and use them to censure a person like *me*?

The old region of Wei west of the Yellow River, from which you come, prospered under the rule of Marquis Wen, and its people still retain something of the ways of the sages Tuan Kan-mu and T'ien Tzu-fang. All of them are men of the most lofty virtue, capable of clearly distinguishing right from wrong. Now, however, you have left your native land and are acting as governor of Ting-an. Ting-an is a mountainous region, the old home of the K'un-yi barbarians, and its sons are greedy and uncouth. How can you hope to change the customs and habits of such people?

I fully understand from your letter what your ambitions are. Now, when the Han is at the height of its glory, I hope you will pursue them with utmost diligence, and not spend too much time in talk.

TRANSLATED BY BURTON WATSON

Hsi K'ang

Letter to Shan T'ao

[*Yü Shan Chü-yüan chüeh chiao shu*]

Some time ago you spoke of me to your uncle, the Prefect of Ying-ch'uan, and I must say I found your estimate of me just. But I wondered how you could have come to so accurate an understanding without really knowing what my principles are. Last year when I came back from Hotung, Kung-sun Ch'ung and Lü An said you had proposed me as your successor in office. Nothing came of it, but your proposal made it obvious you really did not understand me at all.

You are versatile: you accept most things and are surprised at little. I, on the other hand, am by nature straightforward and narrow-minded: there are lots of things that I cannot put up with. It was only chance that made us friends. When recently I heard of your promotion in office, I was upset and unhappy, fearing that the cook would be shy of doing the carving by himself and would call in the Impersonator of the Dead to help, handing over a kitchen knife soiled with rancid fat. Hence I am writing to make clear what may and may not be done.

It used to be that when in my reading I came across people resolutely above the world, I rather doubted their existence, but now I am convinced that they really do exist after all. One can be so constituted that there are things one cannot endure; honest endorsement cannot be forced. So it is perhaps idle to talk about the familiar "man of understanding" who can put up with anything, who takes no exception to vulgarity around him but who still preserves his integrity within; who goes along with the vacillations of the times without ever feeling a twinge of regret. Lao Tzu and Chuang Chou are my masters: they held mean positions. I would hardly criticize *them*. And Confucius, out of his love for all, was ready to hold a coachman's whip; and Tzu-wen, with no desire for the job, was thrice prime minister: these were gentlemen whose minds were bent on saving the world. This is what is meant by "in success, he shares the benefits with all and does not vacillate; in obscurity, he is content and not depressed."

From this point of view, Yao and Shun's ruling the world, Hsü Yu's retirement to the hills, Tzu-fang's helping Han and Chieh-yü's singing as he walked all add up to the same thing. When you consider all these gentlemen, they can be said to have succeeded in doing what they wanted. Hence all the various modes of conduct of the gentleman take him to the same goal by different paths. He acts in accordance with his nature and rests where he finds his ease. Thus there are those who stick to the court and never emerge. and those who enter the wilderness and never come back.

Moreover, I am filled with admiration when I read the biographies of the recluses Shang Tzu-p'ing and T'ai Hsiao-wei and can imagine what sort of men they were. Add to that the fact that I lost my father when young, was spoiled by my mother and elder brother and never took up the study of the classics. I was already wayward and lazy by nature, so that my muscles became weak and my flesh flabby. I would commonly go half a month without washing my face, and until the itching became a considerable annoyance, I would not wash my hair. When I had to urinate, if I could stand it I would wait until my bladder cramped inside before I got up.

Further, I was long left to my own devices, and my disposition became arrogant and careless, my bluntness diametrically opposed to etiquette; laziness and rudeness reinforcing one another. But my friends were indulgent, and did not attack me for my faults.

Besides, my taste for independence was aggravated by my reading of Chuang Tzu and Lao Tzu; as a result any desire for fame or success grew daily weaker, and my commitment to freedom increasingly firmer. In this I am like the wild deer, which captured young and reared in captivity will be docile and obedient. But if it be caught when full-grown, it will stare wildly and butt against its bonds, dashing into boiling water or fire to escape. You may dress it up with a golden bridle and feed it delicacies, and it will but long the more for its native woods and yearn for rich pasture.

Juan Chi[1] is not one to talk about people's faults, and I have tried to model myself after him, but in vain. He is a man of finer

---

1. See his poems below, pp. 179-181.

character than most, one who never injured another. Only in drinking does he go to excess. But even so the proper and correct gentlemen with their restrictions hate him as a mortal enemy, and it is only thanks to the protection of Generalissimo Ssu-ma Chao that he survives. But I, without Juan Chi's superiority, have the faults of being rude and unrestrained, ignorant of people's characters and blind to opportunity, not careful like Shih Fen, but driven to carry things to their end. The longer I were involved in affairs the more clearly would these defects show. I might want to stay out of trouble, but would it be possible?

Furthermore, in society there are prescribed courtesies, and the court has its rules. When I consider the matter carefully, there are seven things I could never stand and two things which would never be condoned. I am fond of lying late abed, and the herald at my door would not leave me in peace: this is the first thing I could not stand. I like to walk, singing, with my lute in my arms, or go fowling or fishing in the woods. But surrounded by subordinates, I would be unable to move freely—this is the second thing I could not stand. When I kneel for a while I become as though paralyzed and unable to move. Being infested with lice, I am always scratching. To have to bow and kowtow to my superiors while dressed up in formal clothes—this is the third thing I could not stand. I have never been a facile calligrapher and do not like to write letters. Business matters would pile up on my table and fill my desk. To fail to answer would be bad manners and a violation of duty, but I would not long be able to force myself to do it. This is the fourth thing I could not stand. I do not like funerals and mourning, but these are things people consider important. Far from forgiving my offence, their resentment would reach the point where they would like to see me injured. Although in alarm I might make the effort, I still could not change my nature. If I were to bend my mind to the expectations of the crowd, it would be dissembling and dishonest, and even so I would not be sure to go unblamed—this is the fifth thing I could not stand. I do not care for the crowd and yet I would have to serve together with such people. Or on occasions when guests fill the table and their clamor deafens the ears, their noise and dirt contaminating the place, before my very eyes they would indulge in their double-dealings. This is the sixth thing I could not stand. My heart cannot bear trouble, and official life is full of it. One's mind is bound with a thousand cares, one's thoughts are involved with worldly affairs. This is the seventh thing I could not stand.

Further, I am always finding fault with T'ang and Wu Wang, or running down the Duke of Chou and Confucius. If I did not stop this in society, it is clear that the religion of the times would not put up with me. This is the first thing which would never be condoned. I am quite ruthless in my hatred of evil, and speak out without hesitation, whenever I have the occasion. This is the second thing which would never be condoned.

To try to control these nine weaknesses with a disposition as narrow and niggling as mine could only result in my falling ill, if indeed I were able to avoid trouble with the authorities. Would I be long in the world of men? Besides, I have studied in the esoteric lore of the Taoist masters, where a man's life can be indefinitely prolonged through eating herbs, and I firmly believe this to be so. To wander among the hills and streams, observing fish and birds, is what gives my heart great pleasure. Once I embarked on an official career, this is something I would have to give up forthwith. Why should I relinquish what gives me pleasure for something that fills me with dread?

What is esteemed in human relationships is the just estimate of another's inborn nature, and helping him to realize it. When you see a straight piece of wood, you do not want to make it into a wheel, nor do you try to make a rafter of a crooked piece, and this is because you would not want to pervert its heaven-given quality, but rather see that it finds its proper place. Now all the four classes of people have each their own occupation, in which each takes pleasure in fulfilling his own ambition. It is only the man of understanding who can comprehend all of them. In this you have only to seek within yourself to know that one may not, out of one's own preference for formal clothes, force the people of Yüeh to wear figured caps, or, because one has a taste for putrid meat, try to feed a phoenix a dead rat.

Of late I have been studying the techniques of prolonging one's life, casting out all ideas of fame and glory, eliminating tastes, and letting my mind wander in stillness: what is most worthwhile to me is Inaction. Even if there were not these nine concerns, I could still pay no attention to your wishes. But beyond this, my mind tends toward melancholy, increasingly so of late, and I am personally convinced that I would not be able to stand any occupation in which I took no pleasure. I really know myself in this respect. If worse comes to worst and there is no way out, then I shall simply die. But you have no grudge against me that you should cause me to lie lifeless in the gutter.

I am continually unhappy over the recent loss of the company of my mother and elder brother. My daughter is thirteen, my son eight years old—neither grown to maturity, and I am in ill health. This is another fact that pains me so much I cannot bear to speak further of it.

Today I only wish to stay on in this out-of-the-way lane and bring up my children and grandchildren, on occasion relaxing and reminiscing with old friends—a cup of unstrained wine, a song to the lute: this is the sum of my desires and ambitions.

If you keep on relentlessly nagging me, it can only be because you are anxious to get someone for the post who will be of use to the world. But you have always known what an irresponsible, bungling sort of person I am, not at all up on current affairs. I know myself that I am in all respects inferior to our modern men of ability. If you think me unlike ordinary men in that I alone do not find pleasure in fame and distinction, this is closest to my true feelings and deserves to be considered. If a man of great ability and endowments, able to turn his hand to anything, were able to be without ambition, he would be worth your respect. But one like me, frequently ill, who wants to stay out of office so as to take care of himself for the remaining years of his life—in me it is rather a deficiency. There is not much point in praising a eunuch for his chastity. If you insist on my joining you in the king's service, expecting that we will rise together and will be a joy and help to one another, one fine day you will find that the pressure has driven me quite mad. Only my bitterest enemy would go so far. The rustic who took such pleasure in the warm sun on his back, or the one who so esteemed the flavor of celery that they wanted to bring these things to the attention of the Most High: this showed them to be well-meaning, but it also showed their complete ignorance. I hope you will not do as they did. This being the way I feel about it, I have written to explain it to you and at the same time to say farewell.

TRANSLATED BY J. R. HIGHTOWER

T'ao Ch'ien
[T'ao hua yüan chi]
Peach Blossom Spring

During the reign-period T'ai yuan [326-97] of the Chin dynasty there lived in Wu-ling a certain fisherman. One day, as he followed the course of a stream, he became unconscious of the distance he had travelled. All at once he came upon a grove of blossoming peach trees which lined either bank for hundreds of paces. No tree of any other kind stood amongst them, but there were fragrant flowers, delicate and lovely to the eye, and the air was filled with drifting peachbloom.

The fisherman, marvelling, passed on to discover where the grove would end. It ended at a spring; and then there came a hill. In the side of the hill was a small opening which seemed to promise a gleam of light. The fisherman left his boat and entered the opening. It was almost too cramped at first to afford him passage; but when he had taken a few dozen steps he emerged into the open light of day. He faced a spread of level land. Imposing buildings stood among rich fields and pleasant ponds all set with mulberry and willow. Linking paths led everywhere, and the fowls and dogs of one farm could be heard from the next. People were coming and going and working in the fields. Both the men and the women dressed in exactly the same manner as people outside; white-haired elders and tufted children alike were cheerful and contented.

Some, noticing the fisherman, started in great surprise and asked him where he had come from. He told them his story. They then invited him to their home, where they set out wine and killed chickens for a feast. When news of his coming spread through the village everyone came in to question him. For their part they told how their forefathers, fleeing from the troubles of the age of Ch'in, had come with their wives and neighbours to this isolated place, never to leave it. From that time on they had been cut off from the outside world. They asked what age was this: they had never even heard of the Han, let alone its successors the Wei and the Chin. The fisherman answered each of their questions in full, and they sighed and wondered at what he had to tell. The rest all invited him to their homes in turn, and in each house food and wine were set before him. It was only after a stay of several days that he took his leave.

"Do not speak of us to the people outside," they said. But when he had regained his boat and was retracing his original route, he marked it at point after point; and on reaching the prefecture he sought audience of the prefect and told him of all these things. The prefect immediately despatched officers to go back with the fisherman. He hunted for the marks he had made, but grew confused and never found the way again.

The learned and virtuous hermit Liu Tzu-chi heard the story and went off elated to find the place. But he had no success, and died at length of a sickness. Since that time there have been no further "seekers of the ford."

TRANSLATED BY CYRIL BIRCH

K'ung Chih-kuei

Proclamation on North Mountain
[*Pei shan yi wen*]

The Spirit of Bell Mountain,
The Divinity of Grass Hut Cloister,
Hasten through the mist on the post road
To engrave this proclamation on the hillside:
     A man who
Incorruptible, holds himself aloof from the vulgar,
Untrammeled, avoids earthly concerns,
Vies in purity with the white snow,
Ascends straightaway to the blue clouds—
     We but know of such.
     Those who
Take their stand outside things,
Shine bright beyond the mist,
Regard a treasure of gold as dust and do not covet it,
Look on the offer of a throne as a slipper to be cast off,
Who are heard blowing a phoenix flute by the bank of the Lo,
Who are met singing a fagot song beside the Yen-lai—
     These really do exist.
     But who would expect to find those
Whose end belies their beginning,
Vacillating between black and yellow,
Making Mo Ti weep,
Moving Yang Chu to tears,
Retiring on impulse with hearts still contaminated
Starting out pure and later becoming sullied—
     What impostors they are!
     Alas!

Master Shang lives no more
Mister Chung is already gone
The mountain slope is deserted,
A thousand years unappreciated.
At the present time there is Chou Tzu
An outstanding man among the vulgar,
Cultured and a scholar
Philosopher and scribe.
      But he needs must
Imitate Yen Ho's retirement
Copy Nan-kuo's meditation,
Occupy the Grass Hut by imposture
Usurp a hermit's cap on North Mountain,
Seduce our pines and cassia trees
Cheat our clouds and valleys.
Although he assume the manner by the river side
His feelings are bound by love of rank.
      When first he came, he was going to
Outdo Ch'ao-fu
Surpass Hsü-yu
Despise the philosophers
Ignore the nobility.
His flaming ardor stretched to the sun
His frosty resolve surpassed the autumn.
He would sigh that the hermits were gone forever
Or deplore that recluses wandered no more.
He discoursed on the empty emptiness of the Buddhist sutras
He studied the murky mystery of Taoist texts.
A Wu Kuang could not compare with him
A Chüan-tzu was not fit to associate with him.
      But when
The belled messengers entered the valley
And the crane summons reached his hill,
His body leapt and his souls scattered
His resolve faltered and his spirit wavered.
      Then
Beside the mat his eyebrows jumped,
On the floor his sleeves danced.

He burned his castalian garments and tore his lotus clothes
He raised a wordly face and carried on in a vulgar manner.
Wind-driven clouds grieved as they carried their anger
Rock-rimmed springs sobbed as they trickled their disappointment.
Forests and crags appeared to lack something
Grass and trees seemed to have suffered loss.
      When he came to
Tie on his brass insignia
Fasten the black ribbon,
He was foremost of the leaders of provincial towns
He was first among the heads of a hundred villages.
He stretched his brave renown over the coastal precincts
He spread his fine repute through Chekiang,
His Taoist books discarded for good
His dharma mat long since buried.
The cries and groans from beatings invade his thoughts
A succession of warrants and accusations pack his mind.
The Lute Song is interrupted
The Wine Poem is unfinished.
He is constantly involved in examinations
And continually swamped by litigation.
He tries to cage Chang Ch'ang and Chao Kuang-han of past fame
And seeks to shelve Cho Mao and Lu Kung of the former records.
He hopes to succeed the worthies of the Three Capital Districts
He wants to spread his fame beyond the governors of the Nine
      Provinces.
      He has left our
High haze to reflect the light unwatched
Bright moon to rise in solitude
Dark pines to waste their shade
White clouds with no companion.
The gate by the brook is broken, no one comes back
The stone pathway is overgrown, vain to wait for him.
      And now
The ambient breeze invades his bedcurtains
The seeping mist exhales from the rafters.
The orchid curtains are empty, at night his crane is grieved
The mountain hermit is gone, mornings the apes are startled.

In the past we heard of one who cast away his cap-pin and retired
    to the seashore
Today we see one loosen his orchids and tie on a dirty cap instead.
    Whereupon
The Southern Peak presents us with its scorn
The Northern Range raises its laughter
All valleys strive in mockery
Every peak contends in contempt.
We regret that this vagrant has cheated us
We grieve that no one comes to condole.
    As a result
Our woods are ashamed without end
Our brooks humiliated with no reprieve.
Autumn cassia sends away the wind
Spring wisteria refuses the moon.
We spread the word of the retirement to West Mountain
We broadcast the report of the resolve to East Marsh.
    Now today
He is hurrying to pack in his lowly town
With drumming oars to go up to the capital.
Though he is wholly committed to the court
He still may invade our mountain fastness.
    How can we permit our
Azaleas to be insulted again
Pi-li to be shameless
Green cliffs again humiliated
Red slopes further sullied?
He would dirty with his vagrant steps our lotus paths
And soil the cleansing purity of the clear ponds.
    We must
Bar our mountain windows
Close our cloud-passes
Call back the light mist
Silence the noisy torrent
Cut off his approaching carriage at the valley mouth
Stop his impudent reins at the outskirts.
    Then
Massed twigs shall be filled with anger

Ranked buds shall have their souls enraged
Flying branches shall break his wheels
Drooping boughs shall sweep away his tracks.
Let us turn back the carriage of a worldly fellow
And decline on behalf of our lord a forsworn guest.

TRANSLATED BY J. R. HIGHTOWER

The Poetry of the Recluse

The preceding section hints at the prevalence of retreat from the world in the centuries of division and turmoil between the close of the Han dynasty (219) and the foundation first of the Suei in the year 589, then of the more enduring T'ang (618). The present selection of poems begins with a noble ode inspired by Taoist mystique which offered spiritual sustenance to all for whom the times were out of joint.

Juan Chi (210-263) and Pao Chao (414-466), though two centuries lie between their lifetimes, share the profound melancholy of the years of darkness, and a taste for the macabre, often startling image.

Between the two, comes T'ao Ch'ien (T'ao Yüan-ming, 365-427). After serving for a time in the bureaucracy of the Chin (Tsin) dynasty, T'ao Ch'ien at the age of thirty-three withdrew from official life never to return: an act commemorated in frequent allusion in subsequent literary works. The poetry in which he extols his rustic joys and reflects on the "shadow-play" of life has come to seem most characteristically Chinese to many Western readers.

The Buddhist monk Han-shan, our last recluse, probably lived in the late eighth and early ninth centuries. Gary Snyder identifies him as a man who has "made it," and translates him accordingly. Linguistic justification is added by the colloquial nature of Han-shan's style, which sets him apart from his age. As the translator says, Han-shan (Cold Mountain) is the name of a man, of a place and of a state of mind. If Chinese Buddhist literature as such must

174

be represented in this anthology by these poems alone, Zen will still be served.

All that is known of Han-shan is contained in the essay by Lü-ch'iu Yin with which the translator prefaces his selection.

•

Chang Heng

The Bones of Chuang Tzu [1]

[*K'u lou fu*]

I, Chang P'ing-tzu, had traversed the Nine Wilds and seen their
    wonders,
In the eight continents beheld the ways of Man,
The Sun's procession, and the orbit of the Stars,
The surging of the dragon, the soaring of the Phoenix in his flight.
In the red desert to the south I sweltered,
And northward waded through the wintry burghs of Yu.
Through the Valley of Darkness to the west I wandered,
And eastward travelled to the Sun's extreme abode,
The stooping Mulberry Tree.

So the seasons sped; weak autumn languished,
A small wind woke the cold.

And now with rearing of rein-horse,
Plunging of the tracer, round I fetched
My high-roofed chariot to westward.
Along the dykes we loitered, past many meadows,
And far away among the dunes and hills.
Suddenly I looked and by the road-side
I saw a man's bones lying in the squelchy earth,
Black rime-frost over him; and I in sorrow spoke
And asked him, saying, "Dead man, how was it?
Fled you with your friend from famine and for the last grains
Gambled and lost? Was this earth your tomb,
Or did floods carry you from afar? Were you mighty, were you wise,
Were you foolish and poor? A warrior or a girl?"

---

1. Compare Chuang Tzu on death, above, pp. 82-83.

Then came a wonder; for out of the silence a voice—
Thin echo only, in no substance was the spirit seen—
Mysteriously answered, saying, "I was a man of Sung,
Of the clan of Chuang; Chou was my name.
Beyond the climes of common thought
My reason soared, yet I could not save myself;
For at the last, when the long charter of my years was told,
I too, for all my magic, by Age was brought
To the Black Hill of Death.
Wherefore, O Master, do you question me?"
Then I answered:
"Let me plead for you upon the Five Hill-tops,
Let me pray for you to the Gods of Heaven and the Gods of Earth,
That your white bones may arise,
And your limbs be joined anew.
The God of the North shall give me back your ears;
I will scour the Southland for your eyes;
From the sunrise will I wrest your feet;
The West shall yield your heart.
I will set each several organ in its throne;
Each subtle sense will I restore.
Would you not have it so?"
The dead man answered me:
"O Friend, how strange and unacceptable your words!
In death I rest and am at peace; in life I toiled and strove.
Is the hardness of the winter stream
Better than the melting of spring?
All the pride that the body knew,
Was it not lighter than dust?
What Ch'ao and Hsü despised,
What Po-ch'eng fled,
Shall I desire, whom death
Already has hidden in the Eternal Way—
Where Li Chu cannot see me,
Nor Tzu Yeh hear me,
Where neither Yao nor Shun can praise me,
Nor wolf nor tiger harm me,
Lance prick me nor sword wound me?
Of the Primal Spirit is my substance; I am a wave

In the river of Darkness and Light.
The Maker of All Things is my Father and Mother,
Heaven is my bed and earth my cushion,
The thunder and lightning are my drum and fan,
The sun and moon my candle and my torch,
The Milky Way my moat, the stars my jewels.
With nature am I conjoined;
I have no passion, no desire.
Wash me and I shall be no whiter,
Foul me and I shall yet be clean.
I come not, yet am here;
Hasten not, yet am swift."
The voice stopped, there was silence.
A ghostly light
Faded and expired.
I gazed upon the dead, stared in sorrow and compassion.
Then I called upon my servant that was with me
To tie his silken scarf about those bones
And wrap them in a cloak of sombre dust;
While I, as offering to the soul of this dead man,
Poured my hot tears upon the margin of the road.

TRANSLATED BY ARTHUR WALEY

Juan Chi

From "Poems of my Heart"

[*Yung huai shih*]

1

Being sleepless at midnight,
I rise to play the lute.
The moon is visible through the curtains
And a gentle breeze sways the cords of my robe.
A lonely wild goose cries in the wilderness
And is echoed by a bird in the woods.
As it circles, it gazes
At me, alone, imbued with sadness.

2

In my youth,
I too was fond of singing and dancing.
I went west to the Capital
And frequented the Lis and the Chaos.
Before the fun came to an end,
I realized time had been wasted.
On my return journey,
I looked back at the riverside district
Where I had squandered a great deal,
So that not a coin was left.
Coming to the T'ai-hang mountain path,
I was afraid of again losing my way.

179

3

Inscribe on your heart
Every inch of the time at sunset.
Adjust your sleeves, unsheathe a slender sword,
And look up at the passing clouds.
Among them a dark stork
Raises its head and rattles its beak;
Darting aloft, it vanishes into the sky.
Never again will it be heard.
It is no company for the cuckoos and the crows
That circle round the Court.

4

Day and night
Revolve,
While my face wrinkles
And my spirit wanes,
But the sight of injustice still pains me.
One change induces another
That cannot be dealt with by tact or wit.
The cycle goes on for ever.
I only fear that in a moment
Life will disperse in the wind.
I have always trodden on thin ice.
Yet no one knows!

5

His influence—
        the scorching sun or a torrential river—
Extends a myriad miles.
His bow hangs in the tree
        on which the sun rests.

His sword leans
> against the place where the sky ends.
Mountains are his whetstones;
And the Yellow River just long enough to be his belt.
But in the eyes of a wise recluse,
Size is of the least importance.
For a giant corpse
Only feeds more vultures.
Perhaps it is only for this
That heroes and aspirants achieve fame and merit.

6

I will not learn to ride a winged horse,
Fearing it will leave me to weep at a lonely roadside.
I dive low or fly high
To avoid the trap of a net.
I float a light boat
And gaze into the boundless waves.
It is better to forget in a river or a lake
Than to wet one another with bubbles on stony dry land.
Seldom can I be arrayed to look elegant,
My way is to be sincere and prudent.
The ancient immortals
Will help me
To survive this long and fearful night.

TRANSLATED BY C. J. CHEN AND MICHAEL BULLOCK

T'ao Ch'ien

Two Poems on Returning to Dwell in the Country

[*Kuei yüan t'ien chu*]

1

In youth I had nothing
    that matched the vulgar tone,
For my nature always
    loved the hills and mountains.
Inadvertently I fell
    into the Dusty Net,
Once having gone
    it was more than thirteen years.
The tame bird
    longs for his old forest—
The fish in the house-pond
    thinks of his ancient pool.
I too will break the soil
    at the edge of the southern moor,
I will guard simplicity
    and return to my fields and garden.
My land and house—
    a little more than ten acres,
In the thatched cottage—
    only eight or nine rooms.
Elms and willows
    shade the back verandah,
Peach and plum trees
    in rows before the hall.
Hazy and dimly seen
    a village in the distance,

Close in the foreground
 the smoke of neighbours' houses.
A dog barks
 amidst the deep lanes,
A cock is crowing
 atop a mulberry tree.
No dust and confusion
 within my doors and courtyard;
In the empty rooms,
 more than sufficient leisure.
Too long I was held
 within the barred cage.
Now I am able
 to return again to Nature.

2

Long I have loved to stroll among the hills and marshes,
And take my pleasure roaming the woods and fields.
Now I hold hands with a train of nieces and nephews,
Parting the hazel growth we tread the untilled wastes—
Wandering to and fro amidst the hills and mounds
Everywhere around us we see dwellings of ancient men.
Here are vestiges of their wells and hearthstones,
There the rotted stumps of bamboo and mulberry groves.
I stop and ask a faggot-gatherer:
"These men—what has become of them?"
The faggot-gatherer turns to me and says:
"Once they were dead that was the end of them."
In the same world men lead different lives;
Some at the court, some in the marketplace.
Indeed I know these are no empty words:
The life of man is like a shadow-play
Which must in the end return to nothingness.

Written While Drunk

I built my house near where others dwell,
And yet there is no clamour of carriages and horses.
You ask of me "How can this be so?"
"When the heart is far the place of itself is distant."
I pluck chrysanthemums under the eastern hedge,
And gaze afar towards the southern mountains.
The mountain air is fine at evening of the day
And flying birds return together homewards.
Within these things there is a hint of Truth,
But when I start to tell it, I cannot find the words.

On Reading the Classic of the Hills and Seas

By the early summer
        grasses and trees have grown
And around my roof
        the spaced trees join branches.
The flocks of birds
        are glad to have their refuge,
I no less than they
        love my little house.
Ploughing is done
        and also I have sown—
The time has come
        to return and read my books.
The narrow lane—
        deep ruts on either side—
Rather deters
        the carriages of friends!
Contentedly I sit
        and pour the new spring wine,
Or go out to pluck
        vegetables in my garden.
A gentle shower
        approaches from the east

And a pleasant wind
        comes along with it.
I read at length
        the story of King Mu,
And let my gaze wander
        over pictures of hills and seas.
Thus with a glance I reach
        the ends of the Universe—
If this is not a pleasure
        where could I ever find one?

A Song of Poor Scholars[1]

The snow lay deep
        before Yüan An's door,
But he was "far away"
        and it did not concern him;
And when Duke Yüan
        saw the contributions
On that very day
        he resigned from office.
A bed of straw
        was always warm enough,
And fresh-gathered yams
        were good enough for breakfast.
What they suffered
        was the *real* pain,
Hunger and cold
        they did not feel at all.

---

1. Allusions: In the *Chin History* it is related that there was a great fall of snow in Loyang. The governor passed by Yüan An's door and seeing no footprints in the snow thought that he might have died. Going in he found Yüan An sitting at his ease. When he asked him why he was so unconcerned he replied: "When there is a blizzard like this everybody would be equally hard put to get enough to eat; how could I think of bothering anyone!"

Duke Yüan was noble but poor; when he was appointed to office some of his friends took up a collection for him, whereupon he resigned.

The *real* pain is the pain of realizing that the Way does not prevail in the world.

Poverty and wealth
    will always war within us,
But when the Tao prevails
    there are no anxious faces.
Utmost moral power
    will crown the village entrance
And purest chastity
    shine in the western gateway.

Written in Imitation of an Ancient Bearers' Song

There were often times
    when we had no wine to drink,
However, this morning
    we fill the empty beakers.
Over the new spring wine
    midges hover—
When will we ever
    taste its like again?
Tables with funeral meats
    stand piled high before us,
Old friends and relatives
    come and weep beside us.
We try to speak
    but cannot utter words,
We try to see
    but our eyes are dim.
Once he used to sleep
    within the lofty hall,
Now he will spend the night
    out on the lonely moor.
Leaving the city gate
    we accompanied him thither
But *we* were back again
    before midnight had come.

Putting the Blame on His Sons

White hair covers my temples—
My flesh is no longer firm,
And though I have five sons
Not one cares for brush and paper.
Ah-shu is sixteen years of age;
For laziness he surely has no equal.
Ah-hsüan tries his best to learn
But does not really love the arts.
Yung and Tuan at thirteen years
Can hardly distinguish six from seven;
T'ung-tzu with nine years behind him
Does nothing but hunt for pears and chestnuts.
If such was Heaven's decree
In spite of all that I could do,
Bring on, bring on
"the thing within the cup."

Written on the Ninth Day of the Ninth Month of the Year *yi-yu* (A.D. 409)

Slowly, slowly,
     the autumn draws to its close.
Cruelly cold
     the wind congeals the dew.
Vines and grasses
     will not be green again—
The trees in my garden
     are withering forlorn.
The pure air
     is cleansed of lingering lees
And mysteriously,
     Heaven's realms are high.
Nothing is left
     of the spent cicada's song,

A flock of geese
    goes crying down the sky.
The myriad transformations
    unravel one another
And human life
    how should it not be hard?
From ancient times
    there was none but had to die,
Remembering this
    scorches my very heart.
What is there I can do
    to assuage this mood?
Only enjoy myself
    drinking my unstrained wine.
I do not know
    about a thousand years,
Rather let me make
    this morning last forever.

TRANSLATED BY WILLIAM ACKER

Pao Chao

Three Poems from "Tedious Ways"

[*Hsing lu nan*]

1

Riding through the northern gate
Sorrow suddenly seizes me.
On looking around, I can only see
Pines and cypresses growing on desolate tombs.
In their blue gloom
A nightjar perches.
It is said to be the spirit of an ancient king.
Its dirge never ceases
And its dishevelled feathers
Bristle like the hair of a convict.
It flies from branch to branch
Searching for worms and ants.
Has it forgotten its majesty?
Many changes are not to be expected.
My heart, overladen with grief,
                    knows no answer.

2

Five peach trees grow in my garden.
One of them has begun to bloom.
It is now the charming third moon
And the wind blows the petals
                    to a neighbour's home

Where the lonely mistress weeps
With a hand on her bosom and her lapel wet.
When her husband left,
There was no thought of a long parting.
Yet now dust covers the couch
         and the mirror no longer reflects.
Her robes are growing loose, her hair untidy.
Can she be happy again?
         Can she stop pacing to and fro till midnight?

3

Do you not see the fallen leaves
         that rustle on the pavings and steps;
Will they become green again?
Do you not see the sacrificial food and wine
         that are laid out for the spirits
Who have never once raised the cups?
To you, this should be a loud warning
That life passes like lightning;
Youthful days never return;
And there cannot be time to compete against anyone.
Retain your noble aims;
Enjoy your food and friends.
For they alone can repel
Your worries and fear.
Yet you still look unhappy.
Do you not like my "Tedious Ways"?

The Ruined City

[*Wu ch'eng fu*]

The immense plain
         runs south to the foamy waves of the sea
         and north to the purple passes of the Great Wall.
In it
         canals are cut through the valleys;

and rivers and roads
lead to every corner.
In its golden past,
    axles of chariots and carts
    often rubbed against each other
    like men's shoulders.
Shops and houses stood row upon row
And laughter and songs rose up from them.
Glittering and white were the salt fields;
Gloomy and blue were the copper mines.
Wealth and talents
And cavalry and infantry
Reinforced the strict and elaborate
Regulations and laws.
Winding moats and lofty walls
Were dug and built, to ensure
That prosperity would long endure.
People were busy working
On palaces and battlements
And ships and beacon stations
Up and down, far and wide
At all places.
Magnets[1] were installed at mountain passes;
Red lacquer was applied on doors and gates.
The strongholds and fortresses
    would see to it
That for a myriad generations
    the family's rule should last.
But after five centuries or three dynasties
The land was divided like a melon,
Or shared like beans.

Duckweed flourishes in the wells
And brambles block the roads.
Skunks and snakes dwell on sacred altars
While muskdeer and squirrels quarrel on marble steps.
In rain and wind,

---

1. To attract enemy arrows.

Wood elves, mountain ghosts,
Wild rats and foxes
    Yawp and scream from dusk to dawn.
Hungry hawks clash their beaks
As cold owls frighten the chicks in their nests.
Tigers and leopards hide and wait
    for a draught of blood
    and a feast of flesh.
Fallen tree-trunks lie lifelessly across
Those once busy highways.
Aspens have long ceased to rustle
And grass dies yellow
In this harsh frosty air
Which grows into a cruelly cold wind.
A solitary reed shakes and twists,
And grains of sand, like startled birds,
    are looking for a safe place to settle.
Bushes and creepers, confused and tangled,
    seem to know no boundaries.
They pull down walls
And fill up moats.
And beyond a thousand miles
Only brown dust flies.
Deep in my thoughts, I sit down and listen
To this awesome silence.
Behind the painted doors and embroidered curtains
There used to be music and dancing.
Hunting or fishing parties were held
In the emerald forests or beside the marble pools.
The melodies from various states
And works of art and rare fish and horses
Are all now dead and buried.
The young girls from east and south
Smooth as silk, fragrant as orchids
White as jade with their lips red,
Now lie beneath the dreary stones and barren earth.
The greatest displeasure of the largest number
Is the law of nature.
For this ruined city,

I play the lute and sing:
"As the north wind hurries on,
    the battlements freeze.
They tower over the plain
    where there are neither roads nor field-paths.
For a thousand years and a myriad generations,
I shall watch you to the end in silence."

TRANSLATED BY C. J. CHEN AND MICHAEL BULLOCK

Han-shan

From "Cold Mountain" Poems

[*Han-shan shih*]

Preface to the Poems of Han-shan by Lü-ch'iu Yin,
Governor of T'ai prefecture:

No one knows just what sort of man Han-shan was. There are old people who knew him: they say he was a poor man, a crazy character. He lived alone seventy li west of the T'ang-hsing district of T'ien-t'ai at a place called Cold Mountain (Han-shan). He often went down to the Kuo-ch'ing Temple. At the temple lived Shih-te, who ran the dining hall. He sometimes saved leftovers for Han-shan, hiding them in a bamboo tube. Han-shan would come and carry it away, walking the long veranda, calling and shouting happily, talking and laughing to himself. Once the monks followed him, caught him, and made fun of him. He stopped, clapped his hands, and laughed greatly—Ha Ha!—for a spell, then left.

He looked like a tramp. His body and face were old and beat. Yet in every word he breathed was a meaning in line with the subtle principles of things, if only you thought of it deeply. Everything he said had a feeling of the Tao in it, profound and arcane secrets. His hat was made of birch bark, his clothes were ragged and worn out, and his shoes were wood. Thus men who have made it hide their tracks: unifying categories and interpenetrating things. On that long veranda calling and singing, in his words of reply—Ha Ha!—the three worlds revolve. Sometimes at the villages and farms he laughed and sang with the cowherds. Sometimes intractable, sometimes agreeable, his nature was happy of itself. But how could a person without wisdom recognize him?

I once received a position as a petty official at Tan-ch'iu. The day I was to depart, I had a bad headache. I called a doctor, but he couldn't cure me and it turned worse. Then I met a Buddhist Master named Feng-kan, who said he came from the Kuo-ch'ing Temple of T'ien-t'ai especially to visit me. I asked him to rescue me from my illness. He smiled and said, "The four realms are within the body; sickness comes from illusion. If you want to do away with it, you need pure water." Someone brought water to the Master, who spat it on me. In a moment the disease was rooted out. He then said, "There are miasmas in T'ai prefecture, when you get there take care of yourself." I asked him, "Are there any wise men in your area I could look on as Master?" He replied, "When you see him you don't recognize him, when you recognize him you don't see him. If you want to see him, you can't rely on appearances. Then you can see him. Han-shan is a Manjusri hiding at Kuo-ch'ing. Shih-te is a Samantabhadra. They look like poor fellows and act like madmen. Sometimes they go and sometimes they come. They work in the kitchen of the Kuo-ch'ing dining hall, tending the fire." When he was done talking, he left.

I proceeded on my journey to my job at Tan-ch'iu, not forgetting this affair. I arrived three days later, immediately went to a temple, and questioned an old monk. It seemed the Master had been truthful, so I gave orders to see if T'ang-hsing really contained a Han-shan and Shih-te. The District Magistrate reported to me: "In this district, seventy li west, is a mountain. People used to see a poor man heading from the cliffs to stay awhile at Kuo-ch'ing. At the temple dining hall is a similar man named Shih-te." I made a bow, and went to Kuo-ch'ing. I asked some people around the temple, "There used to be a Master named Feng-kan here. Where is his place? And where can Han-shan and Shih-te be seen?" A monk named Tao-ch'iao spoke up: "Feng-kan the Master lived in back of the library. Nowadays nobody lives there; a tiger often comes and roars. Han-shan and Shih-te are in the kitchen." The monk led me to Feng-kan's yard. Then he opened the gate: all we saw were tiger tracks. I asked the monks Tao-ch'iao and Pao-te, "When Feng-kan was here, what was his job?" The monks said, "He pounded and hulled rice. At night he sang songs to amuse himself." Then we went to the kitchen, before the stoves. Two men were facing the fire, laughing loudly. I made a bow. The two shouted HO! at me. They struck their hands together—Ha Ha!— great laughter. They shouted. Then they said, "Feng-kan—loose-tongued, loose-tongued. You don't recognize Amitabha, why be courteous to us?" The monks gathered round, surprise going through them. "Why has a big official bowed to a pair of clowns?" The two men grabbed hands and ran out of the temple. I cried, "Catch them" —but they quickly ran away. Han-shan returned to Cold Mountain. I asked the monks, "Would those two men be willing to settle down at this temple?" I ordered them to find a house, and to ask Han-shan and Shih-te to return and live at the temple.

I returned to my district and had two sets of clean clothes made, got some incense and such, and sent it to the temple—but the two men didn't return. So I had it carried up to Cold Mountain. The packer saw Han-shan, who called in a loud voice, "Thief! Thief!" and retreated into a mountain cave. He shouted, "I tell you, man, strive hard!"—entered the cave and was gone. The cave closed of itself and they weren't able to follow. Shih-te's tracks disappeared completely.

I ordered Tao-ch'iao and the other monks to find out how they had lived, to hunt up the poems written on bamboo, wood, stones and cliffs—and also to collect those written on the walls of people's houses. There were more than three hundred. On the wall of the Earth-shrine Shih-te had written some short poems, *gatha*. It was all brought together and made into a book.

I hold to the principle of the Buddha-mind. It is fortunate to meet with men of Tao, so I have made this eulogy.

1

The path to Han-shan's place is laughable,
A path, but no sign of cart or horse.
Converging gorges—hard to trace their twists
Jumbled cliffs—unbelievably rugged.
A thousand grasses bend with dew,
A hill of pines hums in the wind.
And now I've lost the shortcut home,
Body asking shadow, how do you keep up?

2

In a tangle of cliffs I chose a place—
Bird-paths, but no trails for men.

What's beyond the yard?
White clouds clinging to vague rocks.
Now I've lived here—how many years—
Again and again, spring and winter pass.
Go tell families with silverware and cars
"What's the use of all that noise and money?"

3

In the mountains it's cold.
Always been cold, not just this year.
Jagged scarps forever snowed in
Woods in the dark ravines spitting mist.
Grass is still sprouting at the end of June,
Leaves begin to fall in early August.
And here am I, high on mountains,
Peering and peering, but I can't even see the sky.

4

I spur my horse through the wrecked town,
The wrecked town sinks my spirit.
High, low, old parapet-walls
Big, small, the aging tombs.
I waggle my shadow, all alone;
Not even the crack of a shrinking coffin is heard.
I pity all these ordinary bones,
In the books of the Immortals they are nameless.

5

I wanted a good place to settle:
Cold Mountain would be safe.
Light wind in a hidden pine—
Listen close—the sound gets better.
Under it a gray-haired man
Mumbles along reading Huang and Lao.[1]

---

1. Huang: the *Book of the Yellow Emperor;* Lao: Lao Tzu, the *Tao te ching.*

For ten years I haven't gone back home
I've even forgotten the way by which I came.

6

Men ask the way to Cold Mountain
Cold Mountain: there's no through trail.
In summer, ice doesn't melt
The rising sun blurs in swirling fog.
How did I make it?
My heart's not the same as yours.
If your heart was like mine
You'd get it and be right here.

7

I settled at Cold Mountain long ago,
Already it seems like years and years.
Freely drifting, I prowl the woods and streams
And linger watching things themselves.
Men don't get this far into the mountains,
White clouds gather and billow.
Thin grass does for a mattress,
The blue sky makes a good quilt.
Happy with a stone underhead
Let heaven and earth go about their changes.

8

Clambering up the Cold Mountain path,
The Cold Mountain trail goes on and on:
The long gorge choked with scree and boulders,
The wide creek, the mist-blurred grass.
The moss is slippery, though there's been no rain
The pine sings, but there's no wind.
Who can leap the world's ties
And sit with me among the white clouds?

9

Rough and dark—the Cold Mountain trail,

Sharp cobbles—the icy creek bank.
Yammering, chirping—always birds
Bleak, alone, not even a lone hiker.
Whip, whip—the wind slaps my face
Whirled and tumbled—snow piles on my back.
Morning after morning I don't see the sun
Year after year, not a sign of spring.

10

I have lived at Cold Mountain
These thirty long years.
Yesterday I called on friends and family:
More than half had gone to the Yellow Springs.
Slowly consumed, like fire down a candle;
Forever flowing, like a passing river.
Now, morning, I face my lone shadow:
Suddenly my eyes are bleared with tears.

11

Spring-water in the green creek is clear
Moonlight on Cold Mountain is white
Silent knowledge—the spirit is enlightened of itself
Contemplate the void: this world exceeds stillness.

12

In my first thirty years of life
I roamed hundreds and thousands of miles.
Walked by rivers through deep green grass
Entered cities of boiling red dust.
Tried drugs, but couldn't make Immortal;
Read books and wrote poems on history.
Today I'm back at Cold Mountain:
I'll sleep by the creek and purify my ears.

13

I can't stand these bird-songs
Now I'll go rest in my straw shack.

The cherry flowers out scarlet
The willow shoots up feathery.
Morning sun drives over blue peaks
Bright clouds wash green ponds.
Who knows that I'm out of the dusty world
Climbing the southern slope of Cold Mountain?

14

Cold Mountain has many hidden wonders,
People who climb here are always getting scared.
When the moon shines, water sparkles clear
When wind blows, grass swishes and rattles.
On the bare plum, flowers of snow
On the dead stump, leaves of mist.
At the touch of rain it all turns fresh and live
At the wrong season you can't ford the creeks.

15

There's a naked bug at Cold Mountain
With a white body and a black head.
His hand holds two book-scrolls,
One the Way and one its Power.[2]
His shack's got no pots or oven,
He goes for a walk with his shirt and pants askew.
But he always carries the sword of wisdom:
He means to cut down senseless craving.

16

Cold Mountain is a house
Without beams or walls.
The six doors left and right are open
The hall is blue sky.
The rooms all vacant and vague
The east wall beats on the west wall
At the center nothing.

---

2. *The Way and Its Power*, i.e. the *Tao te ching*.

Borrowers don't bother me
In the cold I build a little fire
When I'm hungry I boil up some greens.
I've got no use for the kulak
With his big barn and pasture—
He just sets up a prison for himself.
Once in he can't get out.
Think it over—
You know it might happen to you.

17

If I hide out at Cold Mountain
Living off mountain plants and berries—
All my lifetime, why worry?
One follows his karma through.
Days and months slip by like water,
Time is like sparks knocked off flint.
Go ahead and let the world change—
I'm happy to sit among these cliffs.

18

Most T'ien-t'ai men
Don't know Han-shan
Don't know his real thought
& call it silly talk.

19

Once at Cold Mountain, troubles cease—
No more tangled, hung-up mind.
I idly scribble poems on the rock-cliff,
Taking whatever comes, like a drifting boat.

20

Some critic tried to put me down—
"Your poems lack the Basic Truth of Tao"
And I recall the old-timers
Who were poor and didn't care.

I have to laugh at him,
He misses the point entirely,
Men like that
Ought to stick to making money.

21

I've lived at Cold Mountain—how many autumns.
Alone, I hum a song—utterly without regret.
Hungry. I eat one grain of Immortal-medicine
Mind solid and sharp; leaning on a stone.

22

On top of Cold Mountain the lone round moon
Lights the whole clear cloudless sky.
Honor this priceless natural treasure
Concealed in five shadows, sunk deep in the flesh.

23

My home was at Cold Mountain from the start,
Rambling among the hills, far from trouble.
Gone, and a million things leave no trace
Loosed, and it flows through the galaxies
A fountain of light, into the very mind—
Not a thing, and yet it appears before me:
Now I know the pearl of the Buddha-nature
Know its use: a boundless perfect sphere.

24

When men see Han-shan
They all say he's crazy
And not much to look at—
Dressed in rags and hides.
They don't get what I say
& I don't talk their language.
All I can say to those I meet:
"Try and make it to Cold Mountain."

TRANSLATED BY GARY SNYDER

On Literature

Examples of rhyme-prose gathered in an earlier section gave evidence of the tendency of the genre towards exuberant word-play. We come now to a most remarkable work in which the authentic élan of this exacting form is controlled and sustained throughout a long, intense meditation.

The object of study is literature itself: literature as a vocation, as a craft and as a means to truth. Lu Chi (261-303) wrote the essay three years before he was executed, victim of a cutthroat struggle for power at the Chin court. With both eloquence and precision he images forth the nature of man's commitment to art, the joys and the fret of literary practice, the response to inspiration.

But the essay enters also into specific criticism, as when the fifth section defines the desired characteristics of the ten branches of fine writing. Although no "monumental inscription," "mnemonic" or "epigram" is included in the present anthology, examples of all Lu's remaining classifications will readily be found.

•

Lu Chi

Essay on Literature

[*Wen fu*]

Often have I studied the works of talented men of letters and thought to myself that I obtained some insight into their minds at work. The ways of employing words and forming expressions are indeed infinitely varied. But, accordingly, the various degrees of beauty and excellence achieved needs must bear criticism. When I compose my own works, I am more keenly aware of the ordeal. Constantly present is the feeling of regret that the meaning apprehended does not represent the objects observed; and, furthermore, words fail to convey the meaning. The fact is, it is not so hard to know as it is to do.

I am therefore writing this essay on literature to tell of the glorious accomplishments of ancient men of letters, and to comment on the causes of failure and success in writing. Perhaps some other day the secret of this most intricate art may be entirely mastered. In making an axe handle by cutting wood with an axe, the model is indeed near at hand. But the adaptability of the hand to the ever-changing circumstances and impulses in the process of creation is such that words can hardly explain. Henceforth follows only what can be said in words.

1. THE MOTIVE

Erect in the Central Realm the poet views the expanse of the whole universe,
And in tomes of ancient wisdom his spirit rejoices and finds nurture.

His lament for fleeting life is in observance of the four seasons that
    ever revolve,
His regard for the myriad growing things inspires in him thoughts
    as profuse.
As with the fallen leaves in autumn's rigour his heart sinks in grief,
So is each tender twig in sweet spring a source of joy.
In frost he finds sympathy at moments when his heart is all frigid
    purity,
Or far, far, into the highest clouds he makes his mind's abode.
The shining, magnanimous deeds of the world's most virtuous are
    substance of his song,
As also the pure fragrance which the most accomplished goodness
    of the past yields.
The flowering forest of letters and treasuries of poetic gems are his
    spirit's favourite haunts,
Where he delights in nothing less than perfection of Beauty's form
    and matter.
Thus moved, he will spread his paper and poise his brush
To express what he can in writing.

2. MEDITATION BEFORE WRITING

                                     In the beginning,
All external vision and sound are suspended,
Perpetual thought itself gropes in time and space;
Then, the spirit at full gallop reaches the eight limits of the cosmos,
And the mind, self-buoyant, will ever soar to new insurmountable
    heights.
                             When the search succeeds,
Feeling, at first but a glimmer, will gradually gather into full
    luminosity,
When all objects thus lit up glow as if each the other's light
    reflects.
Drip-drops are distilled afresh from a sea of words since time out
    of mind,
As quintessence that savours of all the aroma of the Six Arts.
Now one feels blithe as a swimmer calmly borne by celestial waters,
And then, as a diver into a secret world, lost in subterranean currents.
                                              Hence,

Arduously sought expressions, hitherto evasive, hidden,
Will be like stray fishes out of the ocean bottom to emerge on the
    angler's hook;
And quick-winged metaphors, fleeting, far-fetched
Feathered tribes, while sky-faring are brought down from the curl-
    clouds by the fowler's bow.
Thus the poet will have mustered what for a hundred generations
    awaited his brush,
To be uttered in rimes for a thousand ages unheard.
Let the full-blown garden flowers of the ancients in their own
    morning glory stand;
To breathe life into late blossoms that have yet to bud will be his
    sole endeavor.
Eternity he sees in a twinkling,
And the whole world he views in one glance.

3. THE WORKING PROCESS

Henceforth,
To obtain choice ideas in close observation of things in categories,
And elect expressions that will fall in happy order,
All objects visible under the sun or moon will the poet in experi-
    ment strike aglow,
All that can give out a sound he will ring to test their resonance.
He makes barren twigs put forth luxuriant foliage as they sway,
Or by endless waves he traces to the remote fountainhead.
He may either work from the obscure to the obvious,
Or, following an easy course, find the hardly obtainable.
Shapes of tame animals by the sudden shining forth of a tiger are
    illuminated,
Or amid the surf-tossed gulls the vision of a dragon emerges.
Sometimes with sure touches and smooth rhythm his ideas in utmost
    ease flow on,
At other moments, as if beset by mountainous obstacles, he is in a
    fret.
But not until the heart attains calm transparency does thought
    crystallize
Into such words as no man before fancied or pronounced.

Then, both heaven and earth find new embodiment in the shape
  desired,
And all things become plastic under the tip of his brush,
Which after all parching anxiety and hesitations
Is saturated and sweeps forth in a wave.

When the substance of a composition, trunk of a tree, is by Truth
  sustained,
Style aids it to branch into leafy boughs and bear fruit.
Indeed, feeling and expression should never fail to correspond,
As each emotional change wears a new complexion on a sensitive
  face.
Thought that swells with joy bursts into laughter;
When grief is spoken, words reverberate with endless sighs;
No matter if the work be accomplished in one flash on the page,
Or is the result of the most deliberate brush.

4. THE JOY OF WRITING

Writing is in itself a joy,
Yet saints and sages have long since held it in awe.
For it is Being, created by tasking the Great Void,
And 'tis sound rung out of Profound Silence.
In a sheet of paper is contained the Infinite,
And, evolved from an inch-sized heart, an endless panorama.
The words, as they expand, become all-evocative,
The thought, still further pursued, will run the deeper,
Till flowers in full blossom exhale all-pervading fragrance,
And tender boughs, their saps running, grow to a whole jungle of
  splendor.
Bright winds spread luminous wings, quick breezes soar from the
  earth,
And, nimbus-like amidst all these, rises the glory of the literary
  world.

5. ON FORM

The forms of things differ in a myriad ways,
For them there is no common measure.

Jumbled and jostled in a ceaseless flux,

Living shapes to all their imitations bid defiance.

Words, each with inherent limitations, do only partial service,

It is the all-harmonizing force of Meaning that integrates and bodies
     forth features supreme.

How the poet's mind toils between Substance and the Void,

And every detail in high and low relief he seeks to perfect,

That the form, although it may transcend the dictates of compasses
     and ruler,

Shall be the paragon of resemblance to all shapes and features
     imitated.

To ravish the eye, rich ornaments may be prized,

But such precision must be wrought that it appeals to the heart as
     true.

Words may in time be exhausted, but not so that their sense is
     immured withal;

A far-reaching thought attains its object only in the realm of the
     infinite.

                                                    (To be specific),

The lyric (*shih*), born of pure emotion, is gossamer fibre woven into
     the finest fabric;

The exhibitory essay (*fu*), being true to the objects, is vividness
     incarnate;

In monumental inscriptions (*pei*) rhetoric must be a foil to facts;

The elegy (*lei*) tenderly spins out ceaseless heartfelt grief.

The mnemonic (*ming*) is a smooth flow of genial phrases, succinct
     but pregnant;

The staccato cadences of the epigram (*chen*) are all transparent
     force.

While the eulogy (*sung*) enjoys the full abandon of grand style,

The expository (*lun*) must in exactitude and clarity excel.

The memorial (*tsou*), balanced and lucid, must be worthy of the
     dignity of its royal audience,

The argument (*shuo*) with glowing words and cunning parables
     persuades.

Meticulous as these classifications are,

Lest passion and thought, given free rein, may wantonly go astray,

The maxim: Let Truth in terms most felicitous be spoken,
While of verbiage beware.

6. THE MAKING OF A COMPOSITION

A composition comes into being as the incarnation of many living
    gestures.
It is (like the act of Tao) the embodiment of endless change.
To attain Meaning, it depends on a grasp of the subtle,
While such words are employed as best serve beauty's sake.
The interactions of sounds and tones are like
The five colours that each the others enhances:
Although they dwell and vanish by no common rule,
And their tortuous, intricate ways permit no liberty,
Yet if a poet masters the secret of change and order,
He will channel them like directing streams to receive a fountain;
But once a false move leads to reckless floundering,
The end and the beginning are thrown into confusion,
Celestial blue and earthy yellow confounded,
Dull mud and dregs to chaos return, all light fails.

                                        A composition is ruined
When a later passage swells to engulf its forerunners,
Or a downright statement encroaches on all that follows.
Apposite truth in words too ill expressed,
And pleasing phrases which utter senseless cant,
To redeem virtues of both, must be set apart
From the harmful company they keep.
For literary merits high and low are by grains and scruples measured,
The elect and the forsaken are separated no wider than a hair's
    breadth.
After the choice is made on the most accurate balance,
The Master Carpenter's tape it must also fit.
Lavish expressions may contain abundant truth,
But fail to direct and drive the Meaning home.
For the highest perfection to be attained will exclude duality,
And consummation admits of no surfeit.
A pithy saying at a crucial point
May whip all parts into a whole.
Though all the words are in nice order arrayed,

Such a "rallying whip" is needed to make them serve.
The utmost is achieved at slightest cost,
When the kernel, unequivocal, suffices.
Sometimes inspired thoughts weave themselves into the finest
    fabrics,
And grow ever fresher and more comely as they expand,
Glistening with colours of the most exquisite embroidery,
And tuned to the poignant music of a thousand strings.
But the accomplished piece of imitation must be so perfected
That it is in the ancient tradition, yet remains a nonpareil.
Even though all the warp and woof are of my own heart's tissue,
In constant fear must I be lest others before me have spun the
    same.
When honor and integrity are menaced,
Even gems most cherished must I sacrifice.

Or a thought may, like a lone plant, burst and burgeon with a life
    all its own,
So individual that on this earth it seems to have no species,
Until it becomes mirage-like, forever a fugitive from form,
Or a phantom voice that no sound audible can echo,
A being isolated from all contexts, a singular eminence,
That no common words or vocables can express.
The heart then feels like a forlorn lover, doomed to desolation,
Yet haunted by a Meaning evasive, intangible, but never to be
    shaken off.
Let it, then, be contained like jade in rocks, that a mountain loom
    in radiance,
Or cast it like a pearl in water that a whole river gleam with
    splendour.
For even shrubberies, when allowed to flourish,
Will by their opulent verdure claim a share of beauty.
In humble tunes that may mingle with the most exalted strains,
I find resources, too, for any grandeur they may augment.

7. FIVE SHORTCOMINGS

A verse limps and falls short
When it is a single train of thought by too indigent vision hampered.
'Tis then like one in bereavement around whom the world is mute,

The heaven above, out of reach, empty and vast:
A weak string plucked alone,
Without resonance, its sound into thin air vanishes.

Or a composition is so marred by languid tones
That its words may flash but never rise to glory.
Fair is confounded with foul,
And qualities are drowned in blemishes:
'Tis as if pipers down the hall pipe hurried notes at random,
Resonant but out of tune, that only throw the hymn into discord.

Or, to attain the unique at truth's expense,
The poet is so bent on a search for the illusory and the minuscular
That his words, lacking true emotion and void of love,
Will waft and drift, homeless, nowhere to return:
'Tis like a zither, too high-strung and hard pressed by rapid fingers;
Although the melody is played in tune, it fails to move with pathos.

Or, a work may swing itself into such a symphony
That it rings and clangs with many bewitching colours.
It may thus please the eye and win popular acclaim,
While its lowly tunes are exalted by loud performance.
Beware of resemblance to the "Dew Shelter" and "Mulberry Grove,"[1]
Which, though full of pathos, are an offense to grace.

Or, aerial purity and simple elegance are so cultivated
That the work is rid of all trimmings and ornaments,
A rarefied feast without relish of seasoned gravy.
A concert of wrought-silk strings that twang with too pure a tone,
Although it trills on with endless reverberations,
For all its grace, is innocent of glamour.

8. THE SECRET OF ARTISTRY

Luxuriance and terseness of style,
And the different aspects of form,
Vary according to laws of propriety,
Whose intricacies hinge upon a feeling so subtle:

---

1. Allusions to ancient folk tunes typified as very lowly.

Once grasped, uncouth language may divulge clever parables,
A truism by light verbal touches is turned into epigram,
The older the model, the fresher the imitation,
The duller the beginning, the more brilliant the final illumination.
Whether this superb artistry becomes apparent at first sight
Or is comprehended only after arduous toils of wit,
It is like the dancer's, whose each whirl of the sleeve is borne by a
    rhythm,
Or the singer's, whose each note responds to the twang of the
    string,
Guided by a force which even the Master Wheelwright Pien could
    not express in words;
Therefore its secret lies beyond smoothest speech.

9. THE SOURCE OF LITERATURE AND DISCIPLINE

To the all-pervasive law of word order and literary discipline
I have devoutly dedicated myself.
In its light I have seen much of the ills in vogue today
And perceived the merits of masters of the past,
Although an art truly wrought from the depths of a master mind
Is oft by untrained eyes with ridicule regarded.

Coral gems and jade filigree, however, are in their origins none
    too rare,
But common as wild beans of the Central Plain that all can gather:
Thus the source of poetry is like the air from the Bellows, the
    eternally generative Void,
And it will forever breed with Heaven and Earth.

But be it soever bounteous and ubiquitous in this world,
Alas, how much of it can my fingers mould?
Dismayed as the holder of a vessel that is too often empty,
I feel harassed by the thought that Great Eloquence is hard to
    achieve.
Hence limping verses, born dwarfed, are let live,
And perfunctory notes are fiddled to round out a vapid tune.
Often have I finished my work with pangs of remorse;
When has my heart rejoiced with self-content?

Always fearful am I lest mine were the earthenware, dust-muffled
    and jarring,
A coarse mockery of tinkling jade.

10. OF INSPIRATION

Such moments when Mind and Matter hold perfect communion,
And wide vistas open to regions hitherto entirely barred,
Will come with irresistible force,
And go, their departure none can hinder.
Hiding, they vanish like a flash of light;
Manifest, they are like sounds arising in mid-air.

So acute is the mind in such instants of divine comprehension,
What chaos is there that it cannot marshal in miraculous order?
While wingèd thoughts, like quick breezes, soar from depths of the
    heart,
Eloquent words, like a gushing spring, flow between lips and teeth.
No flower, or plant, or animal is too prodigal of splendour
To be recreated under the writer's brush,
Hence the most wondrous spectacle that ever whelmed the eye,
And notes of the loftiest music that rejoiced the ear.

But there are other moments as though the Six Senses were stranded,
When the heart seems lost, and the spirit stagnant.
One stays motionless like a petrified log,
Dried up like an exhausted river bed.
The Soul is indrawn to search the hidden labyrinth;
Within oneself is sought where inner light may be stored.
Behind a trembling veil Truth seems to shimmer, yet ever more
    evasive,
And thought twists and twirls like silk spun on a clogged wheel.
Therefore, all one's vital force may be dispersed in rueful failure;
Yet again, a free play of impulses may achieve a feat without pitfall.
While the Secret may be held within oneself,
It is none the less beyond one's power to sway.
Oft I lay my hand on my empty chest,
Despairing to know how the barrier could be removed.

11. THE USE OF LITERATURE

The use of literature
Lies in its conveyance of every truth.
It expands the horizon to make space infinite,
And serves as a bridge that spans a myriad years.
It maps all roads and paths for posterity,
And mirrors the images of worthy ancients,
That the tottering Edifices of the sage kings of antiquity may be
    reared again,
And their admonishing voices, wind-borne since of yore, may resume
    full expression.
No regions are too remote but it pervades,
No truth too subtle to be woven into its vast web.
Like mist and rain, it permeates and nourishes,
And manifests all the powers of transformation in which gods and
    spirits share.
Virtue it makes endure and radiate on brass and stone,
And resound in an eternal stream of melodies ever renewed on
    pipes and strings.

TRANSLATED BY SHIH-HSIANG CHEN

T'ang Dynasty

618 - 907

Poets of a Generation: One

Wang Wei (699-759) *and Li Po* (699-762), *two of the best-loved poets in all the long course of Chinese literature, were born in the same year; Tu Fu* (712-770), *whose name stands supreme, was their junior by thirteen years. The age of the T'ang emperor Hsüan-tsung (Ming-huang, the Illustrious) was the golden age of the shih, the common vessel of Chinese poetry which was shaped by these hands into an erudite and exquisite perfection.*

Wang Wei is represented in this brief selection chiefly by an exchange of poems which he conducted with his friend P'ei Ti. If more of Wang's paintings had survived, they would have won fame to rival that of his verse. In painting and poetry alike he made more than a record or interpretation of nature: he achieved perhaps the closest union with the natural world that has ever been expressed. This sense of harmony, or even of dissolution of the self in nature emerges already from the short letter to his friend which here prefaces their exchange.

From the unearthly beauty of "On the Mountain" we descend, as sooner or later we must with Li Po, to the haze of an elegant drinking-bout. But it is a haze shot through with the gleams of a philosophy now epicurean, now Taoist in characteristic admixture. Something of the sophistication of the world from which wine opened a refuge is to be glimpsed in Li Po's precious begging-letter to a potential patron.

The translator of Tu Fu's "Autumn Meditation" sequence provides the following introductory note:

"Tu Fu wrote this sequence in 766 at K'uei-chou, a town adjoin-

ing and apparently no longer distinguished from Pai Ti (White Emperor City) on the Yangtze River, among mountains a little upstream from the gibbon-haunted Ch'ü-t'ang and Wu gorges, during his second autumn of exile in this region. (The dewy chrysanthemums have 'opened twice, in tears of other days.') The eight poems, although not necessarily written at one time, show a definite continuity. The first three give impressions of K'uei-chou during twentyfour hours, from morning to morning. In these Tu Fu is already thinking of the capital Ch'ang-an far to the north; he imagines it beyond the Dipper in the night sky, and in bed thinks of night duty at the Executive Division (Shang-shu sheng), among maids burning incense and murals of ancient heroes. In the third poem the returning fishing boats and the swallows not yet driven south by the cold remind him of his isolation, of the political failures which have led to it, and of his more successful friends, whom he imagines at Wuling (place of five imperial mausolea) north of Ch'ang-an. The meditation now settles finally on Ch'ang-an, since 755 a 'chessboard' not only in appearance, with its grid of vertical and horizontal streets, but as the scene of a game won and lost in turn by loyalists, rebels and Tibetan invaders. The last four poems recall scenes from the time of Ch'ang-an's greatness and of Tu Fu's own brief glory in the office of 'Reminder' at court (757-58)."

The section ends with two of Tu Fu's passionate and outspoken protests against the frontier wars which in his lifetime seemed to yield place only to bloody rebellion. Tu Fu's poetry is often so encrusted with jewels of compressed esoteric allusion as to be wellnigh untranslateable: his war-poems, in contrast, are simple, direct and immediate of impact.

●

Wang Wei

Letter to the Bachelor of Arts P'ei Ti

[Shan chung yü P'ei hsiu ts'ai Ti shu]

Of late during the sacrificial month, the weather has been calm and clear, and I might easily have crossed the mountain. But I knew that you were conning the classics and did not dare disturb you. So I roamed about the mountain-side, rested at the Kan-p'ei Temple, dined with the mountain priests, and, after dinner, came home again. Going northwards, I crossed the Yüan-pa, over whose waters the unclouded moon shone with dazzling rim. When night was far advanced, I mounted Hua-tzu's Hill and saw the moonlight tossed up and thrown down by the jostling waves of Wang River. On the wintry mountain distant lights twinkled and vanished; in some deep lane beyond the forest a dog barked at the cold, with a cry as fierce as a wolf's. The sound of villagers grinding their corn at night filled the gaps between the slow chimes of a distant bell.

Now I am sitting alone. I listen, but cannot hear my grooms and servants move or speak. I think much of old days; how hand in hand, composing poems as we went, we walked down twisting paths to the banks of clear streams.

We must wait for spring to come: till the grasses sprout and the trees bloom. Then wandering together in the spring hills we shall see the trout leap lightly from the stream, the white gulls stretch their wings, the dew fall on the green moss. And in the morning we shall hear the cry of curlews in the barley-fields.

It is not long to wait. Shall you be with me then? Did I not know the natural subtlety of your intelligence, I would not dare address to you so remote an invitation. You will understand that a deep feeling dictates this course.

Written without disrespect by Wang Wei, a dweller in the mountains.

TRANSLATED BY ARTHUR WALEY

Wang Wei and P'ei Ti

From "Poems of the River Wang"

[*Wang ch'uan chi*]

1. The Hill of Hua-Tzu

WANG: The birds fly away
        into infinite space:
Over the whole mountain
        returns the splendour of autumn.
Ascending and descending
        Hua-tzu hill,
I feel
        unbounded bewilderment and lamentation.

P'EI: The sun sets,
        the wind rises among the pines.
Returning home,
        there is a little dew upon the grass.
The reflection of the clouds
        falls into the tracks of my shoes,
The blue of the mountains
        touches my clothes.

2. The Deer Enclosure

WANG: On the lonely mountain
        I meet no one,
I hear only the echo
        of human voices.
At an angle the sun's rays
        enter the depths of the wood,

And shine
    upon the green moss.

P'EI: At the end of day
          the mountain looks cold.
      But a belated wanderer
          still passes on his way.
      He knows nothing
          of the life of the wood:
      Nothing remains
          but the tracks of the buck.

3. The Path of the Ash Trees

WANG: On the narrow path,
          sheltered by the ash trees,
      In the secrecy of their shade
          flourishes the green moss,
      Only swept
          when someone answers the gate,
      Fearing that the monk from the mountain
          has come to call.

P'EI: To the south of the gate,
          along by the ash trees,
      Is the path over the hillcrest,
          that leads to Lake Yi.
      When the autumn comes
          it rains much on the mountain;
      No one picks up
          the falling leaves.

4. The Pavilion of the Lake

WANG: Light the boat that carries me
          to meet the gentle guest,
      Who from a great distance
          is coming over the lake.

Then, on the terrace,
before a cup of wine,
On every side
the lotus flowers will open.

P'EI: In front of the balcony,
as the expanse of water
fills with ripples,
The solitary moon
goes wandering without pause.
From the depth of the valley
the cries of the monkeys rise;
Borne by the wind
they reach me in my room.

5. *The Stream at the House of the Luans*

WANG: Gusts of wind
in the autumn rain;
The water falls headlong,
it spills from the rocks in torrents.
The waves leap capriciously
one on the other in flight;
The startled white heron
comes down to earth again.

P'EI: The voice of the stream
resounds to the farthest bay.
I walk along the shore
towards the southern ford.
Here and there on the water
ducks and egrets glide,
Always they return, impelled
to the proximity of men.

6. *The Cove of the Wall of Meng*

WANG: My new house
is at the beginning of the wall of Meng,

Among old trees
    and remains of decaying willows.
The other, after me,
    who will he be?
Vain his grief
   for this which was mine.

P'EI: My new hut
    is under the old wall:
Occasionally I go up
    to the ancient enclosure.
There is nothing of the past now
    about the old wall;
Men of today, uncaring,
    come and go.

TRANSLATED BY C. J. CHEN AND MICHAEL BULLOCK

Wang Wei

Seeing Master Yüan Off on His Mission to Kucha

City on Wei
          the morning rain
                    wet
                    on light dust
Around the inn
          green willows
          fresh
I summon you:
          Drink one more cup
No old friends, my friend
When you start westward
                    for Yang Kuan

TRANSLATED BY C. H. KWÔCK AND VINCENT MC HUGH

To the Assistant Prefect Chang

In evening years given to quietude,
The world's worries no concern of mine,
For my own needs making no other plan
Than to unlearn, return to long-loved woods:
I loosen my robe before the breeze from pines,
My lute celebrates moonlight on mountain pass.
You ask what laws rule "failure" or "success"—
Songs of fishermen float to the still shore.

TRANSLATED BY CYRIL BIRCH

Li Po

On the Mountain: Question and Answer

You ask me:
            Why do I live
on this green mountain?
      I smile
      No answer
                  My heart serene
On flowing water
                  peachblow
                  quietly going
                  far away
This is   another earth
           another sky
No likeness
            to that human world below

Spring Thoughts

O grass of Yen
                  like green silk flowing
Green boughs low
                  on mulberries of Ch'in
All that time!
            you've been thinking of home
and all that time!
                  my heart breaking
In my silk bedcurtain
                  spring wind

It does not know me
                    Why does it come
slipping in?

To Someone Far Away

When she was here
        pretty darling
                flowers filled the hall
Now she's gone
        pretty darling
                left her bed behind
On her bed
        th'embroidered coverlet
                rolled up
                never slept in again
Three years to the day
                still keeps
                the scent of her
Fragrance never lost
        pretty darling
        never came back
Yellow leaves falling
                when I think of her
white dew
        on green moss

Night Mooring at Cow's Creek: I Think of the Old Man

At Cow's Creek
                on Western River
                                the night
Sky still blue
                not a rag of cloud
I go on deck
                to look at the bright moon

thinking of
>the great General Hsieh of old

I also
>can make poetry
but that man's like
>>will not be found again
In the morning
>we make sail and go
The maple leaves
>fall as they will

TRANSLATED BY C. H. KWÔCK AND VINCENT MC HUGH

Visiting Han-tan: The Dancers at the Southern Pavilion

They sang to me and drummed, the boys of Yen and Chao,
Lovely girls plucked the sounding string.
Their painted cheeks shone like dazzling suns;
The dancers' sleeves shook out like blossoming boughs.
Bringing her wine I approached a handsome girl
And made her sing me songs of Han-tan.
Then lutes were played, and coiling away and away
The tune fell earthward, dropping from the grey clouds.
Where is the Prince of Chao, what has he left
But an old castle-moat where tadpoles breed?
Those three thousand knights that sat at his board,
Is there one among them whose name is still known?
Let us make merry, get something in our own day
To set against the pity of ages still unborn.

To Yüan Tan-ch'iu[1]

My friend is lodging high in the Eastern Range,
Dearly loving the beauty of valleys and hills.
At green spring he lies in the empty woods,

---

1. The "Friend Tan-ch'iu" (Taoist adept and friend of the poet's) of the fourth of the drinking songs below.

And is still asleep when the sun shines on high.
A pine-tree wind dusts his sleeves and coat;
A pebbly stream cleans his heart and ears.
I envy you who far from strife and talk
Are high-propped on a pillow of grey mist.

To His Old Friend Hsin

Long ago, among the flowers and willows,
We sat drinking together at Ch'ang-an.
The Five Barons and Seven Grandees were of our company,
But when some wild stroke was afoot
It was we who led it, yet boisterous though we were
In the arts and graces of life we could hold our own
With any dandy in the town—
In the days when there was youth in your cheeks
And I was still not old.
We galloped to the brothels, cracking our gilded whips,
We sent in our writings to the Palace of the Unicorn,
Girls sang to us and danced hour by hour on tortoise-shell mats.
We thought, you and I, that it would always be like this.
How should we know the grass would stir and dust rise on the
    wind?
Suddenly foreign horsemen were at the Hsien-ku Pass
Just when the blossom at the Palace of Ch'in was opening on the
    sunny boughs.
Now I, unhappy, am on my way to banishment at Yeh-lang,
Wondering if a day will come when the Golden cock[1]
Will bring me pardon and return.

Fighting South of the Ramparts[2]

Last year we were fighting at the source of the Sang-kan;
This year we are fighting on the Onion River road.
We have washed our swords in the surf of Parthian seas;
We have pastured our horses among the snows of the T'ien Shan.

---

1. Hoisted when an amnesty was proclaimed.
2. Li Po wrote this poem to an old tune, the original words of which, by

The King's armies have grown grey and old
Fighting ten thousand leagues away from home.
The Huns have no trade but battle and carnage;
They have no fields or ploughlands,
But only wastes where white bones lie among yellow sands.
Where the house of Ch'in built the Great Wall that was to keep
    away the Tartars,
There, in its turn, the House of Han lit beacons of war.
The beacons are always alight, fighting and marching never stop.
Men die in the field, slashing sword to sword;
The horses of the conquered neigh piteously to Heaven.
Crows and hawks peck for human guts,
Carry them in their beaks and hang them on the branches of with-
    ered trees.
Captains and soldiers are smeared on the bushes and grass;
The general schemed in vain.
Know therefore that the sword is a cursed thing
Which the wise man uses only if he must.[3]

TRANSLATED BY ARTHUR WALEY

---

an anonymous writer of about the first century, run as follows:

They fought south of the ramparts,
They died north of the wall.
They died in the moors and were not buried.
Their flesh was the food of crows.
"Tell the crows we are not afraid:
We have died in the moors and cannot be buried.
Crows, how can our bodies escape you?"
The waters flowed deep
And the rushes in the pools were dark.
The riders fought and were slain;
Their horses wandered neighing.
By the bridge there was a house:
Was it south, was it north?
The harvest was never gathered:
How can we give you your offerings?
You served your prince faithfully,
Though all in vain.
I think of you, faithful soldiers:
Your service shall not be forgotten.
For in the morning you went out to battle
And at night you did not return.
    3. Quotation from the *Tao te ching*.

Four Poems on Wine

1

Amidst the flowers
      a jug of wine—
I pour alone
      lacking companionship,
So raising the cup
      I invite the moon,
Then turn to my shadow
      which makes three of us.
Because the moon
      does not know how to drink
My shadow merely
      follows my body.
The moon has brought the shadow
      to keep me company a while,
The practice of mirth
      should keep pace with spring.
I start a song
      and the moon begins to reel,
I rise and dance
      and the shadow moves grotesquely.
While I'm still conscious
      let's rejoice with one another,
After I'm drunk
      let each one go his way.
Let us bind ourselves for ever
      for passionless journeyings.
Let us swear to meet again
      far in the Milky Way.

2

If Heaven itself
      did not love wine,
Then no Wine Star
      would shine in the sky.

And if Earth also
     did not love wine,
Earth would have no such
     place as Wine Fountain.
Have I not heard
     that pure wine makes a sage,
And even muddy wine
     can make a man wise?
If wise men and sages
     are already drinkers
What is the use
     of seeking gods and fairies?
With three cups
     I understand the great Way
With one jar
     I am at one with Nature.
Only, the perceptions
     that one has while drunk
Cannot be transmitted
     after one is sober.

3

In the third month
     the city of Hsien-yang—
Thousands of flowers
     at noon like brocade.
Who is able
     in spring to be sad alone?
Faced with this
     to drink is the shortest way
Infinite things
     as well as short and long
Alike have early been
     offered us by Creation.
A single cup
     may rank with life and death,
The myriad things
     are truly hard to fathom.

Once I am drunk
    losing Heaven and Earth,
Unsteadily
    I go to my lonely pillow.
Not to know
    that my self exists—
Of all my joys
    This is the highest.

TRANSLATED BY WILLIAM ACKER

4

    Have you not seen
How the Yellow River, which flows from heaven and hurries
        toward the sea, never turns back?
Have you not seen
How at the bright mirrors of high halls men mourn their
        white hairs,
At dawn black silk, by evening changed to snow?
While there is pleasure in life, enjoy it,
And never let your gold cup face the moon empty!
Heaven gave me my talents, they shall be used;
A thousand in gold scattered and gone will all come back again.
Boil the sheep, butcher the ox, make merry while there is time;
We have never drunk at all till we drink three hundred cups.

    Master Ts'en,
Friend Tan-ch'iu,
Here comes the wine, no standing cups!
I have a song to sing you,
Kindly turn your ears to me and listen.
It is nothing to feast on jade to the sound of bells and drums.
I ask only to be drunk for ever and never wake!
They lie forgotten, the sages of old;
Only the great drinkers have left us their names.
In time gone by, when the Prince of Ch'en feasted in the hall of
        Peace and Joy,
At ten thousand a quart he never stinted the revellers.
Why must our host say he is short of money?

Send to the shop at once, keep the cups filled.
My five-flower horse,
My fur which cost a thousand,
Call the boy, send him out to change them for good wine,
And let me forget with you the sorrows of ten thousand ages!

TRANSLATED BY A. C. GRAHAM

Letter to Han Ching-chou

[*Yü Han Ching-chou shu*]

In the most brilliant society in the empire, I have heard it said that the highest rank is not worth as much as acquaintance with Governor Han. How have you brought men to such a pitch of admiration? Has it not been by acting as did the Duke of Chou, who thrice spat out a half-chewed mouthful of food as he left the table to answer the door and who three times caught up his dripping hair and left the washbasin to meet a caller—and thus, do not you too have the heroes of the empire come running to serve under you? Once they mount your dragon gate, their renown and worth are multiplied tenfold. Hence the coiled-dragon, retired-phoenix gentlemen all wish to have their fame from you and have your excellency establish their value. Your excellency is not arrogant by reason of wealth and rank, nor do you disregard those who are poor and humble. Mao Sui stood out among three thousand retainers as an awl sticks out through a cloth bag; if you will give me the chance to show my abilities, then I shall be a Mao Sui among your followers.

I am a commoner from Lung-hsi. I have been a vagabond through Ch'u and Han. At fifteen, I was fond of swordplay, and went around visiting often the feudal lords. At thirty, I had perfected my literary style and was in touch with the Prime Minister. Although I am not a full six feet in height, still in my heart there is the courage of ten thousand men, and every prince, duke and nobleman will vouch for my moral rectitude. Such is my character: would I dare not expose it entire before your excellency?

Your excellency writes like an angel; your pen plumbs creation and change; your virtuous conduct moves Heaven and Earth; your learning embraces the human and the divine. I hope you will be willing to open your heart and your countenance to me and will not break off our interview because I do not bow deeply enough.

Certainly if you were to receive me with a great banquet and give me free rein in refined conversation, I would ask that you try me, whether I could not dash off ten thousand words while you wait. The whole world considers your excellency to be the judge of writers and the final arbiter in literature. Once appraised and approved by you, a man's worth is recognized. So, on this occasion your excellency surely will not grudge me the square foot of ground I occupy before you, but will rather give me reason to open wide my eyes and blow out my breath, exalting myself to the blue skies. When Shan T'ao[1] became governor of Chi-chou, he sought out and brought to light more than thirty persons, some of whom became *ssu-chung* and *shang-shu*. Your excellency himself has recommended several men, some of whom you recognized for their abilities, and some you rewarded for their purity. Whenever I see one of them, sensible of benefits received, examining himself, or through a sense of loyal duty, striving with might and main, I am profoundly moved and realize that your excellency has succeeded in inspiring the worthy men of the country with your own ardent spirit.

It is for this reason that instead of turning to someone else, I put myself at the service of the country's great man. If in time of stress or difficulty you should have need of me, I am at your disposal. Since not every man is a Yao or a Shun, and no one is perfect, how can I be complacent about the worth of my advice? But when it comes to literary work, I have assembled some scrolls with which I would wish to soil your sight and sully your hearing, though I fear my minuscule talent of writing poetry is unworthy of attention from such a great man as yourself. If you would deign to look over this wastepaper, I will ask you for pen and paper and a scribe therewith; afterwards I could retire and sweep out an empty room and have copies made of my work, which I would offer to you, that it might have the more value by being appreciated by a connoisseur. I hope you will condescend to give me a fair share of your encouragement and praise. Only your excellency can arrange this matter.

TRANSLATED BY J. R. HIGHTOWER

1. Shan T'ao: see above, p. 162.

Tu Fu

Autumn Meditation

[*Ch'iu hsing*]

1

Gems of dew wilt and wound the maple trees in the wood:
From Wu mountains, from Wu gorges, the air blows desolate.
The waves between the river-banks merge in the seething sky,
Clouds in the wind above the passes meet their shadows on the
    ground.
Clustered chrysanthemums have opened twice, in tears of other
    days;
The forlorn boat, once and for all, tethers my homeward thoughts.
In the houses winter clothes speed scissors and ruler;
The washing-blocks pound, faster each evening, in Pai Ti high on
    the hill.

2

On the solitary walls of K'uei-chou the sunset rays slant,
Each night guided by the Dipper I gaze towards the capital.
It is true then that tears start when we hear the gibbon cry thrice;
Useless my mission adrift on the raft which came by this eighth
    month.[1]

---

1. The cries of gibbons in the gorges downstream remind Tu Fu of the
fisherman's song:

> Of the three gorges east of Pa the Wu gorge is longest,
> When I hear the gibbon cry thrice the tears wet my clothes.

The moonlit river running straight to the horizon suggests the legend of
a fisherman who saw a raft floating out to sea every year in the eighth month
(mid-autumn), mounted it, and was carried to the Milky Way. Tu Fu sees
himself as drifting too far from home ever to return.

Fumes of the censers by the pictures in the ministry elude my
     sickbed pillow,
The whitewashed parapets of turrets against the hills dull the
     mournful bugles.
               Look! On the wall, the moon in the ivy
Already, by the shores of the isle, lights the blossoms on the reeds.

               3

The thousand houses, the circling mountains, are quiet in the
     morning light;
Day by day in the house by the river I sit in the blue of the hills.
Two nights gone the fisher boats once more come bobbing on
     the waves,
Belated swallows in cooling autumn still flutter to and fro.
K'uang Heng writing state papers, which earned me no credit,
Liu Hsiang editing classics, my hopes elsewhere . . .[2]
Yet many of my school friends have risen in the world.
By the Five Tombs in light cloaks they ride their sleek horses.

               4

Well said, Ch'ang-an looks like a chessboard—
Won and lost for a hundred years, sad beyond all telling.
The mansions of princes and nobles all have new lords,
And another generation wears the caps and robes of office.
Due north on the mountain passes the gongs and drums shake,
To the chariots and horses campaigning in the west the winged
     dispatches hasten.
While the fish and dragons fall asleep and the autumn river
     turns cold
My native country, untroubled times, are always in my thoughts.

               5

The gate of P'eng-lai Palace faces the southern hills,
Dew collects on the bronze stems high in the Misty River.

---

2. Tu Fu as "Reminder" at the capital (757-58) lost favour by writing
critical memorials, and later he resigned his post as Commissioner of Education at Hua-chou (758-59). He contrasts himself with K'uang Heng and Liu
Hsiang, both of the last century B.C., successful respectively as statesman and
editor of ancient documents.

Behold in the west on Jasper Lake the Queen Mother descend,
Approaching from the east the purple haze fills the Han-ku pass.[3]
The clouds roll back, the pheasant-tail screens open before
    the throne:
Scales ringed by the sun on dragon robes! I have seen the
    majestic face.
I lay down once by the long river, wake left behind by the years,
Who so many times answered the roll of court by the blue
    chain-patterned door.

6

From the mouth of Ch'ü-t'ang gorges here to the side of Crooked
    River there
For ten thousand miles of mist and wind the touch of pallid autumn.
Through the walled passage from Sepal Hall the royal
    splendour coursed,
To the little park Hibiscus Blossom the griefs of the frontier came.
Pearl blinds and embellished pillars closed in the yellow cranes,
Embroidered cables and ivory masts startled the white seagulls.
            Look back and pity the singing, dancing land!
Ch'in from most ancient times was the seat of princes.

7

K'un-ming Pool was the Han time's monument,
The banners of Emperor Wu are here before my eyes.
Vega threads her loom in vain by night under the moon
And the great stone fish's plated scales veer in the autumn wind.[4]
The waves toss a zizania seed, over sunken clouds as black:

---

3. Tu Fu refers variously to the P'eng-lai Palace in Ch'ang-an, named after one of the fairy islands in the Eastern sea; the copper pans raised on pillars which the Emperor Wu (140-87 B.C.) made to collect dew for the elixir; the Misty River is the empyrean; the Western Queen Mother (Hsi-wang-mu) who banqueted King Mu (1001-947 B.C.) at Jasper Lake in her country far to the west, an incident which the poet fuses with her later descent from the sky to teach the arts of immortality to the Emperor Wu; the philosopher Lao Tzu coming through the passes preceded by a purple cloud on his final journey to the west.

4. K'un-ming Pool near Ch'ang-an was made by the Emperor Wu for naval exercises. Near it was a statue of the Weaver girl (the star Vega), and in it a stone whale with movable fins and tail.

Dew on the calyx chills the lotus, red with dropped pollen.
—Over the pass, all the way to the sky, a path for none but the birds.
On river and lakes, to the ends of the earth, a single old fisherman.

8

The K'un-wu road by Yü-su River ran its meandering course,
The shadow of Purple Turret Peak fell into Lake Mei-p'i.
Grains from the fragrant rice-stalks, pecked and dropped by
        the parrots:
On the green *wu-t'ung* tree branches which the perching
        phoenix aged.
Beautiful girls gathered kingfisher feathers for spring gifts:
Together in the boat, a troop of immortals, we drifted late into
        the evening . . .
                This brush of many colours once forced the elements.
Chanting, gazing, in anguish my white head droops.

Looking Out Over the Plains

Clear autumn, sight has no bounds;
High in the distance piling shadows rise.
The farthest waters merge in the sky unsullied;
A neglected town hides deep in mist.
Sparse leaves, which the wind still sheds,
Far hills, where the sun sinks down.
How late the solitary crane returns!
But the twilight crows already fill the forest.

TRANSLATED BY A. C. GRAHAM

Thoughts on a Night Journey

Reeds by the bank bending, stirred by the breeze,
High-masted boat advancing alone in the night,
Stars drawn low by the vastness of the plain,
The moon rushing forward in the river's flow.

How should I look for fame to what I have written?
In age and sickness, how continue to serve?
Wandering, drifting, what can I take for likeness?
—A gull that wheels alone between earth and sky.

TRANSLATED BY CYRIL BIRCH

Recruiting Officer at Shih-hao Village

[*Shih hao li*]

Came at dusk into Shih-hao village
Draft officer there
                    rounding up people by night
Old man
        climbed over the wall
                        escaped
Old woman came out the door
                        staring
Officer roared
            Angry as a bull!
Old woman cried
                Enough to twist your bowels!
I heard her
            She went up and spoke to him:
"I had three sons
                on the border at Yeh
The first one
            sent me a letter
My other two sons
                a while back
                            killed in battle
Survivors
        lucky to be alive at all
The dead
        gone for good
There are no more men in this house

only
        my grandson at the breast
His mother
                stayed here to look after him,
in and out of the house
                        without a decent
                        skirt on her legs
I'm an old woman
                    weak in the back
but please! sir
            let me follow you
                        when you return tonight
hurrying to meet
                the draft at Ho-yang
I'll be in time to cook
a morning meal
                for the soldiers"
Night late
            talk dwindled away
I seemed to hear
                low sobbing
At dawn
            resumed my journey
The old man alone
            when I said goodbye to him.

TRANSLATED BY C. H. KWÔCK AND VINCENT MC HUGH

A Song of War Chariots

[*Ping ch'e hsing*]

The war-chariots rattle,
The war-horses whinny.
Each man of you has a bow and a quiver at his belt.
Father, mother, son, wife, stare at you going,
Till dust shall have buried the bridge beyond Ch'ang-an.
They run with you, crying, they tug at your sleeves,

And the sound of their sorrow goes up to the clouds;
And every time a bystander asks you a question,
You can only say to him that you have to go.
. . . We remember others at fifteen sent north to guard the river
And at forty sent west to cultivate the camp-farms.
The mayor wound their turbans for them when they started out.
With their turbaned hair white now, they are still at the border,
At the border where the blood of men spills like the sea—
And still the heart of Emperor Wu is beating for war.
. . . Do you know that, east of China's mountains, in two
        hundred districts
And in thousands of villages, nothing grows but weeds,
And though strong women have bent to the ploughing,
East and west the furrows all are broken down?
. . . Men of China are able to face the stiffest battle,
But their officers drive them like chickens and dogs.
Whatever is asked of them,
Dare they complain?
For example, this winter
Held west of the gate,
Challenged for taxes,
How could they pay?
. . . We have learned that to have a son is bad luck—
It is very much better to have a daughter
Who can marry and live in the house of a neighbour,
While under the sod we bury our boys.
. . . Go to the Blue Sea, look along the shore
At all the old white bones forsaken—
New ghosts are wailing there now with the old,
Loudest in the dark sky of a stormy day.

TRANSLATED BY WITTER BYNNER

Prose Essays

Han Yü (768-824) stood in the front line of defence of Confucian principles against what he considered the heresies and decadence of the age. The "Ancient Style" (ku-wen) movement, which he led, prized lucidity and artful simplicity in prose and despised the vacuities of the ornamental styles (parallel prose and the like) which had been the rage. But in the hands of scholar-officials no movement could remain purely literary in scope. Hence the political conservatism of the lament over contemporary morals ("An Enquiry into Slander") or the vehemence of attack in "The Bone of the Buddha."

What is under fire in this last piece, Han Yü's most famous memorial, is not so much Buddhism as such, but rather the eunuchs and unscrupulous politicians who pandered to the Emperor Hsien-tsung's quest for increased longevity. Against these men with their patronage of wizards and their promotion of charms Han Yü champions orthodox values and modes of conduct. Distinguished Confucians rallied behind him on the issue—and succeeded in reducing the sentence provoked by the memorial to mere banishment.

Banished as governor to Ch'ao-chou in the south, Han Yü found the inhabitants suffering from the depradations of a crocodile. He performed the ceremony described in the introduction to the "Proclamation," below. The result, it is recorded, was a violent storm which rose that same evening and lasted for several days. It was found that the crocodile had removed to a distance of sixty li to the west; nor was Ch'ao-chou again plagued with crocodiles for several hundred years.

In the opinion of the translator, Han Yü would not have disputed the propensity of wild creatures, whatever their powers, to understand and obey orders issued on the authority of the Son of Heaven himself.

Of the first of the pieces by Han Yü which follow the translator writes: "It is not to be thought that Han Yü ever attempted to perform the curious ceremony here described. His essay amounts to a highly sophisticated form of begging letter, intended to attract the reader's sympathy and excite his indignation against a regime which would permit the poverty of a man of obvious literary ability and upright moral character."

The essay "Against the God of the Wind" is actually "rhyme-prose," and a heavily veiled satire. The emperor (the Sun Crow, in reference to an ancient mythological explanation of the sun's passage across the sky) had shown readiness to remit taxes in a bad year, but Li Shih, the object of Han Yü's lampoon, rapaciously demanded their payment.

Liu Tsung-yüan (773-819), celebrated for his depictions of natural scenery in prose and verse, wrote also one of the best-loved of all the allegories, which concludes our selection.

Han Yü

Farewell to Poverty

[*Sung ch'iung wen*]

In the first month of the sixth year of Yüan-ho [811], early in the morning of the day *yi-ch'ou*, the master bade his servant Hsing plait a cart from willows, weave a boat from grasses, and load them with wet rice and with dry. When the oxen had been tied beneath the yokes, the mast hoisted and the sail unfastened, the master bowed three times to the Demon of Poverty and addressed these words to him: "They tell me that you are going any day. This humble person does not venture to ask by what road, but has had a boat and a cart made ready and loaded with wet rice and with dry. The day is auspicious, the time favourable; you may profitably go to which-ever of the four quarters you please. Do you eat a bowlful, do you sip a goblet-ful, and take with you your friends and companions from this old scene to a new. Ride upon the dust, fly upon the wind, contend for first place with the lightning. As you have no deformity to cause you to delay, and as I have had the kindness to provide for your journey, you and yours will surely be ready to go."

He held his breath, and as he listened in silence he seemed to hear a noise like a whistle or a cry, shrill and piercing, that stood all his hair on end. He hunched his shoulders and drew in his neck, suspecting that there was something yet seeing nothing: and after much time there could be clearly heard a sound as of a voice which said: "You and I have lived together forty years and more. When you were still a child I did not befool you: whether you were studying or ploughing or seeking office and fame, I was always with you, nor did I ever swerve from my first affection. The gods of the gates, the guardians of the doors cursed me and reviled me, but though I was wrapped in shame and pursued by falsehood my devotion never strayed. When you were transferred to the wild country of

244

the south, to be baked in heat and cooked in steam, I went also, though it was not my native place and all the other demons heaped insults on me. When for four years you served in the *t'ai-hsüeh,* with leeks for your breakfast and salted food for your dinner, it was only I who protected you, and though all the rest hated you, I myself from first to last never turned my back upon you. My mind has harboured no traitorous design, no word of departure has ever fallen from my mouth. From whom have you heard that I was due to go? This means that you have permitted a libel to divide us. I am a demon and not human, what use could I find for carts or boats? It is only my nose that smells the stench or the fragrance: your wet rice and your dry may as well be thrown away. I am one and one alone. Who are my friends and my companions? If you are so full of knowledge, can you say how many we are? If you can tell our whole story, you may well be called wise: and once the whole truth is revealed, how should we dare not to turn away and keep aloof?"

To this the master replied: "Do you think that I do not really know you? Your friends and your companions are not six, not four: their number is ten less five, it fills seven all but two. Each has his own special quality and bears his own name. Between you, you have jogged my arm and made me upset my broth: you have twisted my throat and made me say what I should not. All that has made my countenance hateful to myself and my speech tasteless to other men has been of your designing. The name of your first companion is Poverty through Intelligence. He is proud, he is haughty, hates the round and loves the square; and though shamefully deceived by evildoers he cannot bear to do them harm nor hurt. The name of the next is Poverty through Learning. He disdains luck and fame. He unmasks hidden secrets. From his height he pours scorn on common speech and holds in his hand a power that is divine. The name of the next is Poverty through Writing. He does not concentrate on any one talent, but is full of wonders and marvels. He will not go the way of the world, but seeks only to please himself. The name of the next is Poverty through Fate. His shadow is different from his shape. His face is ugly, and his heart beautiful. In the search for material advantage he stands behind the rest of mankind, but in the demands he makes of himself he is before them all. The name of the last is Poverty through Friendship. He wears out his skin and bone. He gives out the whole of himself, waiting on tiptoe upon others, only to be plunged into feuds and enmities. All these five demons are my five plagues. They have exposed me to hunger and cold, cast me down to slander and calumny. They can lead my steps astray, so that no man can come between us: and though I may repent of my actions in the morning, by the evening I have repeated them. They are like buzzing flies and barking dogs, no sooner driven away than they are back again."

Together the five demons stretched their eyes and stuck out their tongues, leaped into the air and sprawled upon the ground, clapped their hands and stamped their feet, burst into laughter and looked at one another. Then after a little they spoke to the master as follows: "You know our names and all that we do. But to drive us and bid us go is to show yourself wise in little and foolish in much. Man's life is but an age span, his time is but short. We have made you a name that a hundred ages will not efface. The small man and the great are not the same in heart, and only when you are in opposition to the world can you be at one with heaven. Yet you take your precious jewel and exchange it for a single sheepskin; you are sated with the fat and the sweet and yearn for thin gruel. No one in the world knows you better than we. Though you suffer dismissal and exile, we will never desert you: and if you think you cannot believe us, look, we beg you, in your classics."

At this the master hung his head in dismay, raised his hands and offered his apology: and having burnt the boat and the cart, he led the demons to the place of honour.

TRANSLATED BY J. K. RIDEOUT

Lament for His Nephew Shih-erh Lang

[*Chi Shih-erh Lang wen*]

It was full seven days, Shih-erh Lang, after I, your uncle Yü, had been told of your death that I could contain my grief, express the feelings of my heart, and send Chien-chung on a far journey to prepare choice and seasonable meats and speak these words to your spirit.

Alas, a little child I was left an orphan. When I grew up, I could not recall the faces of my father and mother. It was solely to my elder brother and his wife that I turned. When in middle life that brother died in the south country you and I were both young, and with his wife we went back to Ho-yang to bury him. After this I went again with you to Chiang-nan to find a living, and together in bitterness and sorrow never for one day were we parted from one another. I had three elder brothers; all had the ill fortune to die early, and to continue my late father's line there were left of grandsons only you, of sons only myself, two generations with but one body, one form, one shadow. My brother's wife once took you on her knee, and pointing at me said "of two generations of the house of Han, these are all that are left." At the time you were very young, and her words could not have remained in your mind; and though I was of an age to retain them I did not understand their full sadness. When I was nineteen years of age, I went for the first time to the capital. Four years later I came home to see you, and four years later again when I had come to Ho-yang to see the graves of my family, I met you following my brother's wife's bier on the way to burial. Two years later again, when I was in Pienchou as assistant to the *ch'eng-hsiang* Tung, you came to see me and stayed for a year, then asked to go home and bring your wife and children. But as in the next year the *ch'eng-hsiang* died and I left Pienchou, you did not come as we had planned. In that year I was attached to the military staff at Hsüchou and no sooner had the messenger sent to fetch you set out, than again I was dismissed and left; and again failed our plan that you should come. But I felt that had you followed me eastwards, it could not have been for long, as the east was a strange land to us. As a lasting plan, I felt it would be better to go back to the west, where I could make a home to which to bring you. Alas! Who could have told that as soon as you had left me you would die? When you and I were both young, I thought that though we might be parted for a little while, in the end we would surely live the rest of our lives together; and it was for that reason that I left you and so-journed in the capital to get myself some small salary. Had I known how it would be, not even for the ten thousand chariots of a great noble or chief minister would I have deserted you for a single day. Last year when Meng Tung-yeh came here I wrote you a letter saying, "Though I am still not forty, my sight is failing, my hair is greying and my teeth are loose. When I think how my father's and brothers' generation, healthy and strong as they were, all died early, I doubt whether so frail a one as I myself can live for long. But I cannot leave here, and as you will not come, I am afraid that if I suddenly die you will be left to take up the burden of an immeasurable sorrow." Who could have told that the younger would be taken and the elder left, the strong cut off and the sickly spared whole?

Alas! is it real, or it is a dream? What they told me surely cannot be true. Can it be real that my brother's excellence has brought an early death upon his heir? That with a nature so pure and clear you should be unable to enjoy its blessings? That the younger and stronger has been taken untimely, the elder and feebler spared whole? It cannot be real. It is a dream. What they tell, surely is not true. Yet this letter from Tung-yeh, this report from Keng-lan, what are they doing by my side? Alas! it is real. My brother's excellence has not saved his heir from untimely death, nor will it be permitted for you to enjoy the blessings of that pure and clear nature which should have been the stay of your household. It is as they say. Truly Heaven is hard to fathom, and the gods hard to understand. Reason is beyond conjecture, and life beyond knowledge. Even so from now on my greying hairs will turn to white, my loosening teeth will drop and fall, and as my hairs and blood grow daily thinner and my mind and spirit daily more weak, it will not be long before I follow you to death. If after death there be a knowing, this parting will be but for a little while. If there be not, this sorrow will be but for a little while, then freedom from sorrow for ever and without end.

Your son is beginning his tenth, mine his fifth year. If you, young and strong as you were, cannot be spared, what hope have these young children of realising maturity? Alas, alas, for sorrow! You said in your letter of last year, "I have recently contracted beri-beri, which is at times acute." "This disease," I said, "is one from which the people of Chiang-nan constantly suffer. There is no need to worry." Alas! was it through this that your life was cut short, or was it some other illness that brought you to your end? Your letter is dated the seventeenth of the sixth month, while Tung-yeh tells me that you died on the second of that month, and the message from Keng-lan bears no date. What happened was that Tung-yeh's messenger had not the sense to ask your household the date of your death, while Keng-lan in his message did not realise that he ought to have mentioned it. When Tung-yeh wrote me his letter he evidently enquired of his messenger, who satisfied him by answering at random. And so I know not what to believe.

I have now sent Chien-chung to make my offering to you, and to condole with your orphans and your foster-mother. If they have the means and can subsist until your funeral is completed, he is to wait until the end of the funeral and then bring them here to me. If they have not, he is to bring them back at once, and leave the rest of the servants to take charge of your funeral. If it be within my powers to change the place of your burial, I will at the last have you buried in the grave of your forefathers. For I know that only when this is done will you have your wish.

Alas! you were sick, and I knew not the time; you are dead, and I know not the day. While you lived, I could not support you or keep you with me; now that you are dead, I cannot touch you or pour out my sorrow. When you are enshrouded I shall not lean upon your bier, when you are committed to the earth I shall not stand by your grave. It is through conduct offensive to the heavenly powers that I have caused your untimely death: it is lack of piety and affection that has prevented me from supporting you in life or watching over you in death. Part of you is on the bounds of heaven, part in a corner of the earth. Alive your shadow was not cast upon my form, dead your spirit may not haunt my dreams: and of this I am the true cause; who else can bear the blame? My grief can no more know limits than these blue skies above me.

From now on I will think no more of the world of men. I will find a few score acres of land on the banks of the Yi or the Ying and spend the rest of my years teaching your son and mine, in the hope that they may grow strong and great, while your daughter and mine await the day of their marriage. This will be the whole of my existence.

Alas! Words are bounded, emotions know no ending. Do you hear me or do you hear me not? Alas, for sorrow!

Humbly I present my offering.

TRANSLATED BY J. K. RIDEOUT

Against the God of the Wind

[*Sung Feng Po*]

Of this drought, who is the cause? I know the author: it is the God of the Wind who is to blame. The hills made the clouds to rise, the marshes sent up their vapour. The thunder whipped the chariot, the lightning shook the banner. The rain was promising, ready to fall; but the God of the Wind was angry, and the clouds could not stay still. The Sun Crow in his kindness had pity upon the people. He dimmed his radiance, and sent not his fiery spirit to battle. But you, God of the Wind, instead what did you do?

For you what else could we have done? We looked for a suitable time, we made ready the materials for the sacrifice. The lamb was full fat, the wine was full sweet. There was food enough for repletion, drink enough for drunkenness. The God of the Wind's anger, what brought it about? The clouds were banked thick, you blew and thinned them. The vapour was ready to condense, you blew and scattered it. You melted the vapour so that it could not transform, you froze the clouds so that they could not shed their rain.

You, God of the Wind, should you wish to escape this crime, what further have you to say? Heaven above, which sees all things, has records, has laws. I now present my charge and for this crime who shall pay? The sentence of Heaven will fall upon you; when it does there can be no repentance; and God of the Wind, even if you die, what man will mourn for you?

Memorial on the Bone of Buddha

[*Lun Fo ku piao*]

I humbly submit that Buddhism is but one of the religious systems obtaining among the barbarian tribes, that only during the later Han dynasty did it filter into the Middle Kingdom, and that it never existed in the golden age of the past.

In remote times Huang-ti ruled for a hundred years, and lived to the age of a hundred and ten; Shao Hao ruled for eighty years and lived to the age of a hundred; Chuan Hsü ruled for seventy-

nine years and lived to the age of ninety-eight; Emperor Ku ruled
for seventy years to the age of a hundred and five; Emperor Yao for
ninety-eight years to the age of a hundred and eighteen; while
both emperors Shun and Yü lived to be a hundred. During this time
the empire was in a state of perfect equilibrium and the people lived
to ripe old age in peace and prosperity; but as yet the Middle Kingdom did not know of Buddha. After this T'ang of Yin lived to be
a hundred. His grandson T'ai Mou ruled for seventy-five years, and
Wu Ting for fifty-nine years; and though the histories do not tell us
to what age they lived, it cannot in either case be reckoned at less
than a hundred. In the Chou dynasty Wen Wang lived to be ninety-
seven, and Wu Wang to be ninety-three, whilst Mu Wang was on
the throne for a hundred years. As Buddhism had still not pene-
trated to the Middle Kingdom, this cannot be attributed to the
worship of him.

It was not until the reign of Ming-ti of Han that Buddhism
first appeared. Ming-ti's reign lasted no longer than eighteen years,
and after him disturbance followed upon disturbance, and reigns
were all short. From the time of the five dynasties, Sung, Ch'i, Liang,
Ch'en and Yüan Wei onwards, as the worship of Buddha slowly increased, dynasties became more shortlived. Wu-ti of Liang alone
reigned as long as forty-eight years. During his reign he three times
consecrated his life to Buddha, made no animal sacrifices in his
ancestral temple, and ate but one meal a day of vegetables and fruit.
Yet in the end he was driven out by the rebel Hou Ching and died
of starvation in T'ai-ch'eng, and his state was immediately destroyed.
By worshipping Buddha he looked for prosperity but found only
disaster, a sufficient proof that Buddha is not worthy of worship.

When Kao-tsu succeeded the fallen house of Sui, he determined
to eradicate Buddhism. But the ministers of the time were lacking
in foresight and ability, they had no real understanding of the way
of the ancient kings, nor of the things that are right both for then
and now. Thus they were unable to assist the wise resolution of their
ruler and save their country from this plague. To my constant regret
the attempt stopped short. But you, your majesty, are possessed
of a skill in the arts of peace and war, of wisdom and courage the
like of which has not been seen for several thousand years. When
you first ascended the throne you prohibited recruitment of Buddhist monks and Taoist priests and the foundation of new temples

and monasteries; and I firmly believed that the intentions of Kao-
tsu would be carried out by your hand, or if this were still impossible, that at least their religions would not be allowed to spread
and flourish.

And now, your majesty, I hear that you have ordered all
Buddhist monks to escort a bone of the Buddha from Feng-hsiang
and that a pavilion be erected from which you will in person watch
its entrance into the Imperial Palace. You have further ordered
every Buddhist temple to receive this object with due homage.
Stupid as I am, I feel convinced that it is not out of regard for
Buddha that you, your majesty, are praying for blessings by doing
him this honour; but that you are organising this absurd pantomime
for the benefit of the people of the capital and for their gratification
in this year of plenty and happiness. For a mind so enlightened
as your majesty's could never believe such nonsense. The minds of
the common people however are as easy to becloud as they are
difficult to enlighten. If they see your majesty acting in this way,
they will think that you are wholeheartedly worshipping the Buddha,
and will say: "His majesty is a great sage, and even he worships
the Buddha with all his heart. Who are we that we should any of
us grudge our lives in his service?" They will cauterize the crowns
of their heads, burn off their fingers, and in bands of tens or hundreds cast off their clothing and scatter their money and from daylight to darkness follow one another in the cold fear of being too
late. Young and old in one mad rush will forsake their trades and
callings and, unless you issue some prohibition, will flock round
the temples, hacking their arms and mutilating their bodies to do
him homage. And the laughter that such unseemly and degenerate
behaviour will everywhere provoke will be no light matter.

The Buddha was born a barbarian; he was unacquainted with
the language of the Middle Kingdom, and his dress was of a different cut. His tongue did not speak nor was his body clothed in the
manner prescribed by the kings of old; he knew nothing of the
duty of minister to prince or the relationship of son to father. Were
he still alive today, were he to come to court at the bidding of his
country, your majesty would give him no greater reception than
an interview in the Strangers' Hall, a ceremonial banquet, and the
gift of a suit of clothes, after which you would have him sent under
guard to the frontier to prevent him from misleading your people.

There is then all the less reason now that he has been dead so long for allowing this decayed and rotten bone, this filthy and disgusting relic to enter the Forbidden Palace. "I stand in awe of supernatural beings," said Confucius, "but keep them at a distance." And the feudal lords of olden times when making a visit of condolence even within their own state would still not approach without sending a shaman to precede them and drive away all evil influences with a branch of peach-wood. But now and for no given reason your majesty proposes to view in person the reception of this decayed and disgusting object without even sending ahead the shaman with his peach-wood wand; and to my shame and indignation none of your ministers says that this is wrong, none of your censors has exposed the error.

I beg that this bone be handed over to the authorities to throw into water or fire, that Buddhism be destroyed root and branch for ever, that the doubts of your people be settled once and for all and their descendants saved from heresy. For if you make it known to your people that the actions of the true sage surpass ten thousand times ten thousand those of ordinary men, with what wondering joy will you be acclaimed! And if the Buddha should indeed possess the power to bring down evil, let all the bane and punishment fall upon my head, and as heaven is my witness I shall not complain.

In the fullness of my emotion I humbly present this memorial for your attention.

TRANSLATED BY J. K. RIDEOUT

Proclamation to the Crocodile

[*Chi o yü wen*]

On the twenty-fourth day of the fourth month of the fourteenth year of Yüan-ho, Han Yü, Governor of Ch'ao-chou, had his officer Ch'in Chi take a sheep and a pig and throw them into the deep waters of Wu creek as food for the crocodile. He then addressed it as follows:

When in ancient times the former kings possessed the land, they set fire to the mountains and the swamp, and with nets, ropes, fish-spears and knives expelled the reptiles and snakes and evil creatures that did harm to the people, and drove them out beyond the four seas. When there came later kings of lesser power who could not hold so wide an empire, even the land between the Chiang and the Han they wholly abandoned and gave up to the Man and the Yi, to Ch'u and to Yüeh: let alone Ch'ao which lies between the five peaks and the sea, some ten thousand li from the capital. Here it was that the crocodiles lurked and bred, and it was truly their rightful place. But now a Son of Heaven has succeeded to the throne of T'ang, who is godlike in his wisdom, merciful in peace and fierce in war. All between the four seas and within the six directions is his to hold and to care for, still more the land trod by the footsteps of Yü and near to Yangchou, administered by governors and prefects, whose soil pays tribute and taxes to supply the sacrifices to Heaven and to Earth, to the ancestral altars and to all the deities. The crocodiles and the governor cannot together share this ground.

The governor has received the command of the Son of Heaven to protect this ground and take charge of its people; but you, crocodile, goggle-eyed, are not content with the deep waters of the creek, but seize your advantage to devour the people and their stock, the bears and boars, stags and deer, to fatten your body and multiply your sons and grandsons. You join issue with the governor and contend with him for the mastery. The governor, though weak and feeble, will not endure to bow his head and humble his heart before a crocodile, nor will he look on timorously and be put to shame before his officers and his people by leading unworthily a borrowed existence in this place. But having received the command of the Son of Heaven to come here as an officer, he cannot but dispute with you, crocodile: and if you have understanding, do you hearken to the governor's words.

To the south of the province of Ch'ao lies the great sea, and in it there is room for creatures as large as the whale or roc, as small as the shrimp or crab, all to find homes in which to live and feed. Crocodile, if you set out in the morning, by the evening you would be there. Now, crocodile, I will make an agreement with you. Within full three days, you will take your ugly brood and remove southwards to the sea, and so give way before the appointed officer of the Son of Heaven. If within three days you cannot, I will go to five days: if within five days you cannot, I will go to seven.

If within seven days you cannot, this shall mean either that finally you have refused to remove, and that though I be governor you will not hear and obey my words; or else that you are stupid and without intellect, and that even when a governor speaks you do not hear and understand.

Now those who defy the appointed officers of the Son of Heaven, who do not listen to their words and refuse to make way before them, who from stupidity and lack of intellect do harm to the people and to other creatures, all shall be put to death. The governor will then choose skilful officers and men, who shall take strong bows and poisoned arrows and conclude matters with you, crocodile, nor stop until they have slain you utterly. Do not leave repentance until too late.

TRANSLATED BY J. K. RIDEOUT

An Enquiry Into Slander

[*Yüan hui*]

The demands that the great men of the past made of themselves were heavy and comprehensive. What they expected of others was light and simple. The first saved themselves from laziness; the second made men glad to do good. They knew that in antiquity there had been a certain Shun, a man possessed of humanity and sense of duty; and when they had discovered what made Shun the man he was, they reproached themselves with these words: "He was a man. I too am a man. But what he could do, I cannot do." Morning and evening they reflected upon this; they put aside what in themselves was unlike Shun, and pursued what was like Shun. They knew that in antiquity there had been a certain Chou Kung, distinguished as a man by many talents and accomplishments; and when they had discovered what made Chou Kung the man he was, they reproached themselves with these words: "He was a man. I too am a man. But what he could do, I cannot do." Morning and evening they reflected upon this; they put aside what in themselves was unlike Chou Kung, and pursued what was like Chou Kung. Both Shun and Chou Kung were great sages, and the world has not seen their like again. Yet that these men should have said "It is a great grief to me that I am not equal to Shun or Chou Kung" surely proves that the demands they made of themselves were heavy and comprehensive.

In dealing with others they said "If he has acquired this, surely we can call him good. If he can do this, surely we can call him accomplished." They accepted this one, and demanded no more; they took him as he was, and did not enquire what he had been. Their only fear was that a man might fail to derive the advantage of the good he had done. Now one virtue is easy to cultivate, a single accomplishment is easy to acquire. Then for these men to say "It is enough if he has acquired this, or can do that" surely shows that what they expected of others was light and simple.

With the great men of the present day, however, things are quite different. They make the most searching demands of others, but are sparing in what they ask of themselves. In consequence others have become most reluctant to try to do good, while from themselves the great men obtain but little. Before they have acquired any skill, they say "I am good at this, and that is quite enough." Before they have obtained any ability, they say "I can do this, and that is quite enough." They impose upon other men without and upon their own hearts within. Before they have made even the smallest advance, they give up. Does not this show that they are very sparing in what they ask of themselves?

But in dealing with other men, they say "He may be good at this, but that is no reason to commend his character," or "He may be able to do this, but that is no reason to commend his services." They pick upon one shortcoming to the exclusion of ten merits. They search into a man's past and take no account of what he is now. Their only fear is that other men may gain a reputation. Is this not to make the most searching demands of others?

In fact it may be said that they fail to apply even ordinary standards to themselves, but demand from others those of a sage. How they can have any self-respect passes my understanding. Such conduct, however, has its root and its source: and these are laziness and jealousy. Laziness prevents their own development; jealousy makes them dread development in others. And this I have proved.

To test my theory I have publicly pronounced this gentleman to be good, or that gentleman to be good. Those who have agreed have been either his associates, or persons so far removed from him that their interests could in no way clash, or persons who were afraid of him; while of those who disagreed, the bolder expressed their fury in speech, the more timid by their expression. By way of further proof I have publicly proclaimed that this gentleman is not good, or that gentleman is not good. Those who disagreed were either his associates, or persons so far removed from him that their interests in no way clashed, or persons who were afraid of him; while of those who agreed, the bolder expressed their satisfaction in speech, the more timid by their expression. In this way does good work provoke slander and high character attract calumny.

Alas! to expect that the pursuit of truth and goodness will bring in this world the glory of fame and praise is to expect the impossible. If only those who are destined to work in high places would understand and abide by my words, this land might yet be well governed.

TRANSLATED BY J. K. RIDEOUT

Liu Tsung-yüan

Camel Kuo the Gardener

[Chung shu Kuo T'o-t'o chuan]

Whatever name Camel Kuo may have had to begin with is not known. But he was a hunchback and walked in his bumpy way with his face to the ground, very like a camel, and so that was what the country folk called him. When Camel Kuo heard them he said, "Excellent. Just the right name for me."—And he forthwith discarded his real name and himself adopted "Camel" also.

He lived at Feng-lo, to the west of Ch'ang-an. Camel was a grower of trees by profession; and all the great and wealthy residents of Ch'ang-an who planted trees for their enjoyment or lived off the sale of their fruit would compete for the favour of his services. It was a matter of observation that when Camel Kuo had planted a tree, even though it was uprooted from elsewhere, there was never a one but lived, and grew strong and glossy, and fruited early and abundantly. Other growers, however they spied on him and tried to imitate his methods, never could achieve his success.

Once, when questioned on the point, Camel replied: "I cannot make a tree live for ever or flourish. What I *can* do is comply with the nature of the tree so that it takes the way of its kind. When a tree is planted its roots should have room to breathe, its base should be firmed, the soil it is in should be old and the fence around it should be close. When you have it this way, then you must neither disturb it nor worry about it, but go away and not come back. If you care for it like this when you plant it, and neglect it like this *after* you have planted it, then its nature will be fulfilled and it will take the way of its kind. And so all *I* do is avoid harming its growth—I have no power to make it grow; I avoid hindering the fruiting—I have no power to bring it forward or make it more abundant.

"With other growers it is not the same. They coil up the roots and they use fresh soil. They firm the base either too much or not enough. Or if they manage to avoid these faults, then they dote too fondly and worry too anxiously. They inspect the tree every morning and cosset it every night; they cannot walk away from it without turning back for another look. The worst of them will even scrape off the bark to see if it is still living, or shake the roots to test whether they are holding fast. And with all this the tree gets further every day from what a tree should be. This is not mothering but smothering, not affection but affliction. This is why they cannot rival my results: what other skill can I claim?"

"Would it be possible to apply this philosophy of yours to the art of government?" asked the questioner.

"My only art is the growing of trees," said Camel Kuo in answer. "Government is not my business. But living here in the country I have seen officials who go to a lot of trouble issuing orders as though they were deeply concerned for the people; yet all they achieve is an increase of misfortune. Morning and evening runners come yelling, 'Orders from the government: plough at once! Sow right away! Harvest inspection! Spin your silk! Weave your cloth! Raise your children! Feed your livestock!' Drums roll for assembly, blocks are struck to summon us. And we the common people miss our meals to receive the officials and still cannot find the time: how then can we expect to prosper our livelihood and find peace in our lives? This is why we are sick and weary; and in this state of affairs I suppose there may be some resemblance to my profession?"

"Wonderful!" was the delighted cry of the man who had questioned him. "The art I sought was of cultivating trees; the art I found was of cultivating men. Let this be passed on as a lesson to all in office!"

TRANSLATED BY CYRIL BIRCH

Poets of a Generation: Two

After two poems by Han Yü, whom we have already seen as an essayist, comes a page of "linked verse," the product of one of those games which filled the cultivated ease of the Chinese man of letters. In a garden, over wine or tea, a topic was given, a metre set, and each friend would cap another's impromptu lines. Of the group here assembled the name of Po Chü-yi will be best known. But P'ei Tu (765-839) was an eminent statesman, the most influential figure of his day. Chang Chi (c. 765-830) was one of the writers who most influenced Po Chü-yi's early poetry. Liu Yü-hsi was a lifelong friend of Po's who was born in the same year and predeceased him by four years.

Of all the many Chinese poets reborn in English from the understanding of Arthur Waley, one feels it was Po Chü-yi (772-846) whose personality most attracted his translator. Waley's biography of Po is a work of love as well as of scholarship. The moods of the poems here reprinted vary widely, from the sublimity of "The Temple" to the quiet whimsy of the contemplation of baldness, but wisdom is the keynote always.

"A Song of Unending Sorrow" is a long narrative poem which in later centuries inspired much work by dramatists. The quatrain "The Poem on the Wall" leads to two poems of Yüan Chen (779-831), another great friend of Po's. He is also the author of the "Story of Ts'ui Ying-ying," given later.

It is a far cry even from the passion of Yüan Chen's grief in "The Pitcher" to the halloween world of Li Ho (791-817). This shortlived poet is one of the great eccentrics of Chinese tradition.

He rode out each morning followed by a servant on foot. The servant carried a bag, into which Li Ho would toss scraps of paper bearing the lines which in the evening he would work into the elegant abandon of his verses.

Lu T'ung (d. 835), minor poet and friend of Han Yü, shared with Li Ho what the translator calls "an exuberance of metaphor and a talent for the grotesque." He is best known for "an extraordinary long poem on the lunar eclipse of 810, in which the moon serves as a symbol of the Emperor misled by wicked advisers." Two extracts from it conclude this section.

•

Han Yü

The Withered Tree

Leaf and twig are gone from the old tree,
Winds and frosts can harm it no more.
Its hollow belly has room for a man,
Circling ants quest under its peeling bark.
Its single lodger, the toadstool which lives for a morning;
The birds no longer visit in the evening.
But its wood can still spark tinder.
It does not care yet to be only the void at its heart.[1]

TRANSLATED BY A. C. GRAHAM

A Poem on the Stone Drums

[*Shih ku ko*]

Chang handed me this tracing, from the stone drums,
Beseeching me to write a poem on the stone drums.
Tu Fu has gone. Li Po is dead.
What can my poor talent do for the stone drums?
... When the Chou power waned and China was bubbling,
Emperor Hsüan, up in wrath, waved his holy spear
And opened his Great Audience, receiving all the tributes
Of kings and lords who came to him with a tune of clanging
    weapons.
They held a hunt in Ch'i-yang and proved their marksmanship:
Fallen birds and animals were strewn three thousand miles.
And the exploit was recorded, to inform new generations. . . .

---

1. The phrase equates the hollow heart of the tree and the Void Mind
of Buddhism, emptied of desire and illusion.

Cut out of jutting cliffs, these drums made of stone—
On which poets and artisans, all of the first order,
Had indited and chiselled—were set in the deep mountains
To be washed by rain, baked by sun, burned by wildfire,
Eyed by evil spirits, and protected by the gods.
. . . Where can he have found the tracing on this paper?—
True to the original, not altered by a hair,
The meaning deep, the phrases cryptic, difficult to read,
And the style of characters neither square nor tadpole.
Time has not yet vanquished the beauty of these letters—
Looking like sharp daggers that pierce live crocodiles,
Like phoenix-mates dancing, like angels hovering down,
Like trees of jade and coral with interlocking branches,
Like golden cord and iron chain tied together tight,
Like incense-tripods flung in the sea, like dragons mounting heaven.
Historians, gathering ancient poems, forgot to gather these,
To make the two Books of Musical Song[2] more colourful and
      striking;
Confucius journeyed in the west, but not to the Ch'in Kingdom,
He chose our planet and our stars but missed the sun and moon. . . .
I who am fond of antiquity was born too late
And, thinking of these wonderful things, cannot hold back
      my tears. . . .
I remember, when I was awarded my highest degree,
During the first year of Yüan-ho,
How a friend of mine, then at the western camp,
Offered to assist me in removing these old relics.
I bathed and changed, then made my plea to the college president
And urged on him the rareness of these most precious things.
They could be wrapped in rugs, be packed and sent in boxes
And carried on only a few camels: ten stone drums
To grace the Imperial Temple like the Incense-pot of Kao—
Or their lustre and their value would increase a hundred fold,
If the monarch would present them to the university,
Where students could study them and doubtless decipher them,
And multitudes, attracted to the capital of culture
From all corners of the empire, would be quick to gather.

---

2. "Ta-ya" and "Hsiao-ya," two of the major divisions of the *Book of Songs*.

We could scour the moss, pick out the dirt, restore the
    original surface,
And lodge them in a fitting and secure place for ever,
Covered by a massive building with wide eaves,
Where nothing more might happen to them as it had before.
. . . But government officials grow fixed in their ways
And never will initiate beyond old precedent;
So herdboys strike the drums for fire, cows polish horns on them,
With no one to handle them reverentially.
Still aging and decaying, soon they may be effaced.
Six years I have sighed for them, chanting toward the west . . .
The familiar script of Wang Hsi-chih, beautiful though it was,
Could be had, several pages, just for a few white geese!
But now, eight dynasties after the Chou, and all the wars over,
Why should there be nobody caring for these drums?
The empire is at peace, the government free.
Poets again are honoured and Confucians and Mencians . . .
Oh, how may this petition be carried to the throne?
It needs indeed an eloquent flow, like a cataract—
But alas, my voice has broken, in my song of the stone drums,
To a sound of supplication choked with its own tears.

TRANSLATED BY WITTER BYNNER

Linked Verse

A Garland of Roses

Like brocade flushed with sunset color,
Following the spring, they open at summer's touch.

Liu Yü-hsi

Waves of pink weave shadows that catch our eye;
A gentle wind carries the fragrance hither.

P'ei Tu

They take their place beside the eastern pavilion,
Before the stairs they salute the upper terrace.

Hsing-shih

Pale or dark in hue, each has perfect shape;
The buds in secret urge each other to blossom.

Liu Yü-hsi

We mourn the falling petals that cover the ground,
By the embankment lament the oars returning.

P'ei Tu

The fragrance is heavy, moist with rain and dew;
The bright vision stands apart from worldly dust.

Hsing-shih

Their faces are bright as if with rouge,
Sharp-cut, as by a clever housewife's shears.

Po Chü-yi

What to do? the flowers leave me no other plans;
I have only these last few cups of wine.

Chang Chi

TRANSLATED BY DONALD KEENE

Po Chü-yi

A Song of Unending Sorrow

[*Ch'ang hen ko*]

China's Emperor, craving beauty that might shake an empire,
Was on the throne, for many years, searching, never finding,
Till a little child of the Yang clan, hardly even grown,
Bred in an inner chamber, with no one knowing her,
But with graces granted by heaven and not to be concealed,
At last one day was chosen for the imperial household.
If she but turned her head and smiled, there were cast a hundred
    spells,
And the powder and paint of the Six Palaces faded into nothing.
. . . It was early spring. They bathed her in the Flower-Pure Pool,
Which warmed and smoothed the creamy-tinted crystal of her skin,
And, because of her languor, a maid was lifting her
When first the Emperor noticed her and chose her for his bride.
The cloud of her hair, petal of her cheek, gold ripples of her crown
    when she moved,
Were sheltered on spring evenings by warm hibiscus-curtains;
But nights of spring were short and the sun arose too soon,
And the Emperor, from that time forth, forsook his early hearings
And lavished all his time on her with feasts and revelry,
His mistress of the spring, his despot of the night.
There were other ladies in his court, three thousand of rare beauty,
But his favors to three thousand were concentered in one body.
By the time she was dressed in her Golden Chamber, it would be
    almost evening;
And when tables were cleared in the Tower of Jade, she would
    loiter, slow with wine.
Her sisters and brothers all were given titles;
And, because she so illumined and glorified her clan,

She brought to every father, every mother through the empire,
Happiness when a girl was born rather than a boy.
. . . High rose Li Palace, entering blue clouds,
And far and wide the breezes carried magical notes
Of soft song and slow dance, of string and bamboo music.
The Emperor's eyes could never gaze on her enough—
Till war-drums, booming from Yü-yang, shocked the whole earth
And broke the tunes of "The Rainbow Skirt and the Feathered Coat."
The Forbidden City, the nine-tiered palace, loomed in the dust
From thousands of horses and chariots headed southwest.
The imperial flag opened the way, now moving and now pausing—
But thirty miles from the capital, beyond the western gate,
The men of the army stopped, not one of them would stir
Till under their horses' hoofs they might trample those
    moth-eyebrows . . .
Flowery hairpins fell to the ground, no one picked them up,
And a green and white jade hair-tassel and a yellow-gold hair-bird.
The Emperor could not save her, he could only cover his face.
And later when he turned to look, the place of blood and tears
Was hidden in a yellow dust blown by a cold wind.
. . . At the cleft of the Dagger-Tower Trail they crisscrossed through
    a cloud-line
Under O-mei Mountain. The last few came.
Flags and banners lost their color in the fading sunlight . . .
But as waters of Shu are always green and its mountains always blue,
So changeless was his majesty's love and deeper than the days.
He stared at the desolate moon from his temporary palace,
He heard bell-notes in the evening rain, cutting at his breast.
And when heaven and earth resumed their round and the dragon-car
    faced home,
The Emperor clung to the spot and would not turn away
From the soil along the Ma-wei slope, under which was buried
That memory, that anguish. Where was her jade-white face?
Ruler and lords, when eyes would meet, wept upon their coats
As they rode, with loose rein, slowly eastward, back to the capital.
. . . The pools, the gardens, the palace, all were just as before,
The Lake T'ai-yi hibiscus, the Wei-yang Palace willows;
But a petal was like her face and a willow-leaf her eyebrow—
And what could he do but cry whenever he looked at them?

. . . Peach-trees and plum-trees blossomed, in the winds of spring;
Lakka-foliage fell to the ground, after autumn rains;
The Western and Southern Palaces were littered with late grasses,
And the steps were mounded with red leaves that no one
      swept away.
Her Pear-Garden Players became white-haired
And the eunuchs thin-eyebrowed in her Court of Pepper-Trees;
Over the throne flew fireflies, while he brooded in the twilight.
He would lengthen the lamp-wick to its end and still could never
      sleep.
Bell and drum would slowly toll the dragging night-hours
And the River of Stars grow sharp in the sky, just before dawn,
And the porcelain mandarin-ducks on the roof grow thick with
      morning frost
And his covers of kingfisher-blue feel lonelier and colder
With the distance between life and death year after year;
And yet no beloved spirit ever visited his dreams.
. . . At Ling-ch'ün lived a Taoist priest who was a guest of heaven,
Able to summon spirits by his concentrated mind.
And people were so moved by the Emperor's constant brooding
That they besought the Taoist priest to see if he could find her.
He opened his way in space and clove the ether like lightning
Up to heaven, under the earth, looking everywhere.
Above, he searched the Green Void, below, the Yellow Spring;
But he failed, in either place, to find the one he looked for.
And then he heard accounts of an enchanted isle at sea,
A part of the intangible and incorporeal world,
With pavilions and fine towers in the five-colored air,
And of exquisite immortals moving to and fro,
And of one among them—whom they called The Ever True—
With a face of snow and flowers resembling hers he sought.
So he went to the West Hall's gate of gold and knocked at the
      jasper door
And asked a girl, called Morsel-of-Jade, to tell The Doubly-Perfect.
And the lady, at news of an envoy from the Emperor of China,
Was startled out of dreams in her nine-flowered canopy.
She pushed aside her pillow, dressed, shook away sleep,
And opened the pearly shade and then the silver screen.

Her cloudy hair-dress hung on one side because of her great haste,
And her flower-cap was loose when she came along the terrace,
While a light wind filled her cloak and fluttered with her motion
As though she danced "The Rainbow Skirt and the Feathered Coat."
And the tear-drops drifting down her sad white face
Were like a rain in spring on the blossom of the pear.
But love glowed deep within her eyes when she bade him thank
    her liege,
Whose form and voice had been strange to her ever since their
    parting—
Since happiness had ended at the Court of the Bright Sun,
And moons and dawns had become long in Fairy-Mountain Palace.
But when she turned her face and looked down toward the earth
And tried to see the capital, there were only fog and dust.
So she took out, with emotion, the pledges he had given
And, through his envoy, sent him back a shell box and gold hairpin,
But kept one branch of the hairpin, and one side of the box,
Breaking the gold of the hairpin, breaking the shell of the box;
"Our souls belong together," she said, "like this gold and this shell—
Somewhere, sometime, on earth or in heaven, we shall surely meet."
And she sent him, by his messenger, a sentence reminding him
Of vows which had been known only to their two hearts:
"On the seventh day of the Seventh-month, in the Palace of
    Long Life,
We told each other secretly in the quiet midnight world
That we wished to fly in heaven, two birds with the wings of one,
And to grow together on the earth, two branches of one tree."
. . . Earth endures, heaven endures; sometime both shall end,
While this unending sorrow goes on and on for ever.

TRANSLATED BY WITTER BYNNER

On the Lotuses Newly Planted at the Municipal Headquarters

A muddy ditch filled with dirty water,
And on the water leaves, disk on disk.
The moment I saw them I heaved a long sigh,

For I knew they were lotus brought from the Eastern Brook.
Up from below comes green slime to foul them;
Never again will they smell fresh and sweet.
Down from above drops red dust to soil them;
Never again will their colour be clear and bright.
It is not only things whose nature is thus;
In human matters it also must be so.
It is better for a man to be utterly cast away
Than torn from his roots and put where he is not in place.
You in the days when you grew in the Eastern Brook—
Your flowers and leaves bewitched the blue stream.
Now, wrested from the scene to which you belong,
In front of a government building you wilt and pine.

The Temple

[*Yu Wu-chen-ssu shih*]

Autumn: the ninth year of Yüan-ho;
The eighth month, and the moon swelling her arc.
It was then I travelled to the Temple of Wu-chen,
A temple terraced on Wang Shun's Hill.
While still the mountain was many leagues away,
Of scurrying waters we heard the plash and fret.
From here the traveller, leaving carriage and horse,
Begins to wade through the shallows of the Blue Stream,
His hand pillared on a green holly-staff,
His feet treading the torrent's white stones.
A strange quiet stole on ears and eyes,
That knew no longer the blare of the human world.
From mountain-foot gazing at mountain-top,
Now we doubted if indeed it could be climbed;
Who had guessed that a path deep hidden there
Twisting and bending crept to the topmost brow?
Under the flagstaff we made our first halt;
Next we rested in the shadow of the Stone Shrine.
The shrine-room was scarce a cubit long,
With doors and windows unshuttered and unbarred.

I peered down, but could not see the dead;
Stalactites hung like a woman's hair.
Waked from sleep, a pair of white bats
Fled from the coffin with a whirr of snowy wings.
I turned away, and saw the Temple gate—
Scarlet eaves flanked by steeps of green;
'Twas as though a hand had ripped the mountain-side
And filled the cleft with a temple's walls and towers.
Within the gate, no level ground;
Little ground, but much empty sky.
Cells and cloisters, terraces and spires
High and low, followed the jut of the hill.
On rocky plateaux with no earth to hold
Were trees and shrubs, gnarled and very lean.
Roots and stems stretched to grip the stone;
Humped and bent, they writhed like a coiling snake.
In broken ranks pine and cassia stood,
Through the four seasons forever shady-green.
On tender twigs and delicate branches breathing
A quiet music played like strings in the wind.
Never pierced by the light of sun or moon,
Green locked with green, shade clasping shade.
A hidden bird sometimes softly sings;
Like a cricket's chirp sounds its muffled song.

At the Strangers' Arbour a while we stayed our steps;
We sat down, but had no mind to rest.
In a little while we had opened the northern door.
Ten thousand leagues suddenly stretched at our feet!
Brushing the eaves, shredded rainbows swept;
Circling the beams, clouds spun and whirled.
Through red sunlight white rain fell;
Azure and storm swam in a blended stream.
In a wild green clustered grasses and trees,
The eye's orbit swallowed the plain of Ch'in.
Wei River was too small to see;
The Mounds of Han, littler than a clenched fist.
I looked back; a line of red fence,

Broken and twisting, marked the way we had trod.
Far below, toiling one by one
Later climbers straggled on the face of the hill.

Straight before me were many Treasure Towers,
Whose wind-bells at the four corners sang.
At door and window, cornice and architrave
A thick cluster of gold and green-jade.
Some say that here the Buddha Kāśyapa
Long ago quitted Life and Death.
Still they keep his iron begging-bowl,
With the furrow of his fingers chiselled deep at the base.
To the east there opens the Jade Image Hall,
Where white Buddhas sit like serried trees.
We shook from our garments the journey's grime and dust,
And bowing worshipped those faces of frozen snow
Whose white cassocks like folded hoar-frost hung,
Whose beaded crowns glittered like a shower of hail.
We looked closer; surely Spirits willed
This handicraft, never chisel carved!

Next we climbed to the Chamber of Kuan-yin;
From afar we sniffed its odours of sandal-wood.
At the top of the steps each doffed his shoes;
With bated stride we crossed the Jasper Hall.
The Jewelled Mirror on six pillars propped,
The Four Seats cased in hammered gold
Through the black night glowed with beams of their own,
Nor had we need to light candle or lamp.
These many treasures in concert nodded and swayed—
Banners of coral, pendants of cornaline.
When the wind came jewels chimed and sang
Softly, softly like the music of Paradise.
White pearls like frozen dewdrops hanging,
Dark rubies spilt like clots of blood,
Spangled and sown on the Buddha's twisted hair,
Together fashioned his Sevenfold Jewel-crown.
In twin vases of pallid tourmaline
(Their colour colder than the waters of an autumn stream)

The calcined relics of Buddha's Body rest—
Rounded pebbles, smooth as the Specular Stone.
A jade flute, by angels long ago
Borne as a gift to the Garden of Jetavan!
It blows a music sweet as the crane's song
That Spirits of Heaven earthward well might draw.

It was at autumn's height,
The fifteenth day and the moon's orbit full.
Wide I flung the three eastern gates;
A golden spectre walked at the chapel-door!
And now with moonbeams jewel-beams strove,
In freshness and beauty darting a crystal light
That cooled the spirit and limbs of all it touched,
Nor night-long needed they to rest.
At dawn I sought the road to the Southern Tope,
Where wild bamboos nodded in clustered grace.
In the lonely forest no one crossed my path;
Beside me faltered a cold butterfly.
Mountain fruits whose names I did not know
With their prodigal bushes hedged the pathway in;
The hungry here copious food had found;
Idly, I plucked, to test sour and sweet.

South of the road, the Spirit of the Blue Dell,
With his green umbrella and white paper pence!
When the year is closing, the people are ordered to grow,
As herbs of offering, marsil and motherwort;
So sacred the place, that never yet was stained
Its pure earth with sacrificial blood.

In a high cairn four or five rocks
Dangerously heaped, deep-scarred and heeling—
With what purpose did he that made the World
Pile them here at the eastern corner of the cliff!
Their slippery flank no foot has marked,
But mosses stipple like a flowered writing-scroll.
I came to the cairn, I climbed it right to the top;
Beneath my feet a measureless chasm dropped.

My eyes were dizzy, hand and knee quaked—
I did not dare bend my head and look.
A boisterous wind rose from under the rocks,
Seized me with it and tore the ground from my feet.
My shirt and robe fanned like mighty wings,
And wide-spreading bore me like a bird to the sky.
High about me, triangular and sharp,
Like a cluster of sword-points many summits rose.
The white mist that struck them in its airy course
They tore asunder, and carved a patch of blue.

And now the sun was sinking in the north-west;
His evening beams from a crimson globe he shed,
Till far beyond the great fields of green
His sulphurous disk suddenly down he drove.

And now the moon was rising in the south-east;
In waves of coolness the night air flowed.
From the grey bottom of the hundred-fathom pool
Shines out the image of the moon's golden disk!
Blue as its name, the Lan River flows
Singing and plashing forever day and night.
I gazed down; like a green finger-ring
In winding circuits it follows the curves of the hill,
Sometimes spreading to a wide, lazy stream,
Sometimes striding to a foamy cataract.
Out from the deepest and clearest pool of all,
In a strange froth the Dragon's-spittle[1] flows.

I bent down; a dangerous ladder of stones
Paved beneath me a sheer and dizzy path.
I gripped the ivy, I walked on fallen trees,
Tracking the monkeys who came to drink at the stream.
Like a whirl of snowflakes the startled herons rose,
In damask dances the red sturgeon leapt.
For a while I rested, then plunging in the cool stream,

---

1. Ambergris.

From my weary body I washed the stains away.
Deep or shallow, all was crystal clear;
I watched through the water my own thighs and feet.
Content I gazed at the stream's clear bed;
Wondered, but knew not, whence its waters flowed.

The eastern bank with rare stones is rife;
In serried courses the azure malachite,
That outward turns a smooth, glossy face;
In its deep core secret diamonds lie.
Pien of Ch'u died long ago,
And rare gems are often cast aside.
Sometimes a radiance leaks from the hill by night
To link its beams with the brightness of moon and stars.

At the central dome, where the hills highest rise,
The sky is pillared on a column of green jade;
Where even the spotty lizard cannot climb
Can I, a man, foothold hope to find?
In the top is hollowed the White Lotus Lake;
With purple cusps the clear waves are crowned.
The name I heard, but the place I could not reach;
Beyond the region of mortal things it lies.

And standing here, a flat rock I saw
Cubit-square, like a great paving-stone,
Midway up fastened in the cliff-wall;
And down below it, a thousand-foot drop.
Here they say that a Master in ancient days
Sat till he conquered the concepts of Life and Death.
The place is called the Settled Heart Stone;
By aged men the tale is still told.

I turned back to the Shrine of Fairies' Tryst;
Thick creepers covered its old walls.
Here it was that a mortal long ago
On new-grown wings flew to the dark sky;
Westward a garden of agaric and rue

Faces the terrace where his magic herbs were dried.
And sometimes still on clear moonlit nights
In the sky is heard a yellow-crane's voice.

I turned and sought the Painted Dragon Hall,
Where the bearded figures of two ancient men
By the Holy Lectern at sermon-time are seen
In gleeful worship to nod their hoary heads;
Who, going home to their cave beneath the river,
Of weather-dragons the writhing shapes assume.
When rain is coming they puff a white smoke
In front of the steps, from a round hole in the stone.

Once a priest who copied the Holy Books
(Of purpose dauntless and body undefiled)
Loved yonder pigeons, that far beyond the clouds
Fly in flocks beating a thousand wings.
They came and dropped him water in his writing-bowl;
Then sipped afresh in the river under the rocks.
Each day thrice they went and came,
Nor ever once missed their wonted time.
When the Book was finished they sent for a holy priest,
A disciple of his, named Yang-nan.
He sang the hymns of the Lotus Blossom Book.
Again and again, a thousand, a million times.
His body perished, but his mouth still spoke,
The tongue resembling a red lotus-flower.
To-day this relic is no longer shown;
But they still treasure the pyx in which it lies.

On a plastered wall are frescoes from the hand of Wu,
Whose pencil-colours never-fading glow.
On a white screen is writing by the master Ch'u,
The tones subtle, as the day it first dried.

Magical prospects, monuments divine—
Now all were visited.
Here we had tarried five nights and days;
Yet homeward now with loitering footsteps trod.

I, that a man of the wild hills was born,
Floundering fell into the web of the World's net.
Caught in its trammels, they forced me to study books;
Twitched and tore me down the path of public life.
Soon I rose to be Bachelor of Arts;
In the Record Office, in the Censorate I sat.
My simple bluntness did not suit the times;
A profitless servant, I drew the royal pay.
The sense of this made me always ashamed,
And every pleasure a deep brooding dimmed.
To little purpose I sapped my heart's strength,
Till seeming age shrank my youthful frame.
From the very hour I doffed belt and cap
I marked how with them sorrow slank away.
But now that I wander in the freedom of streams and hills
My heart to its folly comfortably yields.
Like a wild deer that has torn the hunter's net
I range abroad by no halters barred.
Like a captive fish loosed into the Great Sea
To my marble basin I shall not ever return.
My body girt in the hermit's single dress,
My hand holding the Book of Chuang Chou,
On these hills at last I am come to dwell,
Loosed forever from the shackles of a trim world.
I have lived in labour forty years and more;
If Life's remnant vacantly I spend,
Seventy being our span, then thirty years
Of idleness are still left to live.

The Red Cockatoo

Sent as a present from Annam—
A red cockatoo.
Coloured like the peach-tree blossom,
Speaking with the speech of men.
And they did to it what is always done
To the learned and eloquent.
They took a cage with stout bars
And shut it up inside.

On His Baldness

At dawn I sighed to see my hairs fall;
At dusk I sighed to see my hairs fall.
For I dreaded the time when the last lock should go . . .
They are all gone and I do not mind at all!
I have done with that cumbrous washing and getting dry;
My tiresome comb for ever is laid aside.
Best of all, when the weather is hot and wet,
To have no top-knot weighing down on one's head!
I put aside my messy cloth wrap;
I have got rid of my dusty tasselled fringe.
In a silver jar I have stored a cold stream,
On my bald pate I trickle a ladle full.
Like one baptized with the Water of Buddha's Law,
I sit and receive this cool, cleansing joy.
Now I know why the priest who seeks Repose
Frees his heart by first shaving his head.

To a Talkative Guest

The town visitor's easy talk flows in an endless stream;
The country host's quiet thoughts ramble timidly on.
"I beg you, Sir, do not tell me about things at Ch'ang-an;
For you entered just when my lute was tuned and lying balanced
    on my knees."

The Poem on the Wall[1]

My clumsy poem on the inn-wall none cared to see;
With bird-droppings and moss's growth the letters were
    blotched away.
There came a guest with heart so full, that though a page to
    the Throne,
He did not grudge with his broidered coat to wipe off the dust,
    and read.

TRANSLATED BY ARTHUR WALEY

1. Yüan Chen wrote that on his way to exile he had discovered a poem
inscribed by Po Chü-yi on the wall of the Lo-k'ou Inn.

Yüan Chen

Temporary Palace

Palace of a few days' visit, long years crumbling,
The gardens blossom red into the silence.
And here a palace maiden, white-haired now,
Takes her ease and tells her tales of the emperor.

TRANSLATED BY CYRIL BIRCH

The Pitcher

[*Meng ching*]

I dreamt I climbed to a high, high plain;
And on the plain I found a deep well.
My throat was dry with climbing and I longed to drink,
And my eyes were eager to look into the cool shaft.
I walked round it, I looked right down;
I saw my image mirrored on the face of the pool.
An earthen pitcher was sinking into the black depths;
There was no rope to pull it to the well-head.
I was strangely troubled lest the pitcher should be lost,
And started wildly running to look for help.
From village to village I scoured that high plain;
The men were gone; fierce dogs snarled.
I came back and walked weeping round the well;
Faster and faster the blinding tears flowed—
Till my own sobbing suddenly woke me up;
My room was silent, no one in the house stirred.
The flame of my candle flickered with a green smoke;
The tears I had shed glittered in the candle-light.
A bell sounded; I knew it was the midnight-chime;

I sat up in bed and tried to arrange my thoughts;
The plain in my dream was the graveyard at Ch'ang-an,
Those hundred acres of untilled land.
The soil heavy and the mounds heaped high;
And the dead below them laid in deep troughs.
Deep are the troughs, yet sometimes dead men
Find their way to the world above the grave.
And to-night my love who died long ago
Came into my dream as the pitcher sunk in the well.
That was why the tears suddenly streamed from my eyes,
Streamed from my eyes and fell on the collar of my dress.

TRANSLATED BY ARTHUR WALEY

Li Ho

The Grave of Little Su

> *I ride a coach with lacquered sides,*
> *My love rides a dark piebald horse.*
> *Where shall we bind our hearts as one?*
> *On West Mound, beneath the pines and cypresses.*

> (*Ballad ascribed to the singing girl*
> *Little Su, c. 500*)

Dew on the secret orchid
Like screaming eyes.
Nowhere, the hearts bound as one.
Evanescent flowers I cannot bear to cut.
Grass like a cushion,
The pine like a parasol;
The wind is a skirt,
The waters are tinkling pendants.
A coach with lacquered sides
Waits for someone in the evening.
The cold green will-o'-the-wisp
Squanders its brightness.
Beneath West Mound
The wind puffs the rain.

The Northern Cold

The sky glows one side black, three sides purple.
The Yellow River's ice closes, fish and dragons die.
Bark three inches thick cracks across the grain;
Carts a hundred piculs heavy mount the River's waters.
Flowers of frost on the grass are as big as coins,
Brandished swords will not pierce the foggy sky,

Flying ice-flakes crash in the swirling seas,
And cascades hang noiseless in the mountains, rainbows of jade.

Don't Go Out of the Door

Heaven is dark,
Earth is secret.
The nine-headed monster eats our souls,
Frosts and snows snap our bones.
Incited dogs snarl, sniff around us,
And lick their paws, partial to the smell of the virtuous,
Till the end of all afflictions, when God sends his chariot to fetch us,
And the sword starred with jewels and the yoke of yellow gold.

I straddle my horse but there is no way back,
On the lake which swamped Li-yang the waves are huge
                as mountains,
Deadly dragons stare at me, jostle the metal wheels,
Lions and chimaeras spit from slavering mouths.
Pao Chiao parted the ferns and for ever closed his eyes,
Yen Hui at twenty-nine was white at the temples;
Not that Yen Hui had thinning blood,
Nor that Pao Chiao had offended heaven;
Heaven dreaded the time when teeth would rend and gnaw them,
For this and no other reason made it so.
Plain though it is, I fear that still you doubt me.
Witness the man who raged at the wall as he carved his
                questions to heaven!

                        TRANSLATED BY A. C. GRAHAM

Ancient Arrowhead

Lacquer flakes, bone-dust and water
                made this vermilion colour;
And fearful, ancient stains
                bloomed on this bronze arrowhead.
Its white feathers and gold rings
                have now gone with the rain,
Leaving only this angular wolf's tooth.

Riding the plain with a pair of horses,
I found it, east of the courier station,
                among the weeds.
The long wind shortened the day,
                while a few stars shivered,
And damp clouds like black banners
                were hoisted in the night.

Thin devils and ghosts sang
                to the left and right.
I offered them pressed mutton and cream,
And crickets were silent, wild geese sick and reeds turned red.
The spirit of the whirlwind spat emerald fire
                to bid me farewell.

I stowed it away with my tears.
Its point, crimson and crooked,
                once bit into flesh.
In various districts, young riders ask me
Why I don't sell it to buy firewood.

The Bronze Bird Platform

A lovely young girl brings up a jar of wine.
The autumnal scene extends a thousand miles.
The stone horse lies in the early mist—
How can I describe the sadness?
The singing now is faint
Because a wind comes up out of the trees.
Her skirt, long and heavy, presses against the floor,
And her tearful eyes are fixed on the flowers on the table.

Magic String

When the witch pours her wine,
                clouds gather in the sky;
In the jade stove,
                fragrant coal burns.

Sea-gods and mountain spirits
        all come to take up their seats.
Paper coins crackle, turn into ashes
        and dance in the whirlwind.
She plucks the lute made of love-sickness wood
        and adorned with a golden phoenix,
She mutters and beats the time
        by screwing up her eyebrows:
Come, Stars and Ghosts, and enjoy the feast.
When spectres eat,
        man shivers.
The sun sinks below the Chung-nan Mountains
And the spirits become visible yet invisible.
Only her face reflects
        their anger or their pleasure.
Then a myriad chariots make ready
        for their departure.

TRANSLATED BY C. J. CHEN AND MICHAEL BULLOCK

Lu T'ung

Two Extracts from "The Eclipse of the Moon"

[*Yüeh shih shih*]

1

> The fifth year of the new Son of Heaven,
> The cyclic year *keng-yin;*
> The season when the handle of the Dipper sticks into Aries,
> The month when the pitch-pipe is Yellow Bell.
>
> Ten thousand forest trees stood rigid in the night:
> The cold air tensed and strained, solid and windless.
> The glittering silver dish came up from the bottom of the sea,
> Lighting as it came the east of my thatched cottage.
> On heaven's smooth and violet surface the freezing light
>   stopped flowing:
> Rays from the ice pierced and crossed the cold glimmer of moonrise.
>
> > At first it seemed that a white lotus
> > Had floated up from the Dragon King's palace.
> > But this night, the fifteenth of the eighth month,
> > Was not like other nights;
> > For now a strange thing came to pass:
> > Something began to eat into the wheel.
>
> The wheel was as though a strong man hacked off pieces with an axe,
> The cassia was like a snowy peak dragged and tumbled by the wind.
> The mirror refined a hundredfold
> Till it shone right through to the gall
> Suddenly was buried in cold ash:
> The pearl of the fiery dragon
> Which flew up out of its brain
> Went back into the oyster's womb.
> Ring and disc crumbled away as I watched,

Darkness smeared the whole sky like soot,
Rubbing out in an instant the last tracks,
And then it seemed that for thousands of ages the sky would
      never open.
    Who would guess that a thing so magical
    Could be so discomfited?
    The stars came out like sprinkled sand
    Disputing which could shine the brightest,
    And the dim lamps lit by the servants
    With a dusky glow like tortoiseshell
    This night spat flames as long as the rainbow
    Shooting from the houses through holes and cracks into
      a thousand roads.
    2[1]

Think how once when Yao was our Heaven
Ten suns burned the Nine Regions.
Metals fused into streaming quicksilver,
Jades cooked to charred cinnabar,
The baking universe became a kiln.
A hundred cares oppressed Yao's heart,
God saw the cares of Yao's heart,
And in sudden fury let loose a mighty torrent,
Planning to drown in the flood the monsters of the nine new suns.
High up into heaven the suns ran, out of reach of the flood;
There was nothing to see in the myriad kingdoms but teeming
    babies growing fish's heads.
At this time nine charioteers drove the nine suns,
Each with an ensign in his hand and flourishing token streamers.
Harnessed to the chariots were six times nine, fifty-four young and
    scaly hornless dragons,
Lightning-swift, at the nine fiery shafts.
    If then you had bitten jagged edges across the wheels,
Grabbed reins and ropes, and scratched and clawed,
Crammed them rumbling down into your gullet,
Crimson scales and fiery birds stinging your mouth with burns,
Wings and back-fins upended and sideways sucked down with a
    gurgling noise,

---

1. Addressed to the frog which swallows the moon in an eclipse.

Propping your belly up as it bulged with lumps like mountains
  and hillocks,
Then you could have gorged yourself to death and finished
  with thievery,
Not only stuffed your hungry pit
But also loosed Yao's heart of cares.
It rankles that when you should have eaten
You buried your head and had no appetite;
But now that you should not eat
With lips stretched wide and gaping jaws you eat insatiably.
You have fed your disobedience by eating the eye of Heaven.
How long before the God on High ordains your execution?

TRANSLATED BY A. C. GRAHAM

T'ang Short Stories

The twentieth-century writer and critic Lu Hsün considered the men of the T'ang period to be the first consciously to practise the art of fiction. Such authors as those of the present section were no mere entertainers but scholars and poets—Yüan Chen we have already seen, an outstanding poet of the dynasty and close friend of Po Chü-yi. The language of the stories is the classical narrative style, often reminiscent of biographical entries in the standard histories. It is a plain style, mostly free from rhetorical devices, but capable of a powerful economy: witness the climactic moment of "The Curly-bearded Hero," the stranger's first glimpse of the man destined for the throne: "at sight of the youth his will had died within him." This is conveyed in the original by four words only, each a monosyllable: "saw him, heart died."

Yüan Chen's is the most famous of all Chinese love stories, and the most subtle and profound, though it was coarsened as well as elaborated when it was reworked for the stage in the Yüan period play Romance of the West Chamber (Hsi-hsiang chi). The incidents are believed to be autobiographical, the author only half hiding his own identity behind the figure of the young student Chang.

For "The Story of Miss Li" we follow the traditional attribution to Po Hsing-chien, the brother of the poet Po Chü-yi.

"Curly-beard" is something of a cri de coeur: in an age of confused rivalries presaging the collapse of the once-mighty dynasty, Tu Kuang-t'ing (850-933) harks back to the years of its founding to depict his ideal hero. This man, the stranger who is entirely fictitious and is given only the name Chang, personifies the Con-

fucian virtue of "yielding." Ambitious for the throne, he yet recognizes in the youth Li Shih-min the "man marked out from his fellows," the future emperor. In consequence of this recognition, Chang cedes all his treasure to Li Shih-min's lieutenant and makes a graceful exit from the contest.

•

Yüan Chen

The Story of Ts'ui Ying-ying

[*Ying-ying chuan*]

During the Cheng-yüan period [785-805] of the T'ang dynasty there
lived a man called Chang. His nature was gentle and refined, and
his person of great beauty. But his deeper feelings were absolutely
held in restraint, and he would indulge in no license. Sometimes
his friends took him to a party and he would try to join in their
frolics; but when the rest were shouting and scuffling their hardest,
Chang only pretended to take his share. For he could never overcome his shyness. So it came about that though already twenty-
three, he had not yet enjoyed a woman's beauty. To those who
questioned him he answered, "It is not such as Master Teng-t'u
who are true lovers of beauty, for they are merely profligates. I
consider myself a lover of beauty, who happens never to have met
with it. And I am of this opinion because I know that, in other
things, whatever is beautiful casts its spell upon me; so that I cannot be devoid of feeling." His questioners only laughed.

About this time Chang went to Puchow. Some two miles east
of the town there is a temple called the P'u-chiu-ssu, and here he
took up his lodging. Now it happened that at this time the widow
of a certain Ts'ui was returning to Ch'ang-an. She passed through
Puchow on the way and stayed at the same temple.

This lady was born of the Cheng family and Chang's mother
was also a Cheng. He unravelled their relationship and found that
they were second-cousins.

This year General Hun Chan died at Puchow. There was a
certain Colonel Ting Wen-ya who ill-treated his troops. The soldiers
accordingly made Hun Chan's funeral the occasion of a mutiny, and
began to plunder the town. The Ts'ui family had brought with them
much valuable property and many slaves. Subjected to this sudden

danger when far from home, they had no one from whom they could seek protection.

Now it happened that Chang had been friendly with the political party to which the commander at Puchow belonged. At his request a guard was sent to the temple and no disorder took place there. A few days afterwards the Civil Commissioner Tu Chio was ordered by the emperor to take over the command of the troops. The mutineers then laid down their arms.

The widow Cheng was very sensible of the service which Chang had rendered. She therefore provided dainties and invited him to a banquet in the middle hall. At table she turned to him and said, "I, your cousin, a lonely and widowed relict, had young ones in my care. If we had fallen into the hands of the soldiery, I could not have helped them. Therefore the lives of my little boy and young daughter were saved by your protection, and they owe you eternal gratitude. I will now cause them to kneel before you, their merciful cousin, that they may thank you for your favours." First she sent for her son, Huan-lang, who was about ten years old, a handsome and gentle child. Then she called to her daughter, Ying-ying: "Come and bow to your cousin. Your cousin saved your life." For a long while she would not come, saying that she was not well. The widow grew angry and cried, "Your cousin saved your life. But for his help, you would now be a prisoner. How can you treat him so rudely?"

At last the girl came in, dressed in everyday clothes, with a look of deep unhappiness on her face. She had not put on any ornaments. Her hair hung down in coils, the black of her two eyebrows joined, her cheeks were not rouged. But her features were of exquisite beauty and shone with an almost dazzling lustre.

Chang bowed to her, amazed. She sat down by her mother's side and looked all the time towards her, turning from him with a fixed stare of aversion, as though she could not endure his presence.

He asked how old she was. The widow answered, "She was born in the year of the present emperor's reign that was a year of the Rat, and now it is the year of the Dragon in the period Chengyüan [800]. So she must be seventeen years old."

Chang tried to engage her in conversation, but she would not answer, and soon the dinner was over. He was passionately in love with her and wanted to tell her so, but could find no way.

Ying-ying had a maid-servant called Hung-niang, whom Chang sometimes met and greeted. Once he stopped her and was beginning to tell her of his love for her mistress, but she was frightened and ran away. Then Chang was sorry he had not kept silence.

Next day he met Hung-niang again, but was embarrassed and did not say what was in his mind. But this time the maid herself broached the subject and said to Chang, "Master, I dare not tell her what you told me, or even hint at it. But since your mother was a kinswoman of the Ts'ui, why do you not seek my mistress's hand on that plea?"

Chang said, "Since I was a child in arms, my nature has been averse to intimacy. Sometimes I have idled with wearers of silk and gauze, but my fancy was never once detained. I little thought that in the end I should be entrapped.

"Lately at the banquet I could scarcely contain myself; and since then, when I walk, I forget where I am going and when I eat, I forget to finish my meal, and do not know how to endure the hours from dawn to dusk.

"If we were to get married through a matchmaker and perform the ceremonies of Sending Presents and Asking Names, it would take many months, and by that time you would have to look for me 'in the dried-fish shop.' What is the use of giving me such advice as that?"

The maid replied, "My mistress clings steadfastly to her chastity, and even an equal could not trip her with lewd talk. Much less may she be won through the stratagems of a maid-servant. But she is skilled in composition, and often when she has made a poem or essay, she is restless and dissatisfied for a long while after. You must try to provoke her with a love-poem. There is no other way."

Chang was delighted and at once composed two Spring Poems to send her. Hung-niang took them away and came back the same evening with a coloured tablet, which she gave to Chang, saying, "This is from my mistress." It bore the title "The Bright Moon of the Fifteenth Night." The words ran:

To wait for the moon I am sitting in the western parlour;
To greet the wind, I have left the door ajar.

When a flower's shadow stirred and brushed the wall,
For a moment I thought it the shadow of a lover coming.

Chang could not doubt her meaning. That night was the fourth
after the first decade of the second month. Beside the eastern wall
of Ying-ying's apartments there grew an apricot-tree; by climbing
it one could cross the wall. On the next night (which was the night
of the full moon) Chang used the tree as a ladder and crossed the
wall. He went straight to the western parlour and found the door
ajar. Hung-niang lay asleep on the bed. He woke her, and she cried
in a voice of astonishment, "Master Chang, what are you doing
here?" Chang answered, half-truly: "Your mistress's letter invited
me. Tell her I have come." Hung-niang soon returned, whispering,
"She is coming, she is coming." Chang was both delighted and
surprised, thinking that his salvation was indeed at hand.

At last Ying-ying entered.

Her dress was sober and correct, and her face was stern. She
at once began to reprimand Chang, saying, "I am grateful for the
service which you rendered to my family. You gave support to my
dear mother when she was at a loss how to save her little boy and
young daughter. How came you then to send me a wicked message
by the hand of a low maid-servant? In protecting me from the
license of others, you acted nobly. But now that you wish to make
me a partner to your own licentious desires, you are asking me to
accept one wrong in exchange for another.

"How was I to repel this advance? I would gladly have hidden
your letter, but it would have been immoral to harbour a record
of illicit proposals. Had I shown it to my mother, I should ill have
requited the debt we owe you. Were I to entrust a message of re-
fusal to a servant or concubine, I feared it might not be truly
delivered. I thought of writing a letter to tell you what I felt;
but I was afraid I might not be able to make you understand.
So I sent those trivial verses, that I might be sure of your coming.
I have no cause to be ashamed of an irregularity which had no
other object but the preservation of my chastity."

With these words she vanished. Chang remained for a long
while petrified with astonishment. At last he climbed back over
the wall and went home in despair.

Several nights after this he was lying asleep near the verandah, when someone suddenly woke him. He rose with a startled sigh and found that Hung-niang was there, with bed-clothes under her arm and a pillow in her hand. She shook Chang, saying, "She is coming, she is coming. Why are you asleep?" Then she arranged the bedclothes and pillow and went away.

Chang sat up and rubbed his eyes. For a long while he thought he must be dreaming. But he assumed a respectful attitude and waited.

Suddenly Hung-niang came back, bringing her mistress with her. Ying-ying, this time, was languid and flushed, yielding and wanton in her air, as though her strength could scarcely support her limbs. Her former severity had utterly disappeared.

That night was the eighth of the second decade. The crystal beams of the sinking moon twinkled secretly across their bed. Chang, in a strange exaltation, half-believed that a fairy had come to him, and not a child of mortal men.

At last the temple bell sounded, dawn glimmered in the sky and Hung-niang came back to fetch her mistress away. Ying-ying turned on her side with a pretty cry, and followed her maid to the door.

The whole night she had not spoken a word.

Chang rose when it was half-dark, still thinking that perhaps it had been a dream. But when it grew light, he saw her powder on his arm and smelt her perfume in his clothes. A tear she had shed still glittered on the mattress.

For more than ten days afterwards he did not see her again. During this time he began to make a poem called "Meeting a Fairy," in thirty couplets. It was not yet finished, when he chanced to meet Hung-niang in the road. He asked her to take the poem to Ying-ying.

After this Ying-ying let him come to her, and for a month or more he crept out at dawn and in at dusk, the two of them living together in that western parlour of which I spoke before.

Chang often asked her what her mother thought of him. Ying-ying said, "I know she would not oppose my will. So why should we not get married at once?"

Soon afterwards, Chang had to go to the capital. Before starting he tenderly informed her of his departure. She did not reproach him, but her face showed pitiable distress. On the night before he started, he was not able to see her.

After spending a few months in the west, Chang returned to Puchow and again lodged for several months in the same building as the Ts'ui family. He made many attempts to see Ying-ying alone, but she would not let him do so. Remembering that she was fond of calligraphy and verse, he frequently sent her his own compositions, but she scarcely glanced at them.

It was characteristic of her that when any situation was at its acutest point, she appeared quite unconscious of it. She talked glibly, but would seldom answer a question. She expected absolute devotion, but herself gave no encouragement.

Sometimes when she was in the depth of despair, she would affect all the while to be quite indifferent. It was rarely possible to know from her face whether she was pleased or sorry.

One night Chang came upon her unawares when she was playing on the zither, with a touch full of passion. But when she saw him coming, she stopped playing. This incident increased his infatuation.

Soon afterwards, it became time for him to compete in the Literary Examinations, and he was obliged once more to set out for the western capital.

The evening before his departure, he sat in deep despondency by Ying-ying's side, but did not try again to tell her of his love. Nor had he told her that he was going away, but she seemed to have guessed it, and with submissive face and gentle voice she said to him softly, "Those whom a man leads astray, he will in the end abandon. It must be so, and I will not reproach you. You deigned to corrupt me and now you deign to leave me. That is all. And your vows of 'faithfulness till death'—they too are cancelled. There is no need for you to grieve at this parting, but since I see you so sad and can give you no other comfort—you once praised my zither-playing; but I was bashful and would not play to you. Now I am bolder, and if you choose, I will play you a tune."

She took her harp and began the prelude to "Rainbow Skirts and Feather Jackets." But after a few bars the tune broke off into a wild and passionate dirge.

All who were present caught their breath; but in a moment she stopped playing, threw down her harp and, weeping bitterly, ran to her mother's room.

She did not come back.

Next morning Chang left. The following year he failed in his examinations and could not leave the capital. So, to unburden his heart, he wrote a letter to Ying-ying. She answered him somewhat in this fashion:

> I have read your letter and cherish it dearly. It has filled my heart half with sorrow, half with joy. You sent with it a box of garlands and five sticks of paste, that I may decorate my head and colour my lips.
>
> I thank you for your presents; but there is no one now to care how I look. Seeing these things only makes me think of you and grieve the more.
>
> You say that you are prospering in your career at the capital, and I am comforted by that news. But it makes me fear you will never come back again to one who is so distant and humble. But *that* is settled forever, and it is no use talking of it.
>
> Since last autumn I have lived in a dazed stupor. Amid the clamour of the daytime, I have sometimes forced myself to laugh and talk; but alone at night I have done nothing but weep. Or, if I have fallen asleep my dreams have always been full of the sorrows of parting. Often I dreamt that you came to me as you used to do, but always before the moment of our joy your phantom vanished from my side. Yet, though we are still bedfellows in my dreams, when I wake and think of it the time when we were together seems very far off. For since we parted, the old year has slipped away and a new year has begun. . . .
>
> Ch'ang-an is a city of pleasure, where there are many snares to catch a young man's heart. How can I hope that you will not forget one so sequestered and insignificant as I? And indeed, if you were to be faithful, so worthless a creature could never requite you. But our vows of unending love—those *I* at least can fulfil.

Because you are my cousin, I met you at the feast. Lured by a maid-servant, I visited you in private. A girl's heart is not in her own keeping. You "tempted me by your ballads" and I could not bring myself to "throw the shuttle" to repulse you.

Then came the sharing of pillow and mat, the time of perfect loyalty and deepest tenderness. And I, being young and foolish, thought it would never end.

Now, having "seen my Prince," I cannot love again; nor, branded by the shame of self-surrender, am I fit to perform the "service of towel and comb," to become your wife; and of the bitterness of the long celibacy which awaits me, what need is there to speak?

The good man uses his heart; and if by chance his gaze has fallen on the humble and insignificant, till the day of his death he continues the affections of his life. The cynic cares nothing for people's feelings. He will discard the small to follow the great, look upon a former mistress merely as an accomplice in sin, and hold that the most solemn vows are made only to be broken. He will reverse all natural laws—as though Nature should suddenly let bone dissolve, while cinnabar resisted the fire. The dew that the wind has shaken from the tree still looks for kindness from the dust; and such, too, is the sum of *my* hopes and fears.

As I write, I am shaken by sobs and cannot tell you all that is in my heart. My darling, I am sending you a jade ring that I used to play with when I was a child. I want you to wear it at your girdle, that you may become firm and flawless as this jade, and, in your affections, unbroken as the circuit of this ring.

And with it I am sending a skein of thread and a tea-trough of flecked bamboo. There is no value in these few things. I send them only to remind you to keep your heart pure as jade and your affection unending as this round ring. The bamboo is mottled as if with tears, and the thread is tangled as the thoughts of those who are in sorrow. By these tokens I seek no more than that, knowing the truth, you may think kindly of me for ever.

Our hearts are very near, but our bodies are far apart. There is no time fixed for our meeting; yet a secret longing can unite souls that are separated by a thousand miles.

Protect yourself against the cold spring wind, eat well—look after yourself in all ways and do not worry too much about your worthless handmaid,

Ts'UI YING-YING

Chang showed this letter to his friends and so the story became known to many who lived at that time. All who heard it were deeply moved; but Chang, to their disappointment, declared that he meant to break with Ying-ying. Yüan Chen, of Honan, who knew Chang well, asked him why he had made this decision.

Chang answered: "I have observed that in Nature whatever has perfect beauty is either itself liable to sudden transformations or else is the cause of them in others. If Ying-ying were to marry a rich gentleman and become his pet, she would forever be changing, as the clouds change to rain, or as the scaly dragon turns into the horned dragon. I, for one, could never keep pace with her transformations.

"Of old, Hsin of the Yin dynasty and Yu of the Chou dynasty ruled over kingdoms of many thousand chariots, and their strength was very great. Yet a single woman brought each to ruin, dissipating their hosts and leading these monarchs to the assassin's knife, so that to this day they are a laughingstock to all the world. I know that my constancy could not withstand such spells, and that is why I have curbed my passion."

At these words all who were present sighed deeply.

A few years afterwards Ying-ying married someone else and Chang also found a wife. Happening once to pass the house where Ying-ying was living, he called on her husband and asked to see her, saying he was her cousin. The husband sent for her, but she would not come. Chang's vexation showed itself in his face. Someone told Ying-ying of this and she secretly wrote the poem:

Since I have grown so lean, my face has lost its beauty.
I have tossed and turned so many times that I am too tired to
    leave my bed.
It is not that I mind the others seeing
    How ugly I have grown;

It is *you* who have caused me to lose my beauty,
  Yet it is *you* I am ashamed should see me!

Chang went away without meeting her, and a few days afterwards, when he was leaving the town, wrote a poem of final farewell, which said:

You cannot say that you are abandoned and deserted;
  For you have found someone to love you.
Why do you not convert your broodings over the past
  Into kindness to your present husband?

After that they never heard of one another again. Many of
Chang's contemporaries praised the skill with which he extricated
himself from this entanglement.

TRANSLATED BY ARTHUR WALEY

Po Hsing-chien

The Story of Miss Li

[*Li Wa chuan*]

Miss Li, ennobled with the title "Lady of Chien-kuo," was once a prostitute in Ch'ang-an. The devotion of her conduct was so remarkable that I have thought it worth while to record her story.

In the T'ien-pao era (742-56) there was a certain nobleman, Governor of Ch'ang-chou and Lord of Jung-yang, whose name and surname I will omit. He was a man of great wealth and highly esteemed by all. He had passed his fiftieth year and had a son who was close on twenty, a boy who in literary talent outstripped all his companions. His father was proud of him and had great hopes of his future. "This," he would say, "is the 'thousand-league colt' of our family." When the time came for the lad to compete at the Provincial Examinations, his father gave him fine clothes and a handsome coach with richly caparisoned horses for the journey; and to provide for his expenses at the capital, he gave him a large sum of money, saying, "I am sure that your talent is such that you will succeed at the first attempt; but I am giving you resources for two years, so that you may pursue your career free from all anxiety." The young man also was quite confident and saw himself winning the first place as clearly as he saw the palm of his own hand.

Starting from P'i-ling he reached Ch'ang-an in a few weeks and took a house in the Pu-cheng quarter. One day he was coming back from a visit to the Eastern Market. He entered the city by the eastern gate of P'ing-k'ang and was going to visit a friend who lived in the southwestern part of the town. When he reached the Ming-k'o Bend, he saw a house of which the gate and courtyard were rather narrow; but the house itself was stately and stood well back from the road. One of the double doors was open, and at it stood a lady, attended by her maid-servant. She was of exquisite, bewitching beauty, such as the world has seldom produced.

When he saw her, the young man unconsciously reined in his horse and hesitated. Unable to leave the spot, he purposely let his whip fall to the ground and waited for his servant to pick it up, all the time staring at the lady in the doorway. She too was staring and met his gaze with a look that seemed to be an answer to his admiration. But in the end he went away without daring to speak to her.

But he could not put the thought of her out of his mind and secretly begged those of his friends who were most expert in the pleasures of Ch'ang-an to tell him what they knew of the girl. He learnt from them that the house belonged to a low and unprincipled woman named Li. When he asked what chance he had of winning the daughter, they answered, "The woman Li is possessed of considerable property, for her previous dealings have been with wealthy and aristocratic families from whom she has received enormous sums. Unless you are willing to spend several thousand pounds, the daughter will have nothing to do with you."

The young man answered: "All I care about is to win her. I do not mind if she costs a million pounds." The next day he set out in his best clothes, with many servants riding behind him, and knocked at the door of Mrs. Li's house. Immediately a page-boy drew the bolt. The young man asked, "Can you tell me whose house this is?" The boy did not answer, but ran back into the house and called out at the top of his voice, "Here is the gentleman who dropped his whip the other day!"

Miss Li was evidently very much pleased. He heard her saying, "Be sure not to let him go away. I am just going to do my hair and change my clothes; I will be back in a minute." The young man, in high spirits, followed the page-boy into the house. A white-haired old lady was going upstairs, whom he took to be the girl's mother. Bowing low the young man addressed her as follows: "I am told that you have a vacant plot of land, which you would be willing to let as a building site. Is this true?" The old lady answered, "I am afraid the site is too mean and confined; it would be quite unsuitable for a gentleman's house. I should not like to offer it to you." She then took him into the guest-room, which was a very handsome one, and asked him to be seated, saying, "I have a daughter who has little either of beauty or accomplishment, but she is fond of seeing strangers. I should like you to meet her."

So saying, she called for her daughter, who presently entered. Her eyes sparkled with such fire, her arms were so dazzling white and there was in her movements such an exquisite grace that the young man could only leap to his feet in confusion and did not dare raise his eyes. When their salutations were over, he began to make a few remarks about the weather; and realized as he did so that her beauty was of a kind he had never encountered before.

They sat down again. Tea was made and wine poured. The vessels used were spotlessly clean. He lingered till the day was almost over; the curfew-drum sounded its four beats. The old lady asked him if he lived far away. He answered untruthfully, "Several leagues beyond the Yen-p'ing Gate," hoping that they would ask him to stay. The old lady said, "The drum has sounded. You will have to go back at once, unless you mean to break the law."

The young man answered, "I was being so agreeably entertained that I did not notice how rapidly the day had fled. My house is a long way off and in the city I have no friends or relations. What am I to do?" Miss Li then interposed, saying, "If you can forgive the meanness of our poor home, what harm would there be in your spending the night with us?" He looked doubtfully at the girl's mother, but met with no discouragement.

Calling his servants, he gave them money and told them to buy provisions for the night. But the girl laughingly stopped him, saying, "That is not the way guests are entertained. Our humble house will provide for your wants tonight, if you are willing to partake of our simple fare and defer your bounty to another occasion." He tried to refuse, but in the end she would not allow him to, and they all moved to the western hall. The curtains, screens, blinds and couches were of dazzling splendour; whilst the toilet-boxes, rugs and pillows were of the utmost elegance. Candles were lighted and an excellent supper was served.

After supper the old lady retired, leaving the lovers engaged in the liveliest conversation, laughing and chattering completely at their ease.

After a while the young man said, "I passed your house the other day and you happened to be standing at the door. And after that, I could think of nothing but you; whether I lay down to rest or sat down to eat, I could not stop thinking of you." She laughed and answered, "It was just the same with me." He said, "You must know that I did not come today simply to look for a building site. I came hoping that you would fulfil my lifelong desire; but I was not sure how you would welcome me. What—"

He had not finished speaking when the old woman came back and asked what they were saying. When they told her, she laughed and said, "Has not Mencius written that 'the relationship between men and women is the groundwork of society'? When lovers are agreed, not even the mandate of a parent will deter them. But my daughter is of humble birth. Are you sure that she is fit to 'present pillow and mat' to a great man?"

He came down from the dais and, bowing low, begged that she would accept him as her slave. Henceforward the old lady regarded him as her son-in-law; they drank heavily together and finally parted. Next morning he had all his boxes and bags brought round to Mrs. Li's house and settled there permanently. From this time on he shut himself up with his mistress and none of his friends ever heard of him. He consorted only with actors and dancers and low people of that kind, passing the time in wild sports and wanton feasting. When his money was all spent, he sold his horses and men-servants. In about a year his money, property, servants and horses were all gone.

For some time the old lady's manner towards him had been growing gradually colder, but his mistress remained as devoted as ever. One day she said to him, "We have been together a year, but I am still not with child. They say that the spirit of the Bamboo Grove answers a woman's prayers as surely as an echo. Let us go to his temple and offer a libation."

The young man, not suspecting any plot, was delighted to take her to the temple, and having pawned his coat to buy sweet wine for the libation he went with her and performed the ceremony of prayer. They stayed one night at the temple and came back next day. Whipping up their donkey, they soon arrived at the north gate of the P'ing-k'ang quarter. At this point his mistress turned to him and said, "My aunt's house is in a turning just near here. How would it be if we were to go there and rest for a little?"

He drove on as she directed him, and they had not gone more

than a hundred paces when he saw the entrance to a spacious car-
riage-drive. A servant who belonged to the place came out and
stopped the cart, saying, "This is the entrance." The young man got
down and was met by someone who came out and asked who they
were. When told that it was Miss Li, he went back and announced
her. Presently a married lady came out who seemed to be about
forty. She greeted him, saying, "Has my niece arrived?" Miss Li then
got out of the cart and her aunt said to her, "Why have you not
been to see me for so long?" At which they looked at one another
and laughed. Then Miss Li introduced him to her aunt and when
that was over they all went into a side garden near the Western
Halberd Gate. In the middle of the garden was a pagoda, and round
it grew bamboos and trees of every variety, while ponds and summer-
houses added to its air of seclusion. He asked Miss Li if this were
her aunt's estate; she laughed, but did not answer and spoke of
something else.

Tea of excellent quality was served; but when they had been
drinking it for a little while, a messenger came galloping up on a
huge Fergana horse, saying that Miss Li's mother had suddenly been
taken very ill and had already lost consciousness, so that they had
better come back as quickly as possible.

Miss Li said to her aunt: "I am very much upset. I think I had
better take the horse and ride on ahead. Then I will send it back,
and you and my husband can come along later." The young man was
anxious to go with her, but the aunt and her servants engaged him
in conversation, flourishing their hands in front of him and prevent-
ing him from leaving the garden. The aunt said to him: "No doubt
my sister is dead by this time. You and I ought to discuss together
what can be done to help with the expenses of the burial. What is
the use of running off like that? Stay here and help me to make a
plan for the funeral and mourning ceremonies."

It grew late; but the messenger had not returned. The aunt said:
"I am surprised he has not come back with the horse. You had better
go there on foot as quickly as possible and see what has happened.
I will come on later."

The young man set out on foot for Mrs. Li's house. When he
got there he found the gate firmly bolted, locked and sealed. Astounded, he questioned the neighbours, who told him that the house
had only been let to Mrs. Li, and that, the lease having expired,

the landlord had now resumed possession. The old lady, they said, had gone to live elsewhere. They did not know her new address.

At first he thought of hurrying back to Hsüan-yang and questioning the aunt; but he found it was too late to get there. So he pawned some of his clothes, and with the proceeds bought himself supper and a bed for the night. But he was too angry and distressed to sleep, and did not once close his eyes from dusk to dawn. Early in the morning he dragged himself away to the "aunt's house." He knocked on the door repeatedly, but it was breakfast-time and no one answered. At last, when he had shouted several times at the top of his voice, a footman walked majestically to the door. The young man nervously mentioned the aunt's name and asked whether she was at home. The footman replied: "No one of that name here." "But she lived here yesterday evening," the young man protested; "why are you trying to deceive me? If she does not live here, who *does* the house belong to?" The footman answered: "This is the residence of His Excellency Mr. Ts'ui. I believe that yesterday some persons hired a corner of the grounds. I understand that they wished to entertain a cousin who was coming from a distance. But they were gone before nightfall."

The young man, perplexed and puzzled to the point of madness, was absolutely at a loss what to do next. The best he could think of was to go to the quarters in Pu-cheng, where he had installed himself when he first arrived in Ch'ang-an. The landlord was sympathetic and offered to feed him. But the young man was too much upset to eat, and having fasted for three days fell seriously ill. He rapidly grew worse, and the landlord, fearing he would not recover, had him moved straight to the undertaker's shop. In a short time the whole of the undertaker's staff was collected round him, offering sympathy and bringing him food. Gradually he got better and was able to walk with a stick.

The undertaker now hired him by the day to hold up the curtains of fine cloth, by which he earned just enough to support himself. In a few months he grew quite strong again, but whenever he heard the mourners' doleful songs, would regret that he could not change places with the corpse, burst into violent fits of sobbing and shed streams of tears over which he lost all control; then he used to go home and imitate the mourners' performance.

Being a man of intelligence he very soon mastered the art and finally became the most expert mourner in Ch'ang-an. It happened that there were two undertakers at this time between whom there was a great rivalry. The undertaker of the east turned out magnificent hearses and biers, and in this respect his superiority could not be contested. But the mourners he provided were somewhat inferior. Hearing of our young man's skill, he offered a large sum for his services. The eastern undertaker's supporters, who were familiar with the repertoire of his company, secretly taught the young man several fresh tunes and showed him how to fit the words to them. The lessons went on for several weeks, without anyone being allowed to know of it. At the end of that time the two undertakers agreed to hold a competitive exhibition of their wares in T'ien-men Street. The loser was to forfeit fifty thousand cash to cover the cost of the refreshments provided. Before the exhibition an agreement was drawn up and duly signed by witnesses.

A crowd of several thousand people collected to watch the competition. The mayor of the quarter got wind of the proceedings and told the chief of police. The chief of police told the governor of the city. Very soon all the gentlemen of Ch'ang-an were hurrying to the spot and every house in the town was empty. The exhibition lasted from dawn till midday. Coaches, hearses and all kinds of funeral trappings were successively displayed, but the undertaker of the west could establish no superiority. Filled with shame, he set up a platform in the south corner of the square. Presently a man with a long beard came forward, carrying a hand-bell and attended by numerous assistants. He wagged his beard, raised his eyebrows, folded his arms across his chest and bowed. Then, mounting the platform, he sang the "Dirge of the White Horse." When it was over, confident of an easy victory, he glared round him, as if to imply that his opponents had all vanished. He was applauded on every side and was himself convinced that his talents were a unique product of the age and could not possibly be called into question.

After a while the undertaker of the east put together some benches in the north corner of the square, and a young man in a black hat came forward, attended by five assistants and carrying a bunch of hearse-plumes in his hand. It was the young man of our story.

He adjusted his clothes, looked timidly up and down, and then

cleared his throat and began his tune with an air of great diffi-
dence.

He sang the dirge, "Dew on the Garlic." His voice rose so shrill
and clear that "its echoes shook the forest trees." Before he had
finished the first verse, all who heard were sobbing and hiding their
tears.

When the performance was over everyone made fun of the
western undertaker, and he was so much put out that he immediately
removed his exhibits and retired from the contest. The audience
was amazed by the collapse of the western undertaker and could
not imagine where his rival had procured such a remarkable singer.

It happened that the emperor had recently issued an order
commanding the governors of outside provinces to confer with him
in the capital at least once a year. At this time the young man's
father, who was Governor of Ch'ang-chou, had recently arrived
at the capital to make his report. Hearing of the competition, he
and some of his colleagues discarded their official robes and insignia
and slipped away to join the crowd. With them was an old servant,
who was the husband of the young man's foster-nurse. Recognizing
his foster-son's way of moving and speaking, he was on the point
of accosting him, but not daring to do so he stood weeping silently.
The father asked him why he was crying, and the servant replied,
"Sir, the young man who is singing reminds me of your lost son."
The father answered: "My son became the prey of robbers because
I gave him too much money. This cannot be he." So saying he also
began to weep, and leaving the crowd returned to his lodging.

But the old servant went about among the members of the
troupe asking who it was who had just sung with such skill. They
all told him it was the son of such a one; and when he asked the
young man's own name, that too was unfamiliar for he was living
under an alias. The old servant was so puzzled that he determined
to put the matter to the test for himself. But when the young man
saw his old friend walking towards him he winced, turned away
his face and tried to hide in the crowd. The old man followed him
and catching his sleeve said, "Surely it is you!" Then they embraced
and wept. Presently they went back together to his father's lodging.
But his father abused him, saying, "Your conduct has disgraced the
family. How dare you show your face again?" He took him out of

the house and led him to the ground between the Ch'ü-chiang
Pond and the Apricot Gardens. Here he stripped him naked and
thrashed him with his horse-whip, till the young man succumbed
to the pain and collapsed. The father then left him and went away.

But the young man's singing-master had told some of his friends
to watch what happened to him. When they saw him stretched
inanimate on the ground they came back and told the other members of the troupe.

The news occasioned universal lamentation, and two men were
despatched with a reed mat to cover up the body. When they got
there they found his heart still warm, and when they had held him
in an upright posture for some time his breathing recommenced.
So they carried him home between them and administered liquid
food through a reed-pipe. Next morning he recovered consciousness;
but after several months he was still unable to move his hands and
feet. Moreover, the sores left by his thrashing festered in so disgusting a manner that his friends found him too troublesome, and
one night deposited him in the middle of the road. However, the
passers-by, harrowed by his condition, never failed to throw him
scraps of food.

So copious was his diet that in three months he recovered
sufficiently to hobble with the aid of a stick. Clad in a linen coat—
which was knotted together in a hundred places so that it looked
as tattered as a quail's tail—and carrying a broken saucer in his
hand, he now went about the idle quarters of the town earning his
living as a professional beggar.

Autumn had now turned to winter. He spent his nights in public
lavatories and his days haunting the markets and booths.

One day when it was snowing hard, hunger and cold had driven
him into the streets. His beggar's cry was full of woe and all who
heard it were heart-rent. But the snow was so heavy that hardly a
house had its outer door open, and the streets were empty.

When he reached the eastern gate of An-yi, about the seventh
or eighth turning north of the Hsün-li Wall, there was a house with
the double-doors partly open.

It was the house where Miss Li was then living, but the young
man did not know.

He stood before the door, wailing loud and long.

Hunger and cold had given such a piteous accent to his cry that none could have listened unmoved.

Miss Li heard it from her room and at once said to her servant, "That is so-and-so. I know his voice." She flew to the door and was horrified to see her old lover standing before her so emaciated by hunger and disfigured by sores that he seemed scarcely human. "Can it be you?" she said. But the young man was so overcome by bewilderment and excitement that he could not speak, but only moved his lips noiselessly.

She threw her arms round his neck, then wrapped him in her own embroidered jacket and led him to the parlour. Here, with quavering voice, she reproached herself, saying, "It is my doing that you have been brought to this pass." And with these words she swooned.

Her mother came running up in great excitement, asking who had arrived. Miss Li, recovering herself, said who it was. The old woman cried out in rage, "Send him away! What did you bring him in here for?"

But Miss Li looked up at her defiantly and said, "Not so! This is the son of a noble house. Once he rode in grand coaches and wore golden trappings on his coat. But when he came to our house, he soon lost all he had; and then we plotted together and left him destitute. Our conduct has indeed been inhuman! We have ruined his career and robbed him even of his place in the category of human relationships. For the love of father and son is implanted by Heaven; yet we have hardened his father's heart, so that he beat him and left him on the ground.

"Everyone in the land knows that it is I who have reduced him to his present plight. The Court is full of his kinsmen. Some day one of them will come into power. Then an inquiry will be set on foot, and disaster will overtake us. And since we have flouted Heaven and defied the laws of humanity, neither spirits nor divinities will be on our side. Let us not wantonly incur a further retribution!

"I have lived as your daughter for twenty years. Reckoning what I have cost you in that time, I find it must be close on a thousand pieces of gold. You are now sixty, so that by the price of twenty more years' food and clothing I can buy my freedom. I intend to live separately with this young man. We will not go far away; I shall see to it that we are near enough to pay our respects to you both morning and evening."

The "mother" saw that she was not to be gainsaid and fell in with the arrangement. When she had paid her ransom, Miss Li had a hundred pieces of gold left over, and with them she rented a vacant room five doors away. Here she gave the young man a bath, changed his clothes, fed him with hot soup to relax his stomach, and later fattened him up with cheese and milk.

In a few weeks she began to place before him all the choicest delicacies of land and sea; and she clothed him with cap, shoes and stockings of the finest quality. In a short time he began gradually to put on flesh, and by the end of the year he had entirely recovered his former health.

One day Miss Li said to him, "Now your limbs are stout again and your will strong! Sometimes, when deeply pondering in silent sorrow, I wonder to myself how much you remember of your old literary studies?" He thought and answered, "Of ten parts I remember two or three."

Miss Li then ordered the carriage to be got ready and the young man followed her on horseback. When they reached the classical bookshop at the side-gate south of the Flagtower, she made him choose all the books he wanted, till she had laid out a hundred pieces of gold. Then she packed them in the cart and drove home. She now made him dismiss all other thoughts from his mind and apply himself only to study. All the evening he toiled at his books, with only Miss Li at his side, and they did not retire till midnight. If ever she found that he was too tired to work, she made him lay down his classics and write a poem or ode.

In two years he had thoroughly mastered his subjects and was admired by all the scholars of the realm. He said to Miss Li, "*Now*, surely, I am ready for the examiners!" But she would not let him compete and made him revise all he had learnt, to prepare for the "hundredth battle." At the end of the third year, she said, "Now you may go." He went in for the examination and passed at the first attempt. His reputation spread rapidly through the examination rooms and even older men, when they saw his compositions, were filled with admiration and respect, and sought his friendship.

But Miss Li would not let him make friends with them, saying, "Wait a little longer! Nowadays when a bachelor of arts has passed his examination, he thinks himself fit to hold the most advantageous posts at Court and to win a universal reputation. But your unfortunate conduct and disreputable past put you at a disadvantage beside your fellow-scholars. You must 'grind, temper and sharpen' your attainments, that you may secure a second victory. Then you will be able to match yourself against famous scholars and contend with the illustrious."

The young man accordingly increased his efforts and enhanced his value. That year it happened that the emperor had decreed a special examination for the selection of candidates of unusual merit from all parts of the empire. The young man competed, and came out top in the "censorial essay." He was offered the post of Army Inspector at Ch'eng-tu Fu. The officers who were to escort him were all previous friends.

When he was about to take up his post, Miss Li said to him, "Now that you are restored to your proper station in life, I will not be a burden to you. Let me go back and look after the old lady till she dies. You must ally yourself with some lady of noble lineage, who will be worthy to carry the sacrificial dishes in your Ancestral Hall. Do not injure your prospects by an unequal union. Good-bye, for now I must leave you."

The young man burst into tears and threatened to kill himself if she left him, but she obstinately refused to go with him. He begged her passionately not to desert him, and at last she consented to go with him across the river as far as Chien-men. "There," she said, "you must part with me." The young man consented and in a few weeks they reached Chien-men. Before he had started out again, a proclamation arrived announcing that the young man's father, who had been Governor of Ch'ang-chou, had been appointed Governor of Ch'eng-tu and Intendant of the Chien-nan Circuit. Next morning the father arrived, and the young man sent in his card and waited upon him at the posting-station. His father did not recognize him, but the card bore the names of the young man's father and grandfather, with their ranks and titles. When he read these he was astounded, and bidding his son mount the steps he caressed him and wept. After a while he said, "Now we two are father and son once more," and bade him tell his story. When he heard of the young man's adventures, he was amazed. Presently he asked, "And where is Miss Li?" His son replied, "She came with me as far as here, but now she is going back again."

"I cannot allow it," the father said. Next day he ordered a carriage for his son and sent him on to report himself at Ch'eng-tu; but he detained Miss Li at Chien-men, found her a suitable lodging and ordered a match-maker to perform the initial ceremonies for uniting the two families and to accomplish the six rites of welcome. The young man came back from Ch'eng-tu and they were duly married. In the years that followed their marriage, Miss Li showed herself a devoted wife and competent housekeeper, and was beloved by all her relations.

Some years later both the young man's parents died, and in his mourning observances he showed unusual piety. As a mark of divine favour, magic toadstools grew on the roof of his mourning-hut, each stem bearing three plants. The report of his virtue reached even the emperor's ears. Moreover a number of white swallows nested in the beams of his roof, an omen which so impressed the emperor that he raised his rank immediately.

When the three years of mourning were over, he was successively promoted to various distinguished posts and in the course of ten years was Governor of several provinces. Miss Li was given the fief of Chien-kuo, with the title "The Lady of Chien-kuo."

He had four sons who all held high rank. Even the least successful of them became Governor of T'ai-yüan, and his brothers all married into great families, so that his good fortune both in public and private life was without parallel.

How strange that we should find in the conduct of a prostitute a degree of constancy rarely equalled even by the heroines of history! Surely the story is one which cannot but provoke a sigh!

My great-uncle was Governor of Chin-chou; subsequently he joined the Ministry of Finance and became Inspector of Waterways, and finally Inspector of Roads. In all these three offices he had Miss Li's husband as his colleague, so that her story was well known to him in every particular. During the Cheng-yüan period [785-805] I was sitting one day with Li Kung-tso of Lung-hai, the writer; we fell to talking of wives who had distinguished themselves by remarkable conduct. I told him the story of Miss Li. He listened with rapt attention, and when it was over asked me to write it down for him. So I took up my brush, wetted the hairs and made this rough outline of the story.

TRANSLATED BY ARTHUR WALEY

Tu Kuang-t'ing

The Curly-bearded Hero

[*Ch'iu jan k'o chuan*]

When the Emperor Yang-ti of the Sui dynasty visited Yangchow he left his western capital, Ch'ang-an, in the charge of Councillor Yang Su. This was a man whom high birth had made arrogant, and in the troubled state of the times he had begun to regard his own power and prestige as unrivalled in the land. He maintained a lavish court and departed from the mode of conduct appropriate to a subject. Whether it was a high officer requesting interview or a private guest paying his respects, Yang would receive his visitor seated on a couch; when he rose to leave his hall it would be to walk, supported on either side by a beautiful girl, down between rows of attendant maidens. In these and other ways he arrogated to himself the imperial prerogatives. With age his behaviour grew more extreme, until he no longer seemed aware of the responsibility he owed to sustain the realm against peril.

One day Li Ching, later to be ennobled as Duke of Wei but at that time still a commoner, requested interview with Yang Su in order to present certain policies to which he had given much thought. As with everyone else, Yang Su remained seated to receive him. But Li Ching came forward, bowed and said, "The whole empire is now in turmoil, as would-be leaders strive for mastery. Your highness is supreme in the service of our imperial house. Your first concern should be to win the respect of men of heroic mettle, and this you are hindering by remaining seated to receive those who seek audience."

Yang Su composed his features to an expression of more fitting gravity, rose to his feet and apologized. He derived great pleasure from the discussion which followed, and Li Ching, when the time

314

came for him to withdraw, was assured of the acceptance of his proposals.

Throughout his spirited conversation with the Councillor, Li Ching had been subjected to the gaze of a girl who stood before them, a girl of remarkable beauty who held in her hand a red whisk. When Li had taken his leave this girl followed him into the ante-room and pointed him out to an attendant, whom she asked to ascertain Li's position, family situation and address. Li answered the attendant, and the girl nodded her head and withdrew.

Li Ching returned to his lodging. But that night, towards dawn, suddenly there came a knocking at his door and a call in a low voice. Li Ching rose to find a being dressed in a purple robe and with covered head, who carried a staff and a single travelling-bag.

"Who are you?" asked Li.

"I am the maid-servant from Councillor Yang's residence, the girl with the red whisk," came the reply.

Li at once invited her to enter. The removal of outer robe and headwear revealed a girl of superb beauty, perhaps seventeen or eighteen years old. Her face was free of cosmetics though her clothes were of the gayest style. She bowed to Li Ching, who though startled, returned her greeting.

"I have been for a long time in the service of the Councillor Yang," she said, "and I have seen many of the leading figures of the empire; but none have I seen to equal you. I have come to seek your favour as the creeper, helpless alone, seeks the support of the sturdiest tree."

"But what can I do," Li Ching asked, "when Councillor Yang has such power now in the capital?"

"There is little to fear from him. He is the corpse in which a little breath remains. We his women know him to be a failure, and though many have run away they have not been pursued very far. I have carefully considered all this, and pray that you will not reject me."

Li Ching asked her surname and her position in her family, and she replied that she was the eldest child of the Chang family. Her form and face, her speech and her bearing were all beyond the mortal range, and Li Ching could not find it in him to reject her. But his joy was no greater than the fears her action raised in him.

Each new moment a thousand causes for anxiety would present themselves, and outside the door there was always someone new trying to spy in on them. Then, after a few days, they heard news of a search. Convinced of the danger of their situation, they put on riding dress, left their lodging in the capital and rode out on the Taiyuan road to seek refuge there.

They broke their journey at an inn at Ling-shih. A bed had been made ready for them and meat boiling in a pot on the stove was almost cooked. Miss Chang had to stand up by the bed to comb her hair, which was so long that it reached to the floor. Li Ching was brushing down the horses just outside the door. At this moment there rode up to them a stranger mounted on a lame donkey. The man was of middle height and had a ruddy, curling beard. Dismounting he threw a leather bag down by the stove, took a pillow and lay down on his side, his gaze fixed on Miss Chang as she combed her hair.

Li Ching was infuriated by this behaviour but went on with his grooming while he tried to decide what to do about it. Miss Chang studied the stranger's face. Then, one hand holding out her hair as a screen, with the other she signed to Li not to show anger. She hastily finished her toilet, then approached the stranger, bringing together her sleeves before her in token of greeting and asking to know his name.

"My name is Chang," said the stranger without shifting his position.

"I also have the name Chang," said the girl, "so you should regard me as your younger sister." She swiftly performed the prescribed obeisance, then asked further what position he had in his family.

"I am the third," he replied, and asked what was her position.

"The eldest."

"Then I am most fortunate today in encountering First Sister," said the stranger with a smile.

Now Miss Chang called out to Li Ching, "Come now and greet my Third Brother." Li hastened to salute him, then the three seated themselves round the stove.

"What sort of meat is cooking there?" asked the stranger.

"Mutton. It must be ready by now."

"Good," said the stranger, "for I am hungry."

While Li went out to buy wheaten cakes the stranger drew a dagger from his belt and sliced the meat for them to share. When they had eaten their fill he chopped up what remained and fed it to his donkey. He was extremely swift in all his movements.

"From your appearance I should judge you to be an impover-ished gentleman," said the stranger to Li Ching. "How do you come to be accompanied by such an outstanding beauty as this?"

"It is true that I am poor," Li replied, "yet there is good reason for this. If it were anyone else who asked I should not care to say, but from you I shall hide nothing." And he told him all that had taken place.

"Then where do you plan to go?" asked the stranger.

"We shall take refuge in Taiyuan," answered Li Ching.

"In that case I shall not be able to accompany you," said the stranger. Then, "Do you have wine?" he asked.

"There is a wineshop just to the west of the inn," said Li Ching, and he brought a gallon of wine.

"I have something here just to go with the wine. I hope you will join me, Li," said the stranger when the wine had been passed round. Courteously Li thanked the stranger, who opened his leather bag and drew from it first a human head, then a human heart and liver. The head he dropped back into the bag; the heart and liver he sliced with his dagger and shared with Li Ching.

"This man was unrivalled throughout the empire for mean ingratitude," he said. "For ten years I have nursed my feud with him, but now at last I have taken him and found some vent for my wrath." And he continued: "Li, your bearing is that of a true man of valour. Have you heard, as I have, that there is in Taiyuan a man marked out from his fellows?"

"I have known for some time of a youth whom I consider to be the One Man," replied Li. "Other than this I know only of men destined to be generals or ministers."

"What is his name?" asked the stranger.

"Li, as mine is," said Li Ching.

"How old is he?"

"Nineteen only."

"And what is his position at present?"

"He is the son of a garrison commander," said Li Ching.

"This sounds very like the man I heard of," said the stranger. "I must see him. Li, can you arrange for me to meet him?"

"I have a friend named Liu Wen-ching, who knows him well," answered Li Ching. "I can arrange an introduction through him. But what is it you want of him?"

"A soothsayer spoke of an aura of portent over Taiyuan, and advised me to seek out this man. When do you expect to reach Taiyuan?"

Li Ching told him, and he continued, "Let us agree to meet on the day following your arrival. Wait for me at daybreak at the Fen-yang Bridge."

With these words he mounted his donkey and rode off, so fast that when they looked he was already lost to sight. For some time Li Ching and the girl discussed him with both pleasure and amazement. Then they said, "There is no distrust among true heroes. We have nothing to fear from him." And they hastened on their journey.

They reached Taiyuan by the appointed day, entered the city and awaited Chang's arrival. He was as good as his word and they met with great pleasure. Together they proceeded to the house of Liu Wen-ching. Li Ching disguised their purpose: "This gentleman is a gifted physiognomist who is anxious to meet the youth Li. Would you be so kind as to invite him here?"

Now Liu Wen-ching had long been convinced of the boy's high destiny. On learning that his visitor practised the science of the physiognomist he despatched a messenger to summon him with all speed, and in the shortest possible time he was with them. The youth wore neither outer robe nor shoes, but had on a simple fur-lined jacket. There was about him an air of elation, and his whole appearance was of great distinction.

The bearded Chang remained silent in his seat in the corner of the room: at sight of the youth his will had died within him. They drank a few cups of wine, then Chang summoned Li Ching to him: "This is the true Son of Heaven," he said. Li Ching told this to Liu Wen-ching, who was delighted to be confirmed in his own conviction.

When they had left, the bearded man said to Li Ching, "Now that I have seen him I am almost completely certain, but I need confirmation from a friend of mine, a Taoist. You must take First Sister back to the capital. At noon on such-and-such a day, come to me at the wine-shop to the east of the horse market. Outside you will find this donkey of mine with another one, a very lean beast: this will indicate that my Taoist friend and myself are upstairs together. You must come up to us straight away."

Again he left them, and again Li Ching and the girl Chang followed his instructions and sought him out on the chosen day. They saw the two donkeys as he had described them. Lifting up the skirts of their robes, they climbed the stairs to find the bearded man and the Taoist drinking together. Their arrival gave fresh pleasure to the bearded Chang. He summoned them to be seated, passed wine to them, and after a dozen cups gave them further instructions: "In a cupboard downstairs here, you will find one hundred thousand cash. Find a quiet, safe place to settle First Sister, then on such-and-such a day meet me again at the Fen-yang Bridge."

Li Ching kept the appointment and found the Taoist and the bearded man already there. Together the three of them went to visit Liu Wen-ching. The latter was playing chess when they arrived. He rose, bowed and talked to them, then shortly afterwards sent a messenger in haste to summon the youth Li Shih-min to watch their game. The protagonists were the Taoist and Liu Wen-ching; the bearded man stood with Li Ching at one side, looking on. Very soon Li Shih-min came in, bowed and took a seat. So bright, so distinct was the charm of his manner that the whole room seemed filled with a freshness of spirit; and his eyes, as he looked about him, seemed to glow with an inner light.

At sight of him the face of the Taoist saddened, and he cleared away the chessmen and said, "The game is over! My position had become impossible. Who could have told?—but there was no way out."

The chess at an end, they took their leave, and as soon as they were outside the Taoist addressed the bearded man: "This realm is not to be your realm. But strive hard, and there will be a place for you elsewhere—do not let this bring you to despair."

After this they all returned to the capital together. On the journey the bearded man spoke to Li Ching: "You will not be in the capital before such-and-such a day," he said. "The day after

you arrive, I want you to bring First Sister to my home in such-and-
such a ward of the city. I am afraid you have been put to a great
deal of journeying, and First Sister must fear that you will be
destitute. I should like my wife to meet you, and we can talk things
over then. Please do not decline this request."

With a sigh he left them at this point, while Li Ching and the
girl Chang whipped up their horses and hastened on. Before long
they arrived in the capital. Together they made their way to the
address given them. They found themselves before an unimposing
wooden doorway. Their knock was answered by servants who made
obeisance and said, "We have long been awaiting you, sir, and First
Sister, on our master's orders." And they were led through a series
of gates, each more magnificent than the last. Over thirty maidens
now stood ranged before them, and twenty servants led them into
the eastern wing of the mansion.

Here everything they saw was of the rarest excellence, and there
was an abundance of wardrobes and toilet-cases, of headgear, of
mirrors and hair ornaments, all of a quality seldom seen on earth.
When they had washed and combed their hair they were invited
to change their robes, and the most exquisite garments were brought
for them. No sooner were they ready than word came of the master's
approach, and the bearded Chang entered. In headdress of gauze
and robe of purple, his bearing truly regal, he strode toward them
and greeted them with gladness. His wife, fittingly a being of rare
beauty, he commanded to come forward and make obeisance to
them. Then he brought them to the central hall where a banquet had
been prepared whose lavishness neither king nor noble could have
matched. The two couples seated themselves to face each other,
and delicacies were passed. And now there filed into the courtyard
twenty girl musicians who entertained them with music of a sweetness heard perhaps in heaven, but seldom here below.

The banquet ended, wine was brought, and while they drank, a
procession of household retainers carried in twenty couches from
the western hall, each covered with a sheet of brocade. The covers
were then removed to reveal sets of keys and account-books, which
the bearded Chang explained to Li Ching in the following words:
"Here you will find complete lists of my treasure in jewels and silks.
All that I possess I now give over to you. I must tell you my reason
for this. My design was to carve a place for myself in this realm,

perhaps to establish what power I could after two years or three years of campaigning for the throne. But now that I recognize my overlord there is no cause for me to linger on here. Li of Taiyuan is the true lord of us all: within half-a-dozen years he will have brought the empire to order. You, Li Ching, a man of heroic stature in the service of a prince unrivalled, you must bend your every effort to the supreme tasks of a minister. First Sister, rare beauty matched by great gifts, will support you in your advancement and share in your high nobility. None but First Sister could have foreseen your greatness; none but yourself could have secured her service. As men of wisdom and virtue join with each other in succession, their coming together is as though prearranged: 'storm rises when the tiger roars, clouds gather when the dragon soars'; there is nothing here of mere chance. Put my treasure at the service of our true lord, and strive with all your power to secure his mastery. If in a dozen years from now you hear of stirring happenings in the southeast, a thousand miles away, then you will know that I have found my season of success. You, First Sister, and you, Li Ching, make then together a libation in my honour."

Chang now ordered the servants of his household to assemble and make obeisance, and said, "Li Ching and First Sister are now your master and mistress. Serve them with diligence." And it remained only for Chang and his wife both to put on warrior's clothes and ride off, attended by a single servant; and a few paces took them out of sight.

After taking over the mansion Li Ching became a wealthy man and was able to make his contribution to Li Shih-min's conquest of the empire. By the time of the reign-period Chen-kuan [627-650] he had risen to be Chief Minister of the Left. It was now that reports came from the Man tribes of the southeast: "A force of a thousand ships carrying hundreds of thousands of armed men has invaded the country of Fu-yü. They have killed the king and set up their own leader in his place, and settled down in occupation of the land."

Li Ching realized that the bearded man had found his success. On his return from court he told Madam Chang of the news, and together they made a libation with obeisances towards the southeast in his honour.

From this history we may know that not even a hero, far less a common being, may expect to come forward as the One Man. The subject who harbours foolish thoughts of rebellion is like the mantis which would stop a chariot with its feelers. True it is that our dynastic house shall flourish from age to age, time without end.

TRANSLATED BY CYRIL BIRCH

A Late T'ang Poet

A. C. Graham writes: The T'ang dynasty is the central period of Chinese poetry; the central figure in the last, the overripe phase of the T'ang tradition is Li Shang-yin (?812-858). He is among the few major writers in the classical literature of China for whom the pains of love and the beauty of women are entirely serious themes. His work illustrates the extreme concentration of Chinese poetry at a most advanced point of development: shunning explicit similes, he achieves an extraordinary metaphorical complexity by such devices as the interplay of literary allusions and the parallelism of members within the couplet. Translators have generally avoided him, for the good reason that simpler poets lose much less in translation. But it may be possible to give readers at least a glimpse of a type of Chinese poetry hardly known except to sinologists.

•

Li Shang-yin

Seven Love Poems

1

Passionate. Spring has set.
Together for a moment. The night slants.[1]
Echoes in the house; want to go up, dare not.
Glow behind the screen; wish to go through, cannot.
It would hurt too much, the swallow on a hairpin;
Truly shame me, the phoenix on a mirror.
               On the road back, sunrise over Heng-t'ang.
The blossoming of the morning star shines farewell on the jewelled
    saddle.

2

The east wind sighs, the fine rains come.
Beyond the pool of water lilies, the noise of faint thunder.
A gold toad gnaws the lock. Open it, burn the incense.
A tiger of jade pulls the rope. Draw from the well and escape.
Chia's daughter peeped through the screen, but Han Shou was
    young.
The goddess of the river left her pillow, but the Prince of Wei was
    gifted.
Never let your heart blossom with the spring flowers;
An inch of love's flame is an inch of ashes.

3

When I was eight I stole a look in the mirror;
Already could paint my long eyebrows.

---

1. The sun has set, bringing the end of spring one day nearer; dawn
approaches as the Dipper turns in the sky.

At ten, I went out for the Spring Festival
And made myself a skirt of water lilies.
At twelve, I learned to play the lute;
The silver claws never left my fingers.
At fourteen, I hid away from strangers,
Guessing that I was still to marry.
At fifteen, I weep in the spring wind,
And turn away my face behind the garden swing.

4

Last night's stars, last night's wind,
By the west wall of the painted mansion, east of the hall of cassia.
For bodies no fluttering side by side of splendid phoenix wings,
Between hearts the one minute thread from root to tip of the magic horn.[2]
We sat apart for hook-in-the-palm; the wine of spring warmed.
Teamed as rivals, we guessed what the cup hid; the candle flame reddened.
Alas, I hear the drum, must go where office summons,
Ride my horse to the Orchid Terrace,[3] a wind-uprooted weed.

5

Coming was an empty promise, you have gone, and left no footprint.
The moonlight slants above the roof, already the fifth watch sounds.
Dreams of remote partings, cries which cannot summon,
Hurrying to finish the letter, ink which will not thicken.
The light of the candle half encloses kingfishers threaded in gold,
The smell of musk comes faintly through embroidered water lilies.
Young Liu [4] complained that Fairy Hill is far.
Past Fairy Hill, range above range, ten thousand mountains rise.

6

Where is it, the sad lyre which follows the quick flute?
Down endless lanes where the cherries flower, on a bank where the willows droop.

---

2. The white core of the unicorn's horn is mentioned as a treasure in an early history.
3. Orchid Terrace was the name for a secretariat at the capital.
4. "Young Liu" is a slightly contemptuous reference to the Han Emperor Wu's search for the elixir of life.

The lady of the east house grows old without a husband,
The white sun at high noon, the last spring month half over.
                    Princess Li-yang is fourteen,
In the cool of the day, after the Rain Feast, with him behind the
    fence, look.
—Come home, toss and turn till the last night-watch.
Two swallows in the rafters hear the long sigh.

7

Phoenix tail on scented silk, flimsy layer on layer;
Blue patterns on a round canopy, stitched deep into the night.
The sliced moon of a fan did not hide the shame;
The coach drove out with the noise of thunder, no time to exchange
    a word.
I had waited in the silent room, while the gold of the wick turned
    dark;
Till now no message at all has come, though the pomegranates are
    red.
Only a dappled horse stands tethered on a bank of drooping willows;
Where shall I wait for a kind wind to blow from the southwest?

Ma-wei[1]

> "Where is the house of Never Grieve?
> Never Grieve lives west of Stone City.
> Two oars which beat on the little boat
> Hurry to bring him to Never Grieve." (Folksong)

An empty rumour, that second world beyond the seas.
Other lives we cannot divine, this life is finished.
In vain she hears the Tiger Guards sound the evening rattle;
Never again shall the Cock Man come to report the sunrise.
This is the day when six armies conspire to halt their horses;
The seventh night of another year mocks the Herdboy Star.
Son of Heaven for four decades, what shall we call him now?
Better to be born in the house of Lu and marry Never Grieve.

---

1. Ma-wei is the posting station where the T'ang Emperor Ming-huang's
favorite concubine Yang Kuei-fei was strangled by his mutinous troops in
755. This was the tragic event commemorated in Po Chü-yi's poem "A Song
of Unending Sorrow" (p. 266, above).

The Lady in the Moon

1. Ch'ang O

"The lady Ch'ang O stole the herb of immortality and fled to the moon. Because the moon is white, she is called the White Beauty."

The lamp glows deep in the mica screen.
The River of Heaven slowly descends, the morning star drowns.
Is Ch'ang O sorry that she stole the magic herb,
Above the green sea, beneath the blue sky, thinking night after night?

2. Month of Frost

"In the third autumn month, the Dark Maid comes out to send down the frost and snow."

First calls of the migrant geese. No more cicadas.
South of the hundred-foot tower, water and sky are one.
The Dark Maid and the White Beauty endure the cold together
Rivals in elegance amid the frost on the moon.

Peonies

The brocade curtains have just rolled back. Behold the Queen of
    Wei.
Still he piles up the embroidered quilts, Prince O in Yüeh.
Drooping hands disturb, tip over, pendants of carved jade;
Snapping waists compete in the dance, fluttering saffron skirts.
Shih Ch'ung's candles—but who would trim them?
Hsün Yü's braziers, where no incense fumes.
Though my dream was of handing back the many-coloured brush,
I wish to write on petals a message to the clouds of morning.

PARAPHRASE

    The peonies have just burst their buds, like the Queen of Wei rolling back the brocade curtain behind which she modestly received Confucius. New leaves still grow above the flowers, like the embroidered quilts which Prince O piled over his mistress in the boat when he visited Yüeh.

In a light breeze, the flowers dip like the sleeves of girls in the slow dance "Drooping Hands," upsetting dewdrops like the carved white-jade pendants on the dancers' girdles. In a strong wind, the stalks bend double like girls in the fast dance Snapping Waists, fluttering petals like saffron skirts.

The peonies blaze like the candles on which the epicure Shih Ch'ung cooked his banquet. But their splendour is natural; candles burn only if their wicks are trimmed, and it would be intolerable to cut the peonies. They exhale fragrance like censers; but their scent is as natural as the perfume of Hsün Yü's body, which lingered three days wherever he went.

The poet Chiang Yen dreamed that the ghost of the poet Kuo P'u came to recover his writing-brush of many colours; after Chiang Yen returned it, he woke to find he had lost his genius. The goddess of Mount Wu gave herself to King Huai in a dream, and told him: "At dawn I am the clouds of morning, at sunset the driving rain." I who wish for the second dream have suffered the first; I shall never be able to write as long as you refuse me. I therefore send you this letter, figuring your beauty in the beauty of the peony, and comparing you to the goddess in the clouds of morning.

The Walls of Emerald

[Pi ch'eng]

> "The most ancient God lives in a palace of purple cloud, with walls of sunlit haze the colour of emerald."

1

Twelve turns of the rail on walls of emerald:
A sea-beast's horn repels the dust, a jade repels the cold.
Letters from Mount Lang-yüan have cranes for messengers,
On Lady's Couch a hen-phoenix perches on every tree.
The stars sink down to the ocean bed, see them through your
    window:
The rain has cleared from the River's source, far off you sit watching.
If the pearl of dawn should shine and never leave its place,
All life long we shall gaze in the crystal dish.

2

To glimpse her shadow, to hear her voice, is to love her.
On Jade Pool the lotus leaves spread out across the water.
Unless you meet Hsiao Shih with his flute, do not turn your head:
Do not look on Hung Ya, nor ever touch his shoulder.
The purple phoenix strikes a pose with the pendant of Ch'u in its beak,
Wild is the dance of crimson scales to the plucked strings on the river.
Prince O despairs of his night on the boat
And sleeps alone by the lighted censer beneath the embroidered quilts.

3

On the Seventh Night she came at the time appointed,
The bamboo screens of the inner chamber have never since lifted.
On the white-jade wheel, where the hare watches, the shade begins to grow,
The coral in the iron net has still to put forth branches.
I have studied magic, can halt the retreat of day,
I have fetched phoenix papers and written down my love.
The "Tale of the Emperor Wu" is a plain witness:
Never doubt that the world of men can share this knowledge.[1]

TRANSLATED BY A. C. GRAHAM

---

1. The Taoist arts for attaining immortality are the main sources of erotic symbolism in Chinese. The "Tale of the Emperor Wu" records how the Western Queen Mother descended from the sky on the seventh night of the seventh month to teach the emperor the secret of the elixir. But much of the detail of the poem has defeated the commentators; the poem, in Chinese at least, is a striking illustration of the power of poetic imagery to keep its spell after much of its meaning has been lost.

Sung Dynasty

960 - 1279

Poems in Irregular Metre

The tz'u *form is a striking departure from that staple of Chinese poetry, the* shih *with its absolutely uniform length of line. But the very irregularity of the* tz'u *is still rigidly prescribed. The poet may make his choice from a wide variety of patterns, which came into existence as words were fitted to new tunes of the popular "foreign music" brought into T'ang China from Central Asia. But once he has selected the metrical pattern (which will still bear the name of the song with which it originated) he must "fill in" the words in lines of fixed though uneven length, to a fixed tonal sequence and rhyme scheme. The process of "filling in" gave scope for the incorporation of more colloquial elements of diction than are found in* shih: *something of this colloquial quality may be seen from the poem by Yen Hsüan to the tune* Ho-ch'uan.

One example appears below of Li Po's use of the tz'u *form. But the great age came later. Glen W. Baxter's translations are all from the tenth-century collection* Hua chien chi. *"In this period," he writes, "the songs were mostly about girls of one kind or another—perhaps more of one kind than another. The anthology title might best be freely rendered* The Flowerbeds of Love." *As is clear from the pieces by Su Shih, later poets extended the range of subject matter, though there is almost invariably a romantic, even sentimental chord struck at the close.*

There is one individual genius whose surviving works consist mostly of tz'u. *This is Li Yü (Li Hou-chu), last ruler of the Southern T'ang dynasty. His capital at Nanking was seized by the first Sung emperor, Li himself dethroned and taken captive into exile at*

Pien-liang (Kaifeng) in the north. The selection of his work below constitutes almost an autobiography, lyrical and passionate, of this unhappy king.

A very different life, but eloquent again of that languid melancholy which is at the heart of the tz'u, is told by Li Ch'ing-chao. Of a number of gifted women poets of China, Li Ch'ing-chao is the most highly regarded.

•

Li Po

Tune: "Strangers in Saint's Coif"

[*P'u-sa man*]

Silent planes of woods woven in mist,
Cold hills a tinted thread to knot the heart.
    Dusk ascends the tall tower,
    On the tower, someone grieving.

    Aimless on this moonlit terrace
    Watching the birds' swift homing;
    Try to make out the road back—
    Halt after halt diminishing.

TRANSLATED BY CYRIL BIRCH

Wen T'ing-yün (*fl.* 859)

Five Poems to the "Strangers in Saint's Coif" Tune
[*P'u-sa man*]

1

On the bedscreen's folding panels, gold glimmers and fades.
Clouds of hair verge upon the fragrant snow of cheeks.
Languorous she rises, pencils the moth-eyebrows,
Dawdles over her toilet, slowly washing, combing.
Mirrors front and back reflect her flowers;
Face and blossoms illumine one the other.
Upon her new-embroidered silken jacket
Pairs and pairs of partridges in gold.

2

Blue tail-feathers and markings of gold on a pair of mandarin ducks,
And tiny ripples of water stirring the blue of a pond in spring;
Beside the pond there stands a crabapple tree,
Its branches filled with pink after the rain.
Her figured sleeve covers a dimpled smile
As a flying butterfly lights on the mistlike grass.
Her window gives on all this loveliness—
And news so seldom comes from the Jade Pass! [1]

3

There in her moonlit chamber she is dreaming of him still:
How delicate the willows, how languorous the spring!
In the grasses growing thick outside the gate
She hears his horse neigh as she waves goodbye. . . .

---

1. Frontier garrison west of Tun-huang.

By her colored quilt with kingfishers worked in gold
The scented candle has melted into tears.
Among the falling blossoms a nightjar cries—
And behind her green-gauze window the dream dissolves.

4

In the south courtyard everywhere willow floss covers the ground.
Sadly she listens to the sound of a sudden spring's-end shower;
After the rain, the slanting rays of sunset
And scent of almond blossoms fallen and scattered.
She silently makes up her sleepy face
And sets the folding screen about her pillow.
The time of day is nearing yellow twilight
As languorous and alone she leans by the gate.

5

A brilliant moon has just now reached the zenith of the night.
Behind the lowered blind all's still, no one to say a word.
Secluded there amid perpetual incense
She goes to bed in her same old careless make-up.
Sufficient are her sorrows of this year—
How could she bear to think about the past?
Flowers lie fallen as the moonlight pales,
And under her quilt she knows the chill of dawn.

Three Poems to the "Water-clock" Tune
[*Keng-lou tzu*]

1

The stars grow few
The night-drums cease
Orioles call beyond the blind as the moon sinks into dawn:
Dew heavy on the orchises
Wind aslant the willows
And all the courtyard heaped with fallen flowers.

Up in her empty chamber
Leaning at lattice rail

Is one forlorn as ever she was last year:
Spring's on the wane
But longing is endless,
And bygone joys like something in a dream.

2

Willow boughs long,
Spring rain thin;
Faint beyond the blossoms sounds the night-watch,
Startling migrant geese,
Rousing the crows on the walls . . .
Here on the painted screen, the partridges are gilt.

Tenuous wisps of fragrance
Seep through layered curtains
Where languishes a Lady Hsieh amid her pools and courts.[1]
Shading the crimson candle
She lowers the patterned blind;
Her dreams endure, but he will never know.

3

With my peacock hairpin
And my face powdered pink
There among the blossoms I had my moment with you.
You knew what I felt,
And I was sure you loved me.
Only Heaven can tell of such emotion!

Incense burned to ash,
Candle melted to tears—
The one is just like your heart, the other just like mine.
My pillow moist and clammy,
My pretty quilt all cold,
And I awake as the night-drum fades away.

---

1. Li Teh-yü (787-849) is said to have kept his reluctant concubine
Hsieh Ch'iu-niang in a luxurious mansion with pools and gardens.

Wei Chuang (?858-910)

Four Poems to the "Strangers in Saint's Coif" Tune
[*P'u-sa man*]

1

Every one's always saying how fine it is in the South,
How the best thing for the wanderer is to stay the rest of his days.
In spring the waters are bluer than the skies;
You drowse in your painted boat to the rain's murmur.
The wine-shop girls are lovely as the moon,
Their gleaming arms like paired drifts of snow.
Don't go back to your home until you're old—
Go home and it will surely break your heart.

2

Now they are only memories, the pleasures of the South.
In those days I was young and wore the light attire of spring;
Astride my horse I'd pause on the sloping bridge
As red sleeves beckoned from every room above.
Behind kingfisher screens with golden hinges
I drank and slept in the flowerbeds of love.
Were I to see those flowers once again,
Though white of head I swear I'd not go home.

3

Back in Loyang City now, how fine the spring must be—
While the bright young man of Loyang grows old in another land.
Willows there will be shading the esplanade . . .
Now of all times my heart grows insecure.
Here too is peachbloom over clear spring waters,

And on the waters pairs of ducks are swimming.
With knotted heart I watch the fading sunset
And think of you, of you who cannot know.

4

Gentlemen, I bid you all, tonight we must get dead drunk.
With the cups before us, let us have no talk about tomorrow.
All hail the bounty of our friend and host—
The wine is deep, our feelings no less deep.
We all must sigh that springtime's span is short,
So don't protest when the golden cups are filled.
Whenever you come by wine, then laugh and shout—
After all, how long does a man's life last?

Four Poems to Various Tunes:

1. Tune: "The Long Road Home"
[*Kuei kuo yao*]

Spring's on the wane—
Everywhere fallen blossoms, the very rain stained pink.
In his jewelled cage a melancholy parrot
Perches alone, without a mate.

I gaze to the South—how far the way?
I ask the flowers, but they say nothing.
Oh, when can he or I ever go back home!
I only wish I had his sapphire wings.

2. Tune: "A Visit to Golden Gate"
[*Yeh Chin-men*]

Useless, thinking of him;
No way to get word to each other.
The Lady in the Moon is beyond men's reach—
If you sent her a letter, where would it find her?

I've just awakened, and I feel so helpless.
I couldn't bear to take up his old letters.

All over the garden the flowers have fallen—
A lonely, lonely spring—
The sweet grass is so green it breaks my heart.

3. Tune: "The T'ien-t'ai Fairy"
[*T'ien hsien-tzu*]

I came back in the dead of night, sodden drunk as usual.
They helped me in through the curtains—I still didn't sober up.
The reek of liquor mingled with the scent of musky perfumes.
When they woke me up
I laughed out loud:
As the saying goes—how long does a man's life last!

4. Tune: "Little Ch'ung-shan"
[*Hsiao Ch'ung-shan*]

Shut out of Chao-yang Palace while springs come and go,[1]
Through endless watches of chilly nights
She dreams of his royal love.
She lies there thinking over the past, her soul all but dissolved,
Till her gown of gauze is wet,
Its red sleeves stained with tears.

To the sound of song and flute through door past door,
She walks the courtyard among the sweet green grasses
And leans at the Long Gate.
Her many, many sorrows—to whom can she tell them?
She stands there with her feelings knotted within
As the palaces grow dim in the yellow twilight.

---

1. Han Emperor Ch'eng-ti built this palace for a new favorite, displacing Pan Chieh-yü to whom is attributed the first of the innumerable laments on her fate.

Hsieh Chao-yün (10th Century)

Tune: "The Taoist Priestess"
[*Nü-kuan tzu*]

She has gone to seek the immortals,
Leaving behind her kingfisher pins, leaving her golden combs—
Gone to the cliffs and peaks
Curling the vapors round her for scarf of yellow gauze,
Shaping a cloud for nun's coif of white jade.
Cold the wild mists and the caves of mountain streams,
Chill the forest moon and the bridge of stones
Where in the still of night beneath the wind in the pines
She serves at Heaven's altar.

Ku Hsiung (*fl.* 928)

Tune: "The Willow Branch"
[*Yang-liu chih*]

On an autumn night in her scented room she broods in the lonely
    stillness.
The night wears on and on.
Incense fades among the hangings embroidered with ducks
    and drakes;
The gleam of the candle flickers.
Her thoughts are of her lover, off roaming far and wide—
No telling where he is,
As she listens to the murmur of the rain outside the blind
Where it drips on the plantain leaves.

Sun Kuang-hsien (d. 968)

Tune: "Free and Easy"

[*Feng-liu tzu*]

At a house on the avenue, toward sundown,
I caught a glimpse of a mate for an Immortal!
Daintily touched with powder,
Hair combed loose,
She gleamed in the shadow beneath the painted blind;
Then without word
Or sign,
Slowly trailing her silken sleeves, withdrew.

Lu Ch'ien-yi (*fl.* 931)

Tune: "The Fairy by the River"

[*Lin-chiang hsien*]

Far behind gate on fretted gate the weedgrown court is still;
Curtained windows forlornly face the autumn emptiness.
The feathered banners all are gone, no footfall breaks the silence,
The sound of song and flute from marble pavilions
Long broken off and scattered with the wind.

The misty moon, all unaware of change in men's affairs,
Still shines in the dead of night on the inner palace.
Lotuses huddle in a forgotten pool;
Mutely mourning the fallen kingdom
The pure dew weeps upon the fragrant petals.

Yen Hsüan (*fl.* 932)

Tune: "River Tales"

[*Ho-ch'uan*]

Autumn rain,
Autumn rain!
No moon, no night.
Drip, drip! pour, pour!
Lamp gone out, pallet cold, hating loneliness—
Pretty witch,
Unbearably sad!

West wind rustles faintly in the bamboo by the window,
Stops and begins again.
On her cold-creamed cheeks two teardrops hang like jade.
How many times he promised, "When the wild geese come—"
He broke the date;
The geese came back, he didn't.

Mao Hsi-chen (*fl.* 947)

Tune: "Conquering Tibet"

[*Ting Hsi-fan*]

Bright green, dark shade mottle the garden;
Orioles chirp to each other,
Butterflies dart in pairs
Sporting with the rose.

By the rail in the slant late sunlight, gentle breezes
Draw out the fragrance of a damask dress,
But bring no breath of news about a lover
Or when he's coming back.

Tune: "The Flowers of the Rear Courts"

[*Hou-t'ing hua*]

Her dainty arms are sleeved with freshly scented Southern
   gauze
And circled with thin gold bracelets;
Wordless she leans at the railing and flutters an airy fan,
Half hiding her tinted face.

In fading spring's warm sunshine the orioles grow languid,
The court is strewn with petals.
If only I could stay there with her always,
In the hidden garden by her painted parlor!

TRANSLATED BY GLEN W. BAXTER

Li Yü (937-978)

Tune: "Strangers in Saint's Coif"

[P'u-sa man]

In Paradise Palace a T'ien-t'ai beauty
Is taking a nap in Painted Hall
And no one talks.
She moves her pillow.
Black shines her hair as a black bird's feathers.
From her flowered dress one senses strange perfumes.

As I tiptoe up, a pearl jewel moves
And she wakes from a dream of mandarin ducks.
On her serious face a small smile gathers:
We watch each other in endless love.

Tune: "Joy in the Oriole's Flight"

[Hsi ch'ien ying]

With dawn the moon declines.
The morning clouds disperse.
I lie wordless propped against my pillows,
With longing, longing thoughts of dreams gone back to
        fragrant meadows.
Heaven is high. The geese are scarcely heard.

The orioles twitter and fly away.
The last flowers fall to pieces.
I am lonely in the center of the palace.
"Stop them sweeping up those fallen petals in the garden:
Leave them for the dancing girls to walk on going home."

Tune: "The Butterfly Woos the Blossoms"

[Tieh lien hua]

Nightlong I wander aimlessly about the palace lawn.
The Ching Ming Festival is gone
And suddenly I feel with sadness spring's approaching end.
Now and then a splashing raindrop comes along the wind
And passing clouds obscure the paling moon.

Plum and peach trees, lingering, scent the evening air.
But someone is whispering in the swing,
Laughing and whispering in the swing!
The heart is a single skein, but with a thousand straggling threads
    that tear.
In all the world is no safe place to spread it out and leave it there.

Tune: "Viewing the River Plum-blossom"

[Wang chiang mei]

My idlest dreams go farthest,
South to a land of fragrant springs
And rivers green beneath our boat-borne flutes and strings,
Back to a town of floating catkins mixed with golden dust
And crowds that fought to see the flowers.

Tune: "Viewing the River Plum-blossom"

[Wang chiang mei]

My idlest dreams go farthest,
South to a land of brilliant days in fall,
A thousand miles of hills and rivers, cold-colored sunsets,
Flowering reeds that hid the boats of solitary men,
And flutes played overhead in moonlit rooms.

Tune: "Night Crow Calling"

[Wu yeh t'i]

The flowered woods have dropped their springtime rose festoon,
So soon, so soon.

But night-blowing winds and the cold dawn rain were bound
to be.

Your tear-stained rouge will keep me
Drinking here beside you.
Then—who knows when again?
Our lives are sad like rivers turning always toward the sea.

Tune: "Happiness of Meeting"

[*Hsiang chien huan*]

Wordless, alone, I go upstairs to the western chamber.
The moon is like a sickle.
The lonely trees in the courtyard are locked up there with
the autumn night.
Scissors do not sever,
Nor reason unravel,
The pain of separation.
It lodges in the heart with a taste of its own.

Tune: "Wave-washed Sand"

[*Lang t'ao sha*]

The past is only fit to be regretted.
It stares unbanished in my face
Now autumn winds have claimed the court and moss usurped
the stairs.
The shades hang down in rows, idle and unraised,
Throughout the day, for no one calls.

My golden sword is laid away.
My valor lies in weeds.
When nights are cold, the weather still, and a haloed
moon is out
I think of all that marble palace
Mirrored empty in the Huai.

Tune: "Washing Her Robe in the Creek"

[*Wan ch'i sha*]

One dream that scarce outlasts the burning of a candle or a
petal's fall

And then we go.
I should like to visit ruins and weep for men no longer there,
But heaven makes our circumstances contradict our hearts.

In the river-house I watch the heedless, flowing waters, waiting
　　for the moon,
And when it comes, slanting vaguely on the darkened flowers
　　and the house,
I climb up to look, not minding if my sleeves be wetter still.

TRANSLATED BY SAM HOUSTON BROCK

Tune: "Gazing to the South"

[*Wang Chiang-nan*]

Immeasurable pain!
My dreaming soul last night was king again.
As in past days
I wandered through the Palace of Delight,
And in my dream
Down grassy garden ways
Glided my chariot, smoother than a summer stream;
There was moonlight,
The trees were blossoming,
And a faint wind softened the air of night,
For it was spring.

TRANSLATED BY ARTHUR WALEY

Tune: "The Beautiful Lady Yü"

[*Yü mei-jen*]

When will the last flower fall, the last moon fade?
So many sorrows lie behind.
Again last night the east wind filled my room—
O gaze not on the lost kingdom under this bright moon.

Still in her light my palace gleams as jade
(Only from bright cheeks beauty dies).
To know the sum of human suffering
Look at this river rolling eastward in the spring.

TRANSLATED BY CYRIL BIRCH

Anonymous Woman Poet (10th Century)

Tune: "The Drunken Young Lord"

[*Tsui kung-tzu*]

Outside my door
                the dog barking
I know what it is
                My lover's here
Off with my stockings
                down
                perfumed stairs
My good-for-nothing lover
                    is drunk tonight

I help him into
                my silk-curtained bed
Will he take off the silk gown?
                    O! O! not he
Milord is drunk
                and drunk let him be
Better that
                than sleeping alone

Li Ts'un-hsü (885-926)

Tune: "Memories of Fairy Grace"

[*Yi hsin-tzu*]

Feasted once
          in deep peach glades
one song
      phoenix to phoenix
      danced and sang
I recall
     —how long!
           saying goodbye to her
Tears mingled together
             hand on arm to the door
       like a dream
       like a dream
faded moon
fallen blossoms
      thick mist
         over all

TRANSLATED BY C. H. KWÔCK AND VINCENT MC HUGH

354

Su Shih (1037-1101)

Tune: "The Charms of Nien-nu"

[*Nien-nu chiao*][1]

For ten years the living and the dead have been far severed;
Though not thinking of you,
Naturally I cannot forget.
Your lonely grave is a thousand miles away,
Nowhere to tell my grief.
Even if we could meet, you would not recognize me;
My face is all covered with dust,
The hair at my temples shows frosty.

Last night in a dream I returned home
And at the chamber window
Saw you at your toilet;
We looked at each other in silence and melted into tears.
I cherish in my memory year by year the place of heartbreaking,
In the moonlit night
The knoll of short pines.

Tune: "Water Music Prelude"
[*Shui-tiao ko-t'ou*][2]

When did the moon begin to shine?
Lifting my cup I ask of Heaven.
I wonder in the heavenly palaces and castles
What season it is tonight.
I wish to go up there on the wind

---

1. Written in memory of his wife, who died before either she or Su had reached the age of thirty.
2. Written while thinking of his younger brother, Tzu-yu.

But am afraid the crystal domes and jade halls
Would be too cold on high.
So I dance with my limpid shadow
As if I were no longer on earth.

Around rich bowers,
Into sweet boudoirs,
Shining upon the inmates still awake
The moon should have no regrets.
Why is she always at the full when men are separated?
Men have their woe and joy, parting and meeting;
The moon has her dimness and brightness, waxing and waning.
Never from of old has been lasting perfection.
I only wish that you and I may be ever well and hale,
That both of us may watch the fair moon, even a thousand
        miles apart.

Tune: "The Charms of Nien-nu"

[*Nien-nu chiao*][1]

The waves of the mighty river flowing eastward
Have swept away the brilliant figures of a thousand generations.
West of the old fortress,
So people say, is Lord Chou's Red Cliff of the time of the
        Three Kingdoms. ·
The tumbling rocks thrust into the air;
The roaring surges dash upon the shore,
Rolling into a thousand drifts of snow.
The River and the mountains make a vivid picture—
What a host of heroes once were!

And I recall the young Lord then,
Newly married to the fair Younger Ch'iao,
His valorous features shown forth;
With a feather fan and a silken cap

---

1. A poem on that same Red Cliff which occasioned the two prose poems,
below. Su speaks of it as "Lord Chou's Red Cliff" because it was here, in the
year 208 in the time of the Three Kingdoms, that Chou Yü of Wu won a
decisive victory over the fleet of Wei.

Amid talking and laughing he put his enemy's ships to
    ashes and smoke.
While my thoughts wander in the country of old,
Romantic persons might smile at my early grey hair.
Ah! life is but like a dream;
With a cup of wine, let me yet pour a libation to the moon
    on the River.

TRANSLATED BY CH'U TA-KAO

Li Ch'ing-chao (1081-?1149)

Tune: "Crimson Lips Adorned"

[*Tien chiang ch'un*]

Ride in the swing
                                over
she stands up
                        languid
                        flexing delicate hands
Multitudinous dew
                                on thin flower
a mist of sweat
                        dampens
                        her light dress through
She looks
                A stranger coming
Her stockings down
                        Gold hairpin slipped
Shyly
                she runs
and
        leaning against the door jamb
looks back
lingering
                to sniff at a green plum

Tune: "Magnolia Blossom"

[*T'ien tzu mu-lan hua*]

Bought
                from the flower-peddler's tray

one spring branch
                    just open
                    in bloom
Droplets
                    fleck it evenly
still clouded red
                    with a mist of dew
I'm afraid he'll
                    take it into his head
that my face is not
                    so fair!
                    so fair!
In high-
combed hair
            I fasten
                    a gold pin
                    aslant
There!
let him look
                    Let him compare the two

Tune: "The Butterfly Woos the Blossoms"

[*Tieh lien hua*]

Long placid evening
                    my diversions few
I
            vacantly dreaming of Ch'ang-an
how the road
                    goes up
                    to the old capital
Please tell them:
                    spring
                    is fine
                    this year
Flower glow
moon shadow   set each other off

Pleasant to take   wine
                   food:
              without picking and choosing
Excellent wine
                   a tart plum
—just right for my mood
Tipsy
         I put a flower in my hair
                   O flower! flower!
                   don't make fun of me
Have pity!
                   Spring
                   like all men living
                             will soon
                             grow old

Tune: "Endless Union"

[*Yung yu lo*]

Sunset
              molten bronze
evening clouds
                   marbled white jade
         Where is he?
A mist of light
                             stains the willows
Plum blowing
                   A flute's wail
         Spring reveries
         how much you know!
New Year's Eve
                   the merrymaking festival
Serene weather—
                        wind
              no   in its wake?
                        rain
Friends come
              to invite me out

horses

traveling carts

I thank these wine-drinking friends

poem-making companions

At the capital

joyful days

In my room

much

time to myself

I recall

another New Year's Eve

how I put on

the green-feather headdress

narrow snow-white sash

worked

with gold thread

Headdress and sash

to vie with any beauty

I

haggard now

wind-tangled locks

hair

frosted white

at the temple

Too diffident

to venture among flowers

I loiter

under the window screen

eavesdropping

on the talk

and laughter

of others

Tune: "Spring at Wu-ling"

[*Wu-ling ch'un*]

Wind stopped

earth

smelling of fallen blossoms
Day almost over
Too weary to comb my hair
His belongings here
He here no longer
Everything useless
Before I can say a word
tears flow first

At Twin Stream
they say
the spring still beautiful
I too
would like to go rowing in a light boat
but I'm afraid
that little boat on Twin Stream
would not carry
so much sorrow!

TRANSLATED BY C. H. KWÔCK AND VINCENT MC HUGH

Tune: "One Sprig of Plum"

[*Yi chien mei*]

The scent of red lotus fades, and the mat feels cool.
I loosen my robe
To board the boat alone.
Who sends a message through the clouds?
As the swan formation returns
Moonlight fills the western chamber.
The petals shall fall and the water shall flow:
One kind of longing,
Two victims of unnamed grief.
There is no way to be rid of this thought;
Just as it recedes from the eyebrows
In the heart it swells.

Tune: "The Approach of Bliss"

[*Hao-shih chin*]

The wind dies and fallen petals pile deep—
      Masses of red and snow beyond the curtain.
Long remembered is the season after crabapple has bloomed—
      A time to mourn the vanished spring.
All the wine done, the songs sung, and the cups lying empty,
      See the lamp, how it flickers, now dim, now bright.
My thought already cannot bear this quiet grief
      And yet there should come a cuckoo's call.

Tune: "Dream Song"

[*Ju meng ling*]

Often remembered is the evening on the creek
      When wine flowed in the arbor and we lost our way.
It was late; our boat returning after a happy day
      Entered by mistake a patch of clustering lotus.
          As we hurried to get through,
           Hurried to get through,
A flock of herons, startled, rose to the sky.

TRANSLATED BY K. Y. HSÜ

Two Prose Masters of the Sung Dynasty

Dominating this section is an abridged version of a celebrated letter by Su Shih (1037-1101). Though the longest, this letter was only one of a series which Su addressed to the ambitious young emperor Shen-tsung. The writer was in his middle thirties and in no position of responsibility in the administration, but he took it upon himself to voice widespread indignation against the high-handed measures of the "reformist" premier Wang An-shih. Largely as a consequence of these letters Su was demoted to a provincial post—though this was a minor setback in a career which was to prove a stormy one.

The letter informs the emperor of the precise nature and purposes of the proposed new measures, warns him of possible consequences and boldly confronts him with the gravest threat of all, that of the adverse verdict of history on his own regime. If it were no more than a parliamentary essay in opposition to new taxes and the like, then there would be no place for the letter in an anthology of literature. But in Su Shih's eloquent defence of moral principle as the guiding force in state affairs we see literary effort directed towards its most exalted end: all belles lettres were merely a preparatory exercise, the tempering of a weapon that it might be equal to such a demand. And even more, from Su Shih's desperate earnestness we learn something of the true nobility of the man himself.

Lin Yutang has given the title The Gay Genius *to his biography of Su Shih (Su Tung-p'o). At the heart, as this letter indicates, of the political life of his day, outstanding in his governorship of Hang-chow, ranked among the greatest of poets and essayists, Su Shih* was a truly remarkable example of a remarkable pattern of man, the Chinese scholar-official of imperial times.

Ou-yang Hsiu (1007-1072), under whom Su Shih studied, was a fit heir to Han Yü as leader of the Ancient Style movement of his day. He is represented here only by two short pieces. The first is an exercise in the genre of the preface, a succinct statement whose grace and dignity tell much of the author himself as well as of the two friends he celebrates. Then with his "Sound of Autumn" and Su Shih's two essays under the title of "The Red Cliff" we have in this section three specimens of prose poems. The Chinese term fu is that same generic name we translated as "rhyme prose" for Han times. But with the Sung masters the rhythms have loosened so far in the direction of prose that the inverted phrase "prose poem" seems to fit better, and the translations below are constructed accordingly.

•

Ou-yang Hsiu

Preface to the Collected Poems of the Priest Pi-yen

[*Shih Pi-yen shih chi hsü*]

As a young man, visiting the capital to attend the metropolitan examinations, I had every opportunity to enter into friendships with the most honourable and valiant men of the age. Yet none the less we would remark that for forty years past, the state had held all within the four seas in unity, a stop had been put to armed strife and the world had been nourished and fostered in freedom from troubles of any kind; therefore it must often befall that men of worth, skilled in stratagem, bold and of high purpose, men far removed from the common run would find no scope for their abilities but prefer concealment to emergence on the public scene. Among the wooded hills they might live as butchers or pedlars, grow old and die without ever becoming known to the world; nor was it possible to seek out such men or draw them forth.

Then, later, I found my friend, now dead, Shih Man-ch'ing. Man-ch'ing was a man of broad vision and high mind. If those in power could find no use for such material, neither could Man-ch'ing stoop to seek any compromise. Lacking an outlet for his ambitions, time and again he would carouse with commoners and yokels, never to grow weary though soused and staggering drunk. Feeling that with such ease I had found one of those "concealed and not to be frequented," I welcomed excursions with him and hoped thereby to forward under cover my search for the men of rare worth of this world.

The Buddhist priest Pi-yen was Man-ch'ing's oldest friend. He again was one who could set the world aside, who had the spirit to prize his independence. The two took unreserved delight in each other: where Man-ch'ing's refuge was in wine, Pi-yen's was in his religion, but each was a man of rare quality. Yet in nothing did they find greater joy than the composition of songs and verses. At the far edge of drinking, at the height of the wine they would sing and declaim, laugh and yell for the joy of all that lies beneath the sky— oh, but these were heroes! There was no man of all the flower of the age who did not long to join their company, and I myself went many times to their rooms.

Over the space of ten years Pi-yen travelled, north across the River, east as far as Tsinan and Yün-ch'eng, but never did he meet with a place to suit his purpose. When sore straits forced his return Man-ch'ing was dead, and he himself was aging and in poor health. Ah me, to have seen with my own eyes the vigour and the decline of two such men—and now, that I myself should be drawing close to my dotage!

Man-ch'ing's own verse had limpid depth, yet he in his turn would praise the work of Pi-yen as finely tempered, the product of the true poetic mind.

In stature and countenance Pi-yen is of heroic mould, and there is a greatness in his bosom. Devoting himself to Buddhism he has found no practical application for his gifts. Only his practice of poetry might carry his name before the world, but again he is too idle to care. Now, an old man, he has opened his bundle and brought out some three or four hundred pieces, all of them charming.

Not since Man-ch'ing died has Pi-yen, desolate, found a place to turn. But now he has been learning of the abundant hills and streams of the southeast, the soaring grandeur of whose crests, the booming torrents of whose waters have such power to strengthen and restore; and he has conceived the desire to make a journey there. From this we may know that age has not robbed him of his purpose. On the eve of his departure I compose this preface to his verses, telling of past years of vigour in lament for his decline.

TRANSLATED BY CYRIL BIRCH

The Sound of Autumn

[*Ch'iu sheng fu*]

One night when I was reading I heard a sound coming from the southwest. I listened in alarm and said:

"Strange! At first it was a patter of drops, a rustle in the air; all at once it is hooves stampeding, breakers on a shore; it is as though huge waves were rising startled in the night, in a sudden downpour of wind and rain. When it collides with something it clatters and clangs, gold and iron ring together; and then it is as though soldiers were advancing against an enemy, running swiftly with the gag between their teeth, and you hear no voiced command, only the tramping of men and horses."

I said to the boy, "What is this sound? Go out and look."

The boy returned and told me:

"The moon and stars gleam white and pure, the bright river is in the sky, nowhere is there any sound of man; the sound is over among the trees."

"Alas, how sad!" I answered. "This is the sound of autumn, why has it come? If you wish to know the signs which distinguish autumn, its colours are pale and mournful, mists dissolve and the clouds are gathered away; its face is clear and bright, with the sky high overhead and a sun of crystal; its breath is harsh and raw, and pierces our flesh and bones; its mood is dreary and dismal, and the mountains and rivers lie desolate. Therefore the sound which distinguishes it is keen and chill, and bursts out in shrieks and screams. The rich, close grass teems vivid green, the thriving verdure of splendid trees delights us; then autumn sweeps the grass and its colour changes, touches the trees and their leaves drop. The power by which it lays waste and scatters far and wide is the unexpended fury of the breath of heaven and earth. For autumn is the minister of punishments, the dark Yin among the four seasons. It is also the symbol of arms, metal among the five elements. Hence it is said to be the breath of justice between Heaven and Earth, and its eternal purpose is stern execution. By Heaven's design for all things, spring gives birth, autumn ripens. That is why in music the note *Shang* reigns over the scale of the west, and *Yi-tse* is the pitch-tube of the seventh month. *Shang* means 'grief,' the grief of things which grow old. *Yi* means 'destruction'; things which have passed their prime deserve to be killed.[1]

"Alas! The plants and trees feel nothing, whirling and scattering when their time comes; but mankind has consciousness, the noblest of all intelligences. A hundred cares move his heart, a myriad tasks weary his body; the least motion within him is sure to make his spirit waver, and how much more when he thinks of that which is beyond the reach of his endeavour, worries over that which his wisdom is powerless to alter! It is natural that his glossy crimson changes to withered wood, that his ebony black is soon flecked with stars! What use is it for man, who is not of the substance of metal and stone, to wish to vie for glory with the grass and trees? But remembering who it is who commits this violence against us, why should we complain against the sound of autumn?"

The boy did not answer, had dropped his head and fallen asleep. I heard only the sound of the insects chirping from the four walls, as though to make a chorus for my sighs.

TRANSLATED BY A. C. GRAHAM

---

1. Autumn is the season in which the *ch'i* (breath) which energizes heaven and earth is on the wane, having passed from its Yang or active to its Yin or passive phase. Its place among the four seasons corresponds with that of the board of punishments among the five departments of state, of metal among the five elements, of justice among the five cardinal virtues, of *Shang* among the notes of the pentatonic scale, of the west among the four cardinal points. The seventh month, which is the first month of autumn, corresponds with *Yi-tse* among the twelve tubes which determine musical pitch.

Su Shih

Letter to the Emperor Shen-tsung

[Shang Shen-tsung shu]

Not long ago, ignoring the deficiency of my understanding and the inferiority of my position, I sent to your majesty a confidential letter, in which I spoke of the affair of buying lamps. Being fully aware of the outrage offered to the imperial dignity and of the unpardonable nature of my offence, I lay upon my rush mat in my private chamber and awaited execution by the axe. But though in secret I kept a close watch for some ten days, the dread command did not come; and when I asked the prefect of the city, it was to find that the affair of buying the lamps had been dropped. By this I know that your majesty has not only pardoned my offence, but also has been able to listen to my words; and my surprise and delight, exceeding all my hopes, brought me to shed tears of gratitude. For to be unsparing in the correction of their faults and to follow the better way as naturally as the river its course was the unwearying aim of the sage-kings Yao and Shun, of Yü and T'ang, and a virtue that since the times of Ch'in and Han scarcely has been seen. When I reflect that the buying of the lamps was a blemish too trivial to tarnish a brilliance comparable with that of the sun and moon, and yet your majesty completely reversed your rules and that without an instant's hesitation, this, I can say, is to observe the possessor of surpassing wisdom listening to the words of the most foolish, the wielder of absolute power bending before a common man. I now know that with such qualities your majesty can yourself become a Yao or a Shun, a T'ang or a Wu; that by bringing prosperity to your people you can abjure the use of punishments, and by strengthening your armies secure the submission of the barbarian tribes. To such a ruler, how could I be ungrateful? My sole duty is to pluck out my heart, to sacrifice my life in your service: no other course is open to me but to exercise on your behalf the full extent of my powers.

I said in my previous letter that I realised there were state matters of greater importance than the buying of lamps. My reason for taking so trifling a matter first was that the sage does not approve of offering criticism until confidence has been gained, the man of principle deplores the giving of profound advice upon superficial acquaintance. That was why I made my initial experiment with a trivial matter, and left the more important to be spoken of later. Now the complete forgiveness granted to me by your majesty shows that I have received permission to speak further; and it would be a fault in me if given this permission I remained silent. For this reason I now wish to speak fully and the points I wish to make are three. All that I ask of your majesty is to win the allegiance of your people, to raise the standards of public life, and to maintain discipline.

Every man has some source upon which he depends. It is because your ministers are dependent upon your majesty's commands that they can enforce duties upon the common people, because they are dependent upon your majesty's laws that they can overcome the strong and violent. But the ruler's source of dependence: what is that? "My dominion over the mass of the people," says the *Book of Documents*, "is as precarious as the driving of a team of six horses with rotten reins," meaning that no position in the whole land is so insecure as that of the ruler. When his people are united, they become his subjects: when disunited, his enemies; and the space between union and disunion will not admit even the breadth of a hair or the width of a copper cash. And so when all his people turn to him, he is called ruler; when each follows his personal allegiance, he is called solitary. We can see from this that it is entirely upon the allegiance of his people that the ruler depends. Popular allegiance is as necessary to the ruler as the root to the tree, oil to the lamp, water to the fish, land to the farmer, or goods to the merchant. For as the tree without roots withers, the lamp without oil is extinguished, the fish without water dies, the farmer without land starves, and the merchant without goods becomes impoverished, so the ruler, if he lose the allegiance of his people, will perish. This is the inevitable law, the inescapable calamity, which rightly should be held in terror. From the earliest times it has been so, and none but a madman who courted death and disaster would venture to give free rein to the desires of his own heart in defiance of the will of his people.[1] This is what I mean by begging your majesty to secure the allegiance of the people.

There is no lack of scholars ready to proffer advice, but has any of them ever told your majesty of the true reason why a state survives or falls, why its life is long or short? A state depends for its survival not upon the measure of its power but upon the loftiness of its ethical standards, and for length of life not upon the degree of its prosperity but upon the soundness of its national character. High standards and sound character will ensure the survival even of the weakest and most impoverished state; but neither power nor prosperity will save a state of low standards and unsound character from speedy destruction. And a ruler who knows this knows what he should value. For this reason the better rulers of the past never allowed weakness to lower the standards nor poverty to injure the character of their state; and it was always by their standards and character that the wise judged the state of another. No state was stronger than Ch'i, yet Chou Kung knew that in time to come some minister would assassinate its ruler and usurp the power; no state was weaker than Wei, yet Chi Tzu saw that it would be the last to fall. Even after Wu had inflicted a total defeat upon Ch'u and entered its capital at Ying, Feng Hua, the chief minister of Ch'en, knew that Ch'u would certainly rise again. I therefore beg that your majesty direct your whole energies to the raising of ethical standards and the improvement of the national character, rather than win quick successes out of greed for power and for prosperity. The possession of the wealth of Sui and the power of Ch'in, the conquest of the Hsi-hsia in the west and of the Liao in the north would rightly be credited to your majesty as successes; but it is not upon such successes that the life of your empire depends. For the

---

1. At this point the writer enters on the detailed enumeration and discussion of abuses. These include a new "coordinating commission," suspected of being merely a "tool for getting money"; an impracticable new dam; various new taxes; the imposition of public service on families having no male or only a single male member; and government interference in the activities of merchants. The bulk of Su Shih's discussion of these matters is given in de Bary, ed.: *Sources of Chinese Tradition*, pp. 481-86. For reasons of space, and because of the extremely specific and technical nature of the questions at issue, this entire middle section of the letter is omitted here.

life of the state is like the life of man; as the life of the state depends upon its national character, so the life of man depends upon
his vital force. Many men have reached old age in spite of infirmity;
many have met a violent death in spite of bodily vigour. Infirmity
will not prove harmful so long as the vital force remains intact; but
once it is all expended vigour becomes all the more dangerous.
That is why those who are careful of their lives are cautious in
their movements and moderate in their eating and drinking, taking
a regular course of exercise, and breathing out the old and taking
in the new; if they are compelled to use drugs, they choose those
of the best quality and the soundest ingredients, which can be
taken over a long period without harmful effects. Then their five
organs will work in concert, and length of life will be assured. But
those who are careless despise the results of caution and modera-
tion, and ignore the effects of correct breathing; hating the herb
drugs they use those of inferior quality, and promote their physical
strength at the expense of their vital force. But once the root of
the tree is in danger, it will not be long before it falls; and of the
state of the empire, this is no less true. For this reason I beg your
majesty to guard the national character as jealously as you would
guard your vital force.

The sages of the past were not unaware that remorseless leg-
islation will bring the masses into line, and that the ruthless can
achieve results; that faithful honesty is not far removed from the
unpractical, and that mature experience at first sight may seem
like dilatory obtuseness. Even so, they were never prepared to exchange the one for the other, for they knew that they stood to lose
far more than they would gain. Tsao San was a chancellor of more
than ordinary wisdom, and his advice was: "Be careful not to upset
the prisons and the markets"; Huang Pa, who was among the good
officials, said, "The art of government is to avoid extremes." When
Hsieh An was reproached for neglecting state affairs from principles of quietism he merely laughed and said, "The First Emperor
of Ch'in employed the legalists, and his dynasty fell in the second
generation." The government of our own emperor Jen-tsung was
characterised by a kindly tolerance in the operation of the law,
and a respect for precedence in the granting of promotion; he was
anxious to conceal rather than expose the faults of his system, and
would never lightly alter existing regulations. It is true that his

practical achievements were not spectacular, that his armies were defeated nine times out of ten, and that his budgets barely balanced. His whole concern was to make a generous example felt and a sense of duty appreciated by all his people. For these reasons when he died the whole empire felt as though they had lost a father or mother, and for the long continuation of his line some credit is certainly due to him. For Jen-tsung knew what was of real value. This, however, our present reformers fail to appreciate; and because they see only that in Jen-tsung's latter years the official class as a whole was compliant rather than energetic, they wish now to regiment it by burdensome supervision and discipline it by the exercise of cleverness and ingenuity. To this end they have produced a number of enterprising and newly promoted persons, with whose help they will lay all plans with an eye to speedy results; but long before their benefits are received, the whole country will be completely demoralised.

When even heaven's seasons are irregular, who among men can be free from faults? The ruler of a state must swallow some dirt; the hypercritical have no friends. If you, your majesty, will open your arms to all, talent will be fairly employed; but if you insist upon establishing a far-flung network of spies and are bent upon the detection of small blemishes, men will lose their peace of mind and devise excuses for temporary retirement. This would be to the detriment of your court and not at all what your majesty would wish. Long ago Han Wen-ti would have given office to the keeper of the Tiger Park had not Chang Shih-chih feared the corrupting influence of his ready tongue. But now you seem prepared to choose your officers for mere fluency and dismiss them for slowness in repartee, to mistake empty boasting and disregard of truth for ability, or an arrogant and ungovernable temper for high character: if this be really so, then of the magnanimous example of our late emperor nothing will soon remain.

The custom in official appointments has always been to make every man ascend the ladder of promotion and to demand concrete achievements even from the most exceptionally gifted, partly to ensure that they will have gained enough experience and be sufficiently aware of difficulties to undertake nothing without due consideration, partly to guard against objections by waiting until successful achievements have warranted their reputations. When Liu

Pei of Shu, founder of a dynasty, long ago appointed Huang Chung lieutenant-general, Chu-ko Liang deplored so ill-advised a step. "Chung's reputation," he said, "does not stand as high as those of Kuan Yü or Chang Fei. There will certainly be discontent if they are suddenly made equal in rank"—and later Kuan Yü did raise objections as he had feared. Now Huang Chung was a very gallant general, and the relations between Liu Pei and his followers were extremely intimate: if, even so, he was prepared to reconsider this question, how much less should it be ignored by others.

It is the hope of titles and of emoluments that spurs the ambitions of the majority. If these are granted only to men who have rendered good service and it is thus made clear that they can be attained only with difficulty and after patient waiting, every man will restrain himself from overeagerness and bear his lot contentedly. But now by widely opening doors to rapid advancement, you raise hopes of unexpected aggrandisement and possibilities of reaching the highest honours at a single bound; and as the successful will not admit to having been lucky, the unsuccessful who have been passed over will nourish a grievance. Who knows what may not happen if the normal official who has risen in the ordinary way is made to feel so unreasonably ashamed of his inferiority? Any hope that you may have of raising the national character will certainly disappear. Normally ten or more years elapse before selected candidates are transferred to duties at the capital: and this promotion is granted only after arduous probation and the most rigorous inspection of their previous records. For the discovery of a single false step taken during those early days will normally condemn them to a life of obscurity and neglect. But now, if office is to be given them on the recommendation of a single individual, and as if that were not enough, honours are to be heaped upon them, how do you propose to satisfy those who have arrived only after rendering distinguished services and after long waiting for their due? These ordinary officials may become provincial or district governors; but they have so long complained that vacancies are far too few for the number of candidates that the opening of further doors to clever careerists must surely be unthinkable. A really strong invasion by these clever people will fill with apprehension and anxiety all those who are less able to look after their own interests, and you should not lose sight of the fact that this may have its disadvantages no less than

its benefits. As it is, in recent years, as the number of clever careerists has increased the number of the less astute has diminished, and
for encouragement, pity, sympathy, and assistance they have only
your majesty to look to. Yet such a request as that made for the
Three Fiscal Offices the other day, that one man be selected from
each district to take over their accounts and receive permission to
apply for some post out of his due turn as a reward for his services,
means that in a few years' time the inspectorate will be swelled
by some three hundred additional men, each with a prior claim to
fill any vacancy that may occur. This must make the position of the
ordinary official who has to wait his turn all the harder. Besides
these, there are controllers of the various grain transports and su-
pervisors of agriculture and irrigation, already wielding the authority of inspector, and all full of ambition for rapid advancement;
there are officials at question time hoping for speedy promotion by
fitting in with your majesty's wishes, and official informers looking
for quick preferment by demonstrating their own superiority; and
when all of these raise their officious and rival voices, the truth
is thrown to the winds. I ask your majesty to consider the virtues
of simple laws and of a quiet mind, leave no foothold for wicked-
ness, and give the standards of the people a chance for improvement. This is what I mean when I beg you to raise the national
character.

In the government of the earliest days a proper balance was
preserved between the power vested in internal and in external
hands. By such dynasties as the Chou and the T'ang also, much
power was placed in external hands with the regrettable result that
a powerful state might enquire the weight of the imperial tripods.[2]
But dynasties like the Ch'in and Wei made the opposite mistake,
the effects of which were equally disastrous: for under them were
to be found dishonest ministers who were prepared to call a deer
a horse. At a time of great prosperity the sage anticipates a period
of decline, and will endeavour by means of precautionary legisla-
tion to save his state from possible disaster. Now the taxes of the
whole empire are being entered in the books of the Three Offices
and large bodies of troops are concentrated in the capital, which

---

2. With a view to appropriating to itself these symbols of rule.

judging by the past, looks as if too much power were being placed in internal hands.

Now I am well aware that so humble a servant as I cannot fully appreciate or comprehend the deep-laid and farsighted plans of emperors of the past; but the single example of the power delegated to the censors seems to me a preventive measure of supreme wisdom. Though several hundred men from the Ch'in and Han down to the Five Dynasties paid for their criticism with their lives, since the beginning of our dynasty no man has ever suffered for a single word. On the contrary the slightest criticism has won for the censors immediate promotion. Permission has been given them to lay anonymous charges against officers of the highest rank; no man however great or however humble is safe from their denunciations. Even the Son of Heaven has changed countenance when their remonstrances have been directed against his person; even the chancellor has awaited punishment. A lesser age cannot be expected to appreciate the profound wisdom of the sages; but merely because not all the censors selected have been good, nor all their criticisms justified, there is no reason to condemn as futile the practice of giving great power to men of acute perception. Its justification is that by breaking the first shoots of ministerial dishonesty, it guards against the evil of too great a concentration of internal power. For though the censor's criticism is enough to break the first beginnings of ministerial dishonesty, even armed force cannot remove it once it has spread. Now, I know, the laws are scrupulously administered, the court is sincerely honest, and there could be no possible ground for the rise of what I call ministerial dishonesty. None the less cats are kept to get rid of mice, and freedom from mice is no excuse for keeping a cat that could not catch one; dogs are there to keep away thieves, and the absence of thieves is no reason for keeping a dog that will not bark. The emperors of the past established the office of censor as a protection for their descendants for all time; can your majesty afford to ignore the motives of the one or the needs of the other? Can court discipline ever have any stronger support?

Judging from notes made when I was young, and from what I heard my elders say, the criticisms made by the censors always followed public opinion, upholding what the people approved, and condemning what they attacked. When Ying-tsung first ascended the throne, he laid before his ministers a proposal to confer a title upon his father. This the censors of the period were prepared to fight to the death, not because it was a bad mistake on the part of their emperor, nor because it lacked justification, but simply because it aroused popular dissension and failed to meet with unanimous approval. But now when the whole air is charged with criticism indignation is encountered on every side, and the trends of public opinion are plain for all to see, the censors look at one another and utter not a word, and the hopes of all are dashed to the ground. For even the most moderate will rouse themselves if wrong is successfully denounced by the censors; but let them once lose their authority, and even the boldest will be impotent. What I fear is that the subservience of censors, once established as a habit, will become widespread, that they will degenerate into the personal tools of the powerful, and that the emperor will thus be completely isolated. For who knows what may not happen once their corrective influence is lost?

"In the service of a ruler," said Confucius, "no place should be found for the unprincipled. For first they will fear failure to gain their ambitions; next they will fear to lose what they have gained, and this fear may drive them to anything." When I first read these words, I wondered whether they did not go too far; for it seemed to me that fear to lose what they had gained could involve the unprincipled in no greater crime than sycophancy to keep their positions. But when I read how Li Ssu set the Second Emperor on the throne and so brought to an end the dynasty of Ch'in, because he was afraid that Meng T'ien might rob him of his power, and how Lu Chi deceived Te-tsung and provoked a second rebellion because he feared that Li Huai-kuang would enumerate his misdeeds, I saw that Confucius' words were in fact accurate. For these two men, inspired originally by fear of losing what they had gained, did harm great enough to destroy their country. It is this that convinces me that if the ruler of a state in time of peace always employs ministers disinterested enough to defy him to his face, he may expect them to follow their sense of duty far enough to die for him in times of danger. But how can he demand from them this last sacrifice at such a juncture, if even in normal times they are unable to utter a single word. Staffed exclusively by such ministers this empire, too, will be in daily peril. For the man of principle will mix, but will not imitate; the unprincipled man will imitate but not mix. Mixing is like the blending of soup, imitation like the meeting of waters parted by a boat. Sun Pao aptly said, "Chou Kung was a very wise and Chao Kung a very good man. None the less their disagreements were recorded in the annals, without any disgrace to either." Wang Tao of Chin may well claim the title of elder statesman, and every word he spoke to his followers was applauded by the whole company. This, however, did not please Wang Shu, who expressed the opinion that no man who was not a Yao or a Shun could be right in everything that he said; and Tao himself withdrew his hands into his sleeves, and thanked him. When all speak the same words, think the same thoughts, and sing the same tune, every single one will pass for better; and should there be by any chance any unprincipled person present, then what means will the ruler have of recognising him for what he is? That is what I mean when I speak of maintaining discipline.

It is not my wish to criticise the new measures one by one nor to raise mere tiresome objections. Such recent acts as the curtailment of the civil list, the compulsory examinations for privileged sons, and the re-equipment and review of the armed forces are examples of your majesty's divine wisdom and unswerving determination; and when public opinion has been satisfied, how should I venture to object? The three requests, however, which I have made to your majesty do not express a personal opinion, but embody a natural grievance, universally felt and known to all. If the court be entirely innocent of the matter of my three requests, this empire is fortunate indeed, and in that good fortune I hope to share; but if there be the smallest justification for them your majesty should not fail to take them to heart.

However, that I should lay any proposals before you may well seem as foolish as for the short-lived ant to try to wield the power of the thunder; nor for these repeated exhibitions of my folly can I continually expect pardon. At the most I deserve that my head be severed from my body and my whole family exterminated, at the least that I be deprived of my official titles and exiled to some desert on the road to which I should perish. Nevertheless I know that your majesty will not inflict such punishment; for though my natural gifts are poor in the extreme, I am at the least honest and sincere. In my recent comment upon the new scheme of training and examinations, I directly opposed the fundamental ideas of a high minister, and for that expected banishment, nor dared even to think that I should escape unscathed. But your majesty instead allowed my criticisms and graciously granted me an audience. After opening your heart to me most freely for a long time you even said to me, "You have our permission to tell us wherein lie the merits and demerits of the present regime, even though they be errors and omissions of our own." To this I answered, "You, your majesty, are possessed of innate wisdom, and of heaven-sent skill in the arts of peace and of war. Fear then no lack, whether of understanding, energy, or determination; guard only against being too hasty in seeking to govern or too precipitate in granting promotion, and be tolerant in listening to advice." Then when you bade me explain in full for what reasons I had said these words, you bowed your head in agreement, and said, "We will give our fullest consideration to the three points which you have made." And so my foolish temerity was not limited only to that single day, nor was the pardon granted me for that one moment, but extended over a long space of time. Your majesty, I know, would not pardon me at the outset, and fail to forgive me at the finish; and it is because I rely on this that I have spoken without fear.

My real fear is that I have many sharp critics and resentful enemies who will so slander me with cunning arguments and so entrap me in their deadly toils that it may well be impossible for your majesty to pardon me, even though you should be so minded. This is my greatest danger. For death for myself I care nothing: I fear only that the empire may be deterred by my example, and that no one will speak freely again. For this reason I have pondered night and day for many months, and two or three times destroyed what I had written. But the gratitude I feel to your majesty for having once listened to a single word from me will not be restrained, and in the end I send to you this letter, asking only that you show pity for my foolish loyalty, and pardon me at the last. Thus fortified it will not be too much for me humbly to await my sentence, and the coming of misery and fear.

TRANSLATED BY J. K. RIDEOUT

The Red Cliff, I

[*Ch'ih pi fu*]

In the autumn of the year *jen-hsü* (1082), on the sixteenth day of the seventh month, I took some guests on an excursion by boat under the Red Cliff. A cool wind blew gently, without starting a ripple. I raised my cup to pledge the guests; and we chanted the Full Moon ode, and sang out the verse about the modest lady. After a while the moon came up above the hills to the east, and wandered between the Dipper and the Herdboy Star; a dewy whiteness spanned the river, merging the light on the water into the sky. We let the tiny reed drift on its course, over ten thousand acres of dissolving surface which streamed to the horizon, as though we were leaning on the void with the winds for chariot, on a journey none knew where, hovering above as though we had left the world of men behind us and risen as immortals on newly sprouted wings.

Soon, when the wines we drank had made us merry, we sang this verse tapping the gunwales:

Cinnamon oars in front, magnolia oars behind
Beat the transparent brightness, thrust upstream against
    flooding light.
So far, the one I yearn for,
The girl up there at the other end of the sky!

One of the guests accompanied the song on a flute. The notes were like sobs, as though he were complaining, longing, weeping, accusing; the wavering resonance lingered, a thread of sound which did not snap off, till the dragons underwater danced in the black depths, and a widow wept in our lonely boat.

I solemnly straightened my lapels, sat up stiffly, and asked the guest: "Why do you play like this?"

The guest answered:

"'Full moon, stars few
Rooks and magpies fly south . . .'

"Was it not Ts'ao Ts'ao who wrote this verse? Gazing toward Hsia-k'ou in the west, Wu-ch'ang in the east, mountains and river wind-

ing around him, stifling in the close green . . . was it not here that
Ts'ao Ts'ao was hemmed in by young Chou? At the time when he
smote Ching-chou and came eastwards with the current down from
Chiang-ling, his vessels were prow by stern for a thousand miles,
his banners hid the sky; looking down on the river winecup in hand,
composing his poem with lance slung crossways, truly he was the
hero of his age, but where is he now? And what are you and I com-
pared with him? Fishermen and woodcutters on the river's isles,
with fish and shrimps and deer for mates, riding a boat as shallow
as a leaf, pouring each other drinks from bottlegourds; mayflies
visiting between heaven and earth, infinitesimal grains in the vast
sea, mourning the passing of our instant of life, envying the long
river which never ends! Let me cling to a flying immortal and roam
far off, and live for ever with the full moon in my arms! But knowing that this art is not easily learned, I commit the fading echoes
to the sad wind."

"Have you really understood the water and the moon?" I said.
"The one streams past so swiftly yet is never gone; the other for
ever waxes and wanes yet finally has never grown nor diminished.
For if you look at the aspect which changes, heaven and earth
cannot last for one blink; but if you look at the aspect which is
changeless, the worlds within and outside you are both inexhaustible,
and what reasons have you to envy anything?

"Moreover, each thing between heaven and earth has its owner,
and even one hair which is not mine I can never make part of me.
Only the cool wind on the river, or the full moon in the mountains,
caught by the ear becomes a sound, or met by the eye changes to
colour; no one forbids me to make it mine, no limit is set to the
use of it; this is the inexhaustible treasury of the creator of things,
and you and I can share in the joy of it."

The guest smiled, consoled. We washed the cups and poured
more wine. After the nuts and savouries were finished, and the wine-
cups and dishes lay scattered around, we leaned pillowed back
to back in the middle of the boat, and did not notice when the sky
turned white in the east.

The Red Cliff, II

In the same year, on the fifteenth of the tenth month, I went on foot from Snow Hall on my way back to Lin-kao, accompanied by two guests. When we passed the slope of Huang-ni the frost and dew had fallen already. The trees were stripped of leaves, our shadows were on the ground; we looked up at the full moon, enjoyed its radiance around us; and as we walked we took turns to sing. At last I said with a sigh:

"I have guests but no wine; and if I did have wine there would be nothing to eat with it. The moon is white and the wind is cool; what shall we do on a fine night like this?"

"Today at twilight," a guest said, "I went out with a net and caught some fish with big mouths and little scales; they look like the perch of Pine River. But where shall we get wine?"

After we reached home I consulted my wife.

"I have a quart of wine," she said. "I have been keeping it for a long time, in case you needed it in some emergency."

So we took the wine and fish and went on another excursion under the Red Cliff. The river flowed noisily, the banks rose sheer for a thousand feet; the moon was small between the high mountains, and stones stood out from the sunken water; even after so few months and days river and mountains were no longer recognisable. I lifted the hem of my coat and stepped ashore. Treading on the steep rocks, parting the dense thickets, I squatted on stones shaped like tigers and leopards, climbed twisted pines like undulating dragons, drew myself up to the perilous nests of perching falcons, looked down into the underwater palace of the River God. Neither of the guests was able to keep up with me.

I called them with a long slicing whistle. The grass and trees stirred and shook, cries in the mountains were answered in the valleys, the wind rose and the water seethed. I felt uneasy and dispirited, frightened by the eeriness of it; I shivered, it was impossible to stay there. We turned back and climbed into the boat, loosed it in midstream, and moored it where it drifted to a stop. At that time it was nearly midnight, and there was silence all around us. Just then a single crane came from the east across the river, with wings turning like cartwheels, white jacketed and black underneath. With a long dragging wail it dived at our boat and flew on westwards.

The guests left at once, and I too retired to sleep. I dreamed of a Taoist monk who passed below Lin-kao swaggering in a feathered robe. He asked me with a bow:

"Did you enjoy your trip to the Red Cliff?"

I asked his name; he looked down and did not answer.

"Ah, I know you! Last night, the thing which flew past me wailing, wasn't it you?"

The Taoist looked back at me smiling. I woke with a start and opened the door to look for him, but did not see him anywhere.

TRANSLATED BY A. C. GRAHAM

A Poet of the Sung Dynasty

Gerald Bullett's translations furnish a rare example of the success-ful use of rhyme in English translation from Chinese verse. The ten shih *below are selected from a sequence of sixty in which Fan Ch'eng-ta (1126-93), somewhat in the manner of T'ao Ch'ien almost eight centuries earlier though with a less profound philosophical commitment, sings the seasonal joys of the countryman.*

●

Fan Ch'eng-ta: From "A Rural Sequence"

[*Ssu shih t'ien yüan tsa hsing*]

Early Spring

But for the cockerel calling the noon hour,
No voice is heard in the lane of willow-flower.
The young leaves of the mulberry, half-uncurl'd,
Are showing their green tips to the warm world.
Waking from quiet dreams, where I drowse in my chair,
With nothing to do but enjoy the bright air,
I look from my window, flooded now with noon,
And see the silkworm break from her cocoon.

Swink how we may, evenings or early morn,
Our garden crops bring only a bare return.
The seeds once planted, set in careful rows,
Children and birds must be accounted foes.
Here is a needling thorn-hedge, finger-high;
Here young bamboos shoot up to greet the sky.
Let's now, to trick these thieving friends of ours,
Turn fishermen and net the cherry-flowers.

Late Spring

On the shores of a desolate region of lake and sky
The new-dug ivory roots of lotus lie.
Green coins of water-lily, lying so still,
Persuade us half to forget the gradual swell.
Now is the plum season, gusty and quick,
With petals flying and fruit soon to pick.
Savouring the hour I mark where bulrush shoots
Come sidling up from long lateral roots.

386

Few come this way, and if a stranger should,
See how the birds dart off, into the wood!
Shadows of dove-grey dusk the hills obscure,
And gathering reach my fagot-builded door.
In a boat light as a leaf, still visible,
My lad-of-all-work plies his single scull.
Alone, I weave my fence, of lithe bamboo,
And ducks go primly homewards, two by two.

Summer

Heavy the trees with load of golden plum,
To mellow age the almond fruit is come,
Flowers of the rape-turnip bloom and blow,
And the long barley blossoms into snow.
Long and serene my solitary day
Hedged in with summer, and never a passer-by,
Except these bright-wing'd insect-travellers
Going about their glittering affairs.

Cocoons, in boiling vats put to proof,
Thicken the rising water with snow-white surf.
The wheels of the spinning-cart buzz: the spray falls
Pat on the workers' dried-leaf overalls.
These mulberry-girls cross hands, as for a game,
To give each other joy of the great time,
Pleased that the coarser silk has proved to be rare
And the fine filament plentiful this year.

Autumn

Here Madam Spider spins and weaves
Her web under the low eaves,
Plotting to take and hold in snare
The wing'd unwary passenger.
A dragonfly and bees, in dire suspense,
Hang there for evidence:
Which sight so little pleases my old age,
I send my rustic boy to raise the siege.

Nightlong endures this unexpected frost,
A sign that autumn nears her end at last:
The woods, where yesterday only greenness was,
Wear now a richly-embroidered silken dress.
Here, in my orange-garden's secret air,
Another transformation is astir:
Hidden among these leaves of emerald
Ten thousand golden spheres are safe in fold.

Winter

Low lie the hills as day goes slowly down:
High above is a pale slice of moon.
Drowsy from sleep I swallow my due potion,
Then take a stroll to set my blood in motion.
Tall trees, assaulted by the frosty wind,
With thrice ten thousand leaves scatter the ground.
Leaning upon my staff, I noddingly
Compute how many herons' nests there be.

Now add we to the roof another patch
Of dried rushes to reinforce the thatch;
Like monks' pavilions safe from winter's harm,
With thicker clay-cast make our houses warm.
So we be safe inside, and he without,
Let the wind roar at his pleasure and tear about,
While we within enjoy the music he makes,
Playing his flute in the fence of bamboo-stakes.

TRANSLATED BY GERALD BULLETT

Yüan Dynasty

1280-1367

Two Yüan Plays

Yüan was the dynastic title taken by the Mongols, who ruled China for about a century. Their regime inflicted a severe shock on the established pattern of life of the scholar-official. The most notable repercussion in the world of letters was the emergence of more popular modes of writing. Of stage entertainment only rudimentary kinds seem to have been known to earlier generations, although judgment is difficult when so little has survived. But with the Yüan a particular style of drama, the tsa-chü, came to its full flowering and for the first time engaged the talents of leading writers.

Properly in the Yüan tsa-chü only one character has a singing role (Li K'uei in the first play below, the emperor in the second): an interesting mark of the evolution of the form from the Sung period "recitation" of songs interspersed with prose narrative sections. The sections for singing, the "arias" so to say, carry a kind of poetry which itself may trace its ancestry back to the tz'u, the poems of irregular metre, via the longer and looser song form san-ch'ü. Each act of a Yüan play consists, in effect, of a sequence of these song patterns set to a given key. Dialogue bears forward the action of the play and may establish dramatic situations of some power; but it is largely functional in the service of the poetry of the arias. In these, word-pictures are painted, moods defined and the inner feelings of the central figure vividly expressed.

Mostly devoid of poetic value are the regular-metre verses spoken by various characters (J. I. Crump, like Donald Keene who bases his translation of the arias on blank verse, rhymes these spoken verses for a deliberate doggerel effect). Conventional also

391

*are the soliloquies in which characters identify themselves on each
appearance and further risk the displeasure of the reader (if not the
casual spectator) by recapitulating the action with every new act.*

Autumn in the Palace of Han *is a tragedy justly famed for the
portrayal in its closing scenes of the autumnal loneliness of an emperor.* Li K'uei Carries Thorns *provides a complete contrast. It is
one of a large number of plays built upon incidents from the cycle
of legends about Sung Chiang and his twelfth-century bandit
brotherhood, that cycle which eventually took form as the novel*
The Men of the Marshes (Shui hu chuan). *This play about Li K'uei
is in fact the only surviving piece which tallies exactly with incidents
in the novel itself. Dr. Crump's translation recaptures the lusty
comedy of the original, the fun of slapstick, the play of verbal wit
and the incongruities arising from the assumption of the role of
knight-errant by the bloodthirsty "Black Whirlwind": "who says
we've no scenery at Liang-shan P'o?" asks our knight as he ends an
idyllic descriptive aria; "—I'll knock his teeth out!" Wu Hsüeh-
chiu, who appears briefly in the play, is the Schoolteacher, Wu Yung,
who figures so prominently in the extract from* The Men of the
Marshes *given below.*

●

K'ang Chin-chih (*fl.* 1279)

Li K'uei Carries Thorns

[*Li K'uei fu ching*]

ACT I

SUNG CHIANG, WU HSÜEH-CHIU *and* LU CHIH-SHEN *enter with attendants.*

SUNG CHIANG (*recites*): By the camp gate tumbles the quarrelling
mountain stream,
Wild flowers thrust aslant under sweat-stained headbands.
Black stroked words against the yellow banner's gleam:
"Delivering the people and aiding heaven's way."

I am Sung Chiang, also known as Sung Kung-ming, and called
the Herald of Justice. Once I was a clerk in the yamen at Yün-
ch'eng but having killed the hag Yen P'o-hsi while I was drunk,
I was sent to the prison garrison at Chiang-chou. Where the
road passed near the foot of Mt. Liang I met brother Ch'ao Kai,
who rescued me and brought me up here to the mountain.
Afterwards, when Ch'ao Kai died during the three battles at
Chu-chia village, the men made me their leader and I have
brought together thirty-six large bands, seventy-two small bands
and a host of followers. My power holds Shantung in awe and
my orders are obeyed in Hopei.

Of all the festivals in the year the two I like best are the
third of the third month, called *ch'ing-ming* and the ninth of
the ninth month, called *ch'ung-yang*. Today is *ch'ing-ming* and
I've given my men three days leave to visit the graves of their
ancestors. When three days are up, all must return to the mountain and whoever disobeys the order will be beheaded.

(*recites*): Who does not fear my strict command
And rigid limits to his leave,

393

But loiters longer half an hour
Returns to find there's no reprieve.   (*Exit.*)

(*Enter the elderly* WANG LIN.)

WANG LIN (*recites*): The straw[1] hangs high on its springy staff,
A *p'i-p'a* sounds in the willows' shade.
Disciples of Kao-yang[2] linger with us
For mine host's wines are wondrously made.

My name is Wang Lin, I live in Hsing-hua Village where I run a little business in wines to make a living. Of the three in my family, my wife died long ago and left me and my daughter, Man-t'ang Ch'iao, who is now eighteen and as yet unbetrothed. My place is quite close to the foot of Mount Liang and the leaders of the band all buy their wine from my shop. I've got the wine vessel warmed, so I'll go see if anyone's coming.

(*Enter* SUNG KANG *and* LU CHIH-EN *in villain-clown makeup.*)

SUNG KANG: Firewood's cheap, rice isn't dear, and we're glib rascals, two to the pair! I'm Sung Kang and the name of my mate here is Lu Chih-en. Because we come from around Mt. Liang we're pretending to be from there. So I'm calling myself Sung Chiang and he's supposed to be Lu Chih-shen. We're here at old Wang Lin's wineshop in Hsing-hua Village to get a drink. (*He sees* WANG LIN.) Old Wang, is there any wine?

WANG LIN: There is indeed, brother, please be seated inside.

SUNG KANG: Give us five hundred coppers' worth. Old Wang, do you recognize the two of us?

WANG LIN: My old eyes are rather bad. I don't recognize you gentlemen.

---

1. Bundles of straw and banners were used as wineshop signs.
2. A warrior named Li Shih-ch'i tried to see the first emperor of Han while the latter was still battling for the throne. "What does this Li Shih-ch'i look like?" the emperor asked his aide. "A Confucianist," was the reply. "Send him off," said the emperor. Li Shih-ch'i heard the conversation and hooted, "I'm a disciple of Kao Yang-chiu (i.e. the wine of Kao-yang), not Confucius." Almost the identical poem is used in Yüan operas whenever a tavern-keeper appears on the stage.

SUNG KANG: Well, I'm Sung Chiang and this is Lu Chih-shen. A lot of our men from the mountain come to your place and cut up a bit. If any of them give you trouble you come up the mountain and let me know. I'll take care of things for you.

WANG LIN: You men on the mountain are all good fellows, helping the way of heaven. No, there's been no trouble, but I hope you will forgive an old man for not recognizing your honor. If I had known it was you I would have gone out to meet your honor. Very inhospitable, I hope you'll not hold it against me. Many thanks to you captains for patronizing my place. (*Hands him wine.*) Please, your honor, drink it down. (SUNG KANG *drinks.*) Here's more.

LU CHIH-EN (*drinking*): That's good wine, brother.

SUNG KANG: Are there any more in your family, old Wang?

WANG LIN: No one to speak of, your honor, only an eighteen-year-old unbetrothed daughter called Man-t'ang Ch'iao. Since I've no one else to do the honors, let me bring her out to pass your excellency his cup. It will show my respect.

SUNG KANG: Since she's not yet betrothed perhaps you'd better not.

LU CHIH-EN: There's nothing wrong with that, brother; bring her out.

WANG LIN (*calls*): Man-t'ang Ch'iao, my child, come here.

MAN-T'ANG CH'IAO: Why did you call me, Father?

WANG LIN: You may not realize it, but Sung Kung-ming from the mountain is here today in person. Come and serve him a cup.

MAN-T'ANG CH'IAO: Wouldn't that be improper, Father?

WANG LIN: No harm. (*She sees the guests.*)

SUNG KANG: I've been afraid of the smell of make-up all my life. Back a little, please.

WANG LIN: Give the two gentlemen a cup, my child. (*She hands them wine.*)

SUNG KANG: And I'll give old Wang a cup of wine. (*He hands* WANG LIN *a cup.*) My, an old gentleman like you shouldn't have holes in his clothes. Here, let me give you my red sash to patch them. (WANG LIN *takes the sash.*)

LU CHIH-EN: Hah! you didn't know it, but the wine we handed you was the betrothal wine and the sash was the red wedding gift. Now we'll just take your daughter with us to be mistress of Sung Kung-ming's fort. We'll borrow her for three days and we'll return her on the fourth. We're leaving for the mountain. (*They lead the girl off.*)

WANG LIN: My old eyes, my arms, lived only for my daughter. Oh, what shall I do now? (*Weeps.*)

(*Enter* LI K'UEI, *drunk.*)

LI K'UEI: Drinking without getting drunk is worse than being sober. I am Li K'uei from Liang-shan P'o. Because of my dark skin men call me the Black Whirlwind. Brother Sung Chiang has given us three days leave to enjoy ourselves and "dance among the new shoots"[3] so of course I had to come down from the mountain to buy a few pots from old Wang Lin and get rotten drunk.

(*sings*): The spirit of drink is hard to lay,
        And laid, the intemperate ghost rises again.
        Seeking wine in the village I asked of Wang Liu—

(*speaks*): Said I to him can you find me some wine?
        But that rascal said nothing, only made a bee line
        from my hand. So I yelled to him, whoa!
        And I chased him and grabbed him so he couldn't go.
        I lifted my hand just to tap him a bit,
        then he splits his whiskers yelling, "Daddy, don't hit."

(*sings*): Said Wang Liu, they have some over there.
        But this is the time of Ch'ing-ming.
        The wind and rain are sadly tender with the flowers.
        The soft breeze gently rises,
        At evening the showers cease.

---

3. This seems once to have been a peasant dance in the fields, but it means simply to enjoy the *ch'ing-ming* festival in most operas where it appears.

Yonder, half hid in willows, lies the tavern.
From the bright blaze of peach blossoms peeks
The fisherman's little boat, blending with
Ripples in the green waters of spring.
Migrant swallows fly to and fro,
Sand gulls wheel far and near.

(*speaks*): Who says we have no scenery at Liang-shan P'o?
I'll knock his teeth out!

(*sings*): For there green mountains stand in cloud-locked
beauty
And willow isles lie caught in nets of mist.

(*speaks*): There's a golden oriole peck, peck, pecking at a blossom on the peach tree and the petals are falling into the
water. They're beautiful! Where did I hear something of
that sort? Let me think—ah, it was brother Wu Hsüeh-
chiu who said it.

(*sings*): Light, impudent blossoms chasing the water's flow.

(*speaks*): Let me pick up a petal and look at it. How red it is!
(*Laughing.*) And how black the finger!

(*sings*): But how its make-up glows through a coat of white
powder.

(*speaks*): Ah, but I take pity on you, little petal, and toss you
back to join the others. And I'll follow you, chase you, eager
to run after blossoms.

(*sings*): And so I reach the shop at Meadowbridge hard by
Willowford.

(*speaks*): This won't do! I'd be disobeying Sung Chiang's orders.
I'd better go back.

(*sings*): I try not to drink, but the waving of the wineshop
Flag has made my steps waver.
How it dances in the east wind atop its springy staff.

(*speaks*): Wang Lin, have you any wine? And it won't be on
the house, either. Look, gold chips, and they're yours if
you'll bring me a drink.

WANG LIN (*wiping tears away*): What would I want with gold chips?

LI K'UEI (*laughing*): His mouth says what would I want with them, but see how fast he snugs them away in his bosom! Bring me wine, Wang Lin.

WANG LIN: It's coming, coming. (*Strains the wine into a cup.*)

LI K'UEI: If I get this into my belly I'll be back again and again. But if I don't drink I'll get drier.

(*sings*): In former days I had wine debts everywhere I went;
    Of every ten taverns nine carried my bill.

(*speaks*): Old Wang,

(*sings*): Your shop in Hsing-hua Village need not blush before
    the Hsieh pavilion.
    Set me down your Ch'un-p'ei wine, smooth as warm oil,
    Cook me up a fat lamb, the prize of your stock.
    On one side cooking meat, on the other wine new-poured
        and fuming,
    Make fragrance such as steals from spice bags
        yet unopened.
    Now while the senses urge shall I drink three cups one
        upon another.
    How true: "one cup dissolves a thousand woes."

(*speaks*): Old Wang, I have finished the wine,

(*sings*): All my cares are gone. Indeed, lost somewhere behind
    my brain.
    And I have drunk the time away without a halt.

(*speaks*): I *am* drunk!

(*sings*): What matter if I fall by the road
    Or sleep with my head on a wine vat?

(*speaks*): I tell you old Wang Lin,

(*sings*): I'll pour it in till the vessel itself perishes!

(*speaks*): Old Wang, this wine is cold. Heat me some more.

WANG LIN: Yes sir. (*Changes the wine, weeping.*) Oh, Man-t'ang ch'iao . . .

LI K'UEI: Come, warm up the wine.

WANG LIN (*still weeping*): Oh, my Man-t'ang Ch'iao.

LI K'UEI: Old Wang, haven't I already given you the money? What's bothering you?

WANG LIN: It's not because of you, brother. It's just that I have troubles I can't hide. Please, drink your wine.

LI K'UEI (*sings*): Times past haven't we stood before the jug and talked quite readily?
Then why today do you feign to see me not at all?

WANG LIN: You don't understand, I've just given my daughter away . . . that's what troubles me.

LI K'UEI (*sings*): Ai! You addled old egg, how far you go in search of complaints.

(*speaks*): If it bothers you so much, why did you marry her off in the first place?

WANG LIN: Aiya! My Man-t'ang Ch'iao.

LI K'UEI (*sings*): You should have kept her by you till her face was blue-veined
And her hair hoary white.

(*speaks*): Don't you know there are three things in the world that cannot be kept as they are?

WANG LIN: What three?

LI K'UEI: A silkworm when it ages, a man when he ages, and

(*sings*): You foolish old man, as it's often said,
A woman grown cannot be kept as she was.

(*speaks*): But, tell me, who did your daughter marry?

WANG LIN: Oh my brother, if my daughter had married do you think I would be troubled as I am? To my sorrow she has been carried off by a bandit.

LI K'UEI: Bandit is it! Next you'll be telling me I stole her!

> (*sings*): Here stand I staring with rage
> And there he with his tricky tongue
> And mouth too ready to open in gossip.
> One instant of deceit now and I'll be stung to wrath.
> A torch will change your little thatch gourd
> To crumbling ashes, and its wine vats to shattered
> potsherds.

> (*speaks*): Up with my two broadaxes and

> (*sings*): Down come your fruit trees of the serpent roots
> And your brown buffalo of the flaring horns.

> (*speaks*): Listen Old Wang, if what you say is true, that's an
> end of it. But if it is false, you will never get by me!

WANG LIN: Please your honor! Rest your anger and its shouts and listen to an old man while he tells it all slowly. Two men came here for wine. One said he was Sung Chiang and the other was Lu Chih-shen. I said, since it's really two gentlemen from Liang-shan P'o, and I had no others to come pay their respects except an eighteen-year-old, unbetrothed daughter, I would call her out to present herself and serve the gentlemen their wine, which would show my deference. Well, I called her out and she passed the wine and then Sung Chiang passed me three cups and thrust a red sash into my bosom. Lu Chih-shen said the three cups were marriage wine and the red cloth was a wedding gift. He said Sung Chiang had one hundred and eight leaders under him and lacked only one thing. He said, take this eighteen-year-old girl as mistress of the fort. He said today was an auspicious day for such things so they would take her back to Liang-shan P'o. They said they would keep her for three days and then send her back to me. Then they left, taking her with them. And left me, an old man whose very eyes and arms live for that girl, to watch her led away in broad daylight. Oh, brother, would you still have me untroubled?

LI K'UEI: But what proof have you of this?

WANG LIN: Here's the red sash, that's proof.

LI K'UEI: I wouldn't believe the story, but only the gentry have those things. Old Wang, you draw off a good crock of wine, slaughter a fine calf, and in three days I'll bring your daughter, Man-t'ang Ch'iao, back here just as nice as you please. How's that?

WANG LIN: Oh, brother, if you can bring her home, a crock of wine, a slaughtered calf, even killing myself would be too little to repay you your kindness!

LI K'UEI (*sings*): I'll handle your enemies, but please
No more sputtering of thanks like crackling bamboo
From a mouth which dangles like a handleless dipper.

(*speaks*): Sung Chiang,

(*sings*): Taking your pleasure you have done a grievous wrong.
I swear, though spilt water is water lost, yet I'll
Have reasons from you, not rubbish.
You'd best have your case by heart,
No substitution of what isn't for what is,
Only what happened, first first and last last.

(*speaks*): Now I'm off to Sung Chiang to tell him his crimes. I'll have him take leave of his thirty-six bands, seventy-two groups and host of followers and bring him, along with Lu Chih-shen, down from the mountain to your village. And when I call you, don't you pull in your head like a turtle!

WANG LIN: If I don't see them I can say nothing. But I'll know the both of them if I do see them. And as for not identifying them— it will be strange if I don't bite a hole in that Sung Chiang!

LI K'UEI: Alas for poor Sung Chiang, what an awful death! Hey, old Wang, I do believe that's brother Sung Chiang coming right now!

(WANG LIN *stares about him in fright*.)

No, it's not, old one, I do but tease you. However,

(*sings*): Mind you don't become my spear with a point of wax.

(*Exit*.)

WANG LIN: Brother Li has left. I suppose I should straighten up the shop. Oh, Man-t'ang Ch'iao, I shall die of grief over you.

(*Exit.*)

ACT II

SUNG CHIANG, WU HSÜEH-CHIU *and* LU CHIH-SHEN *enter with attendants.*

SUNG CHIANG (*recites*): Our flag is dyed in the blood of men
The oil of our lamps is fat from their brains.
The dogs we give their skulls and scalps
And the crows their livers and reins.

(*speaks*): I am Sung Chiang. I've given my men three days leave for *ch'ing-ming* to leave the mountain, dance among the new shoots and enjoy themselves. This is already the end of the third day. When the watch-drum sounds three times in the Hall of Justice the men must all assemble. Guards, to the main gate and watch for arrivals.

SOLDIER: Yes sir.

(LI K'UEI *enters.*)

LI K'UEI: It is I, Li K'uei, and I carry the red sash to see Sung Chiang.

(*sings*): Shaking black anger that bristles my brown beard.
Now no halt can be called. Crushing my hands together in eagerness,
Time and again I lose the battle against
Passions which assail my heart.
Oh Sung Chiang, why was this done? What reason
Was it, I wonder, what compelled him?
My anger swells like thunder.
But no matter who he is or I am, or that we have
Half a lifetime without a rift,
Today the sun and the moon reach eclipse!
Only a few words may pass between us,
Yet I fear the mark it can leave on our friendship.
Hesitation besets me again . . .

(*speaks*): Guard, report to Sung Chiang that Li K'uei has arrived.

SOLDIER: Yes sir. (*Reports to* SUNG CHIANG:) Brother Li K'uei has arrived.

SUNG CHIANG: Send him in.

SOLDIER: He is here.

LI K'UEI: Brother Hsüeh-chiu: "How bright the hat on the new groom, how tight fit the sleeves to welcome a new son-in-law." And where is our Sung Kung-ming? Come forth and exchange bows with me. I have a little silver here to send my new sister-in-law in salutation.

SUNG CHIANG: What impertinence the rascal has! He salutes Hsüeh-chiu and ignores me; and what drivel he's talking!

LI K'UEI (*sings*): Ai! To you my friend-till-death
Heartiest congratulations!

SUNG CHIANG: Congratulations . . . ?

LI K'UEI (*sings*): But where do I find the lady of our fortress?

(*Points to Lu Chih-shen, speaking*): Tonsured donkey, a fine deed you've done.

(*sings*): You've kept your own bed-cover clean
But I'll not let you off.

SUNG CHIANG: What? Now he's after you, Chih-shen!

LI K'UEI (*sings*): Their eyes bulge with innocence as they stoutly deny it,
But we shall have it out right here.

SUNG CHIANG: Li K'uei, when you left the mountain something happened down there. Why don't you tell me exactly what? (LI K'UEI *stands mute and looking troubled.*) Well, since you don't wish to tell me, tell it to brother Hsüeh-chiu from the beginning.

LI K'UEI (*sings*): If my brother wanted a wife
The bald one would make plans for him.

SUNG CHIANG: He says you make plans, Chih-shen. What plans?

LU CHIH-SHEN: The man has guzzled so much wine that he's whizzing around like a gadfly out of reach of the fly-whisk. Who can understand his bzz bzz?

LI K'UEI (*sings*): So it is then. Liang-shan P'o's a heaven without a sun.

(*Snatches out his axe to chop the flagstaff.*)

Then I must bring our yellow banner down!

(*Everyone wrestles him for the axe.*)

SUNG CHIANG: You Iron Ox! Before anything is straightened out you ·draw your axe to cut down the yellow flag. What's the meaning of this?

WU HSÜEH-CHIU: Brother, you're too direct and violent.

LI K'UEI (*sings*): Too direct, you say, and violent.
Then I must dress the scene to please.

(*Calls to others.*) Come here, all you men.

SUNG CHIANG: What should they come here for?

LI K'UEI (*sings*): To attend a banquet for the happy families.

SUNG CHIANG: A banquet?

LI K'UEI (*sings*): Yes, we'll not let you off so lightly,
Oh, noble matchmaker-monk, oh veritable Tripitaka,
Nor you, radiant bridegroom, true Robber Chih.[4]

SUNG CHIANG: Brother, where did you go to drink when you left the mountain, and who did you meet? I think he must have said a good deal about me! Tell us from the beginning, but tell it clearly.

LI K'UEI (*sings*): Not only did you carry off his fair flower of spring,
You now abandon him to die of grief, that old, white head at Meadowbridge.

SUNG CHIANG: There must be something hidden in all this.

---

4. The patron saint of robbers, cf. Ssu-ma Ch'ien's "Biography of Po Yi and Shu Ch'i," p. 104, above.

LI K'UEI (*sings*): Plainly was it hidden, this deed!
    And such grief for him to be severed, living, from his life.

    (*speaks*): Oh, Sung Chiang,

    (*sings*): He has just grievance against you.

SUNG CHIANG: Ah, so it's old Wang Lin's girl; and you say I took her? No need to say I didn't, but if I had he should be happy, not grieved. But you tell me about it and I'll listen.

LI K'UEI (*sings*): Sometimes the old man weakly weeps in his thatched shop;

    (*speaks*): He looks toward our mountain, crying his hatred for Sung Chiang,

    (*sings*): He restlessly rises to his feet
        Then whimpers with wrath outside his wicker door,

    (*speaks*): Crying, "Oh, Man-t'ang Ch'iao;"

    (*sings*): And sighingly sobs his suffering.

SUNG CHIANG: What does he do with his sorrow?

LI K'UEI (*sings*): He then gloomily looms by his wine vats,

    (*speaks*): Picks up a dipper, takes the straw lid from the crock, dips up cold wine and drinks it in gulps;

    (*sings*): Then dully, dizzily drunk,
        Clutching his scrap of matting
        He listlessly lays it out on his brick bed.

    (*speaks*): He goes outside again to look; sees no sign of her, and then,

    (*sings*): He sadly sinks to his bed
        And snuffles and whines to sleep.
        This will not do, brother,
        This will not do!

SUNG CHIANG: What does he mean now?

LI K'UEI (*sings*): The old man says there are no sweet waters on our mountain,
        Nor honor in our men.

SUNG CHIANG: Brother Hsüeh-chiu, it seems some footpads have dared assume our names and have done this thing. But we cannot be sure. Our brother should have brought some proof so we could be certain.

LI K'UEI: But I have, I have! Isn't this red sash proof?

SUNG CHIANG: Li K'uei, I'll make a wager with you now. If it was I who took that girl you win my head, the seat of all my senses. Now, what will you be willing to lose?

LI K'UEI: My wager will be a whole banquet for you, brother.

SUNG CHIANG: A banquet indeed! That's good, that is. You must match my wager.

LI K'UEI: All right, all right! Brother, if it wasn't you then I'll willingly give you my own bullhead.

SUNG CHIANG: Since that's settled, we'll write it down as part of our military oaths and Hsüeh-chiu will hold it.

LI K'UEI: Do you mean to say the Gay Monk is going to be let off?

LU CHIH-SHEN: Leave my bald head out of this: It would bring you bad luck!

(*They write out the military form for the wager.*)

LI K'UEI (*sings*): My fate's in the hands of a man powdered prettily
On both sides. One whose words make true become false in an instant.
Who acts like a dog but thinks like a wolf. Tiger at one end,
Snake at the other. I make no twigs grow on twigs to form a maze,
Nor carry awls in a sack;
None made you steal another's child to ease your itch . . .

SUNG CHIANG: Hear the Black Ox becoming crude.

LI K'UEI (*sings*): You must forgive my crudities
Which raise a single hillock on the flat plain.

SUNG CHIANG: Since I didn't do the deed, how can I forgive you?

LI K'UEI (*sings*): Your finger at heaven or scratches on the earth
May fool the spirits, but embroider as you will
You'll not deceive me—not that you don't do it well and
cleverly.

SUNG CHIANG: We'll go down the mountain together . . .

LI K'UEI (*sings*): Yes, down from the fort to the wineshop.
We'll know the facts,
See the truth, then
I'll cut off your head to close your mouth.

SUNG CHIANG: The Iron Ox tries insolence now!

LI K'UEI (*sings*): No, not insolence; but since we've made this deadly
wager
Am I likely to stick at anything?
What's more, I do it for thirty-six of my sworn brothers.

(*speaks*): Come here, all you men!

SUNG CHIANG: Now what are you doing?

LI K'UEI: Men, I am now leaving with Sung Chiang and Lu Chih-
shen to go to Hsing-hua Village. As soon as old Wang Lin has
said "yes," then you, you matchmaking Gay Monk need not be
surprised when my axe cleaves your skull nicely into two bowls
—who told you to make off with young Man-t'ang Ch'iao anyway? But Sung Chiang I will leave till last, for I would like
to serve him prostrate.

SUNG CHIANG: What? You'll serve me prostrate?

LI K'UEI: Absolutely prostrate! I shall take your collar in one hand
and your belt in the other and then, buckety-bump you'll be
flat as a bedboard with feet. While you're prostrate I'll serve you
—by hopping on to your chest, raising my broad-axe and bringing it down on your neck, kerchop!

(*sings*): Though all your ancestors to the seventh generation
Leap from their graves and beseech me not to do it.
[*Exit.*]

SUNG CHIANG: Well, he's gone. Guard, prepare two horses. Brother Chih-shen and I will leave the camp together and go to confront old Wang Lin.

> (*recites*): Wang Lin has mischief on misdeed bred,
> Li K'uei's confounded "yes" with "no";
> Since one of us will lose his head
> To Hsing-hua Village both must go.

ACT III

WANG LIN *enters weeping.*

WANG LIN: Oh, my Man-t'ang Ch'iao, worry over you will be the death of me. I am Wang Lin, whose daughter was carried away by the two bandits. Today is the third day. Yesterday brother Li K'uei went up Mount Liang to search for Sung Chiang and Lu Chih-shen to bring them here for me to identify as the ones who did this deed. I guess I'd better have something for them to eat when they arrive. [*Weeps.*] Oh, Man-t'ang Ch'iao. They said they'd return her on the third day but will they or won't they? I shall die of worry.

(SUNG CHIANG, LU CHIH-SHEN *and* LI K'UEI *enter.*)

SUNG CHIANG: Brother Chih-shen, let us hurry a little. Look at our friend: when we go on ahead he comes right behind us, when we hang back he stays close in front of us. I dare say he thinks we'll escape.

LI K'UEI: Wait up for me! Thinking of getting to your in-law's makes you eager, eh?

SUNG CHIANG: There goes that devil with his riddles again, do you hear, brother Chih-shen? Never fear, when Wang Lin doesn't identify us, I'll take care of you, Li K'uei.

LI K'UEI (*sings*): Skirting the blue-green foothills I see afar
    The tavern's banner signaling in the wind, and think
    On the emotions felt there last night. I know
    They must be otherwise today; truth and falsehood
    Will both be known this day.

(*speaks*): How now Gay Monk, why the tiny steps? Is such a
laggard pace perhaps because of belated twinges of the
go-between's conscience?

LU CHIH-SHEN: Listen to him!

LI K'UEI (*sings*): Lu Chih-shen resembles much
A serpent dragged reluctant from its lair.

(*speaks*): Sung Chiang, move along. It couldn't be that the
shame of stealing another's child slows you down?

SUNG CHIANG: Insolent pup!

LI K'UEI (*sings*): Hurrying Sung Chiang is as easily done
As brushing the nap off a rug.

Oh, alabaster princess of Chou, such a
Wang Tzu-ch'iao awaits you here. "But where
Do the maidens of jade play their pipes?"[5]
Yet, have my footsteps broken up the dusty
Struggles of sparrows, or ended the wedded union of
phoenixes?

(*speaks*): No matter, I've come with you two to Hsing-hua
Village and

(*sings*): I'll hew me a road as each mountain demands.

LU CHIH-SHEN: You should have said, "I'll build a bridge when I
come to the river," brother.

LI K'UEI (*sings*): Ah, you who merely sailed a boat with the stream
Would not now let me burn my bridge when I've crossed it.

(*Sung Chiang advances.*)

He likes this ill and will throw his weight about.

SUNG CHIANG: Do you not remember the oath of brotherhood we
swore on the mountain, the oath of eight salutations?

LI K'UEI (*sings*): You, my brother, mention our past bond,
Solemnized by the eight-fold bow, that now seems

---

5. This is a quotation from Tu Mu's poem *Ehr-shih-ssu Ch'iao* and adds
nothing more than an elegant touch to the song since the allusion is not particularly apposite.

> Only a bright bottle-gourd—all shell and no meat.
> Scarce can I suppress scornful laughter.
> What is it you wish? To match your talents with mine?
> To contest sensitivity and readiness to shame?

> (*speaks*): Here is Wang Lin's door. Brother, say nothing till I've called him out.

SUNG CHIANG: I understand.

LI K'UEI (*calling out*): Old Wang, Old Wang, open up. (WANG LIN *nods and dozes.*)

> Open up, I say. I've brought your daughter back!

WANG LIN (*waking with a start*): She's truly here? I'm opening the door! (*He embraces* LI K'UEI.) Oh, my Man-t'ang Ch'iao . . . ugh! It's not her!

LI K'UEI (*sings*): Poor fellow, once he earned the nickname "Half-barrel,"

> Now here he is, stupid on just a spoonful.
> 'Tis just the loss of Man-t'ang Ch'iao
> That's added such weight to his burden of years.

> (*speaks*): I called twice to open the door. The third time I said we'd brought his daughter. He threw open the door and hugged my black neck, crying Man-t'ang Ch'iao!

> (*sings*): Old one, you've been so constantly in grief.
> And now I've got you rubbing your eyes,
> Wiping your tears and sobbing again.

> (*speaks*): Brothers, go into the shop and be seated. (*They enter and sit.*) He's an old man. Don't you frighten him now. I'm going to have him identify you. Old Wang, come here and see if you recognize them.

WANG LIN: Yes, I want to.

SUNG CHIANG: Old man, come close. I am Sung Chiang, and I must tell you that Li K'uei and I have bet our heads on whom you will identify as the one who stole your daughter.

LI K'UEI: Go, look at him, old Wang: isn't he the one?

WANG LIN (*looking carefully at* SUNG CHIANG): No, it wasn't this one.

SUNG CHIANG: Just as I said!

LI K'UEI: Wait till he's taken a good look, brother; don't glare at him and scare him. How can he recognize you if he's scared? Come, old Wang, the two of us have bet our heads because of your daughter. Isn't that one your "in-law," the stealer of Man-t'ang Ch'iao, Sung Chiang?

WANG LIN (*looking carefully again, wags his head*): No, he's not.

SUNG CHIANG: You see!

LI K'UEI (*sings*): Why did you not sit still and bow your head?
What made you widen your eyes and stare him down?
You are so hard and haughty in your power, Sung Chiang,
That you must glare and scare him witless.
If this is aiding heaven's way then I am happy
To leave mercy to my pitiless broad-axe.

(*speaks*): Old Wang, come and look at this bald one. He's the go-between Lu Chih-shen. See if you don't recognize him.

LU CHIH-SHEN: Yes, and make it quick!

WANG LIN (*now looks carefully at Lu*): No, no, he's not one. One of the two who did it was good looking and tall, but your Sung Chiang is dark and short. The other had a mangy scalp and sparse hair, but this one is a tonsured monk. No, no . . .

LU CHIH-SHEN: You see, brother, I was right.

LI K'UEI: You bald rascal, why did you have to yawp at him just as he was about to identify you?

(*sings*): Everyone knows you, Lu Chih-shen of Chen-kuan,
And knows you took to the greenwood having left Mount Wu-t'ai.
If he but fingered your face in the dark he would know who it was.
When you bellowed your thunderclap
You turned the old simpleton's wits upside down.
Now he'd not remember any name.

(*speaks*): He was just about to recognize you.

(*sings*): See him now wagging his head and tilting his brain in wasted conjecture.

SUNG CHIANG: Since he has said we're not the ones who did it, brother Chih-shen, we'll return to the mountain and wait till the Iron Ox comes back to settle up.

LI K'UEI: Old Wang, my son, try again.

WANG LIN: I said they're not the ones and they're not. What good would another try be?

(LI K'UEI *raises his hand to strike* WANG LIN.)

Mercy, take pity or you'll kill an old man!

LI K'UEI (*sings*): I'll beat this old clod whose fear has frozen what little guts he had.
I'm bound I'll thump his pot and break his ladle.

SUNG CHIANG: Boy, bring the horses. Brother Lu and I are returning to the mountain.

LI K'UEI: You say let's return to the camp, but I say, brother, please sit a while and let him try again carefully.

(*sings*): My brother cries ready the horses, back to camp . . .

(*speaks*): Ai! Oh brother, this brings the shame home, but,

(*sings*): Like one stuck on a plank-bridge with his mule
Here I stand and suffocate with rage . . .
But the sauce-pot's spilled. My rope's cut short at the windlass
And won't draw water from the well.
My barrel's empty, my dipper's smashed, my cleaver's broken in two.
Oh, but I long to hear the crackle of your thatched
Gourd burning down. You who lead men into pitfalls, enrage me so
I hop and bounce like a stranded minnow.
But how can I do what I want?
"The young must be protected, the aged respected."

SUNG CHIANG: Come, brother Chih-shen, back to camp.

> (*recites*): Head wagered in an empty cause—
> Ridiculous warrior, errant knight—
> Return to the camp and stretch your neck
> To meet my axe's heavy bite. (*Exeunt.*)

LI K'UEI (*with a sigh*): This time I was wrong.

> (*sings*): And now I believe what is oftenest said,
> "How hard to know the heart of a man; for a lamp
> Casts only shadows on its own base." My eyes are
> Opened now and see the difference between
> The noble and the base.
> Heedless, I wagered my head with Sung Chiang,
> And now "the hope of three generations" has found
> His own tongue heavy enough to cut off his head. (*Exit.*)

WANG LIN: Brother Li K'uei has left. To be sure, he brought two men to me to identify if I could—one was the real Sung Chiang and the other the actual Lu Chih-shen—but neither was one of those who took my daughter. May heaven smite those who did steal her! . . oh, how I long for you, Man-t'ang Ch'iao.

> (*Enter* SUNG KANG, *sneezing, accompanied by* LU CHIH-EN *and the girl.*)

SUNG KANG: I'm sneezing and my ears are hot; someone must be talking about me. Well, here we are in Hsing-hua Village. Where is my "father-in-law"? You see, we promised to bring your daughter back in three days and here we are.

WANG LIN (*sees her, embraces her and weeps*): Oh, Man-t'ang Ch'iao!

SUNG KANG: You see, we weren't lying. Exactly three days and your beloved daughter is back.

WANG LIN: Many thanks, your honor, accept my praises. Because this is a poor household and has been much upset, there is no wine ready to toast you. If you'll go to my daughter's room and have a drink of plain wine, I will kill a hen tomorrow and entertain you.

LU CHIH-EN: Old Wang, in our camp we've more than enough of meat and wine. I'll order one of the boys to bring you twenty or thirty fat lambs and forty or fifty loads of wine.

WANG LIN: Thank you, your honor. Unhappily I've no gift for the go-between: a dreadful thing.

SUNG KANG: Come, let us to the lady's room for a drink. (*Exeunt.*)

WANG LIN: So those two thieves aren't leaders from Liang-shan P'o. They stole my daughter and both of them have cracked her jug. Well, let that be. But what a pity brother Li K'uei, always a hot-hearted fellow, has bet his head on the matter. This is no time to dally. I'll fill two bowls, one with warm and one with cold wine, and help those two thieves get dead drunk. Then tonight I'll wait till they're asleep and quietly slip up Mt. Liang, report the whole thing to Sung Chiang, and save Li K'uei. That ought to work.

(*recites*): Why does Old Wang Lin walk by night
    Up Liang-shan? Because he must requite
    The kindnesses of Li K'uei.
    Yet I fear
    That false Sung Chiang's evil deeds
    Will bring the valorous Li K'uei here
    And send Man-t'ang Ch'iao untimely into widow's weeds.

A C T   I V

SUNG CHIANG, LU CHIH-SHEN *and* WU HSÜEH-CHIU *enter leading attendants.*

SUNG CHIANG: I am Sung Chiang. Brother Hsüeh-chiu, the insolence of Li K'uei was insufferable. I bet my head against his, and now we've been to Hsing-hua Village and been identified as innocent of the abduction, brother Lu and I have returned to await Li K'uei's arrival—at which time he'll lose his head. Guard, go to the crest and keep a lookout. It's about time for Li K'uei to arrive.

(*Enter* LI K'UEI *carrying a fagot of thorn branches.*)

LI K'UEI: Oh, Black Whirlwind, how needlessly you have acted, losing your life for another. Having no other way left to me I have cut this fagot of thorns to carry back to camp and see brother Sung Chiang.

(*sings*): I've arrived in my present plight only because
I pursued it. I needlessly wagered my head against
My brother.
I've thrown off my red coat and burst the stitches
Of my worn sandals.
I must think . . .

(*speaks*): When I return to camp my brother will want my head at once.

(*sings*): But how can I hand over this familiar old thing
Atop my neck?
I'd rather give up my body.

(*speaks*): This steep green cliff overhanging the bottomless stream below. If I were to leap it would swallow me up —even ten Black Whirlwinds could disappear into it.

(*sings*): Time and again I've thrown myself down that cliff,
But still the camp draws nearer. Each step is
The last one up to the headsman's block.
When I am dead, who will fix a marker on
My tomb naming my native heath?
And who in the land of the quick will chant beside
My spirit tablet to pray me into paradise?
Would that a man could be cut asunder, yet leave
A whole corpse for burial . . .
Ah, that would be the thing!

I've come to the gates of the palisade and see within
The men drawn up in ranks like migrant geese.

(*speaks*): Before, when I arrived

(*sings*): The sentry stood to and hurried toward me,

(*speaks*): But today,

(*sings*): He acts the simpleton and stares right through me.

(*Peers surreptitiously about him.*)

(*speaks*): Oh, brother Sung Kung-ming and all the men have
   gone to the hall.

(*sings*): He faces the heroes assembled there.
   Each and all sit gravely and with chins firm set.
   I shall speak to the point and say: here stands a loutish
   Lien P'o[6] to confess his crimes,
   And he should die!

(SUNG CHIANG *and* LI K'UEI *see each other.*)

SUNG CHIANG: You have arrived, brother, but what do you carry on
   your back?

LI K'UEI: My brother, I cut this bundle of thorny sticks to ask you
   to beat me for my moment of stupidity which caused this all to
   happen.

(*sings*): I call upon my brother, Herald of Justice,
   To see to my punishment. Give Li K'uei a feast
   Of thorns: first, because we are brothers, and second,
   To reduce my awful debt of blood and dissolution!
   Say not that I fear death and burial, but rather,
   If you don't thrash this stubborn fool until
   The full moon rises, he'll never change his stripes!

SUNG CHIANG: We wagered our heads. There was no mention of
   beating. Guard, take Li K'uei to the Hall of Justice to be beheaded and report back to me.

LI K'UEI: Brother Hsüeh-chiu, intercede for me! Chih-shen, plead
   for me!

(*They pantomime intercession for* LI K'UEI.)

SUNG CHIANG: No! I will not beat him. This is a military oath. All
   I want is his head.

LI K'UEI: What did you say, brother?

SUNG CHIANG: I said I'll not beat you, I only want your head.

---

6. A general of the Warring States period, and the most famous person
to have used the ritual baring of the back to beg pardon.

LI K'UEI: But are you sure, brother? Each blow causes pain in a flogging, but beheading—one stroke and it's over and isn't painful at all.

SUNG CHIANG: I won't beat you.

LI K'UEI: Well, if you won't, I thank you. (*Starts to go.*)

SUNG CHIANG: Where are you going?

LI K'UEI: My brother said he wouldn't beat me so I . . .

SUNG CHIANG: We wagered our heads and I will have your head, the seat of all senses!

LI K'UEI: Very well, then, so be it! But suicide is better than execution. If I may borrow my brother's sword I shall cut my throat.

SUNG CHIANG: All right. Guard, give him my sword.

LI K'UEI (*taking the sword*): Why, this was mine! Well I remember the day I was out with you driving game for the hunt. Alongside the highroad there were people gathered saying that a snake lay across the path. I pushed my way to the front and found that it was no snake, but a perfect T'ai A[7] of a sword And I gave it to you, brother, to hang at your waist. Some days ago I thought I heard the hum of a sword. I said to myself someone will be slain—never thinking that it might be me.

> (*sings*): My heart startled when I heard *leng-leng*
> The cry of the sword.

> (*speaks*): And *what* a sword!

> (*sings*): To blow a hair against its edge is to cleave it
> Asunder. With such a weapon one would shear
> A coin in half as he would a hemp stalk.

> (*speaks*): I am remembering ten years of friendship and close feelings now ended.

> (*sings*): Enough of former feelings and off
> With my well-beloved head.

---

7. A proper name for the sword which is as famous in China as Excalibur is in English-speaking countries.

(WANG LIN *rushes on shouting.*)

WANG LIN: Stay the knife! I have to report to your honor. Those two villains who stole my daughter have come back! I've got them soaking drunk at my place. I came straightway to tell you. Please be my champion against them.

SUNG CHIANG: Li K'uei, I'll let you go on this condition: if you take these two footpads, I'll use your merit in that to absolve you of the other matter. If you don't take them you'll answer for both. Will you go?

LI K'UEI (*laughing*): Oh, this scratches just the place that itches! I'll take them like two turtles in a jug and bring them here in my hand.

WU HSÜEH-CHIU: Nonetheless, they have two horses ready. How could you take them both? If by chance you did not do it, the reputation of Liang-shan P'o would suffer. Brother Lu, go with Li K'uei and help.

LU CHIH-SHEN: He called me a bald go-between more times than once and had Wang Lin try to identify me time and again. What kind of an idea is this? If he can do it let him go take them both himself. He'll wait a long time till I help him!

HSÜEH-CHIU: Think of our watchword, "Assembled Justice," brother, and don't let a small grudge harm our greater goal.

SUNG CHIANG: That's the right of it. Brother Chih-shen, go with him and help bring in those two masquerading thieves.

LU CHIH-SHEN: If that is your order, I'll go with him. (*Exeunt.*)

(LI K'UEI, LU CHIH-SHEN *and* WANG LIN *enter.*)

LU CHIH-EN: What wine! We were both drunk last night. The sun is already three rods high in the sky—I wonder where your "father-in-law" is. Was he stiff too?

LI K'UEI: You thieves! Here's your father-in-law. (*Strikes* SUNG KANG.)

SUNG KANG: We don't even know your name and you hit us!

LI K'UEI: When I do tell you, you'll wet your pants. I'm old Papa

Black from Liang-shan P'o and this is the real Gay Monk, Lu Chih-shen. (*Hits them.*)

(*sings*): Borrow the devil's name and buy his troubles.
　　　　Today heaven has caught you up!

　　　　Never will Man-t'ang Ch'iao be mistress of your
　　　　Lustful camp. And what is to be done is not
　　　　The fault of Papa Black's black anger.

SUNG KANG: These are the real ones! We haven't a chance, run, run!

LI K'UEI: Where are you going? (*Catches up with them and hits them again.*)

(*sings*): I'll beat you curs till your skin's scragged,
　　　　Your bones broken and your flesh flayed.
　　　　And could you leap right through the blue
　　　　Veil of heaven, my hand would catch you
　　　　On the other side. You . . . you . . . you . . .
　　　　A fine Lu Chih-shen you are, who never abstained
　　　　From meat! And you, a Herald of Justice lost
　　　　To lechery! Now you'll confront those men themselves.
　　　　And from you let there be no cry of outrage;
　　　　Not brutality, but calamity of your own making
　　　　Has found you out. (*Catches hold of both.*)

(*speaks*): Now we've got the thieves!

(WANG LIN *and his daughter bow deeply to* LI K'UEI.)

LU CHIH-SHEN: Save your bows, old one. Come to our camp and present them tomorrow to Sung Chiang, our leader. (*Exit* LU *and* LI *guarding the thieves.*)

WANG LIN: There they go, taking those villains with them, and we are rid of a mouthful of foul breath. Tomorrow, my child, we'll lead a lamb and carry wine up Liang-shan to thank Sung Chiang, the chief. (*Daughter pantomimes shaking with sobs.*) Come my dear, don't carry on so. What good is a thief like that? Bide your time till I can pick out a good man to marry you to. (*Exeunt.*)

(SUNG CHIANG *and* WU HSÜEH-CHIU *enter leading attendants.*)

SUNG CHIANG: Brother Li and Lu Chih-shen went to Hsing-hua Village a long time ago, Hsüeh-chiu, my brother: I wonder why they haven't returned. Perhaps I'd best send someone from here to meet them.

HSÜEH-CHIU: It won't matter where those thieves have gone, you won't have to send anyone else. They'll be here soon.

GUARD: I beg to report, brother, two of our leaders have returned victorious.

(*Enter* LI K'UEI, LU CHIH-SHEN, SUNG KANG *and* LU CHIH-EN.)

LI K'UEI: We've brought the two devils in and now wait for you to pronounce sentence, brother.

SUNG CHIANG: A fine Sung Chiang! A likely Lu Chih-shen! How dared you masquerade in our names and soil the honor of our families? Guards, bind them to the flagpole, cut out their hearts and livers and we'll have them with our wine. Then hang up their heads as a warning to all their kind.

GUARD: Yes sir. (*Exit taking the thieves.*)

LI K'UEI (*sings*): In a green pool of shade the feast will be set.
　　　　　Beneath the flagpole, fat lambs
　　　　　Will be carved. When cups are drained
　　　　　They will fill again.

　　　　　Their eyes are out, limbs hang useless,
　　　　　Their hearts and livers torn grisly from them.
　　　　　I snatched a bone from the maw of the tiger,
　　　　　Plucked a pearl from the chin of the dragon
　　　　　And took it upon myself to bring them ruin.

(*speaks*): Brother Chih-shen,

(*sings*): I must absolve you: never were you a go-between
　　　　　Of violence.

(*speaks*): Brother Kung-ming,

(*sings*): I must let you off: no yearning to paint eyebrows
　　　　　Possessed you.

SUNG CHIANG: Today we hold a feast in the Hall of Justice to reward Li K'uei and Lu Chih-shen for their deed.

(*recites*): The will of heaven was served by Sung Chiang
And greenwood justice done by his men.
Li K'uei's sword was drawn in a cause,
Uniting Wang Lin and his child again.

TRANSLATED BY J. I. CRUMP

Ma Chih-yüan (*fl.* 1251)

Autumn in the Palace of Han

[*Han kung ch'iu*]

PROLOGUE

HU-HAN-YEH, *the Tartar Khan, and his followers enter.*

KHAN (*recites*): The autumn winds wander in the grass by my tent;
A lonely flute sounds through the moonlit firmament.
A million brave archers acknowledge me their khan,
Yet I affirm allegiance to the House of Han.

I am the Khan Hu-han-yeh. For many years I have lived
in the deserts, and I rule the north alone. Hunting is my people's
livelihood, and conquest our business. Once Emperor T'ai Wang
fled before us to the east, and Wei Chiang, trembling before
our might, begged us for peace. Huns, Tartars, northern savages
—each Chinese dynasty has had its own abusive name for my
people, and the Chinese title for our Tartar Chieftain has
changed as often. When China was torn by fighting between the
Ch'in and Han, my country was strong and prosperous, and had
a million archers and warriors under arms. My ancestor, the
Khan Mao-tun, besieged the Han Emperor Kao at Po-teng
for seven days. The emperor, adopting the policy proposed by
Lou Ching, sued for peace between our two nations, and a
Chinese princess was sent in marriage to our khan. This practice has been followed in every generation since the time of
the Emperor Hui and the Dowager Empress Lü. In the time
of the Emperor Hsüan a dispute among my brothers about the
succession weakened the country somewhat, but now the tribes
of my people have established me as their khan.

I myself on my mother's side am a member of the house

of Han. Now, with my hundred thousand armed warriors, I have moved south and approached the Han borders, intending to declare myself a feudatory of the Han empire. Recently I despatched an envoy to offer tribute and to request that a princess be given me as my bride. As yet I do not know whether or not the Han emperor is willing to renew our treaty of alliance.

Today the heavens are high, the air is clear. Chiefs—would not a round of hunting on the sandy banks be pleasant sport? Truly Tartars own no land, no houses; bows and arrows are our only wealth. (*Exeunt.*)

(*Enter* MAO YEN-SHOU. *He recites*):

> I have a hawk's claws, a vulture's beak;
> I deceive the great and oppress the weak.
> Thanks to flattery and an avaricious bent
> I've built a fortune too huge to be spent.

I am no other person than Mao Yen-shou. I now serve the Han court as middle counsellor. I have employed a hundred arts of deceit and steady flattery to dupe that old man, the emperor, and I keep him in sufficiently good spirits. My words are heeded; my plans are followed. Within and without the court, is there a man who does not respect me, does not fear me?

I have been studying a new plan: if I can persuade the emperor to devote as little time as possible to his learned ministers, and to give himself instead to fleshly pleasures, my command over the imperial favor will truly be secure. But while I've been talking, the emperor has arrived.

(*Enter the* EMPEROR HAN YÜAN-TI, *with a retinue of eunuchs and women.*)

EMPEROR (*recites*): Ten reigns since Fiery Liu who founded our line,
China's four hundred counties, the whole world, are mine.
The borders long have been secured by solemn vow;
At night I sleep in peace, no cares afflict me now.

I am Han Yüan-ti. My ancestor, the first Han emperor, arose from among the common people, began his career at Feng-p'ei, crushed the Ch'in dynasty and destroyed Hsiang Yü. It was he who established the imperial authority passed down to me through ten reigns. Ever since I ascended the throne, the country in all its length and breadth has been at peace, not because of my own virtue, but thanks entirely to the civil and military officials on whose support I depend. The palace ladies were all dismissed after my father's death, and now the women's palace is lonely and deserted. What would be best for me to do?

MAO YEN-SHOU: Your majesty, even a country fellow, when he harvests ten more loads of wheat than he had expected, will want to change his wife. Why should your majesty, whose rank is supreme, and whose riches encompass the nation, not enjoy as much? Would it not be wise to send an official throughout the empire to select maidens for the palace? These girls should be chosen without respect to their families' position, the only condition being that they are between fifteen and twenty years of age, and of pleasing features. You should fill the women's palace with the maidens selected. What objection could there be to this plan?

EMPEROR: You have spoken well. I therefore appoint you, in addition to your other duties, commissioner in charge of the selection. When you receive my written edict you will travel over the empire choosing maidens for the palace. You will have a portrait painted of each girl you pick, and send that portrait to me. I shall bestow my favors in accordance with the pictures. When you have returned successful from your mission, I shall reward you as you deserve.

(*sings*): The world's at peace; no more of swords and horses.
   The harvest is rich; war and conquest are ended.
   I look to you to choose my palace maids.
   I know your search will cost much weariness,
   But see that you discover in your quest
   A beauty worthy of an emperor. (*Exeunt.*)

ACT I

MAO YEN-SHOU *enters.*

MAO (*recites*):

> I'll snatch my fill of gold with both my hands,
> And fear no seas of blood nor royal commands.
> Alive, I only ask for wealth to spare;
> When dead, let men spit on me for all I care.

I, Mao Yen-shou, have received a mandate from the emperor directing me to travel far and wide over the country selecting beautiful maidens for the palace. I have already chosen ninety-nine. The family of each of these girls was only too glad to offer me whatever worldly goods it possessed. I have in this manner amassed quite a fortune. Recently, I visited the Tzu-kuei district of Ch'eng-tu, where I chose Chaochün, the Elder Wang's daughter, a girl of dazzling beauty. She is endowed with every grace and charm, truly without peer in all the world. Unfortunately, her family were originally farmers and have no great wealth. When I asked her father for one hundred ounces of gold to have her name placed at the head of the list, he at first pleaded his poverty, then refused altogether, relying on his daughter's extraordinary beauty to gain her preference. I intend therefore to remove her name from the list.

(*Considers a while, then says*): But would not my removing her name actually prove a kindness? Let me think a moment, some good plan is sure to come. I have it! I'll disfigure the girl's portrait a little, so that when she arrives in the capital she will certainly be relegated to the palace of neglected ladies. I shall make her lead a lifetime of suffering. Truly is it said that a man with little power of hatred is no man at all. Every real man has his venom. (*Exit.*)

(*Enter* WANG CHAO-CHÜN *with two palace maids. She recites*):

> One day by royal command I came to this sad place;
> It seems ten years—I've yet to see my sovereign's face.

This lovely, lonely evening, who will join my song?
My lute alone has brought me joy the whole night long.

I am Wang Chao-chün. I come from the Tzu-kuei district in Ch'eng-tu. My father, the Elder Wang, has been a farmer all his life. When my mother was about to give me birth, she dreamt that moonlight entered her breast and laid her on the ground. Soon afterwards I was born. When I grew to be eighteen, I was honored by being chosen to enter the women's palace. I did not realize, when I could not give Mao Yen-shou the money he demanded, that he would take his revenge by disfiguring my portrait, so that I could never be seen by His Majesty. Now I have been relegated to this dungeon of neglect.

When I was still in my father's house I was very fond of music, and I learned to play many pieces for the lute. Now, in the lateness and solitude of the night, I shall try to while away the tedium by playing on my lute.

(*She plays. Enter* EMPEROR *with eunuchs bearing lanterns.*)

EMPEROR: In all the time that has passed since the selection of maidens for my palace, there are many I have never favored with my affections. How terribly unhappy they must be! Today I have a little respite from my innumerable duties, and the thought came to me to take a walk through the palace grounds. I shall see which lady is destined to meet me.

(*sings*): My carriage wheels crush the fallen flowers,
    A girl in the moonlight puts down her flute.
    Some palace lady I have never met
    Has aged with grief, and white now streaks her hair.
    I see the rolled-up blinds, the eyes that stare
    Towards Chao-yang Palace,[1] every step a world.
    On windless nights they jump at bamboo shadows
    And loathe their curtains that only moonbeams touch.
    Our carriage moving past midst flutes and strings
    Must seem some magic raft, rising to the stars.

(CHAO-CHÜN *plays her lute.*)

EMPEROR: Is that a lute being played somewhere?

---

1. The residence of the emperor's consort; see above, p. 341.

EUNUCH: It is, your majesty.

EMPEROR (*sings*): Who plays in secret plaintive melodies?

EUNUCH: I shall hasten to inform her of your majesty's approach.

EMPEROR: No, do not.

(*sings*): Do not too quickly tell her of my will:
> Too sudden favors might upset her so
> Her broken notes would startle nesting birds,
> And frighten crows atop the palace trees.

Eunuchs, discover what palace lady is playing her lute. Command her to come into my presence, but beware lest you alarm her.

(EUNUCHS *go to investigate.*)

EUNUCH: Which of you ladies is playing her lute? The emperor approaches. Prepare at once to meet him. (CHAO-CHÜN *comes forward.*)

EMPEROR (*sings*):

> I forgive you, you're guilty of no crime.
> I myself ask you, who lives in these quarters?
> Do not blame me that I've not come before,
> Nor take fright at my sudden visit now.
> I've come to make amends for all the tears
> That have soaked your handkerchiefs of gossamer,
> And to warm your satin slippers chilled by dew.
> Heaven has sent this lovely girl to earth
> That I might offer her my tenderness.
> I'm sure the candle on her silver stand
> Sputtered tonight and left auspicious forms.

(*says*): Eunuchs! See how the candle-flame within the gauze lantern flares brighter! Lift it up that I may see her better!

(*sings*): It strives to shine more brightly than her beauty:
> Look—do you see that slender elegance,
> Lovely enough to kill a man with joy?

CHAO-CHÜN: Had your humble slave known that your majesty was coming, she would have gone to meet you and not kept you waiting so long. She deserves ten thousand deaths.

EMPEROR (*sings*): She greets me with the words "'your majesty,"
She bows and calls herself my "humble slave."
This surely is no simple peasant girl.

(*says*): What perfection I see in her features! She is truly a lovely girl!

(*sings*): She paints her brows in the palace fashion,
Her face she tints and powders to perfection,
And scented pins and plumes flash in her hair:
A smile from her is worth a captured city.
Had King Kou-chien seen *her* on Soochow Terrace,[2]
He'd have rejected Hsi Shih's wiles and lost
His house and kingdom ten years earlier.

(*says*): Maiden, most beautiful of all, who are you?

CHAO-CHÜN: My name is Wang Chao-chün. I come from the district of Tzu-kuei in Ch'eng-tu, where my father cultivates the fields our ancestors have left us. We are country rustics, and know nothing of court etiquette.

EMPEROR (*sings*): When I see your brows painted with mascara,
Your hair swept up like piles of ravens' wings,
Your waist as slim as swaying willow boughs,
Your face as lovely as bright-colored clouds,
I wonder which of all my palace halls
Is worthy of you? Who asked if your father
Furrowed the soil to earn his livelihood?
By favor of your lord you'll share his bed:
Heaven that causes the rains and dews to wet
The mulberry and hemp has destined you for me.
If not, in all the breadth of my domains,
Could I have found you in a hut of thatch?

When I see such beauty before me, I wonder why you have never been favored by my visit.

---

2. Apparently an error for King Fu-ch'a of Wu. King Kou-chien of Yüeh sent the beautiful Hsi Shih to Fu-ch'a, hoping to distract him from state business. The plan was successful, and Fu-ch'a lost his kingdom.

CHAO-CHÜN: At the time of the first selection, the commissioner Mao Yen-shou asked my father for money, but my family was so impoverished that we could raise none. Mao Yen-shou took his revenge by disfiguring the eyes in my portrait. That is why I was sent to the cold palace.

EMPEROR: Eunuch! Bring me her portrait that I may examine it!

(EUNUCH *shows* EMPEROR *the picture*.)

(*sings*): One question only have I for the artist—
Why did he fail to give your face its due?
Eyes clear as autumn stream he has made muddy—
Surely the painter's own eyes must be blind!
I doubt that my eight hundred palace maids
Can match this portrait, even with its flaw.

Eunuch! Transmit my order to the imperial guard that Mao Yen-shou be apprehended and decapitated. Report to me his execution.

CHAO-CHÜN: Your majesty, my parents in Ch'eng-tu are commoners. I entreat you in your generosity to show them your favor.

EMPEROR: That is easily done.

(*sings*): Mornings you picked greens, at night watched the melons;
In spring you sowed grain, in summer watered hemp.
You'd like a proclamation on the wall
Exempting all your family from tax:
Lucky that you are married to a prince!
My rank is higher than a village chief,
My palace bigger than a judge's court.
Heaven and earth! Have mercy on this groom!
Who now will dare to mock your father's house?

Approach and hear my command. I appoint you now Princess of the Court.

CHAO-CHÜN: What have I done to deserve your majesty's favor?

EMPEROR (*sings*): Tonight a while we'll give ourselves to love;
Ask not about tomorrow morning's levee.

CHAO-CHÜN: Your majesty, please come early tomorrow morning. I shall be waiting here for your arrival.

EMPEROR (*sings*): Tomorrow morning—who knows?—I may lie
　　　　In drunken sleep upon my consort's bed.

CHAO-CHÜN: I am a poor and insignificant person. Though I have received your favors, how could I aspire to share your couch?

EMPEROR (*sings*): Don't take offense: I merely joked with you:
　　　　I jested, but you took my words for truth.
　　　　My carriage glided smoothly to your door—
　　　　Could I again condemn you to neglect?
　　　　Tomorrow night wait by the western gate.
　　　　You must be silent when you greet my chair:
　　　　Your music might awaken other lutes. (*Exit.*)

CHAO-CHÜN: The emperor has returned. Attendants, shut the gates now. I shall sleep awhile.

ACT II

The KHAN *enters with his followers.*

KHAN: I am the Khan Hu-han-yeh. Recently I sent envoys to offer my allegiance to the Han and to ask in return for a Han princess. The Chinese emperor refused, claiming that the princesses of his palace are still too young for marriage. I am most annoyed. I am sure that the Chinese court holds countless palace ladies, and it would by no means embarrass the emperor to give me one. I shall recall my envoys at once. I intend to raise troops and invade the Han lands to the south. But I fear to destroy the peace of several years' standing. I shall examine conditions and act accordingly.

(*Enter* MAO YEN-SHOU.)

MAO: I am Mao Yen-shou. When I was charged with selecting maidens for the palace, I demanded money from their families. Later, I defaced the portrait of the beautiful Wang Chao-chün, and she was sent to the cold palace. I never imagined that the emperor would visit her personally and ask how she happened to have been relegated to neglect. I learned that he intended to execute me, but I managed to escape from the Han territories. I have found no refuge as yet. I have with me a portrait of Wang Chao-chün which I intend to present to the khan. I'll induce him to demand this girl. The Chinese court will assuredly yield her.

I have traveled for days, and now I am here. I can see in the distance an immense number of men and horses. This must be the khan's tent here. (*Shouts to a soldier.*) Chief! Inform his majesty, the khan, that a minister from the Han court has come to see him. (*The soldier reports.*)

KHAN: Ask him to come before me. (*Sees* MAO.) Who are you?

MAO: I am the Middle Counsellor of the Han court, Mao Yen-shou. The women's pavilion of the Han palace holds a lady of surpassing beauty named Wang Chao-chün. When your majesty sent an envoy to ask the Chinese court for a princess, this lady begged to go, but the Han emperor, unable to bear to part with her, refused to release her. I repeatedly remonstrated with the emperor, asking him how he could be so given to lust for a woman as to destroy the friendly relations between our two countries, but the emperor, for an answer, ordered that I be beheaded! I have escaped here, bringing with me a portrait of this beauty for your majesty's approval. If her picture pleases you, your envoy should demand the princess. You will undoubtedly be successful. Here is her likeness.

(*Presents the picture.*)

KHAN: Is it possible that the world contains such a woman? My wishes would all be fulfilled if I could have her for my queen. I shall despatch an official and some retainers with a letter to the Chinese emperor asking for Wang Chao-chün. In exchange for the princess, I shall offer peace between our two nations. If the emperor refuses, I shall invade his domains without delay, and he will not find it easy to defend his rivers and mountains. Meanwhile I and my soldiers will make a foray within the Han borders, pretending it is for a hunt, and when we see our chance, we shall strike. (*Exit.*)

(*Enter* WANG CHAO-CHÜN *with palace maids.*)

CHAO-CHÜN: A month or more has passed since the emperor first favored me with a visit. His majesty has devoted so much attention to me that he has not held court for a long time. I hear that today he has gone to the Hall of Audience. I shall sit before my dressing stand and touch up my rouge and powder. I want to be ready when he comes. (*She applies cosmetics before a mirror. Enter* EMPEROR.)

EMPEROR: Ever since I met Chao-chün in the Western Palace I have been inebriated by love for her. It steals my senses away and has kept me from attending court for weeks. Today I went to the Hall of Audience, but could not wait for the levee to end. I had to return to the Western Palace to see her again.

(*sings*): The rains and dews have fallen in good time;
My country everywhere is prosperous.
My loyal statesmen all are worthy men;
No cares harass my pillow when I sleep.
My love has dazzling teeth and starry eyes;
How could I bear even the daytime without her?
But recently some ailment has assailed me,
One that comes in part from cares of state,
In part from melancholy and from wine.

When with my ministers I try to show
The courtesy that well becomes a king,
But separation from my princess brings
The autumn sorrow Sung Yü once described.
How could I keep from clinging to the sleeves
Of dragon robes scented with her rare perfumes?
Her every feature is adorable,
Her every action matches my desires.
She dissipates all gloom and weariness,
And shares with me my leisure-time delights.
How wonderful to climb with her the terrace
When moonlight lies upon the pear in bloom,
And play at fortunes under gauzy lanterns.
She radiates a warmth and gentleness
That twenty years have polished and perfected.

Ours is a match decreed by destiny
Five hundred years before we even met.
Her face reveals a thousand nameless charms:
I would there were some fit comparison—
She's like the Kwan-yin of Lo-chia Mountain
Although she lacks the sacred willow branch;
A single glance at her adds long years to life.
The love that binds my heart will some day cease,
But only when desire has been sated.

(*Sees her at a distance.*) I must not startle her. I shall watch her secretly awhile.

How deeply once she hated my neglect;
She could not know my dreams would turn to her.
I love her when, as now, her make-up done,
Lovelier than an artist's brush could paint,
She still looks shyly at her mirrored face.

(*Comes up behind* CHAO-CHÜN.)

I watch you from behind your dressing-stand;
The goddess of the moon shines from your glass.

(CHAO-CHÜN *sees the emperor and gestures in welcome. Enter the* PRIME MINISTER *with eunuch.*)

MINISTER: A minister should give his mind to affairs of state,
And to the public good his efforts consecrate,
But most at banquets their abilities display,
When have they ever served their lord a single day?

I am the Prime Minister Wu-lu Ch'ung-tsung and this is the eunuch Shih Hsien. Today, when court was dismissed, a messenger came from the Tartars to ask for the Lady Chao-chün as the condition of making peace. I must report this to the emperor. I have come to the Western Palace and shall now enter. (*Sees* EMPEROR.) I wish to report to your majesty that the Khan Hu-han-yeh of the northern barbarians has sent an envoy here to say that Mao Yen-shou presented him with a portrait of Lady Chao-chün. The khan demands her in marriage as requisite for making peace and ending hostilities. If his demand is refused, he will march south with great numbers of men, and you will not be able to defend your territories.

EMPEROR: I have maintained my armies for a thousand days just so that I might use them on one occasion. In vain is my court filled with civil and military officials—who of them all will drive back the enemy for me? They all fear the Tartar swords and are anxious to escape the Tartar arrows. How can you let my lady be exiled without lifting a finger to prevent it?

(*sings*): Success is ever followed by decay,
And respite from the wars will never come.
Should not the fate of those who eat my food
Be mine to order any way I choose?
In time of peace you boast of your achievements,
But now that trouble threatens you would send
The girl I love to lonely banishment.
Falsely you accept a stipend from our house—
In what way will you share your sovereign's griefs?
Brave ministers, afraid to draw your bows!
Bold counsellors, who fear to lose your lives!

MINISTER: In Tartary they say that your rule is deteriorating because of your majesty's excessive fondness for Wang Chao-chün, and they foresee the ruin of the nation. They declare that if you refuse to surrender Chao-chün to the khan, he will use his troops to enforce his demands. Consider the example of King Chou who, for the love of Ta-chi, destroyed his kingdom and lost his life.

EMPEROR (*sings*): I am no evil emperor like Chou
Who raised a palace to pluck down the stars:
And why speak only of a wicked king,
Not of a loyal minister like Yi Yin?
Once you're dead and reach the underworld,
If you should meet Chang Liang, the great lieutenant,
I'm sure you'll feel a shame too great to stifle.
You sleep beneath thick quilts, rich dishes grace
Your board, you ride sleek horses, wear soft furs;
You do not think of Chao-chün's slender waist,
A willow branch the winds of spring will sway.

How could you let the shadow of her sash
Tremble in moonlight by the verdant tomb,[3]
Or make the echoes of her lute die out
Beside the autumn-wasted Amur River?

MINISTER: Your majesty, our soldiers are not prepared to fight, and
we have no skilled generals to lead them. What would happen
if our forces were defeated? Your majesty, I pray you will re-
nounce your attachment to the princess and save the country.

EMPEROR (*sings*): Who was it once displayed his bravery
When he exposed Hsiang Yü's severed head
As sign the land belonged to fiery Liu?
All this we owe to Marshal Han's success
In battles staged before the Nine Mile Mountain—
Perfected, in one man, the ten great deeds.
You wear within these halls your golden badges,
Your purple tassels, hollow marks of glory,
You love to entertain inside your gates
Your singing girls with dancing, twisting sleeves;
Yet if the Tartars break through our defenses,
You'll ask my wife to intercede for you!
Like ducks with arrows sticking through your bills,
Not one of you will even dare to cough!
It wounds my heart when I recall Chao-chün,
So young, so bright a vision—and none to save her!
What harm did Chao-chün ever do to you?
Did she kill your parents, is that your grievance?
No, what's the use? My court will soon become
A swarming den of rogues like Mao Yen-shou.
Three thousand strong my corps of officers,
Four hundred the divisions of my land,
And yet I wait only to cede, to yield.
Simpler by far to raise a thousand troops
Than find a single general to lead them.

OFFICIAL: The Tartar emissary is waiting for an audience with your
majesty.

---

3. Chao-chün's tomb in the desert was celebrated because it remained
perpetually green; this remark anticipates the future miracle.

EMPEROR: Very well, very well. Let the barbarian approach.

(*Tartar eunuch enters.*)

TARTAR EUNUCH: The Khan Hu-han-yeh has sent me to report to the great Han emperor. The northern countries and the southern court have long been united by ties of marriage. The khan has twice sent emissaries to ask for a princess, but without success. Recently Mao Yen-shou presented the khan with a portrait of a beautiful lady. The khan sent me here especially to ask for this lady. He wishes to make Chao-chün his consort. He will then end all hostilities between our two countries. If your majesty does not grant this request, the khan has a million brave soldiers ready to start marching south at a moment's notice to settle the issue. I earnestly implore your majesty not to make an unwise decision.

EMPEROR: Let the emissary rest for a while at his lodgings. (*Exit emissary.*) Deliberate now, my civil and military officers! If you have some plan for driving back the barbarians, present it— anything to save Chao-chün from being delivered over to the Tartars. It must be easy to despise so gentle and good a princess. If the Empress Lü[4] were alive now, who would dare disobey if she uttered a word? In light of this experience, I shall henceforth know better than to trust civil or military officers to settle affairs of state. Beautiful women will be my statesmen.

(*sings*): Tell me at once, if you have things to tell.
   You need not fear. I have no cauldrons filled
   With boiling oil to punish those I hate.
   I thought you civil ministers would bring
   Our country peace. I thought you generals
   Would settle strife with spear and shield. Alas!
   Your only wisdom, only bravery,
   Consists in trying to be first to cry,
   "Long life, your majesty!"—in posturing,
   And with your scrapings stirring up the dust.
   Oft have you said, "We tremble and we bow,"
   But now you'd have Chao-chün take Yang Kuan Road

4. Wife of the first Han emperor and empress-dowager during the reign of her son the Emperor Hui; a woman known for her strong will.

Across the border. Once an empress ruled
In Wei-yang Palace, inside lowered screens.
I hardly think, officials, you'd have dared
Exile the Empress Lü to save the peace.
It's useless now to hope for martial deeds;
My only weapons are my palace maids.

CHAO-CHÜN: I have been favored by your majesty's great kindness.
Now it is my turn to repay you by my death. I am willing to be
married to the barbarian. If, because of my sacrifice, swords are
not raised, I shall enjoy a good name in the histories to come.
But how can I give up the love I shared with you?

EMPEROR: I cannot let you go.

MINISTER: Your majesty must give up this love, and think instead of
your country's good. Send away the princess at once.

EMPEROR (*sings*): Today she will be wedded to the khan—
You must be satisfied, my ministers!
The Chinese princess has a country still,
Yet nowhere can she turn. She must go forth
Where yellow clouds rise not from hills of green.
Reduced to distant gazing, our eyes will strain
To sight a lonely goose cross the autumn sky:
This year, my fate decreed I'd suffer grief,
And Chao-chün languish too with wasting sorrow.
Her crown of kingfisher feathers, her sash,
All her Chinese clothes she must now exchange
For brocade hoods and beaded robes of fur.

(*says to officials:*) Today you will escort the princess to the
emissary's residence, and deliver her to him. Tomorrow I
myself shall go to Pa-ling Bridge and drink with her a farewell cup of wine.

MINISTER: I am afraid that would not be seemly, your majesty. You
will only arouse the contempt of the barbarians.

EMPEROR: I have agreed with everything you have proposed. Why
can't you in this one point follow my desires? Come what may,
I insist on seeing her off. How I detest that loathesome Mao
Yen-shou!

(*sings*): I only hate that beast who could forget
My kindnesses and bite his master's hands.
His portrait could have hung in the Hall of Fame,[5]
My trusted nobles, the court was in your hands!
In what did I not share my plans with you,
In what not follow your memorials?
How could you cause my first dreams to go astray?
From now on, instead of Ch'ang-an she will see
The Dipper hanging in the northern sky:
Wrenched apart, we'll drift like never meeting stars.

MINISTER: It is not we, your servants, who are forcing the lady to marry the Tartar king. We have no other course; he asked for Chao-chün by name. Many men have lost their kingdoms because of amorous entanglements.

EMPEROR (*sings*): For ordinary people like Chao-chün
There is at least the chance of happiness:
Who is less obeyed than an emperor?
How will she ride a massive camel's back?
She always went by scented palanquins.
She needs a servant's help to leave her chair,
And lacks the strength to lift her bamboo blinds.
Who now will think of her? The empty moon
Will drop reflections in the flowing water;
Her lonely, bitter thoughts run on forever.

CHAO-CHÜN: I go now into exile. It is for my country's sake, but I shall never forget your majesty.

EMPEROR (*sings*): I fear that when Chao-chün desires to eat,
There'll be no food but tasteless salted flesh;
When thirsty, only clabbered milk and gruel.
I'll break a sprig of willow as a pledge,
And drink a parting cup of wine with her.
I'll watch as long as she remains in sight,
My heart consumed by grief to see her turn
Her head to look again, and still again.
She never more will see our phoenix halls.
This night, our last, we'll spend by Pa-ling Bridge. (*Exeunt.*)

___

5. An anachronistic reference to a gallery hung by command of the Emperor T'ai-tsung of T'ang with portraits of 28 meritorious ministers.

ACT III

TARTAR ENVOY *enters escorting* CHAO-CHÜN. *He plays Tartar music.*

CHAO-CHÜN: I am Wang Chao-chün. I was selected to serve the Emperor, but my portrait was disfigured by Mao Yen-shou, and I was sent to the cold palace. When at last I began to enjoy his majesty's favors, Mao Yen-shou showed another picture of me to the Tartar khan, and the khan sent an army to demand me. I did not wish to go, but I was afraid that our country would otherwise be lost. I have no choice. I have been sent across the frontier to marry the Tartar khan. The winds and frost are cruel in the northern lands. How shall I endure them? Many tales are told from ancient times of beautiful women who have suffered unhappy fates. But I must not resent the sorrows my beauty has brought on me.

(*Enter* EMPEROR *with officials.*)

EMPEROR: Today I am to bid farewell to my princess at Pa-ling Bridge. The time of parting has come so quickly.

(*sings*): Now she will put aside her Chinese clothes
And change to robes of fur and coarse brocades.
I must look at her portrait once again.
Old pleasures are as short as golden reins;
New grievances outreach jade-handled whips.
We who were once a pair of mandarin ducks
Dwelling in golden chambers, never dreamt
That we should fly apart on lonely wings.

My civil and military officers, why can you think of no way to repel the Tartar soldiers, and save my princess from marrying a Tartar!

My ministers, consider what has happened—
The Tartar envoy will bring rich rewards,
But leave us to despair, my wife and me.
The humblest household shakes with grief at parting

When someone merely takes a little trip.
The willows at Wei-ch'eng increase the gloom;
The flowing water adds its mournful note
At Pa-ling Bridge. Do you alone grieve not?
A world of sadness clings to Chao-chün's lute.

(*Dismounts. Grieves with* CHAO-CHÜN.)

Attendants! Sing slowly as you can. I will drink a last cup of wine with the princess.

Now play that song, "The Parting at Yang Kuan":
Let it not trip too lightly from the strings.
A foot from her will seem a world away.
Slowly, slowly I lift my cup of jade:
If I could but delay this final hour!
It does not matter if your lute be tuned,
As long as you prolong the melody;
Sing slow and sad a farewell verse for me.

TARTAR ENVOY: I beg the princess to start at once. It is growing late.

EMPEROR (*sings*): Alas, how heavy is this separation!
I know how anxious you must be to leave.
My heart will go before her to the north;
When I return, I'll look for her in dreams.
Oh, never say that great men soon forget.

CHAO-CHÜN: When shall I see your majesty again? Put away my Chinese clothes.

(*recites*): Today I lead a Chinese palace life,
Tomorrow I shall be a Tartar's wife.
How could I wear your gifts of former days
To flaunt my charms and win another's praise?

(CHAO CHÜN *lays aside her robes.*)

EMPEROR (*sings*): Why do you leave behind your dancing robes?
The wind will blow away their faded scent.
I truly dread the day my carriage again
Passes your quarters, overgrown with moss,
Suddenly to reach the palace of the queen.
Then I'll remember how you looked when once

> I saw your beauty in a mirror framed,
> That loveliness will brush my heart again.
> Today Chao-chün must leave her native land.
> How long before this banishment will end?

TARTAR ENVOY: I beg the princess again to leave. We have already wasted too much time.

EMPEROR: Very well, very well. Chao-chün, now you must go. Do not hate me for what I have done. (*Leaves her.*) And I am the emperor of the Great Han!

MINISTER: Your majesty must not take these matters too heavily to heart.

EMPEROR (*sings*): She's gone! And none of you is man enough
> To save her! In vain have I maintained my guards
> Along the border. Even you must need
> Someone to serve you—why must I lose my wife?
> You wave your swords and spears, but well I know
> Your hearts are pounding like a frightened fawn's.
> Today you forced the princess to consent:
> Is that the way you choose to prove your valor?

MINISTER: Let us return to the palace, your majesty.

EMPEROR (*sings*): You fear I may refuse to loose the bridle:
> It's true—how could I now return triumphant
> With cracking whip and jingling golden stirrups?
> You are presumed to know the yin and yang,
> To hold the reins of court, to calm the nation,
> To swell our borders and extend our lands:
> Supposing now the emperor had doomed
> Your only serving maid to banishment,
> Away from native heath, to lie in snow
> And sleep in frost—would she not miss your home?
> Tell me so; I'll name you Prince Imperial!

MINISTER: Your majesty should not be grieved to leave her. Allow her to depart.

EMPEROR (*sings*): The Tartar king—I can't recall his name—
> What right had he to fall in love with her?

How could I bear to look when last she turned,
Or stand to watch the distant storm-whipped flags?
Such doleful drums and horns—they shake the mountains!
Before me lie the bleak and ravaged plains,
The grass has yellowed, stricken by the frost,
The mottled coats of dogs grow gray and shaggy.
Men raise their tasseled lances in the chase,
And horses struggle under heavy loads.
Wagons bear provisions for the journey,
And all is ready for the hunt to start.
She, yes, she brokenhearted said good-bye;
I, yes, I took her hand and climbed the bridge.
She and her train ride into the desert;
I in my carriage return now to the palace.
I return now to the palace and pass the wall,
I pass the wall and follow a twisting lane,
A twisting lane that leads close to her room,
Close to her room where the moon grows dusky;
The moon grows dusky and the night turns cold,
The night turns cold and the cicadas weep.
The cicadas weep by green-curtained windows,
By green-curtained windows that feel nothing.
To feel nothing! Only a man of steel
Could feel nothing. No! Even a man of steel
In grief would shed a thousand trickling tears.
Tonight I'll hang her portrait in the palace
And have a service chanted for her there.
Then I'll lift high the silver candlestick
And let the light fall on her painted form.

MINISTER: May your majesty return to your palace. The princess is
    already far on her journey.

EMPEROR (*sings*): I must make some excuse, tell my council
        I cannot meet them. They will want to prate
        Of state affairs. I cannot bear to talk.
        Without her here in flower-like loveliness
        What solace do my palace gardens offer?
        No doubt she often pauses, paces to and fro,
        Irresolute; then suddenly she hears

Caw! Caw! the cries of southward-flying geese:
But all that fills my eyes is sheep and kine,
The sound I heard was but the creaking wheels
Of the felt-covered cart bearing its load
Of sorrow up the slopes of northern hills. (*Exeunt.*)

(*Enter* TARTAR KHAN *with followers leading* CHAO-CHÜN.)

KHAN: Today the Han court has shown itself faithful to our old alliance. The emperor has given me Wang Chao-chün, and made peace between our two houses. I have named Chao-chün my consort. She shall live with me in my chief palace. Now there will be no warfare between our countries. All has been for the best. Officers! transmit my command to the ranks that we are to start marching north. (*They march.*)

CHAO-CHÜN: Where are we now?

ENVOY: This is the Amur River, the boundary between our territories and those of the Han. The lands to the south belong to the Han, and those to the north to us.

CHAO-CHÜN: Will your highness gave me a cup of wine that I may pour a libation facing the south, and take a last leave of China before my long journey? (*She pours a libation.*) Mighty emperor of the Han! Now is this life ended. I await you in the next. (*She throws herself into the river.*)

(*The* KHAN, *alarmed, tries to save her, but fails.*)

KHAN (*in tears*): Alas, alas. Chao-chün was so unwilling to enter my domains that she threw herself into the river and died. Let her be buried, then, on the bank of this river at a place we shall call the Green Mound. She whom I thought to marry is dead. In vain did I create enmity between myself and the Han. It was all schemed by that knave, Mao Yen-shou. Men! Bring Mao Yen-shou here, then despatch him under guard to the Han court, where he will meet his punishment. I shall resume our traditional alliance with the Emperor of Han, and remain forever to him as nephew to uncle. All may have proved for the best.

I see it now: it was because his picture had done an injustice to Chao-chün that Mao Yen-shou betrayed the Han ruler and secretly absconded. Then he beguiled me with another portrait of the beauty, and my armies crossed the border to demand her as a condition of peace. How could I know that she would throw herself into the river and die? To no avail was my spirit melted by one glimpse of her. But such a wicked, treacherous villain will prove the ruin of my court if I keep him here. It is better to send him for execution to the Han court. Then, by virtue of the long-standing courtesy between nephew and uncle, our two countries will prosper forever. (*Exit.*)

ACT IV

EMPEROR *enters with officials.*

EMPEROR: A hundred days have passed since my princess was sent away to appease the barbarians, but I have been unable to hold court all this time. Tonight is bleak and desolate. I feel unbearably depressed. Perhaps if I hang her portrait on the wall it may dissipate my melancholy a little.

(*sings*): The palace chills. The night is far advanced,
        And in the women's quarters all is still.
        I face a cold lamp on its silver stand.
        My empty pillow when I go to bed
        Is testimony to my wretched lot.
        I wonder where she rests, my soul, tonight,
        Ten thousand miles from this my dragon hall.

Eunuch! The incense in the stand has burnt out. Put a little more on the stand.

        The royal jar of incense is consumed,
        I place another yellow stick on the stand.
        My thoughts of her remain, but she is gone,
        Vanished without a trace, like a mirage,[6]
        This portrait here is all that I retain.

6. Allusion to a Buddhist story of a pilgrim who, after visiting the Chu-lin Temple, turns his head and discovers it has vanished.

She is not dead, she lives this day, and yet
I truly offer her my veneration.

Of a sudden I feel worn and weary. I shall sleep awhile.

How sad I cannot dream the dreams I'd choose:
Oh, dearest, where are you, my dearest one?
Why do you show no sign of your presence
But refuse the joys of love, even in a dream?

(*Falls asleep. Enter* CHAO-CHÜN.)

CHAO-CHÜN: I was sent to the northern lands to appease the barbarians, but I have secretly escaped and returned. Is that not my lord? Your majesty, I have come.

(*Enter* TARTAR SOLDIER.)

SOLDIER: While I was dozing a while ago, Chao-chün stole away from me and escaped to her own country. I have rushed as quickly as I could to the Han Palace. There she is now! (*Seizes her, and leads her off.*)

(EMPEROR *wakens.*)

EMPEROR: I thought just now I saw my princess. Why has she vanished so quickly?

(*sings*): A soldier came here from the Tartar khan
And called Chao-chün by name, but when I called
She would not come into the candlelight.
It must have been her portrait, not Chao-chün.
But suddenly I hear a phoenix flute,
Ghost sounds within the Hall of Fairy Music.
Is this the ancient melody of Shun?
By daytime there was none to wait on me,
My griefs denied me sleep, though dawn had come,
And would not grant a single pleasant dream.

(*A wild goose cries.*)

Listen—a wild goose, calling twice or thrice
At Chao-chün's empty palace. How could it know
Another, lonelier than she, waits here?

(*Wild goose cries again.*)

Probably it is old and strengthless now;
And must be hungry, bones and feathers light.
It would turn back, but fears for southern nets;
It would go forward, but dreads the Tartar bows.
Its mournful notes are like a voice that tells
Of Chao-chün's longing for the Lord of Han:
Sad as the dirges for a fallen hero,
Heart-rending as the odes of Ch'u at night,
Doleful as thrice-chanted songs of parting.

(*Wild goose cries again.*)

That cursed bundle of feathers—its cries make me all
the lonelier!
My thoughts already filled me with despair,
But now another torturer has come.
Sometimes you moan in long protracted notes,
At other times come rapid, nervous cries:
You harmonize your calls to the watch of night.
What now? You wheel above the palace roofs
And all below responds to your lament.
But surely you mistake the time of year?[7]
Are you searching for Su Wu, for Li Ling's tomb?
Is that why you wake me by the candle stand?
The shadow on the wall stirs bitter grief.
The Han princess, in that distant land, still lives,
But sees and hears you not, you bag of feathers!

Wearisome goose!
It brings my heart no joy to hear your cries:
The sound is like the soughing forest wind
Or icy murmurs of a rocky stream.
I seem to see an endless mountain range
And water that reflects a distant sky.
You surely must have wandered from your way:
You desolate the twilit Hsiao and Hsiang[8]
And stir again the pangs of separation.

---

7. The goose should be flying south, not north, in autumn.
8. The rivers Hsiao and Hsiang were famous for their twilight scenery,
when wild geese alighted; but this wild goose will not be there for twilight.

What voices sick with parting do you echo?
How can I pass this everlasting night?
I loathe the moonlight on the palace steps.

EUNUCH: Your majesty, put aside this sorrow and think more of your august person.

EMPEROR: How can I help but be afflicted?

(*sings*): You must not say my feelings conquer me—
You ministers—how loathesome you seem again!
That bird was not a swallow chattering
On sculptured beams, nor yet the oriole
Singing on a gaily colored tree: it was
The bird of sorrow that Chao-chün of Han
Somewhere, far from home, will hear in misery.

(*Wild goose cries again.*)

Honking, the other geese have flown across
The weed encumbered banks; one lonely bird
Still lingers by the Phoenix Hall of State.
Below the painted eaves the little bells
Tinkle thinly: the palace couch is cold.
The falling leaves are sighing in the wind.
The lamps are dark—her quarters hemmed in silence.
One voice has circled round the palace of Han;
Another goes to Chao-chün at Wei-ch'eng.
My hair has grayed, my body is sick and weak:
My sorrows lie too deep to be assuaged.

MINISTER: Today after the morning council was dismissed, an envoy came from Tartary with Mao Yen-shou in chains. The envoy declared that Mao Yen-shou's treachery had caused the rupture in our alliance and all the ensuing calamities. He further reported that Chao-chün is now dead, and that the khan desires peace between the two nations. The envoy humbly awaits your word.

EMPEROR: If that be so, execute the traitor and offer his head to the spirit of the princess. Make preparations in the Imperial Banqueting Hall for a feast to honor the envoy before his return.

(*recites*): Leaves fell in the courtyard as the wild goose
            cried above,
        Bringing to my lonely pillow dreams and thoughts of love.
        O   lady of the verdant tomb, sign to me where you are—
        I'll put to death the painter who dared your beauty mar.

                        TRANSLATED BY DONALD KEENE

A Yüan Novel

The Men of the Marshes (Shui hu chuan) *is a novel of massive size and scope which probably took shape in the years about 1368, when the Yüan dynasty yielded place to the native Chinese Ming. Little is known about the putative authors, Shih Nai-an and Lo Kuan-chung, although the latter (who lived from about 1330 to about 1400) is credited with several other lengthy historical novels. They had at their disposal a mass of material, part factual but mainly legendary, which storytellers for some two hundred years past had woven about the historical figures of Sung Chiang and his band of thirty-six. The novel Shih and Lo created continued to grow for another two centuries: the extract which follows is from chapters 14 to 16 of the most complete version, which appeared in 120 chapters toward the close of the Ming dynasty. Pearl S. Buck has translated, under the title* All Men Are Brothers, *all of a later "truncated" version of the first 70 chapters only.*

The novel is rich in incident and in vivid portraits of hao-han *or "bravos." These, from sneak-thieves to murderers, are presented as men of goodwill and generous heart driven outside the law by the injustices of the men in power over the land. The economic plight of the three fishermen brothers in our extract is a case in point; as for Yang Chih, it is his failure, on a mission for the governor, to counter the stratagem hatched by Wu Yung that forces him into the "greenwood," the marsh-protected mountain lair of Sung Chiang's group. When one by one Sung has assembled his "thirty-six major and seventy-two lesser chiefs," the episodic structure of the novel tightens: the band operates as a whole, first against*

449

and then later (after amnesty) by the side of government troops, until at last its leaders are betrayed and liquidated by jealous enemies at court.

It would be wrong to claim that The Men of the Marshes *was often taken seriously as a work of literature. Its popular origins, "vulgar" colloquial language and dangerous message all precluded the possibility. But Chinese scholars of modern times have recognized in it the first full masterpiece in that long line of novels which began with mass entertainment and progressed to include some of the finest literary products of later ages.*

From "The Men of the Marshes"

The Plot Against the Birthday Convoy

[Shui hu chuan, XIV-XVI]

Wu Yung dragged shut the door of his schoolroom and put a lock on it, then went off with Ch'ao Kai and Liu T'ang to the Ch'ao Clan Village. Ch'ao Kai took the other two right through to the inner-most room of his house and seated them as guests.

"Alderman Ch'ao, who is this companion of yours?" asked Wu Yung.

"He is Liu T'ang of Eastern Luchou, a bravo of river and lake," replied Ch'ao Kai. "He came on purpose to find me with news of a treasure. But last night as he lay dead drunk in the Temple of Officials of the Tao he was seized by runner Lei Heng and brought here, and it was only by identifying him as my nephew that I was able to have him released. This is his story: Governor Liang of Ta-ming, the northern capital, has got together a fortune in gold and jewels worth a hundred thousand strings of cash. This he is sending to the eastern capital as a birthday present for his father-in-law the chief minister, the Grand Tutor Ts'ai Ching himself. At some time on their journey they must pass by here; and these are ill-gotten goods, ours for the taking! Liu T'ang's wish to see me fits a dream I had: it was only last night that I dreamed the seven stars of the Big Dipper descended onto my roof. And on the handle of the Dip-per was another star, a smaller one, which turned into a ray of white light and vanished. I said to myself, surely some good must come to a house lighted by stars. And so now here I am seeking your advice, Schoolmaster Wu. What is your opinion on all this?"

Wu Yung smiled. "When I saw how eager brother Liu was to get here," he said, "I guessed three-quarters of the truth. There's only one problem I can see in this matter: we shall fail if we have too many men and we shall fail if we have too few. Not one of all these villagers of yours is any use to us, and that leaves only you, Alderman, with brother Liu and myself—and how can three of us handle a job like this? Both of you may well be men to be feared, but this is too much for us. We need seven or eight bravos for it —and again, more than that would make it impossible."

"Then we must match the number of stars in my dream?" said Ch'ao Kai.

"This dream of yours is no light matter," said Wu. "Surely it must mean we shall have helpers from the north?" He thought for a while, then his eyebrows lifted as a plan sprang to his mind: "Got it! Got it!"

"If you know of bravos you can trust, send for them at once so that we can bring about our scheme," said Ch'ao Kai.

Slowly and deliberately Schoolmaster Wu laid one forefinger across the other and said, "I have just thought of three men, great of heart and just of will, outstanding exponents of the military arts, who would go through fire or boiling cauldrons to live and die together. Only if we can lay hold of these three is our scheme to be accomplished."

"What kind of men are these?" asked Ch'ao Kai. "What are their names, and where do they live?"

"They are three brothers," Wu told him, "who live in Stone Tablet Village, by Liang-shan Marsh in Chichou. They are fishermen by trade, and at odd times they have practised a little smuggling on the waterways of the marsh. They are the Juan brothers: Number Two, nicknamed the 'Earthly Jupiter,' Number Five, the 'Ill-starred Demon Erh-lang,' and Number Seven, the 'Living Pluto.' They are blood brothers. I once lived up there for several years, and when I met those three I found that, though none of them could boast of an education, in their friendships they were true and upright, good fellows all. And so I spent much time with them, though it is now at least two years since last I saw them. If we can get these three we cannot fail."

"I also have heard the names of these three Juan brothers, though I have never met them," said Ch'ao Kai. "Stone Tablet Village is no more than some thirty-odd miles from here. Why not send someone to invite them to talk things over?"

"How do you expect them to come at the request of a mes-

senger?" asked Wu Yung. "I must make the trip myself, and trust
to the quickness of my tongue to talk them into joining us."

Highly pleased, Ch'ao Kai asked, "When may you leave,
honoured sir?"

"The matter brooks no delay," replied Wu. "I shall leave this
very night in the small hours, and by midday tomorrow I should
be there."

"Excellent," said Ch'ao Kai. And he ordered his men to set
out food and drink for them then and there.

"I have travelled the road between the northern and the eastern capitals," said Wu Yung, "but I find myself wondering which
route they will take with the birthday present. Perhaps brother
Liu would also undertake to leave tonight, to make his way to the
northern capital and there scout out the date of departure and exactly what route they are to take?"

"I shall set out this very night," agreed Liu T'ang.

"Wait, though," said Wu, "the birthday is the fifteenth of the
sixth month and we are still only at the beginning of the fifth,
still forty or fifty days away. Let us wait until I return from my
discussions with the Juan brothers before we send out brother Liu."

"Very well then," agreed Ch'ao Kai, "our comrade Liu can
stay here in this village while we wait."

No need to describe at length how they spent much of that
day in feasting. When the small hours came Wu Yung rose, washed
and rinsed his mouth. He ate a little breakfast, then requested some
silver from Ch'ao Kai, which he secreted about his person. Finally
he donned his straw sandals and, escorted to the gates of the village
by Ch'ao Kai and Liu T'ang, he there left them and strode through
the night towards Stone Tablet Village. By midday he had reached
his destination, where he saw:

> Emerald hills cresting the purple haze,
> Clouds resting on green groves of mulberry,
> All about the lone village, flowing waters,
> Here and there by its paths a patch of bamboo.
> > Thatched roof overhangs a creek,
> > Hoary trees lean together,
> High over a hedge hangs the flag of a tavern,
> Fishing skiffs lie moored in the willows' shade.

Schoolmaster Wu knew his own way about and needed no directions. Reaching the centre of Stone Tablet Village he made his way straight to the home of Juan Number Two. Looking about him there, he saw a number of small fishing-boats tied up to rotting piles, a tattered net drying in the sun on a straggly hedge, a dozen or so reed huts facing the water, their backs to the hills. He called out, "Is Second Brother at home?"

In reply a man came striding out, whose appearance:

> Craggy features
> Brows steep-slanting
> Lantern-jaw
> Curly whiskers
> Brown hair tangled on his chest
> Mighty shoulders jutting square
> Arms of strength to lift ten hundredweight
> Eyes with glint of ice-cold steel—
> Call me this no village fisherman,
> Truly a Jupiter come on earth!

—Juan Number Two came striding out, barefoot, in ragged head-cloth and ancient jacket. Seeing Wu Yung he hurried to greet him: "What are you doing here, Schoolmaster? What wind has blown you this far?"

"I've come to ask a small favour of you," replied Wu Yung.

"Tell me right away what it is then."

"It is already two years since I left you," said Wu Yung. "I have now found a post as tutor in a rich man's household. He is preparing to give a banquet and needs a dozen or so gold carp of not less than nineteen or twenty pounds. That's why I thought of coming to ask your help."

Juan Number Two gave a laugh, and said, "Let's talk about it after we've had three bowls of wine together."

"That's the other reason I came, to have three bowls with you," said Wu Yung.

"There are several taverns across the lake," said Juan. "We'll row over there."

"Excellent," said Wu Yung. "I wanted a few words with Fifth Brother also. Is he at home?"

"We'll go and find him," said Juan.

They walked down to the edge of the water, where Juan untied one of the boats moored by the rotting piles and handed Wu Yung down into it. Taking up an oar from the foot of a tree he set himself to rowing, and soon they were out in the lake. All at once Juan stopped rowing to wave his hand, and called out, "Seventh Brother! Have you seen Number Five?"

And Wu Yung saw a small boat come gliding out from a clump of reeds. In the boat was a fellow:

> Mottled face bursting with boils
> Veined eyes popping from their sockets
> Rusty hairs sprout from his cheeks
> Black spots jostle for space on his skin.
> Was he beaten out of iron
> Or cast whole from molten bronze?
> Surely a being from the netherworld—
> Known to the villagers as "Living Pluto."

—Juan Number Seven wore a black coolie-hat against the sun, a checked vest and an apron of unbleached cloth. He came rowing up and asked, "Second Brother, what do you want with Number Five?"

But Wu Yung greeted Number Seven, and said, "I've come on purpose to put something to you."

"Forgive me, Schoolmaster," said Juan Number Seven. "It's so long since we last saw you."

"I'm off for a bowl of wine with your Second Brother," said Wu Yung.

"I too have wanted a bowl of wine with you," said Number Seven, "but I haven't had the chance to see you."

In line the two boats went on along the lake until shortly they reached a place, lapped with water all around, where on a steep islet stood seven or eight reed huts. "Mother," called out Juan Number Two, "is Fifth Brother there?"

"Don't talk to me of that one," said the old woman. "Not a fish does he take, off to his gambling he is day after day, and now that he's lost every last copper he comes and asks me for my hair ornaments and takes those off to town to gamble some more!"

Juan Number Two laughed and rowed off. From the boat behind came the voice of Number Seven: "What's to be done, brother? Every game, nothing but lose, what filthy luck! It's not only Fifth Brother—I've been stripped myself down to my skin."

But Wu Yung was saying to himself, "They're just ripe for my scheme!"

Together the two boats drew towards Stone Tablet Village. After an hour's rowing they caught sight of a big fellow standing by a single plank bridge. He had two strings of cash in one hand while with the other he made ready to cast off the painter of his boat.

"Here's Fifth Brother," said Juan Number Two. And Wu Yung saw:

> Pair of hands like iron clubs
> Two eyes like round bronze bells
> The smiling curves of his cheeks
> Hide not the ferocious brow.
>> Distributor of disaster
>> Cause of calamities fell,
> Before his fists the lion quails
> Where his kick lands the snake despairs.
> For demons of pestilence seek where you will—
> Here truly is the "Ill-starred Erh-lang."

—A ragged cloth was wound aslant round the head of Juan Number Five, a pomegranate flower stuck into it against his temple. An ancient shirt hung open to reveal a chest tattooed with an indigo leopard. His trousers were held at the waist by a knotted kerchief.

Wu Yung called out to him: "Have you been winning, Fifth Brother?"

"So it's the schoolmaster!" said Juan Number Five. "It must be a good two years since we last saw you. I've been standing here at the bridge for half an hour watching you."

"I took the schoolmaster straight to your home," said Number Two, "but Mother said you were off to town for a game so we came here after you. Come on now to the terrace for three bowls of wine with Schoolmaster Wu."

Juan Number Five hastened to cast off, jumped aboard and seized an oar. He shoved off, and the three boats rowed abreast a short while until they reached the tavern with its water terrace. This was the sight they had:

Looking on the lake in front,
Back as well reflected in ripples,
Elm and willow, groves of green mist,
Lotus shining red from the water.
Windows open to painted balcony
Breeze moves the curtains in the terrace room.
Tell no tales of "Thrice drunk in Yüeh-yang"—
Here truly the wanderer finds his Fairyland.

They took the three boats in through lotus pools beneath the balcony and made fast. Wu Yung was helped ashore, then all four entered the tavern and chose for themselves a red-lacquered table and stools on the water terrace.

"We should like you, sir, to take the seat of honour, and not hold it against us three brothers that we are rough and clumsy folk," said Number Two.

"That would not be right," said Wu Yung.

"Brother Two," said Number Seven, "you just sit yourself down at the head of the table and let Schoolmaster Wu have the guest's place—and then Fifth Brother and I can sit down!"

"Seventh Brother was always the hasty one," laughed Wu Yung.

Settled at last, the four called for a gallon cask of wine. The tavern boy laid four places with large bowls and chopsticks, then brought four dishes of vegetables and the cask of wine which he set in the middle of the table.

"What do you have to help down the wine?" asked Number Two.

"There's a newly slaughtered ox," replied the boy, "good fat meat as sweet as dumplings."

"Let's have a dozen pounds, thick-sliced," said Number Two. And Number Five added, "You mustn't laugh at us, Schoolmaster, because we've nothing to offer you."

"On the contrary," said Wu Yung, "I'm putting you to a lot of trouble with my visit."

"Nothing of the kind," said Number Two. He pressed the boy to pour the wine, and soon the meat was sliced and set before them on the table in two dishes. The three Juan brothers invited

Wu Yung to eat and watched until he could eat no more; then they themselves fell to like ravening wolves or tigers.

Then Number Five turned to Wu Yung and asked, "What matter brings you here, sir?"

Number Two explained: "The schoolmaster has a post now teaching as a tutor in a rich man's house, and he's been asked to provide a dozen gold carp of nineteen or twenty pounds, so he's come to us for them."

"If it was forty or fifty of ordinary size it would be all right," said Number Seven. "Never mind a dozen or so, we brothers could manage more than that for you. But as things are nowadays, even if it was only a twelve-pounder you wanted, that's no easy job."

"Since you've come so far, Schoolmaster, we can probably manage a dozen seven- or eight-pounders to give you when you leave," added Number Five.

"I have plenty of silver with me," said Wu Yung. "It's up to you to fix the price. Only, small ones won't do, they'll have to be nineteen or twenty pounds to be of any use."

"But where are we to get them, Schoolmaster?" said Number Seven. "We couldn't even manage the seven- or eight-pounders Fifth Brother promised you, unless you were prepared to wait a few days. But at least I have a bucket of little live ones on my boat, I'll get them now and we can have them with our wine."

Juan Number Seven went off to his boat and returned with his bucket, some eight or nine pounds of fish altogether. He took them himself to prepare at the stove, then set them on the table in three dishes. "Just help yourself to these," he said.

And so they set to eating again. But gradually it grew dark, and Wu Yang said to himself, "This tavern isn't the place for us to talk. I'll have to ask for their hospitality tonight; we can discuss matters further when we get to their home."

And Juan Number Two said, "It's getting towards night. Schoolmaster, will you stay at my house tonight, and then tomorrow we can see what is to be done?"

"It was a hard journey for me here," replied Wu Yung. "But it was my good fortune to find the three of you together. I know you won't let me pay for this supper we've had, and tonight I shall be glad to stay in Second Brother's house. But I have some silver on me: let me buy a jar of wine and some meat here in the inn, then perhaps we can find a couple of chickens in the village, and tonight we can get good and drunk together."

"How can we let you spend your money?" Number Two protested. "We brothers will arrange it all, there's no need to fear we can't manage."

"But my whole idea was to play host to you three gentlemen," said Wu Yung. "If you won't let me do so I shall have to take my leave here and now."

"If this is what the schoolmaster wants, let's go ahead and have our wine and sort it all out later," said Juan Number Seven.

"My thanks to Seventh Brother for a straightforward solution!" cried Wu Yung; and he took out an ounce of silver and handed it to him. Then they bought a jar-measure of wine from the host and borrowed a large jar to carry it home, and bought also twenty-five pounds of meat, some cooked and some raw, and a couple of chickens.

"I'll settle my score later," said Number Two.

"Good enough," said the tavern-keeper.

The four left the tavern and returned to the boats. They placed the wine and meat in the deck-house, cast off and rowed away, straight to the home of Juan Number Two. On arrival there they jumped ashore, made fast the boats again to the piles, took out the wine and food and followed each other through to the back of the house, where they sat down and called for lanterns. As it happened, only Number Two of all the Juan brothers had a wife and family, Number Five and Number Seven had not yet found themselves brides, and so the four men sat themselves down in the lakeside pavilion at the back of Number Two's place. Number Seven killed the chickens and handed them over for preparation to the kitchen-helpers summoned by his sister-in-law. It was about half-way through the evening when the wine and food were set out on the table.

Wu Yung urged the three brothers to drink a few bowls and returned to the matter of his purchase of fish. "How is it that with so much room to fish here you can't find any of the size I want?"

"I might as well tell you, Schoolmaster Wu," said Juan Number Two, "fish as big as that are only to be found in the waters of the Liang-shan Marsh, this narrow little Stone Tablet Lake of ours doesn't hold any that size."

"But it's no distance from here to Liang-shan Marsh," said Wu Yung, "and there are connecting waterways, why don't you go there for them?"

"Better to keep quiet about it!" said Number Two with a sigh.

But Wu Yung pressed him further: "Why do you sigh?"

Then Number Five broke in: "You don't realize, Schoolmaster—Liang-shan Marsh used to be a real ricebowl for us three brothers, but nowadays we don't dare go anywhere near."

"Don't tell me the government can manage to prohibit fishing over an area as great as that!" said Wu Yung.

"I'd like to see the government that would try to prohibit me from fishing!" cried Number Five. "I'd take no prohibition from the Lord of Hades himself!"

"Then if there's no government prohibition why are you afraid to go?"

"It's clear you don't realize what's behind all this," said Number Five. "Perhaps we'd better tell you all about it."

"Well, I certainly don't understand it at all," said Wu Yung.

At this point Juan Number Seven spoke up: "It's hard to describe what's happened at Liang-shan Marsh. The waterways have been taken over by a gang of scoundrels who have just arrived and won't let anyone fish there."

"I'd no idea of this," said Wu Yung. "I had heard nothing in my part of the world about any gang of scoundrels arriving."

"The boss of the gang is one of those failed examination candidates," explained Juan Number Two. "His name is Wang Lun, and they call him the 'White-gowned Scholar.' His number two is the 'Skyscraper' Tu Ch'ien, and the third is the 'Cloud-wrapped Guardian God,' Sung Wan. Then there's a man called Chu Kuei, the 'Dry-land Sharp-ears,' who has opened a tavern now at the entrance to Li-chia-tao Village and spies out the land for the others, but he doesn't count for much. But there is a bravo just arrived, used to be an instructor in the imperial guard at the eastern capital, some fellow called Lin Ch'ung, the 'Leopard-headed,' a past master in the military arts. These bandits have gathered together with six or seven hundred people, men and women, and there they go robbing homes and plundering any traveller who passes. It's been more than a year since we went there to fish, and now that the waterways are closed to us our ricebowl is broken—that's why it's not easy to put it into a few words."

"I had really no idea of all this," said Wu Yung. "Why doesn't the government come and take them into custody?"

"Wherever they poke about nowadays," replied Number Five, "the government men only bring trouble. If they come out to a village they eat up innocent people's pigs and lambs and chickens and geese, and then they won't leave again until they've collected their 'travelling expenses'! And what help can you expect from them? The government thief-catchers daren't go near the villages! If one of the higher-ups orders them out to arrest somebody they daren't look him in the eye, they're so scared they mess their pants back and front!"

And Number Two added, "If we can't take any good-sized fish, at least we're spared a good number of taxes!"

"If that's the way things are," said Wu Yung, "those roughs of yours are well off."

"They fear neither heaven nor earth—nor the government," said Number Five. "I should think they *are* well off, measuring out their gold and silver, decking themselves out in the fanciest brocades, meat in thick slices and wine by the jar! Clever fishermen we might be, my brothers and me, but how could we ever hope to rival them?"

As he listened, Wu Yung was saying to himself delightedly, "This is the time for me to start my scheme!"

" 'A man has one lifetime as the grass has one summer,' " Juan Number Seven went on. "We stick to our fishing for our livelihood, but what a fine thing it would be to have one day of their life!"

"But why should you wish for their way?" asked Wu Yung. "How will they end up but as criminals sentenced to sixty or seventy strokes of a bamboo rod, all their might and majesty gone for good? And if the government does get its hands on them, they've only themselves to blame."

"The government!" said Number Two. "Rest upon it, they haven't a notion, plain stupid the whole lot of them. People get away with a thousand crimes that stink to high heaven and nothing happens to them. There's no getting rich for us brothers as we are, but if we could only find a contact with them, we'd be up there!"

"I've had this idea many a time," Number Five agreed. "We're as capable as anyone else, my brothers and me. But who there knows our worth?"

"Suppose someone did know your worth," said Wu Yung, "would you really go?"

"If someone were to recognize us," said Number Seven, "we'd go through water and we'd go through fire. One day of riches, and if we died for it we could smile in the next world."

And Wu Yung said to himself with glee, "These three are already willing, but I'll lead them on gently for a while."

He pressed another two rounds of wine upon the brothers. Truly,

> How did these flames of violence come incarnate?
> Only through seeking use for their skills in crime.
> Observe now how these three, the brothers Juan,
> From a birthday convoy plunder ill-gotten gains.

"Would the three of you dare to go up into the Liang-shan Marsh and take this gang of bandits?" Wu Yung asked next.

"And if we succeeded in taking them," said Juan Number Seven, "where would we go to collect our reward? We should be laughed to scorn by every bravo of river and lake!"

"Forgive my ignorance," Wu Yung went on. "But if you have this grievance over the interference with your fishing, wouldn't it be better to go over there and make a deal with them?"

"I tell you, sir," said Number Two, "I've talked time and again with my brothers about going off to join the gang. But this 'White-gowned Scholar,' Wang Lun—we've heard his underlings agree that he's a mean and jealous sort, hard to get along with. When that Lin Ch'ung from the eastern capital joined the gang he got mad with rage. No, Wang Lun won't take in just anyone who comes along, and that's why when we heard things were this way we weren't too eager to go."

"It would be all right if they were men of good will like yourself, sir, and had the kind of regard for us that you have," said Number Seven.

And Number Five broke in: "If we could expect the kind of friendship from Wang Lun that we've had from you, Schoolmaster, we'd have been off long ago and not waited till now! The three of us would gladly have faced death for him!"

"I am no one to be spoken of in this way," said Wu Yung. "Not when there are so many noble and heroic bravos here at this time in Shantung and Hopei!"

"Perhaps there are," said Number Two, "but we've never met any."

"What of Alderman Ch'ao, here in East Creek Village in Yünch'eng County, is his name known to you?"

"You must mean the 'Pagoda-lifting God,' Ch'ao Kai?" asked Number Five.

"That's the man I mean," agreed Wu Yung.

"It's been our misfortune that we've only heard of him and not met him, though he is not forty miles away," said Number Seven.

"But how could you have failed to meet him, a good fellow like that who chooses always honour above riches!" said Wu Yung.

"None of us has had any business that's taken him over there," said Number Two, "that's why we have never met him."

"These last few years I have done some teaching in a village school close by Alderman Ch'ao's place," said Wu Yung. "And now I learn that he is expecting to take a certain treasure. In fact, that is the reason I came here, to discuss with you whether we should go over there, meet it on its way and seize it—what do you say?"

"We couldn't do that," said Juan Number Five. "Since he is such a good fellow, and chooses always honour above riches, if we were to go and disgrace him in his own neighbourhood we should be the laughingstock of all the bravos of river and lake when they found out."

"I had been thinking merely that you were men of no fixed purpose," said Wu Yung, "but the truth is that you are honourable and considerate of strangers. Believe me now, if you are truly prepared to join in this, then I have something to tell you. I happen to be staying with Alderman Ch'ao, and when he heard of your exploits he asked me to invite you to his house."

"I speak now for the three of us brothers, words of truth with not a grain of falsehood!" said Juan Number Two. "It must be that Alderman Ch'ao has some great trading venture on foot and wishes to engage our aid, and so has troubled you, Schoolmaster, to come here. If this is really so, let us use the remainder of this wine to make an oath: if we fail to stake our lives on aiding him in this, may nothing but mischance befall each one of us, may loathsome diseases overtake us and may we die each one a violent death!"

And at this Juan Number Five and Juan Number Seven each alike clapped his hand to the nape of his neck and cried, "All we wish is to sell this hot blood of ours to one who knows the worth of what he is buying!"

"I say plainly to you brothers three," said Wu Yung now, "I do not wish to lure you with cunning arts into this matter, for it is no trifling undertaking. Very soon the Grand Tutor Ts'ai at court will celebrate his birthday, on the fifteenth of the sixth month. Governor Liang of Ta-ming, the northern capital, is his son-in-law, and he is preparing to send at once a treasure in gold and jewels worth a hundred thousand strings of cash as a birthday gift to the Grand Tutor. Of all this we have been informed by the bravo Liu T'ang. I am here now to ask you to come for talks. We shall gather together a band of bravos, find a quiet hollow in the hills and take this treasure of ill-gotten wealth, which will make each one of us rich for the rest of his life. This is why I was sent here, on the pretext of buying fish, to ask you three to turn this matter over in your minds so that we may bring it about. What then do you say to it?"

"Enough, enough!" cried Juan Number Five when he had heard all this. And he shouted out, "Seventh brother, what did I tell you?"

But Number Seven had already jumped to his feet: "All the dreams of a lifetime fulfilled this day! This scratches me exactly where I itch! When do we go?"

"As soon as you can," said Wu Yung. "Let us all rise early in the morning and leave together for the village of Ch'ao Kai, the 'Pagoda-lifting God'!"

The delight of the three brothers Juan may be seen from the poem:

> Books, not riches, are Schoolmaster Wu's concern,
> But the brothers Juan have forgotten the joys of fishing!
> Why now this gathering of the brave and true?
> —To take a treasure gotten through injustice!

They spent that night together, and when they rose the next morning and had eaten breakfast the three Juan brothers gave instructions to the members of their household. Then led by School-master Wu they left Stone Tablet Village and strode out on the road for East Creek Village. A day's walking brought them to the Ch'ao Clan Village, where from far off they had sight of Ch'ao Kai sitting with Liu T'ang under a green locust tree, awaiting their arrival. These two watched Wu Yung lead the Juan brothers up to the tree, where all exchanged greetings.

Greatly pleased, Ch'ao Kai cried, "I see that the brave name of the three brothers is no idle rumour. Let me invite you into my house to talk things over."

The six men entered Ch'ao Kai's house and went through to the innermost room, where they seated themselves host and guests in order. Ch'ao Kai listened with great pleasure to Wu Yung's account of all that had been said, and gave orders to his men to butcher pigs and sheep and prepare paper offerings for the spirits. Observing Ch'ao Kai's dignity of appearance and complaisant way of speaking, the three Juan brothers said happily, "It is our greatest joy to join in friendship with true bravos, and this is indeed a place where such abide. Had Teacher Wu not led us here today, how should we have come to know you?"

That evening they spent in eating and talking half into the night. At dawn the next day they returned to the inner room, in the courtyard before which were set out sacrificial money and horses and such of paper, together with incense, lamps and candles, and bowls of the pork and lamb that had been boiling overnight. Before such sincerity of purpose shown by Ch'ao Kai, all present were filled with joy, and each man took a solemn oath: "The money and treasure which Governor Liang is sending to the eastern capital as a birthday gift for the Grand Tutor Ts'ai Ching is the fruit of his misdeeds and extortions against the common people of the northern capital, and is nothing but ill-gotten wealth. If there be one among us six who is moved by selfish desire, may the bright eyes of the spirits seek him out and may heaven and earth destroy him." And having made their oath, they burned the paper offerings.

But as the six of them were feasting and amusing themselves in the inner room a villager came to them with a message: "There is a gentleman at the gate seeking alms from Alderman Ch'ao."

"Ignorant lout!" said Ch'ao Kai. "When you know I am busy entertaining my guests here with wine, why couldn't you just give him three or four pints of rice and leave it at that, instead of coming to bother me?"

"I gave him rice," said the villager, "and he wouldn't take it, but wanted to see you personally."

"Obviously it wasn't enough for him," said Ch'ao Kai. "Go and give him another couple of gallons. But tell him I have guests in for wine today and haven't time to receive him."

The man left, but after some time came back and said, "I gave the gentleman three gallons of rice, but he still wouldn't go. He calls himself 'The Clear-through Man of Tao,' and he says he didn't come for money or food but only to see you, sir, in person."

"If you can't think of anything else, blockhead," said Ch'ao Kai, "just tell him I really haven't the time today, but if he'll call again later I'll offer him a bowl of tea."

"I said that too," persisted the villager, "but the gentleman said, 'I didn't come here for money or food. I have heard the alderman is a true knight, and I am here on purpose to talk with him.'"

"On you go," cried Ch'ao Kai, "and not a scrap of help do you give me! If he still thinks it's not enough, give him another three or four gallons, why do you have to come pestering me! If I weren't drinking with guests just now I'd go and have a word with him and there would be no difficulty. But go and get rid of him, and I don't want to see you come back again!"

But the man had not been gone long when there was a commotion outside the gate and another villager came flying in: "That gentleman's in a rage, and he's knocked a dozen or more of us flat on the ground!"

Ch'ao Kai rose to his feet in alarm and said hurriedly, "Stay on for a while, all of you, I'll go myself and take a look."

He left the inner room and hurried to the gate, and there he saw the visitor, eight feet tall, with the stern visage of a Taoist priest but a most extraordinary appearance, laying about him among a crowd of villagers under the locust tree outside the gate. As Ch'ao Kai looked at him, he saw:

> Hair straggling loose from two crude tufts,
> Short serge jacket like a Szechuan mountaineer,
> Silk sash rainbow-coloured wound round his waist,
> Antique bronze sword mottled like pine-bark.

Bare feet staring from frayed straw sandals,
Purse at wrist, tortoise-shell fan in hand.
Almond eyes,
Brows down-slanting,
Square-set jowl,
Mustachioed cheeks.

As he flailed about he was shouting, "Why don't you recognize a man of worth?"

"Calm yourself, sir!" Ch'ao Kai called to him. "If you are seeking Alderman Ch'ao it must be for the favour of a meal or for alms. When he has already given you rice what cause have you for such a rage as this?"

At this the master roared with laughter: "Poor Taoist as I am, I did not come here for food or wine, for rice or cash. To me a hundred thousand strings are of no account. But I have something to say to the alderman and came here on purpose to find him, and my temper rose because I could not put up with abuse from these ignorant village louts."

"Have you ever met Alderman Ch'ao?" asked Ch'ao Kai.

"I have not met him, only heard of him."

Ch'ao Kai said, "I am the man you seek. What is it you have to say?"

The master looked at him and said, "Do not be angry with me, sir, but allow me to kowtow."

"Then let me invite you into the house for a bowl of tea," said Ch'ao Kai.

"Many thanks," said the master; and the two entered the house, where Wu Yung, seeing them coming, took Liu T'ang and the three Juan brothers and hid.

Ch'ao Kai led the master through to the back room. But when they had drunk tea the master said, "This is not the place for us to talk. Is there somewhere else we can go?"—and Ch'ao Kai took him to a small secluded chamber, where they seated themselves as host and guest.

"May I ask your name, sir, and the noble place of your origin?" said Ch'ao Kai.

"I have the double surname Kung-sun, my personal name is Sheng, and my name in the Tao is 'The Clear-through Master,'" came the reply. "I am a man of Chichou, where as a youth I gave myself to training with spear and staff and became proficient in many of the warlike arts, so that people called me the Gallant Kung-sun Sheng. But among the rivers and lakes I am known as 'The Cloud-soaring Dragon' because of my studies as a Taoist adept, which enable me to summon the wind and rain and to ride the clouds and the mist. I have long been familiar with the great name of Alderman Ch'ao of East Creek Village in the county of Yün-ch'eng, but not until now was it in my fate to meet you. I bring now a gift of treasure worth one hundred thousand strings of cash to mark my respect on this our first meeting, but I do not know whether a knight such as yourself would be willing to accept this gift?"

Ch'ao Kai laughed and said, "Surely what you are speaking of, sir, must be a birthday convoy from the north?"

Greatly startled, the master asked, "How do you know of this?"

"It was just a wild guess on my part, but is that what you had in mind?" said Ch'ao Kai.

"Riches such as these cannot be passed by," said Kung-sun Sheng. "The ancients had a saying, 'If you do not take it when you should, do not regret it when it has gone.' What is your own view, Alderman?"

But as he said these words a fellow burst in from outside the chamber, seized Kung-sun Sheng round the body and cried, "So! In the world of men are the royal statutes, in the world of darkness are gods and spirits! You are bold to discuss such a matter as this— but I have heard every word!"

It was the "Star of Wisdom," Schoolmaster Wu. Ch'ao Kai laughed and said, "Don't be upset, sir, but let me introduce you."

When they had greeted each other Wu Yung said, "Among the rivers and lakes I have long heard men speak of the fame of the 'Cloud-soaring Dragon,' the 'Clear-through' Kung-sun Sheng, but I had not dreamt I might meet you here today."

"This scholar is the 'Star of Wisdom,' Schoolmaster Wu," said Ch'ao Kai.

"I have heard many men of the rivers and lakes praise the fame of the 'Master of Added Lustre,' " said Kung-sun Sheng, "and now it is my happy fate to meet you here in the home of the alderman:

it is because the alderman despises riches but honours justice that valiant men from all the land are presenting themselves before him."

"Some other friends are in there," said Ch'ao Kai, "let me invite you into the back room to meet them."

And the three of them went through to greet Liu T'ang and the brothers Juan. Truly,

> Gold and fabrics hoarded up invite disaster sure,
> Yet such a gathering of heroes, what man could expect?
> Comes the time when valiant friends despoil the palace treasures,
> And seven points of starry light startle the royal seat.

"This meeting here today is no chance encounter," said the friends. "Alderman Ch'ao, you must take the seat of honour."

"I am a poorly endowed host," said Ch'ao Kai, "how should I presume to take the lead?"

But Wu Yung said, "Alderman, you are the eldest of us all, and I am next, so let us sit accordingly." And so Ch'ao Kai took his seat first in rank, with Wu Yung next, Kung-sun Sheng third, Liu T'ang fourth, Juan Number Two in fifth place, Juan Number Five in sixth place and Juan Number Seven last. The servants now replaced the earlier bowls and dishes and brought fresh wine and food, and they set to drinking again.

Then Wu Yung spoke: "Alderman Ch'ao in a dream saw the seven stars of the Big Dipper descend onto his roof. This 'conclave of the just' that the seven of us hold today to plan our campaign: surely it is in accord with that heavenly portent! The treasure is ours, we have only to spit on our hands and take it. The other day it was agreed that we should ask our brother Liu T'ang to discover what route the treasure-bearers will follow. It is late in the day now, but tomorrow morning he should leave on his mission."

"No need for this," said Kung-sun Sheng. "I have already made enquiries and discovered that they will follow the main road itself over Yellow Clay Ridge."

"Three miles to the east of Yellow Clay Ridge," said Ch'ao Kai, "in An-lo village there lives a fellow by the name of Po Sheng, the 'Daylight Rat.' He once sought refuge with me and I helped him with money for his needs."

"That white light on the handle of the Dipper—surely this man was meant!" exclaimed Wu Yung. "We shall find a use for him."

"It is some distance from here to Yellow Clay Ridge. Where are we to station ourselves?" asked Liu T'ang.

Wu Yung replied, "That will be our station—Po Sheng's home; and he himself can work for us."

Ch'ao Kai asked, "Master Wu: are we to take it the soft way or the hard way?"

Wu Yung laughed: "The trap is already set. Our behaviour will depend on the manner they choose: force will be met with force, guile with guile. I have a stratagem to offer which perhaps may win your agreement: this is what I propose . . ."

Ch'ao Kai heard him out with great delight, and stamped his feet and cried, "A marvellous scheme! Not in vain do they call you 'Star of Wisdom.' Truly you excel the wily Chu-ko Liang himself! A scheme to wonder at!"

"We must speak no more of it," said Wu Yung, "for often it is said, 'Is there no ear beyond the wall, no listener by the window?' This must be kept to ourselves."

Then Ch'ao Kai gave his orders: "The three brothers Juan should return to their homes for the time being and meet us again here when the time comes; let Master Wu go back to his teaching as usual; and Master Kung-sun with Liu T'ang will spend the interval here on my farm."

They drank till evening, when each retired to his allotted room. They rose next day at the fifth watch, and when they had eaten breakfast Ch'ao Kai took out thirty taels of patterned silver which he presented to the brothers Juan with the words, "A small token of my esteem, I hope you will not decline this."

The three brothers would have refused to accept the gift, but Wu Yung said, "It is the wish of a friend, you should not decline it." And with this the brothers Juan were persuaded to accept the silver. As they were being seen off from the farm Wu Yung whispered into their ears, "This is what you must do . . . Let there be no mistake when the time comes."

The brothers Juan took their leave and returned to Stone Tablet Village, and Kung-sun Sheng and Liu T'ang stayed on with Ch'ao Kai at his farm, where they were joined from time to time by Wu Yung for further discussions. Truly,

Taking what is not their own, officials all are thieves;
Skimming off this surplus wealth, thieves serve the
    common good.
Plans made ready, now they wait in quiet steadfastness,
And mock the frantic preparations for the treasure-train.

We must not become prolix, but tell now how in the prefecture
of Ta-ming, the northern capital, Governor Liang was collecting
together a treasure worth one hundred thousand strings of cash for
the birthday gift and choosing a date to send it on its way. One
day at this time he was sitting in his hall when his wife, Madam
Ts'ai, the grand tutor's daughter, came to him and asked, "My
lord, when will the birthday convoy be dispatched?"

"The presents are all prepared," answered Governor Liang,
"and I shall send them off tomorrow or the day after. There is just
one thing I am finding difficult to decide."

"And what is the difficulty?"

"Last year also I spent one hundred thousand strings of cash
to amass gold and pearls and precious things, which I dispatched
to the eastern capital; but I failed to pick the right men, the caravan was plundered by robbers and to this day nothing has been
recovered. This year again I can think of no really capable man
on my staff who could escort the treasure. This is what I am finding difficult to decide."

Lady Ts'ai pointed down to the body of the hall: "You have
often spoken of that man as absolutely capable. Why do you not
send him, armed with a written authority, to escort the treasure
on its journey, so that there will be no mistake this time?"

Governor Liang looked at the man she indicated, who was the
"Blue-faced Beast," Yang Chih. Filled with joy, he at once summoned Yang Chih to him and said, "I was forgetting you. If you
will escort this birthday convoy for me, I will see to it that you receive your promotion."

Yang Chih stepped forward with hands folded, bowed and
said, "How should I dare decline your excellency's commission! But
how are the gifts to be carried, and when should I leave?"

"Requisition several flat, four-wheeled carts of the *t'ai-p'ing*
sort from the prefecture," Governor Liang instructed him. "Take
a dozen or so of the prefectural bodyguards from my staff to escort

the carts. On each cart mount a yellow banner bearing the words 'Birthday Gift for the Grand Tutor Ts'ai.' Take a man-at-arms in addition to accompany each cart, and set out within the next three days."

"I am not merely making excuses," said Yang Chih, "but in all truth I am not able to go. I beg your excellency to commission some hand-picked man of valour for this task."

"I have a mind to raise you in rank," said Governor Liang. "Among the documents accompanying the convoy will be a special letter which will commend you highly to the grand tutor, so that you will have a certificate of merit to bring back with you. What do you mean now by producing arguments and refusing to go?"

"With all respect, your excellency," said Yang Chih, "I heard it said that last year the caravan was plundered by robbers and to this day nothing has been recovered. There are just as many bandits about this year; nor is there any route by water to the eastern capital, but the journey must be made all the way by road. The route is by way of Red Gold Mountain, Twin Dragon Mountain, Peach Blossom Mountain, Sunshade Mountain, Yellow Clay Ridge, the White Dunes, Wild Cloud Ford and Red Pine Forest: in every one of these places ruffians lurk. Not even a lone traveller dares pass through these places by himself; and when they know it is a treasure of gold and precious things, what is to stop them from coming to seize it? It is merely throwing away human lives, and that is why I am unable to undertake the mission."

"If this is the case," said Governor Liang, "then take more troops for protection."

"If your excellency were to send five hundred men it would still be no use," said Yang Chih. "Just let them hear one whisper of the approach of bandits, and you would find they'd all vanished."

"From what you say, then," said the governor, "it seems the birthday convoy had better not leave at all!"

But Yang Chih replied, "If you will consider my own plan, I will undertake to escort it."

"Of course your plan will be considered, since it is to you the task is entrusted," said Liang.

"Then if it is done my way," Yang Chih began, "we shall not need carts. The gifts will be made up into a dozen or so porters' loads, as if they were just packages of goods belonging to some merchant. We should pick out ten of the strongest of the prefectural guards and fit them out as porters to carry the loads; then all I should need is one other companion for myself. He and I would dress as merchants and make our way quietly, travelling by night, to the eastern capital, and deliver the gifts. That would be the way to do it."

"You are absolutely right," said Governor Liang. "I shall write a report commending you very highly, so that you will have an official title to bring back with you."

"I am deeply grateful for your excellency's kindness," said Yang Chih.

And so that day Yang Chih had the bundles made ready and selected the soldiers to carry them. On the morrow he went to wait on Governor Liang, who, as he entered his hall of audience asked, "Yang Chih, when will you leave?"

"If it please your excellency," replied Yang Chih, "I shall leave tomorrow morning, and request your written authority."

"My wife," said Governor Liang, "has a package of gifts of her own which she wishes you to deliver to her family. And fearing that you will not know your way about, she has given special orders to her majordomo, Superintendent Hsieh, who is the husband of her old wet nurse, to take two sergeants of the guard and accompany you on your mission."

"Your excellency, I am unable to go," said Yang Chih.

"The gifts are all packed and ready, why is it this time that you can't go?" asked Liang.

"The ten packages are my responsibility alone," Yang Chih now submitted, "and the entire group is under my command. If I want to move early in the day, we move early in the day; if I want to move at night, we move at night. We stop for rests entirely on my orders. But now you would have old Superintendent Hsieh and two sergeants accompany me. Hsieh is under my mistress's orders, a family servant of the grand tutor himself: how should I dare to argue with him if some squabble blew up on the journey? And then, if our whole plan went wrong, what excuse should I be able to make?"

"This is an easy matter," said Governor Liang. "I will simply instruct the three of them to obey your orders."

"Now that I have cleared this," said Yang Chih, "I should

like to receive your excellency's written authority. And if there is any mishap, I shall willingly undergo the severest punishment."

In great glee Governor Liang cried, "I was right to think of exalting you! You are certainly a man of great experience!" And at once he summoned old majordomo Hsieh and the two sergeants into the hall and gave them his orders: "Captain Yang is willing to accept my written authority to escort a birthday convoy consisting of eleven packages of gold, jewels and precious things to the eastern capital and there deliver them to the mansion of the grand tutor. The entire responsibility for this rests with him. The three of you will accompany him, but you are to obey his orders whether for rising in the morning, travelling at night or stopping to rest. In all this there must be no squabbling with him. You all understand the matters entrusted to you by my wife. Act with caution, leave and return as quickly as you can, and let there be no mishap."

To all of this the old superintendent assented.

Having accepted his commission, Yang Chih rose the next morning at the fifth watch. The porters' loads and carrying-poles were all laid out before the prefectural audience-hall. An additional small bundle of valuables had been brought by the old superintendent and the two sergeants, so that there were eleven loads altogether. Eleven of the strongest prefectural guards were selected and dressed as porters. Yang Chih wore a straw coolie-hat against the sun, a dark-coloured silk-gauze vest, a girdle about his waist, and on his feet stout hempen sandals for travelling; for arms he wore a sword and carried a staff in his hand. The old superintendent was likewise dressed in the manner of a travelling merchant, and the two sergeants were got up to look like servants accompanying them. Each of them carried a staff and a number of rattan switches. When Governor Liang had handed over documents to accompany the convoy, the whole group ate a hearty meal and then took formal leave of him in the audience-hall.

And now the men took up their loads and set out, Yang Chih with Superintendent Hsieh and the two sergeants escorting them, a company of fifteen all told leaving the governor's official residence, leaving the city gate of the northern capital and striking out on the main highway for the eastern capital many miles away. It was the middle of the fifth month, and although it was good to have such clear weather the oppressive heat made travelling a hardship. In former days the Prince of Wu wrote these lines:

Jade screens are set for shade about the painted walks,
In garden pools the happy fish play tag with floating weeds,
Matting is hung, eight feet high, woven of the giant
        shrimp's feelers,
And for the coolest pillow, a block of smooth red agate.
Rain-bearing dragons fear the heat and will not venture out,
Even to the shores of the Blessed Isles the sea's waters boil.
And while the young lord wishes for the strength to fan himself
The traveller makes his way along the dusty road.

This poem describes the youth of gentle or noble family who in the blazing heat of the midsummer months takes his ease in the coolest summerhouse or in a lakeside pavilion, quenching his thirst with melons and plums floating in their juice, or preparing dishes of lotus-root, white as snow and ice-cold—and yet deplores the heat. But now think of the traveller!—all for the sake of some slight profit or some petty repute as a trader, even though there be no cangue about his neck nor ropes binding him, through the heat of the dog days he must needs take to the road.

This day Yang Chih and his company also, in order to arrive in time for the birthday on the fifteenth of the sixth month, had to take to the road. For five or six days after leaving the northern capital they did indeed set out in the small hours and travel in the cool of the morning, so that they could rest in the heat of the day. But by the end of this time they were passing fewer dwellings, other travellers were rarely seen and each stage of the journey lay across mountainous country. And now Yang Chih insisted on setting out in full daylight and going on to late afternoon. Each of the eleven prefectural guards carried a heavy load, none was lighter than another, and as the day grew hotter they felt they could not go on. If they saw a copse of trees they would want to rest in the shade, but Yang Chih would urge them on. If one of them stopped he would get at least a violent cursing or even a beating with a rattan switch to force him on.

The two sergeants, though they carried only light bundles of their own baggage, panted and puffed and could not keep up. Yang Chih yelled at them: "An ignorant pair you are! This is all my responsibility, but instead of giving me some support in driving these fellows on, all you do is wander idly along behind! This is no place for games!"

"We are not going slow because we choose to," said the sergeants, "we fell behind because we can't move when it gets so hot. Earlier on you were taking advantage of the morning cool—why do you now insist on travelling in the heat of the day? There is no sense in arranging things this way."

"That kind of talk is about as helpful as a fart," said Yang Chih. "Until now we had good roads to walk on. Now there are steep cliffs everywhere: if we don't get through in daylight, who is going to risk it in the small hours, the middle of the night?"

The two sergeants said nothing more but thought to themselves, "This fellow enjoys cursing people whether they deserve it or not."

While Yang Chih took up his staff in one hand and a switch in the other and went ahead to urge on the porters, the two sergeants sat down in the shade of a willow and waited for the old superintendent to come up. To him they complained: "That fellow Yang is getting too big for himself, lording it over us this way when he's no more than a captain of the guard under our master the governor!"

"We had orders from the governor himself to avoid squabbling with him," said the superintendent. "That is why I have said nothing. The last day or two I haven't been able to stand the sight of him either, but we have to put up with him for the time being."

"Our master was only trying to give him face, and you have only to exert your authority," said the sergeants.

But the superintendent repeated, "We must put up with him for the time being."

They went on that day until late afternoon, when they found an inn for their rest. Sweat poured like rain from the eleven prefectural guards, who went up to the old superintendent gasping for breath and sighing: "When we had the ill luck to become soldiers we knew very well we would be sent on missions. But in this blazing hot weather, and loaded down too with heavy burdens—and then these last two days we weren't allowed to travel in the morning cool, and whatever we do we get beaten with a switch! We are made of flesh and blood like everyone else, why do we have to suffer like this?"

"Don't go on grumbling," said the old superintendent, "just put up with it as far as the eastern capital and I will see that you are rewarded for your pains."

"If only it was someone like you in charge of us, sir," said the soldiers, "we shouldn't be grumbling."

Another night passed, and in the morning the men got up before dawn and wanted to leave while it was still cool. But Yang Chih leapt to his feet and roared, "Where are you off to! Get some more sleep now, and then we'll see!"

"If we don't set out early, when it gets hot we won't be able to move, and then you'll beat us," said the men.

"What do you know about it?" yelled Yang Chih. He snatched up his switch and made to lay about him, and they could only swallow their anger and lie down again to sleep. Not until full daylight did Yang Chih, taking his time, allow them to build a fire, cook breakfast and get under way. He kept after them all the way and would not let them seek out cool spots to rest in. The eleven guards muttered and grumbled among themselves, and the two sergeants chattered and argued with the old superintendent face to face; he took no notice of what they said, but he had his own feelings about Yang Chih.

But we must not become prolix. After fourteen or fifteen days like this there was not one of the other fourteen who did not detest Yang Chih. Then came a day when they slowly made their preparations to leave their inn, lit their fire and cooked breakfast though it was already full daylight. It was now the fourth of the sixth month, and before the day had advanced to noon a great red sun hung in the sky, there was no trace of a cloud and the heat was at its fiercest. There is a verse by a writer of former times:

> Chu-jung the Fire God drives his flame-breathing dragons
> And blazing banners scorch the sky to crimson;
> At noon the sun's great disc seems glued in place
> And every realm melts in a glowing furnace.
> Verdure shrivels from the Five Peaks, every cloud
>   has perished,

Lord Yang the Water Spirit fears the sea will run dry.
O for a precious breeze to rise one night
And sweep away this heat from all the earth!

Their route all that day followed steep, winding mountain trails. Up one ridge and down another they drove the soldier-porters on until they had covered ten miles or so more of their journey. Whenever the men made for a clump of shady willows to take a rest, Yang Chih would come lashing out at them with his rattan switch and yelling, "Faster, faster! Who told you to stop now?"

Looking up at the sky they could see no trace of a cloud, and by this time the heat was unbearable. This is how it was:

Dust kicked up
Into steaming air,
All creation one great cauldron,
The sky an umbrella of fire.
No cloud to be seen, all breezes hushed,
Even at the creek's edge bushes burn.
Mountains aflame:
Rocks split open, ashes fly.
Birds aloft, their lives in peril,
Zigzag their way to the forest's depth;
Fish below cast off their scales
And burrow deep into muddy holes.
Now the stone tiger pants for breath,
The iron statue drips with sweat.

As Yang Chih urged his column of men along the mountain paths, before long the sun stood at high noon and the rocks became so hot to the feet that walking was painful. "A day like this, the heat will kill us all!" said the soldiers. But—

"Faster, faster!" yelled Yang Chih. "We'll get past this ridge in front, and then we'll see." They were just coming up to the ridge, and this is how it looked:

Green trees crowd at the summit,
Yellow sand stretches at the foot,
Rearing crests form dragon shapes,
Storms reverberate on the heights.

Reeds on the hill slopes,
Tangled clumps in array of sword and spear;
Rocks litter the ground,
Jumbled cairns drawn up like slumbering tigers,
Speak not of the perilous highland road to Shu:
Be forewarned: these are the T'ai-hang Mountains.

All fifteen came up to the ridge on the run, and once there, fourteen of them, burdens set down, stretched themselves out in the shade of thick pines to sleep. "More trouble," cried Yang Chih. "What sort of place do you think this is to start resting in the shade? Up with you now, quick!"

"It doesn't matter if you chop us into little pieces, we can't go any farther," said the men.

Yang Chih took up his switch and came slashing at their heads, but as soon as he had brought one man to his feet another would lie down to sleep again and there was nothing he could do to prevent it. And now the old superintendent and the two sergeants came panting desperately up to the top of the ridge, where they sat down beneath the pines to get their breath. Seeing Yang Chih beat his men the old majordomo said, "You mustn't blame them, Captain, it really is too hot to march any farther."

But Yang Chih replied, "You don't realize, Superintendent: this is just one of the places where bandits lurk. This place is called Yellow Clay Ridge. Even in normal times when there is order in the land they come here in broad daylight to rob and plunder—who would be foolhardy enough to halt here now, in times like these?"

Hearing this the two sergeants said, "How many times have you said that now! You are only trying to scare us!"

And the Superintendent added: "How would it be if you let them have a little rest for the time being, and move on again when the middle of the day has passed?"

"You don't understand either!" cried Yang Chih. "How can I do that? There's not a human dwelling for three miles round from this ridge. What sort of place do you think this is for us to risk taking a rest now?"

"Then I'll just sit here by myself for a while," said the superintendent, "while you get the rest of them under way."

Yang Chih took his switch and shouted, "Twenty strokes for anyone who doesn't start moving."

All the men began crying out at once, and one of them started to argue: "We're carrying hundred-weight loads, Captain, we're not like you travelling emptyhanded, why can't you treat us like human beings? Even if it was the governor himself in charge of us he'd let us have our say, but you don't seem to have any feelings at all, all you do is browbeat us all the time!"

"I've had more chattering from you swine than I can stand," said Yang Chih. "The only thing you understand is a good beating" —and seizing a switch he struck the man across the face.

But the old majordomo cried, "Stop that, Captain Yang! Listen to me now: when my wife was wet nurse to the grand tutor's family in the eastern capital I came up against hundreds and thousands of military men, and there wasn't one that didn't treat me with respect. I don't want to say too much, but I know you were an officer before and were disgraced and sentenced; and then the governor took pity on you and promoted you to captain. And now look at you, given some trivial little rank and duty, coming blustering about like this! We can forget that I am the majordomo in the governor's household—even if I were nothing more than an old peasant off the farm you should still be prepared to listen to advice. What sort of way to command men is this when all you can do is beat them?"

"You are a city-dweller, Superintendent," replied Yang Chih. "You've spent your life in official residences, what do you know about the troubles and dangers of the open road?"

"I've travelled through Szechuan and the two Kuang Provinces, but never have I seen anyone behave as you are behaving now," said the superintendent.

"It's very different when there is order in the land," said Yang Chih.

"You deserve to have your tongue cut out for that kind of talk," said the superintendent. "How can you say that order is not kept throughout the empire at the present time?"

Yang Chih's reply was on his lips when suddenly he caught sight of someone sticking his head out and peering at them from a hiding-place among the trees before them. "What was I saying?" he shouted. "Isn't that some scoundrel or other right there?" He

threw aside his switch but grabbed up his staff and charged into
the pine copse yelling, "What impudent fellow is this, coming to
stare at what we are carrying?" Truly,

> Speak of the devil, the devil is here,
> Speak of bandits, bandits appear;
> Men born to be brothers
> Meet now in mistrust and fear.

Hastening up to the pine copse Yang Chih found there seven
wheelbarrows of the Chiangchou type standing one behind the
other all in a row, while seven men lay stark naked resting in the
shade. One of them, who had a cinnabar-red birthmark at his temple,[1] took up a staff and advanced on Yang Chih as the rest all
leapt to their feet with a cry of "Aiya!"

"What are you doing here?" shouted Yang Chih.

"What are you doing here?" asked the seven in return.

But Yang Chih went on, "Don't tell me you aren't a band of
brigands?"

"Haven't you got it the wrong way round?" said the seven.
"We're nothing but small traders, it's no use your expecting money
from us."

"And if you are small traders, I suppose I'm a wealthy merchant," said Yang Chih.

"Well, who are you anyway?" they asked.

"Tell me first where you come from," said Yang Chih.

"The seven of us are men of Haochou," was the reply. "We're
on our way to the eastern capital with a load of dates for sale.
This place lay on our route, and we had often heard tales of travelling merchants being robbed by bandits here on Yellow Clay Ridge.
But as we came along we were saying to each other, 'all we have
between the seven of us is a few dates, we've nothing of value'—
and so we just came on over the ridge. But when we got as far as
this we couldn't stand the heat any longer, and so we are resting
under these trees for the moment, until the evening when it will
be cooler and we can be on our way again. Then when we heard
people coming up the ridge we thought it must be scoundrels of
some kind, and so we sent this brother here to have a look."

---

1. The "Red-haired Devil," Liu T'ang.

"So that's the way it is, you're just traders like ourselves," said Yang Chih. "When I saw this man looking out just now I thought he was a scoundrel and that's why I came running up to find out."

"Would you like a few dates, friend?" asked the seven.

"No, but thank you," said Yang Chih; and staff in hand he went back to where the porters' loads lay on the ground.

"If there are robbers here we'd better be off," said the old majordomo.

"I thought they must be scoundrels, but they're nothing more than date pedlars," said Yang Chih.

"From what you were saying just a while ago, they must surely be desperate villains!" said the majordomo.

"There's no need to be sarcastic, we can just be thankful there's no trouble," said Yang. "All right, have a rest now, we'll go on when it's cooler."

The men began to laugh, and Yang Chih thrust his staff into the ground and went over by the trees to sit in the shade and rest.

Before enough time had passed for you to get through half a bowl of rice, there appeared in the distance a fellow carrying a shoulder-pole with a bucket at either end. As this man came up the ridge he was chanting a refrain:

"Blazing sun like a fi-re burning,
Crops in the fields to a crisp are turning,
Farmer's blood bubbles like boiling soup,
Gentlemen at ease for fans are yearning."

Chanting as he came he climbed the ridge. Reaching the pine copse he set down his buckets and seated himself where it was cool. The soldiers took one look at him and asked, "What have you got in those buckets?"

"Cool wine," came the reply.

"Where are you taking it?" asked the men.

"I'm taking it to the village to sell," said the fellow.

"How much the bucket?"

"Five full strings."

The soldier-porters fell to discussion: "We're all hot and thirsty, why don't we buy some to cool us off a bit?"

But as they were trying to raise the money for the wine Yang Chih saw them and roared, "What are you up to now?"

"We're buying a bowl of wine for ourselves," they replied.

Yang Chih struck at them with the handle end of his staff and yelled, "You've got a nerve, just deciding for yourselves that you'll buy some wine, without bothering about permission from me!"

"Here you are making trouble again with no reason!" said the men. "We've raised money among ourselves to buy wine, what has it to do with you? What are you hitting us for this time?"

"You ignorant bunch of yokels, you've no idea what you're doing, but still you have to argue!" cried Yang Chih. "What do you understand of the perils of life on the open road, where many an honest bravo has been knocked out flat with a drugged drink?"

The wine-vendor sneered as he turned to Yang Chih: "That doesn't show much sense, coming out with an old wives' tale like this before I've even said whether I'll sell you my wine."

As they stood at the edge of the trees grappling and shouting, out from the pine copse across from them came the pedlars of dates, each with staff in hand. "What are you quarrelling about?" they asked.

"Here am I with this load of wine to take over the ridge for sale in the village," said the wine-vendor. "With it being so hot I thought I'd rest here in the shade. These men here wanted to buy something to drink, but before I have said I'd sell them my wine, here comes this boss of theirs and says my wine has some kind of drug in it, what do you think of that for a joke, coming out with a tale like that?"

"We were just thinking there were scoundrels here," said the seven pedlars. "If this is all it is, there's no harm done. We were wishing we had some wine, we're so thirsty. If they're so suspicious about it, you can sell us a bucket instead."

"I'm not selling it at all!" said the wine-vendor.

"What's wrong with you, you stupid lout," said the seven pedlars. "It's not us who have been quarrelling with you. You're going to sell it in the village anyway, you'll get the same price for it, what's the harm in selling us a drop? And then you'd have all the credit for saving our lives from this heat and thirst, without needing to set up as an almsgiver, handing out tea and soup."

"I wouldn't mind letting you have a bucket," said the wine-vendor, "only these fellows have been insulting me. And besides I've no bowls for you to drink from."

"Don't take it so much to heart!" said the seven. "What does a bit of an argument matter? And for ladles, we've got coconut-shells of our own with us."

And two of the pedlars went to fetch a couple of coconut-shell ladles from a barrow. One of them brought out a big bunch of dates as well. The seven of them surrounded the bucket, took off the lid and ladled out the wine, passing the cup round from man to man, with dates to go with it. Not much time passed before one whole bucket of wine had been emptied.

"We never asked you how much you wanted for it," said the pedlars.

"I never haggle over prices," answered the fellow. "Five full strings the bucket, ten strings the load."

"Five strings it is then," said the seven pedlars, "just let us have another ladleful free."

"Nothing free, it's a fixed price," said the vendor.

But while one of the pedlars paid him the money another one went and took the lid off the other bucket, scooped out a ladleful and started to drink it. The vendor made to snatch it away from him, and the pedlar ran off into the pine copse, the half-full ladle still in his hand and the vendor chasing him. Then from the trees on this side emerged another of the pedlars with the other coconut-shell in his hand. This man came up to the bucket and dipped in his ladle. When the vendor saw this he flung out a hand and snatched the ladle, poured the wine back in the bucket, clapped on the lid and hurled the ladle to the ground. "That's no way for men of honour to behave," he muttered. "Folk who should have some self-respect, squabbling like this!"

All this time the soldier-porters were watching with greedy eyes from where they sat. All of them longed for a drink, and one of them said to the old majordomo, "Put a word in for us, will you dad? Those pedlars have bought one bucket from him and drunk it, why can't we just buy the other to moisten our throats? We're all so thirsty with this heat, and there's nowhere on this ridge we can get a drink of water. Do us a favour, sir!"

The old majordomo heard them out, and indeed he himself was longing for a drink. In the end he went up to Yang Chih and said that now the date pedlars had bought one bucket there was only the other one left, why not let them buy a little to drink against the heat, there really was nowhere to get a drink of water anyway.

Yang Chih told himself: "I watched those fellows myself buying his wine and drinking it over there. And I saw one of them right here in front of me drink half a ladleful out of the other bucket, it must be all right. I've been knocking them about for so long, I might just as well let them buy a bowl of wine." And so he said, "Now that you've asked me, Superintendent, we'll let these fellows buy their drink and then we'll move on."

With this the men put together five strings of cash and came up to buy their wine. But the vendor said, "I'm not selling, I'm not selling! This wine has a drug in it!"

"All right, brother, you've got your own back," the men chuckled.

"I'm not selling, stop bothering me!" said the vendor.

The date pedlars tried to pacify him: "You silly fellow, they've upset you again, you take things too seriously. We had to put up with a scolding from you too. It was nothing to do with these men, just let them have a drink and be done with it."

"Well, why did he have to make everybody start suspecting things without any reason?" said the vendor.

The date pedlars shoved the wine-vendor aside and carried the second bucket over to give the men a drink. The men took off the lid, but they had no ladle, and so very politely they asked the pedlars for the loan of their coconut-shells.

"Have these dates to go with the wine," said the pedlars.

"Why are you giving us these?" the men asked.

"No need for politeness, we are all travellers together, what do a few dozen dates matter?" said the pedlars.

The men thanked them and filled the two ladles, offering one to the old majordomo and one to Captain Yang. Yang Chih declined, but the majordomo drank his and then the two sergeants had a ladleful each. Then the men all came at it together and in no time the bucket was almost empty. Yang Chih saw that the men had come to no harm, but he himself had not had a drink. Now for one thing the heat was intense, and for another he was unbearably thirsty: he picked up a ladle and drank only half, and took a few dates to go with it.

Then the wine-vendor said, "Those pedlars took a ladleful of wine out of this bucket, you've been cheated, so I'll let you off half a string of cash."

The men brought out their money to pay him. The fellow took the money, shouldered the empty buckets and went off down the ridge singing his ditty as before.

The seven pedlars of dates now ranged themselves at the edge of the pines and pointed at the fifteen. "Go on, fall down!" they cried.

And the fifteen men, heads heavy, feet light, gaped at each other and one after another crumpled to the ground.

The seven pedlars pushed out their seven Chiangchou wheelbarrows from within the pine copse, dumped their loads of dates out on the ground and filled up the barrows again with the eleven porters' loads of gold and jewels and precious things. They covered them up to conceal them, called out "Excuse us!" and went trundling their barrows off down the ridge. Truly,

> The gift was bought with the people's blood,
> None cared whether they lived or died.
> Now it is clear why thieves come forth,
> This is the way that leads to crime.

All Yang Chih could do was moan aloud, for his limbs were too weak for him to rise to his feet. The fifteen of them with eyes wide open watched the seven load up the precious bundles and make off with them, for they could neither stand nor struggle nor speak.

And now let me ask you who these seven men really were. They were no other than these: Ch'ao Kai, Wu Yung, Kung-sun Sheng, Liu T'ang and the three brothers Juan; and the fellow who just now brought along his load of wine was the "Daylight Rat," Po Sheng.

And how was the drug administered? Well, when the two buckets were carried up the ridge all they contained was perfectly good wine. After the seven had finished off the first bucket it was Liu T'ang who took the lid off the second, scooped up half a ladleful of wine and drank it down: this he did deliberately in full view of the others, to put an end to any doubts they might have. Next, Wu Yung went into the pine copse to get the drug, which he shook into his ladle. Then pretending to be stealing wine for himself he dipped in his ladle and mixed the drug with the wine. He made as if to drink the wine he scooped up, but Po Sheng flung out a hand, snatched the ladle and poured the wine back in the bucket. This then was their ruse, all of it put forward by Wu Yung; and it is known as "The Plot Against the Birthday Convoy."

Now Yang Chih having drunk the least wine was the first to come to his senses. He pulled himself up somehow, though he still swayed on his feet. He surveyed the other fourteen, who lay there drooling at the mouth and making not a move; it was just as the saying goes:

> You may be as sly as any demon
> But you just drank the water I washed my feet in.

Yang Chih said to himself in disgust: "There's nothing I can do about your making off with the birthday convoy—but how am I to go back and face Governor Liang? Not much use delivering these documents"—and he tore them up. "And now here I am, no home to go to, no country to take me in—where shall I hide myself? Best to put an end to myself right here on this ridge." And hoisting up his clothing he strode to the edge of the ridge to throw himself off.

Then suddenly he came to himself. He slowed and stopped and reflected: "My father and mother when they brought me into this world gave me a fine manly presence and a splendid strong body. From my childhood days I have perfected my mastery of the eighteen weapons of war; it is not for me to end my days like this. Rather than leap to my death here and now, let me wait till they've caught those fellows and see what happens then."

And he turned back to look again at the other fourteen, who gazed wide-eyed at him but made no effort to rise. Pointing his finger at them Yang Chih cursed roundly: "All this trouble has come about because you fools wouldn't obey my orders, and it's me you've involved in it all."

He took up his staff from the foot of a tree and thrust his sword in his girdle. He looked about him, but there was nothing else. Yang Chih heaved a sigh and went off down the ridge.

TRANSLATED BY CYRIL BIRCH

A Short Bibliography

GENERAL HISTORY

Eberhard, Wolfram. *A History of China*. Berkeley: University of California Press, 1960.

Goodrich, L. Carrington. *A Short History of the Chinese People*. New York: Harper & Brothers, 1951.

Grousset, René. *The Rise and Splendor of the Chinese Empire*. Berkeley: University of California Press, 1953. Incorporates much material drawn from the author's special interest in the history of Oriental art.

HISTORY OF LITERATURE AND CRITICAL STUDIES

Chen, Show-yi. *Chinese Literature*. New York: Ronald Press, 1961. Appreciations and reading-notes, often informative but not very highly organized.

Feifel, Eugen. *Geschichte der Chinesischen Literatur*. Peking: Catholic University, 1945. Based on the work of Nagasawa Kikuya.

Giles, H. A. *A History of Chinese Literature*. New York: D. Appleton, 1923. Still the only formal "history" in English, and still too full of critical wisdom to discard.

Hightower, J. R. *Topics in Chinese Literature*. Cambridge, Mass.: Harvard University Press, 1953. Accurate and highly informative outlines, definitions and bibliographical aids.

Hung, William. *Tu Fu: China's Greatest Poet*. Cambridge, Mass.: Harvard University Press, 1952. Includes prose versions of almost four hundred of Tu's poems.

Lin Yutang. *The Gay Genius*. New York: John Day, 1947. Biography of Su Shih (Su Tung-p'o).

Liu, James J. Y. *The Art of Chinese Poetry*. Chicago: University of Chicago Press, 1962. Traditional criticism, Western-informed criticism, and a stimulating synthesis of the two.

Lu Hsün. *Brief History of Chinese Fiction*. Peking: Foreign Languages Press, 1959. Pioneer survey of a neglected field, originally published in Chinese in 1925.

Margouliès, G. *Histoire de la Littérature Chinoise*. Paris: Payot, 1949 (Prose), 1951 (Poésie).

Shih, Vincent Yu-chung. *The Literary Mind and the Carving of Dragons*. New York: Columbia University Press, 1959. Translation of the celebrated fifth-century work of literary theory *Wen-hsin tiao-lung* by Liu Hsieh.

Waley, Arthur. *The Poetry and Career of Li Po*. New York: Macmillan, 1950.

——. *The Life and Times of Po Chü-i*. London: George Allen & Unwin, 1949.

Watson, Burton. *Early Chinese Literature*. New York: Columbia University Press, 1962.

ANTHOLOGIES

Bynner, Witter and Kiang Kang-hu. *The Jade Mountain*. New York: A. A. Knopf, 1929; Anchor, 1964. Translation of an eighteenth-century anthology, the "Three Hundred T'ang Poems."

Ch'u Ta-kao. *Chinese Lyrics*. Cambridge: Cambridge University Press, 1937.

Davis, A. R. (ed.) *The Penguin Book of Chinese Verse*. Translations by Robert Kotewall and Norman L. Smith. London: Penguin, 1962.

De Bary, Wm. Theodore (ed.). *Sources of Chinese Tradition*. New York: Columbia University Press, 1960. Texts illustrating the history of Chinese thought and institutions.

Demiéville, Paul. *Anthologie de la Poésie Chinoise Classique*. Paris: Gallimard, 1962. Translations by a group of scholars from an unusually wide range of classical poetry.

Kwôck, C. H. and McHugh, Vincent. *Why I Live on the Mountain.* San Francisco: Golden Mountain Press, 1958.

——. *The Lady and the Hermit.* San Francisco: Golden Mountain Press, 1962.

Margouliès, G. *Anthologie Raisonnée de la Littérature Chinoise.* Paris: Payot, 1948. Verse and prose, but with a very heavy concentration on the T'ang writers Han Yü and Liu Tsung-yuan.

Payne, Robert. *The White Pony.* New York: John Day, 1947.

Von Zach, E. *Die Chinesische Anthologie.* Cambridge, Mass.: Harvard University Press, 1958. Translation of the major early anthology, the sixth-century *Wen-hsüan.*

Waley, Arthur. *Chinese Poems.* London: George Allen & Unwin, 1948. Selected from three earlier books: *The Temple and Other Poems, One Hundred and Seventy Chinese Poems* and *More Translations from the Chinese.*

——. *Ballads and Stories from Tun-huang.* London: George Allen & Unwin, 1960. Rare specimens of early vernacular literature.

——. *Three Ways of Thought in Ancient China.* London: George Allen & Unwin, 1939.

Wang, Chi-chen. *Traditional Chinese Tales.* New York: Columbia University Press, 1944.

TRANSLATIONS OF INDIVIDUAL WORKS OR AUTHORS

Acker, William. *T'ao the Hermit.* New York: Thames and Hudson, 1952. Translations from T'ao Ch'ien (T'ao Yüan-ming).

Buck, Pearl S. *All Men Are Brothers.* New York: John Day, 1933. 2 vols. For this full translation of the seventy-chapter version of the novel *Shui hu chuan,* Pearl Buck evolved a special kind of "Sino-English" which sometimes reads awkwardly.

Bullett, Gerald. *The Golden Year of Fan Ch'eng-ta.* Cambridge: Cambridge University Press, 1946.

Chen, C. J. and Bullock, Michael. *Poems of Solitude.* London: Abelard-Schuman, Ltd., 1960.

Chen, S. H. *Lu Chi: Essay on Literature.* Portland, Me.: Anthoensen Press, 1953.

Hawkes, David. *Ch'u Tz'u: The Songs of the South.* Oxford: Clarendon Press, 1959.

Hsiung, S. I. *The Romance of the Western Chamber.* London: Methuen, 1935. The masterpiece of Yüan drama, *Hsi hsiang chi.*

Pound, Ezra. *The Classical Anthology Defined by Confucius.* Cambridge, Mass.: Harvard University Press, 1954. The *Shih-ching* or "Book of Songs."

Snyder, Gary. "Cold Mountain Poems," *Évergreen Review,* II, 6 (Autumn, 1958), 69-80; reprinted in *Riprap & Cold Mountain Poems.* San Francisco: Four Seasons Foundation, 1965.

Waley, Arthur. *The Book of Songs.* Boston and New York: Houghton Mifflin, 1937.

Watson, Burton. *Records of the Grand Historian of China.* New York: Columbia University Press, 1962. 2 vols. Selections from *Shih-chi.*